The Price of Pride

Abigail Reynolds

Published by White Soup Press, 2020.

THE PRICE OF PRIDE

First edition. December 15, 2020.

Copyright © 2020 Abigail Reynolds.

ISBN: 978-1954417014

Written by Abigail Reynolds.

Table of Contents

Prologue

Darcy rubbed his knuckles against his forehead as he sank into the chair behind his desk. This was not the homecoming he had dreamed of. He had imagined it so often, arriving here at Pemberley with Elizabeth beside him as his bride. Elizabeth, whose fine eyes and sparkling wit made his soul take wings and fly. Elizabeth, who would never be his.

If only she had accepted his offer of marriage! He had thought that was the first step to a brighter future. The four months since then had not been enough to begin to erase the traces of her from his heart. Instead, losing her had only deepened his feelings for her, the woman he loved so passionately but could never have.

Now, instead of laying Pemberley at her feet, proudly showing her those parts of his home that he loved the most, he was alone in his study, having ridden ahead of his party so he could face this pain without witnesses. Elizabeth would never lighten the darkness here with her smiles or bring laughter back to Pemberley, the sort of laughter he remembered from his early childhood. That joy had ebbed away as he grew up and the constant arguments over Drew had poisoned the atmosphere. His mother's death and his father's long illness had completed the process.

He had thought Elizabeth's presence could banish the emptiness, that her wit and warmth could rekindle love and happiness here. And then she had refused him. Bitterly, angrily, and leaving him no room for hope.

The butler appeared at the study door. "Mr. Andrew Darcy is here to see you," said Hobbes.

Darcy straightened. Drew was actually here, at Pemberley, and seeking him out? Wonders never ceased. Perhaps something good had come of this debacle after all, and at least he would have regained one person he had lost. "Show him in."

Hobbes hesitated. In that slight, almost imperceptible shift of tone the old butler used for matters he deemed significant, he said, "Mr. Andrew is in the drawing room."

Darcy glanced around the study. Why did Hobbes want Darcy to see Drew in the more formal setting of the drawing room rather than here? Was something wrong? But Hobbes had known Drew through the years when Darcy had been off at school and university, so perhaps he was aware of something.

Darcy rose to his feet. "Very well; I will see him there."

Was that a flicker of relief in the butler's faded eyes? "Very good, sir."

As Darcy passed between the heavy carved doors of his study, the answer suddenly struck him. This had been his father's study, of course, and the place that gentleman had always delivered tongue lashings and occasional canings to the children of the house. Darcy recalled all too well a few unpleasant visits there, but Drew, who had always been in trouble for one thing or another, must have many bad memories of it. No doubt he had been disowned in this very room. Yes, much better to meet elsewhere.

And Hobbes had realized it, when Darcy had not. Elizabeth had been right when she accused him of a selfish disdain for the feelings of others.

But he was determined to change, to become a better man, one who could be worthy of a woman like Elizabeth. Drew's presence here was proof of it. Elizabeth's refusal had led to his decision to reach out to Drew once more, to offer him the living in Kympton, and to wait patiently – or at least with the external appearance of patience – as Drew warily examined his generous offer for potential traps. Elizabeth had taught him that much; he could not assume anyone would trust his motives simply because he wished them to do so. His patience had paid off; Drew had, in the end, accepted the living, and now he was back at Pemberley where he belonged.

And there was Drew, standing on the far side of the drawing room, studying a small watercolor on the wall.

"Georgiana painted that last year," Darcy said. "I thought she caught the autumn colors particularly well."

Drew started and spun around to face him. "Yes. She appears to have a good eye for the picturesque," he said stiffly. Always stiffly. Would Drew never trust him? But that would take time, and more patience.

2

"She does, although she only sees the faults in her paintings." No. He needed to be warm and approachable. "Welcome. I am glad to see you. Some wine, perhaps?"

Drew's lips tightened. What had Darcy done wrong now? "No, I thank you, and I will not take up much of your time. I am sorry to trouble you when you have only just arrived."

"Not at all. I am very pleased to see you. How have you found the parsonage at Kympton? Is it in satisfactory condition?" Darcy studied him, noticing a bruise darkening his cheek. An accident, or had he been fighting?

His brother plucked at his cuffs, looking uncomfortable. "Yes, very satisfactory, and I thank you again for granting me the living there."

"You have done me a favor in taking it. I am relieved to have it in reliable hands."

Drew plunged on, as if nervous. "But I would not have troubled you on your first night at home, had I not something in particular to tell you, and I wanted you to hear this news from me rather than from someone else."

Oh, no. That sounded ominous. What sort of trouble had Drew got himself into now? Whatever it was, Darcy had to remain calm. "News?"

Drew took a deep breath. "I am engaged to be married."

"Engaged? My congratulations! That is excellent news." At least he knew how to respond properly to this, even if the thought of Drew being married came as shock. Or perhaps it merely brought home his own failure to become engaged. Elizabeth should be sitting beside him as his wife, and instead he was alone, while Drew was engaged. "May I ask who the fortunate lady is?" Not that he had any particular worries in that regard. When he had made inquiries about Drew's recent behavior before offering him the living, there had been nothing about petticoat chasing.

"Actually," he drew out the word, "I believe you are acquainted with her. Her name is Miss Bennet. Miss Elizabeth Bennet."

The world froze as the words echoed inside his head. No. It could not be. This was some horrible joke. Or perhaps he had heard wrong. "Miss Elizabeth Bennet of Longbourn?" Astonishingly, his voice still worked.

"The very one." Drew watched him steadily.

It could not be. Drew, engaged to Elizabeth? How was such a thing possible. How had his brother even met Elizabeth? Why had she never mentioned him? But all the questions in the world could do nothing to calm the agonizing pain ripping through him.

He had known that someday she would marry another man, but not so soon. But not Drew! God help him, not Drew. Darcy would have to witness them together again and again, to know she was in Drew's arms, that she was bearing Drew's children, not his... He drew in a harsh breath, fighting the urge to clutch at his stomach, to scream at Drew that it was impossible.

But if he raised his voice to Drew, or even criticized him, he would never see his brother again. It had taken all these years to reach the point where Drew would converse with him, much less step over the threshold of Pemberley. He could not lose him now.

And how could he blame Drew for loving Elizabeth, when he himself found her so utterly irresistible? But Elizabeth did not want him. She wanted Drew. Blood pounded in his ears.

Finally Darcy managed to say, "I was unaware she was acquainted with you."

Drew shrugged. "She never mentioned you to me, either, until I proposed to her."

"Have you known her long?" He did not know whether he hoped the answer was yes or no. That Elizabeth could refuse him and then enter into an engagement with his brother. It was intolerable.

Drew's eyes narrowed. "Long enough."

Elizabeth had accepted Drew. Agreed to marry him, after telling Darcy he was the last man in the world she could be prevailed upon to marry. But she had chosen to become Drew's wife. His chest grew painfully tight. Would he ever be able to draw a full breath again?

He had to say something, all the proper things, even if his world was breaking into tiny pieces. "You are a fortunate man. I wish you both happiness. When is the wedding?"

"We have yet to set a date. This was only just settled. You are among the first to know." Drew raised an eyebrow and said deliberately, "Miss Bennet feared you might object to the connection, but I told her I did not need your permission to marry."

Darcy swallowed hard. Of course he objected. Objecting did not begin to describe his feelings about it. But he said, "I cannot think why. She is a gentleman's daughter, and thus perfectly suitable." How could laughing, teasing, witty Elizabeth possibly marry stern, angry Drew? Oh, yes, he objected, and with every bone of his body. But he could never, ever say so.

Drew actually smiled. "Good. I am glad of that."

Darcy could not imagine ever feeling glad again.

But there was one thing he had to know, one more bit of salt to pour on the jagged open wound in his heart. "I seem to recall hearing her portion was small. Is this a love match, then?"

The lines on Drew's forehead smoothed. "Yes," he said quietly. "I love her."

Chapter 1

Lambton, two weeks earlier

The small mirror in Elizabeth's room at the White Hart Inn reflected her fatigue as she plaited her hair for the night. It had been a long, trying day. The journey from Bakewell had been pleasant enough, and their tour of Pemberley had lacked neither beauty or interest. But seeing Darcy's home, even in his absence, and hearing the housekeeper's praise of the Master of Pemberley had raised painful memories, not to mention regrets. Fortunately, he was not there himself, and was not due for a fortnight. By then she would be on her way back to Longbourn, so at least she was spared the embarrassment of meeting him again.

A tapping came at the door. "Lizzy? Are you still awake?" It was her aunt's voice.

"Yes. Do come in." What could Mrs. Gardiner want now? They had spent the entire day together. As her aunt slipped inside, Elizabeth said, "Is something the matter?"

"That is what I came to ask you," Mrs. Gardiner said. "You were very quiet today, not at all yourself, and I wondered if perhaps our tour is not to your liking, or if you are displeased with Derbyshire."

"Oh, no! I am enjoying it greatly! You know how I have always longed to travel to new places. The countryside here far exceeds my expectations. I love the steep hillsides and the starkness of the terrain. I believe I could happily remain in Derbyshire for a very long time." It was all true, and perhaps it would distract her aunt.

But Mrs. Gardiner was not easily fooled. "Is something else troubling you, then? I do not wish to pry, but even your uncle noticed you seemed out of spirits at dinner."

It would probably be simplest to tell her the truth, or at least some of it. She had no desire to tell her aunt that seeing Mr. Darcy's home had left her melancholy. "I have been thinking about my future," Elizabeth said quietly. "Jane and I had a talk before I left Longbourn, and it made me see how difficult our position is. Neither of us will find husbands in Meryton. The few marriageable gentlemen there have their sights set elsewhere. Even when the town was overrun by single militia officers, none of them showed serious interest in us, and why should they? Who would be willing to marry one of us, when it would mean someday caring for our sisters and mother as well? Even Jane's beauty and sweetness are not enough to overcome that disadvantage."

"You are afraid of ending up a spinster?" her aunt asked gently.

Elizabeth shook her head. "I do not mind that idea; I have thought it rather likely for some time. But I always assumed Jane would marry, and that after my father's death I could live with her family. But Jane has not had even a hint of an offer, and she is now speaking of finding a tradesman to marry simply to avoid being a burden on our relatives. How selfish I have been to rely on her to secure my future!"

"I do not think the situation is that bleak," her aunt said. "After all, you are but twenty. But there may be something to what you say about being at a disadvantage in Meryton where your family is well known. Perhaps we should make more of an effort to introduce you to eligible gentlemen in London."

"Jane just spent five months with you in London." And came home without an admirer.

Her aunt sighed. "True, but she was pining for Mr. Bingley, and we made little effort to put her forward. I know men who might be interested in you or Jane. Perhaps not the marriages your parents would have dreamed of for you, but good men with reliable work and prospects for the future."

London might be a delightful place to visit, but Elizabeth had no desire to live there. After a time in the city, she always craved the freedom of the countryside. "I am not desperate yet, my dearest Aunt!" She tried to sound amused, even if she did not feel it. "If I cannot marry a man I respect, I would rather find a position as a lady's companion. Perhaps that would allow me to see more of the world." But most lady's companions saw nothing of the world and had to tolerate every whim of the lady they served.

"I hope you know your uncle and I will always do what we can to provide for you."

From the assurance with which Mrs. Gardiner spoke, Elizabeth suspected this discussion had already taken place between her aunt and uncle. The Gardiners were well aware of her situation. More aware than she had been.

She hugged Mrs. Gardiner. "You are all that is good and generous." But the Gardiners had four children of their own. Having to support five Bennet sisters would be an enormous strain on them.

Her aunt smiled. "You are very dear to us."

Elizabeth forced herself to rally her spirits. "But enough of this gloom! What plans have you for tomorrow?"

"I thought we would call on Mr. Morris at the rectory. He was very kind to me after he took over the living when my father died, and I confess I would like to see the house I grew up in once more."

"I should like that, too," said Elizabeth.

"MY DEAR MRS. GARDINER!" The elderly gentleman with a fringe of white hair brought his hands together in delight. "Why, you do not look a day older than when you were keeping house for your father all those years ago."

"What a flatterer you are, Mr. Morris!" exclaimed Mrs. Gardiner warmly. "Why, I have four children now. Pray permit me to present my husband and my niece, Miss Bennet."

The rector shook Mr. Gardiner's hand heartily. "It is a great pleasure, sir. Miss Bennet, are you enjoying your visit to Derbyshire?"

Elizabeth curtsied. "Very much so." There was something about the old man's warm smile that made her trust him instinctively.

Mr. Morris gestured to a tall young man standing in the opposite doorway. "Drew, come meet my new guests! Are you already acquainted with Mrs. Gardiner from the days when she lived in Lambton? She would

THE PRICE OF PRIDE

have been Miss Carlisle then, the daughter of old Mr. Carlisle, who had this living before me. She left Lambton not long after I became rector here."

"That would have been before my time," said the younger man with a friendly smile. "But I am honored to meet you."

"In that case, Mrs. Gardiner, may I present Mr. Andrew Darcy, my former student and – if dare I say it – my current protégé?" asked Mr. Morris. "He has recently been given the living at Kympton."

Elizabeth started. Darcy? Not the Mr. Darcy she knew, thank heavens! Apart from his height, this gentleman bore him no resemblance. His straight, light hair, angled jaw and cleft chin were unlike Mr. Darcy's dark curls and chiseled face, and he lacked the other man's habitual haughty expression. Instead, his open countenance seemed to be all affability. But given his name, and living not five miles from Pemberley, he must be related, perhaps a cousin of some sort. A distant one, most likely, as she had never heard mention of cousins on the Darcy side. His clothing seemed to suggest a poor relation – tidy, but not particularly fashionable, with his coat sleeves showing wear at the elbows. No, obviously not a close relative to Mr. Fitzwilliam Darcy, thank heavens.

Mrs. Gardiner exclaimed, "Kympton – why, that is a lovely village! I remember visiting the parsonage there when I was a child. A charming house."

A shadow seemed to cross the young man's face. "I am still becoming acquainted with Kympton."

"It takes time to settle into a living," said Mr. Morris. "May I invite you to sit down?" He ordered a tea tray and began gently encouraging Mrs. Gardiner to tell him about her travels and her life since leaving Lambton. Almost by default, the two young people were left to sit together on a small settee. Elizabeth felt a certain trepidation that this new Mr. Darcy might yet prove as haughty as the one she could not forget, but, as the conversation between Mrs. Gardiner and Mr. Morris turned to people she had never heard of, she said, "Lambton seems a charming town. Do you know it well?"

He smiled, setting aside his tea and cake untasted. "I lived here for two years when I was a boy, studying with Mr. Morris, but I have been away since then. I am glad to be on familiar ground again, but becoming a rector is quite a change for me. Mr. Morris has been very helpful to me in learning what is expected of me."

"I imagine he would be a good mentor." Elizabeth took a sip of tea. It was so bitter she had difficulty keeping from making a face. No wonder this young clergyman was not drinking it!

"Terrible, is it not?" he said in a cheerful undertone. "My advice is not to try the cake, especially if you are fond of your teeth."

Elizabeth could not help smiling. "I thank you for your advice, but I would not wish to offend our host."

The young man took the teacup from her hand and placed it beside his own. "He will not be offended. He is too gentle-hearted to dismiss his cook when she has nowhere else to go, but he is well aware that her food is nigh inedible."

"A generous gentleman, then," she said.

"The best I have ever known," he said simply. "But I have learned never to pay a call here when I am hungry."

No, this Mr. Darcy was generous in spirit, quite unlike the one she had met in Meryton and whose memory still haunted her, especially after visiting his home the previous day. Why could she not simply forget him?

Mr. Morris leaned towards Mrs. Gardiner, saying something softly. At her nod, he said, "Drew, I believe Mrs. Gardiner might enjoy seeing the upstairs rooms, but my old knees are too tired to give her the tour. Would you be good enough to do the honors?"

"Of course, sir." The young man rose to his feet.

"How very kind of you!" exclaimed Mrs. Gardiner.

"He knows the house almost as well as I do," said Mr. Morris. "Mrs. Gardiner might be interested in hearing about your parsonage, too, Andrew."

"Indeed, sir," he said politely. "This way, Mrs. Gardiner."

After the two had left the room, Mr. Morris rubbed his hands together with a twinkle in his eyes, encompassing both Mr. Gardiner and Elizabeth in his gaze. "Forgive me for failing to offer you the tour as well, but I have my reasons. I believe Mrs. Gardiner may be in a position to offer young Drew some much needed advice. When the Lord is good enough to send a lady who was raised to run a parsonage just at the moment when Drew

10

was begging me for advice on that very subject, the least I can do is to offer them time to speak alone."

"He is unmarried, then?" asked Mr. Gardiner.

"Yes," said Mr. Morris. "He was a curate before coming here, so he is familiar with his pastoral duties, but that position did not include a parsonage. The one that comes with his living was not well-maintained by the last incumbent, and the servants are a slovenly lot. Servants are always a challenging issue for clergymen since they are both our employees and our parishioners, and poor Drew has no experience at running a household."

Mr. Gardiner chuckled. "Whenever I compliment my wife on her household management, she always says it is much easier than running a parsonage. I assumed that was because she was still a girl when she took over the household after her mother died, but she says her duties were different, with parishioners coming by and the responsibility to them."

"You have a very capable wife. She made it look simple. I did not realize how difficult it was until I watched my late wife struggle to learn the duties of a clergyman's wife."

Elizabeth's brows drew together. Her friend Charlotte never complained of finding her duties onerous, but perhaps that was because her servants lived in terror of Lady Catherine de Bourgh's frequent inspections of the parsonage. Charlotte would never have to worry about discharging a bad servant, because Lady Catherine would have long since done so on her behalf.

Mrs. Gardiner and Mr. Andrew Darcy did not reappear for over a quarter of an hour. When they did, Mrs. Gardiner's face was alight with interest as she told the young man, "We shall find a way, never fear!"

"Ah, my dear, I recognize that expression!" said Mr. Gardiner. "You have a new project."

Delicate color rose in Mrs. Gardiner's cheeks. "Only a very small one. It will not take away from our holiday, I promise you. I am simply going to visit this young man's parsonage and perhaps offer some advice on how to manage it; that is all."

Mr. Gardiner smiled broadly. "And help him find a new housekeeper and staff, and suggest how he might redecorate it, and half a dozen things that I cannot even dream of."

Mr. Andrew Darcy drew himself to his full height. "Mr. Gardiner, I have no intention of imposing myself on your wife in any way."

Her uncle guffawed. "Lad, my wife is never happier than when she has a new project! It will undoubtedly be a high point of our trip for her. And now I will not need an excuse to sneak off to find a fishing stream, as Mr. Morris has kindly offered to loan me his tackle."

The younger man visibly thawed. "There is a fine trout stream that runs not far from my parsonage. Perhaps you would care to try your luck there."

Mr. Gardiner beamed. "That sounds delightful."

Elizabeth smiled dutifully, though she had no interest in fishing, refurbishing a parsonage, or calling on even a distant relative of Mr. Fitzwilliam Darcy, no matter how amiable he might be. But her aunt and uncle had been generous enough to invite her on this journey, and it was her job to be pleased by whatever activities they selected.

Chapter 2

Paying a call to Mr. Andrew Darcy's parsonage sounded dull, but Elizabeth loved nothing more than exploring new places, and she certainly could not complain about the drive. The countryside had an invigorating loveliness, with steep hills rising on each side of the road and sheep dotting the hillsides under a clear blue sky. The village of Kympton was delightfully picturesque, with neat stone cottages lining the road and a square-towered church rising above it.

The parsonage stood at the end of a gravel lane, a large house covered with ivy, its lines more impressive than Mr. Collins's parsonage in Hunsford. The ivy needed trimming, and a workman was repairing some missing fence slats. Roses bloomed by the doorway, but the bushes were scraggly.

Elizabeth, still uncomfortable with the idea of spending time with one of Mr. Darcy's relations, hung back while her uncle knocked on the door. She bent down to sniff one of the roses, closing her eyes as the sweet fragrance filled her senses. At the sound of the door opening, she straightened to see the young clergyman himself in the doorway, looking past her aunt and uncle, gazing at her with an arrested expression.

Oh, dear. So much for not attracting his attention. Not that she had been doing anything provocative, and there had been no reason to think he would answer his own door rather than have a servant do it...except that the reason for their visit was that he was having problems with his servants. Of course, she had not thought she had done anything to attract Mr. Fitzwilliam Darcy's interest, either.

She put a practiced social smile on her face as they entered the house and did her best to fade into the background, saying nothing as he instructed her uncle on how to find the trout stream and then showed the ladies to the sitting room.

"I apologize for the furnishings." Mr. Andrew Darcy gestured to the mismatched chairs and side tables. "The previous incumbent used it as his sickroom when he could not manage the stairs, and we are still restoring it."

Mrs. Gardiner stood in the middle of the room and turned around slowly, inspecting it thoroughly. "Still, the structure appears good, as does the woodwork. The paint looks fresh. I think it will do very well."

"The steward at Pemberley made some repairs before I arrived, but I told him I preferred to take responsibility for the rest." He sounded a bit stiff about it, as if he disliked working with the steward. "As I told you before, the staff are my greatest concern. There is conflict between the ones who were already here and the two I brought from London, and I do not know how much to trust the housekeeper. She is now suggesting I hire another maid, which seems excessive to me, but I know nothing of how to manage a household."

Mrs. Gardiner said, "Perhaps that is where I can be helpful. You live here alone, do you not?"

He nodded. "Yes."

"How much entertaining do you intend to do?"

"Entertaining?" He looked surprised at the question. "I suppose I must be ready to receive calls from parishioners and neighbors, but I think it would be inappropriate for a single clergyman to hold any sort of party."

"And how many servants do you have?"

He counted on his fingers. "The housekeeper, the cook, two maids, and a gardener were already here. I brought my personal manservant and his sister, and said that we must dismiss one of the maids. The housekeeper was very unhappy about that."

Mrs. Gardiner's eyebrows rose. "All for taking care of one gentleman who does not entertain? It is a large house, admittedly, but I fear your housekeeper is taking advantage of you."

He sighed. "I was afraid of that, but my lack of domestic knowledge has hindered me in arguing with her. I would be most grateful for your view of how many servants are necessary."

Mrs. Gardiner pursed her lips. "You might need a little extra help while setting up your household, but your housekeeper and cook should be able to take on other duties, so a maid and one manservant should be able to meet your needs adequately. If you were married and had a family, it would be different, although if you had a wife, you would not need a housekeeper at all."

Mr. Andrew Darcy flushed. "Alas, the right young lady has yet to come my way. Your assessment sounds sensible, but leaves me with the question of whom I must ask to leave."

"I would suggest that your housekeeper is already trying to take advantage of you, and you might be better off without her. I assume you would like to keep the servants you brought with you?"

The young clergyman straightened. "I most certainly would. That is part of the problem, too. The cook has taken a strong dislike to them."

Mrs. Gardiner nodded. "I think it would be best if I could meet your staff. Perhaps we could begin with a tour of the house, and you could introduce me to the servants as we go. That way it would appear less as if I am here to judge them."

The young clergyman nodded. "A good plan. Shall we start with the kitchen?"

Elizabeth trailed along behind them as they proceeded to the rear of the house, but before they even reached the kitchen, a woman's raised voice reached her. "Stay away from me, I tell you!"

A quieter voice spoke soothingly, but Elizabeth could not make out the words.

The first woman shrieked, "Keep your filthy hands off me!"

"Oh, dear," groaned Andrew Darcy. "It appears you are about to see my cook at her worst."

"Is she always this temperamental?" asked Mrs. Gardiner.

His mouth twisted. "No. Only when it comes to the servants I brought with me. She hates foreigners."

"Ah. Just as well to know the problem, if we wish to fix it," said Mrs. Gardiner.

"True." He stepped back to usher them in.

The kitchen was large, replete with the aroma of chicken and onions. A pile of chopped turnips and apples sat on the table, perhaps ready to go in the pot hanging over the fire. The sight of half a dozen tiny puppies nursing on a dog in the corner next to the hearth caught Elizabeth's eye and made her smile.

On the opposite side of the room, a lanky, middle-aged woman in a soiled apron stood with her back pressed against a tall cupboard, a bloody cloth clutched around her hand. A smaller, dark-skinned girl with a colorful scarf wrapped around her hair stood before her and spoke in a musical, accented voice. "The master knows I am a healer, and—" She stopped as she noticed the newcomers.

"Myrtilla, what seems to be the matter?" the young clergyman asked.

The dark-skinned woman shrugged. "Cook, she cut her hand, and she won't let me help her. There is no one else, and it must be sewn."

"I want none of her filthy witchcraft," muttered the cook. "She's a devil!"

Elizabeth grimaced. There would be no simple solution for this problem. Africans were a common sight in London, but likely less so in rural Derbyshire.

"It is not witchcraft," said Andrew Darcy. "Myrtilla's master in Antigua was a surgeon, and he trained her to assist him and to provide treatment to other slaves. She can help you."

The cook scowled ferociously. "She's not touching me!"

The young man sighed and turned to Mrs. Gardiner. "You see the difficulty."

"I do indeed." Mrs. Gardiner eyed the cook. "Since you are unwilling to accept your employer's direction, I suggest you find someone else to treat your injury."

With a heave of her shoulders, the cook gave the young clergyman a wounded look and stomped out of the kitchen.

Myrtilla's lip curled. "The maid will stuff that cut with spiderwebs and give her an infection, but only touch her with pure English hands."

Elizabeth stared at her, unused to servants expressing disdain so openly in the presence of their employer, but Andrew Darcy seemed unsurprised.

"I am sorry, Myrtilla," said the clergyman. "It is wrong of her to speak so to you."

Myrtilla's only response to this was a swift, wordless glance.

Mrs. Gardiner said briskly, "Mr. Darcy, might I speak with Myrtilla privately? I would like to understand her situation here better."

He nodded. "Myrtilla, I have asked Mrs. Gardiner's advice on the staffing of the parsonage. Pray speak truly to her about your experience. Do not tell her what you think she wishes to hear, just the truth."

The former slave sniffed. "As you wish."

"We will leave you to discuss it, then. Miss Bennet, would you care to join me in the sitting room?" the young clergyman asked.

Elizabeth glanced at her aunt, who waved her away. This was just the sort of situation Mrs. Gardiner excelled at resolving, and since she looked perfectly in her element, Elizabeth returned to the drawing room with the clergyman. It was so odd to hear him called Mr. Darcy, especially given how very different he was from the one she knew. She imagined servants would scurry to obey that Mr. Darcy, rather than argue with him. Perhaps she should think of this Mr. Darcy by his first name, as inappropriate as that was, or she would be forever comparing two very different men in her head.

Her current companion said, "I dearly hope your aunt can help with this. Myrtilla will not answer my questions about what happens below stairs. It is unlike her to be so resentful and angry, and I suspect there is a reason for it."

"She is a freed slave?" asked Elizabeth.

"Yes, as is her brother."

"People who have lived here all their lives may be predisposed to dislike newcomers," said Elizabeth diplomatically.

He gave her a rueful look. "Perhaps, but I fear there is more to it than that, and I am ill-equipped to deal with it. In the household where I lived in London, there were several freed slaves among the servants, and no one seemed troubled by it."

"In London, it is hardly unusual–" She broke off in mid-sentence when a large ginger tabby jumped onto her lap. One of his ears was bent and scarred from an old injury, but he rumbled a purr. She scratched his cheeks until he turned in a circle and curled up.

"Oliver, you are not supposed to be in here," Mr. Andrew Darcy said mildly.

"Is your name Oliver?" Elizabeth asked the cat. "It suits you."

"Forgive me. He is supposed to stay out of the sitting room, but he is such a friendly fellow that he always wishes to be where people are."

"He is perfectly welcome on my lap." She leaned down and examined his scarred ear. "Apparently he is not as friendly with other cats, or was it perhaps the dog I saw in the kitchen who did this? You must be an animal lover."

He flushed a little. "I am fond of animals, it is true. I never intend to adopt them, but somehow it happens. Oliver came to me when I rescued him from a group of boys who were mistreating him. The dog is not actually mine, only the puppies. A farmer was going to drown them, and I persuaded him to let me take them instead. I had to bring their mother here to care for them, but once they are weaned, the farmer wants her back."

"How kind of you! What will you do with all those puppies?"

He turned his hands up with a wry smile. "I have not the least idea, only that I could not watch them drown. Their mother is a good sheep dog, so perhaps they will take after her and other sheep farmers will want them."

Most likely he would have difficulty placing them, since there were always more dogs than homes, but being soft-hearted was hardly a crime. It showed how different he was from his cousin, the Mr. Darcy she knew, whom she could not imagine taking in a litter of mongrel pups, no matter how generous the Pemberley housekeeper had claimed he was. The very thought of that proud man in such circumstances made her smile. She stroked the cat's back, the vibrating purr soothing her. "It is very hard to resist a puppy."

They chatted for some time before Mrs. Gardiner rejoined them. "That was interesting. Myrtilla tells me you told her she was to be the cook's assistant. Is that correct?"

"Yes. She finds England chilly, and so prefers to work in the kitchen because it is always warm."

"It appears that she is actually working in the scullery because the cook will not permit her to touch any food destined to be served, while the former scullery maid is now the parlor maid. She ran her fingertip along the mantelpiece. "Good enough, I suppose. Your cook disobeyed your direct instructions to your face. Another issue."

Andrew Darcy frowned. "Myrtilla has mentioned none of this to me."

Mrs. Gardiner gave him a sympathetic look. "She grew up in a land where a slave who complained about a white servant would be whipped. While she thinks you are a good employer and a well-meaning person, she is unlikely to trust a white man."

Lines etched between his brows. "No doubt her life has given her reason to believe that. What would you suggest I do?"

"That depends on how much you wish to keep Myrtilla here. The simplest solution would be to find her another position, but that still leaves you with an insubordinate cook."

"Myrtilla stays. She is hard-working and has valuable skills."

Tilting her head to one side, Mrs. Gardiner said, "That is important, though I would be remiss if I did not point out that Myrtilla also tends to insubordination, and she does not show you proper respect."

He smiled ruefully. "It is true that she can be difficult, but I prefer to overlook it because Myrtilla also has non-domestic duties, in which I appreciate those characteristics."

Mrs. Gardiner drew back. "I see," she said coolly.

Andrew Darcy looked confused. "I am sorry if I have offended you. I do take your concerns seriously." He paused, looking inward as if reviewing his words, and then exclaimed, "Good God, if you thought I meant...I assure you, madam, it is nothing of the sort! I would never, ever..." He bit down on his words, obviously struggling to restrain himself. "Myrtilla assists me in my abolitionist work, providing a first-hand account of the experience of slavery. To be willing to argue powerfully when others deny her story requires a certain willingness to be disrespectful and difficult."

Mrs. Gardiner's stiff posture relaxed. "In that case, I apologize most sincerely for my misapprehension. I fear I have seen too much misuse of servants in my day, and I am glad to hear your reasons are quite different. And I understand now why you would not wish to quell Myrtilla's spirit, even when it moves into impertinence."

He looked amused. "I doubt it is in my power. Stronger men than I have tried, and they used weapons I would never employ. Myrtilla's character is set. It has made it difficult for her to retain employment, which is why she was willing to take this post so far from her family and friends in London."

Mrs. Gardiner nodded, as if this answer satisfied her. "My advice, then, would be to tell your cook that her services are no longer required. Give her position to Myrtilla. Tell your upstairs maid that she is expected to assist Myrtilla as needed, including in the scullery."

"The housekeeper will be unhappy. The cook is her friend and ally."

"As your housekeeper does not seem to be working in your best interest, you may do well to look for a new one."

He spread his hands. "How would you recommend I find one who is more trustworthy?"

Mrs. Gardiner pursed her lips. "I would advise you to ask the housekeeper at Pemberley for recommendations. She is likely to be aware of who might be available and who should be avoided."

"Not Pemberley." There was an edge to his voice. "I prefer to leave Pemberley out of my domestic issues."

Elizabeth studied him, her interest piqued. His reaction was odd; after all, he had just been given a valuable Pemberley living, so presumably he was in favor with the Master of Pemberley. What could be the source of the tension? Then she stopped herself. The subject of Mr. Darcy of Pemberley was one she would be wisest to leave alone.

"As you wish," Mrs. Gardiner said equably, but Elizabeth thought she was a little taken aback. "I can make some inquiries among my friends in Lambton. They might have some ideas."

MRS. GARDINER INSISTED on returning to the Kympton parsonage three days later to meet with Mr. Andrew Darcy and his new housekeeper. Elizabeth, given the choice between accompanying her or watching Mr. Gardiner fish, announced she would go to Kympton, but spend her time walking the path behind the parsonage that she had noticed on their last visit. Andrew Darcy tried to convince her to remain with them instead and offered to escort her after their business was concluded, but she was resolute in her desire for an immediate long walk.

Though her feet were tired by the time she returned from her excursion, her spirits were high from the delight of exploring this unknown part of the world and discovering new sights at every turn of the path. Her calf muscles, unaccustomed to the steep hills of Derbyshire, ached, but the views had been well worth the exertion.

As she paused just outside the gate to the garden to scrape the worst of the mud from her half-boots, she heard a male voice say, "Are you enjoying living at the parsonage? It was to have been mine, you know." The voice was familiar, one she had once longed to hear. But it could not be him; he was in Brighton with the militia.

She peeked around the hedge. Good heavens, it truly was George Wickham, talking to Andrew Darcy! She pressed herself back against the hedge, having no desire to meet him.

"I am told you refused it," Andrew Darcy said coldly.

"I always knew Darcy wanted you to have it." Wickham was all geniality, just as he had been in Meryton when he had convinced her to believe his lies.

"Somehow I doubt you had my best interests in mind."

"I have always felt for your position, Drew. It was so close to my own. Living at Pemberley, but always told that you did not belong, that you were not good enough. You always seemed able to ignore the rumors about your father, much more than I could about my own. We have both been treated unfairly because of the sins of our parents."

"The sins of my parents are in the past. All I can do is to live my own life as free of sin as God will permit. What is it you want from me, Wickham?" Clearly the young clergyman trusted Wickham no more than she did.

"Just a little loan to tide me over until I take my new position." Had he left the militia, then?

"Money for you to spend on women and drink? Wickham, you speak of your father's sins, yet you follow in his footsteps. Why not choose a different path?"

"Spare me your sermons! I know how much this living brings in; surely you can spare a few pounds? You would not wish me to repeat what old Mr. Darcy said about you to your new parishioners, would you?"

Andrew Darcy's laugh was like the crack of a pistol shot. "Be my guest. No doubt it is old news to them."

They were coming towards Elizabeth, and soon they would discover her. She took a step backwards, but her foot landed on a twig which broke with a loud snap.

"Who is there?" Andrew Darcy demanded.

There was nothing for it but to brazen it out. Elizabeth lifted the latch and pushed the gate open. "Forgive me for startling you," she said brightly. "Why, if it is not Mr. Wickham! I had thought you were in Brighton, sir."

The young clergyman recoiled. "You know one another?"

"Mr. Wickham was a militia officer in my town in Hertfordshire," Elizabeth explained. She certainly did not wish to claim him as a friend.

Wickham bowed. "Indeed, I had the privilege of meeting Miss Elizabeth there. But what brings you to the wilds of Derbyshire?" Then a knowing look came over his face. "Or perhaps I can guess."

She had no idea what he was attempting to insinuate. "I am traveling with my aunt and uncle."

"Very interesting!" A calculating look came over his face. "So, Drew, are you certain you cannot help me?"

"I will pray for you, Wickham."

Wickham's eyes narrowed, and he snarled, "You and your high and mighty brother may rot in hell." Then, with an abrupt change in attitude, he bowed to Elizabeth with an ingratiating smile. "My apologies, Miss Elizabeth, and my congratulations on a brilliant match. I do hope you will always count me among your friends. I wish you good day." He turned and sauntered back towards the road.

Elizabeth pressed her fingers to her throat. "Good heavens! What was that about?" Despite knowing of Wickham's past, she had never seen him be anything short of charming before. And what had he meant by a brilliant match?

The young clergyman straightened his cuffs, using the action as an excuse not to meet her eyes. "My apologies for his language. Wickham can be intemperate on occasion, although usually not in front of ladies, but he is not a man to be trusted."

"I am aware of that," she said dryly. "I am sorry if my presence made matters more difficult for you."

He looked up, a slight quirk to his lips. "Things are always difficult when Wickham is nearby. Think nothing of it. I hope he has not caused you distress in the past."

"No. He was always perfectly charming to me. I have only heard rumors of his misdeeds, not suffered directly from them." She certainly did not want to explain to Mr. Darcy's cousin precisely where she had learned of Wickham's offenses. Far better to change the subject. "Is my aunt within?"

"Yes, she is going over the accounts with the new housekeeper. I told her it was unnecessary, but she insisted a housewife's eye would see errors a man would miss. I daresay she is right, but I do not know how I will ever repay her for her assistance. The parsonage is a much happier place now."

"She has enjoyed it immensely," Elizabeth assured him. "There is little that gives her more pleasure than to use her skills to solve problems. She will look back on this with pleasure."

"I hope it has not been a disappointment to you," he said. "After all, you might have wished to spend your holiday in a quite different manner."

"Not at all," she said, not completely truthfully. "I would never have discovered this charming village if my aunt had not offered her assistance, and I must say I have grown quite fond of it."

A shy smile grew on his face. "It was a fortunate day that you appeared at Mr. Morris' rectory. I have benefited greatly from your aunt's assistance, but beyond that, it has been a delight to make your acquaintance."

Was he trying, in a timid, clumsy way, to flirt with her? He seemed to have little experience at it. Poor fellow; if his name had not been Darcy, she would have been happy to enjoy a nice flirtation with him. "It is a great pleasure to make new friends in my travels. Now, where might I find my aunt?"

Chapter 3

As the carriage turned into the stableyard at the White Hart Inn, Mrs. Gardiner said, "Are you certain you do not mind being left here alone?"

"Not in the least," Elizabeth said stoutly. "I do not want my little accident to disrupt your day. I would feel exceedingly guilty if you were to miss seeing Peveril Castle simply because I was foolish enough to slip in the mud." Especially when her aunt had warned her against trying to climb those very rocks where she had slipped!

"But I hate to leave you all by yourself," her aunt said worriedly.

"There is no need. One of the chambermaids will be happy to help me change into a clean dress, and I can use the time to catch up on my correspondence."

Mr. Gardiner said, "Perhaps I should walk you to your room, just to be safe."

Elizabeth repressed a desire to give a sharp response, knowing that if she let her aunt and uncle out of the carriage, it would be three times as hard to get them back into it. "Nonsense. This is a perfectly respectable inn where we are well known. I want you to go to Peveril so I can hear all about it later!"

"Very well, if you are certain," said Mrs. Gardiner.

With a warm, reassuring smile, Elizabeth clambered out of the carriage. "It is only twenty feet to the door of the inn. What could happen to me, surrounded by all these fine citizens? Now, off with you!" She stepped back inside the stable doorway to allow the carriage room to turn around, and waved as her uncle and aunt drove through the archway back to the street.

With a sigh of relief, she straightened her skirts to hide the muddy patches as much as she could before crossing the courtyard. Then she spotted Mr. Wickham's familiar figure emerging through the inn door accompanied by a red-haired chambermaid. She certainly did not want to run into him, especially when she was alone, so, at the sound of his cajoling tones, she ducked back into the shadows of the stable.

HALF AN HOUR AND MANY painful blushes later, Elizabeth decided Wickham was finally distracted enough that she could escape unseen and seized her chance to hurry across the stable yard and into the back door of the inn. All she wanted was to reach the privacy of her room and scrub the memory of what she had overheard out of her mind, but ought she to warn the inn proprietor before that? No, first she should change her dress. She did not want to speak to anyone in her current state of muddy, embarrassed dishevelment. If only she could be certain this matter could wait until her uncle's return! It would be so much easier if he managed it in her stead.

The obstacle of the public room stood between her and the stairway. She took a deep breath and tried to creep quietly along the wall, hoping to avoid notice.

She failed.

"Miss Bennet!" Mr. Andrew Darcy stepped forward and bowed over Elizabeth's hand.

She had thought she was out of blushes. "Pray forgive my appearance, sir. A slight accident while climbing Mam Tor."

"I am sorry to hear it. I hope you are uninjured."

"I am perfectly well, I thank you." Apart from a few bruises and a severely sprained dignity, and now a new, distressing problem to solve.

"Is Mrs. Gardiner with you? I called in the hope of seeing her."

"No, she and my uncle dropped me off here and continued on to Peveril Castle. I do not expect them for some hours."

He studied her. "Are you certain you are well? You look distressed."

"I..." She blinked hard, wishing she could run away. "Nothing is truly wrong; I simply had an experience a few moments ago which has discomposed me a little." The echo of Wickham's seduction played in her ears.

"Is there any way I could assist you? A glass of wine; shall I get you one?" His concern was evident.

"No, I thank you," she replied, endeavouring to recover herself. "There is nothing the matter with me. I am quite well. I am only distressed by something I overheard, and I do not know what to do about it." But perhaps this meeting was a blessing in disguise; Andrew Darcy might be the only person in Derbyshire whom she could count on to understand Wickham's ways. "Now that I think on it, if it would not be an imposition, sir, it is a matter in which I would appreciate your advice."

He looked genuinely pleased at her words. "I would be happy to be of service, if I may. Perhaps we might speak in the private parlor? It is empty, and if we leave the door open and remain in full sight of the public room, I do not think anyone could object."

For once she was grateful to have someone else organizing things for her, so she accepted his direction. "Very well, but I must remain standing, lest I spread mud all over a nice, clean chair."

"Of course." He accompanied her inside the parlor, and then added, "Naturally, anything you tell me will be held in confidence."

"Thank you." How was she to begin? She had no desire to explain that she had been an unwilling witness to a seduction scene. "This whole matter is perhaps none of my affair, but I am uncertain what to do about it. It concerns Mr. Wickham, which is why I thought your advice might be helpful."

His look of concern deepened. "I am sorry to hear he has been troubling you."

"Not directly. Yesterday he called when we were out and left a message for me saying that he wished to apologize for his intemperance. I am unsure how he learned where I was staying, but I decided it would be easiest to avoid him. Just now, after my uncle and aunt left me in the stable yard, I heard him talking to a girl who works at the inn. Since I did not wish to encounter him, I hid behind a door to wait for him to pass by." Her cheeks grew hot at the remembrance of what she had heard.

"Did he discover you?"

"No, but he came into the stable, and I could not help overhearing what took place." And there was no need to go into any details on that! "He was promising the girl he would take her to Gretna Green and marry her, but he needed money to get them there. He told her to empty the innkeeper's till and give him the money, and it seemed as if he had persuaded her." She wiped the back of her hand against her mouth, as if she could scrub the words away. "I do not know what to do, whether I should tell the innkeeper or not. Perhaps the girl will not do it, and if I say something, she might lose her position."

Andrew Darcy sucked in a breath through his teeth. "You need do nothing. I will take care of this, and without involving the innkeeper. Is Wickham still out there?"

"I believe so." She expected he would be taking his time making sure the poor girl was thoroughly in his thrall. And to think she had once admired him! "I do not wish to cause any trouble for you."

"You have caused no trouble. Wickham is on the verge of destroying a girl's life, and you are quite right to seek help for her. Leave this to me. Perhaps you might wish to go upstairs and attend to your dress."

Elizabeth had all but forgotten the reason she had returned to the inn. "I will do so, and I thank you for helping that poor girl."

ONCE UPSTAIRS, SHE could not put the situation out of her head. She ought to do as he said and let him handle it, but she could not forget how quickly Wickham's temper had shifted at the parsonage. What if he became angry here? Perhaps she should keep an eye out from a distance, just in case. Her window overlooked the stable yard, so she wrestled with the sticky latch. She had kept it closed until now because of the noise of coaches arriving at all hours. But now, because of her, Andrew Darcy was down there confronting Wickham.

She could not see him, so either Andrew was already in the stable block or had not yet gone into the yard. With a sigh, she turned away from the window and began to unfasten her dress, thankful it was one that did not require assistance to remove. Fortunately, the mud had not reached her shift, so she was able to put her blue muslin on over it. As she was struggling to reach the last of the buttons in the back, she heard a commotion from outside.

She hurried to the window in time to see Andrew Darcy pick himself up from the ground as George Wickham stood over him. A few stable hands loitered around them, urging them to fight, but Andrew shook his head and said something she could not hear. Wickham's fist shot out and connected with the young clergyman's nose. He staggered, blood streaming down his face, but made no effort to defend himself as Wickham hit him again, this time in the stomach. Andrew doubled over.

Elizabeth could not bear it. Throwing a shawl over her shoulders, she raced out of her room and down the steps, pushing past several men in the taproom, and finally out to the stable yard.

"Coward!" Wickham taunted Andrew, who held a handkerchief to his nose. "You may call yourself a pacifist, but I call it cowardice."

"*Resist not evil, but whoever shall smite thee on thy right cheek, turn to him the other also,*" Andrew quoted nasally, and slowly turned his head to the side, exposing his cheek to Wickham.

"Fool," spat Wickham, and struck his chin with a closed fist.

This time the young clergyman fell to the ground again. Wickham kicked him in the ribs, and he curled up, clutching his side. As Wickham drew his foot back again, Elizabeth ran to stand between them.

"Stop this," she cried.

Wickham's lips twisted. "Only for your sake, Miss Elizabeth." He wiped his hand across his mouth and blew on his reddened knuckles.

She could not bear to look at him, so she knelt beside Andrew Darcy, still wrapped in a ball, with blood staining his cravat and spattered across his coat. "How may I assist you, sir? May I help you inside?"

He pulled himself to a sitting position, wincing as he reached for his handkerchief and wiped the blood from his face. "I regret you had to see this. You should go back inside. This is not serious."

She had sent him out here, and he had suffered for it. That made it serious in her mind. "When someone is tending to your injuries, I will do so."

He rose to his feet stiffly. "It is just a few bruises." But he staggered a little.

Of course he would not admit to injuries, not when Wickham had just accused him of cowardice. She thought quickly. "You cannot walk down the street covered in blood. You must clean up first. Come in and I will have someone bring you a basin of water."

Wickham moved beside her. "There is nothing to worry about. I did not hit him hard."

She turned a reproachful glare on him. "Indeed," she said icily.

He leaned closer and whispered, "There is more to this than you know. I hope you will never discover how interfering and meddlesome young Drew can be."

"Miss Bennet, will you come in with me? I would not leave you alone here." Andrew's dignified words were muffled by the handkerchief pressed to his face.

Wickham said smoothly, "Miss Bennet knows she is perfectly safe with me."

She gave Wickham a withering look and took the arm Andrew Darcy offered her. "I have nothing to say to you, Mr. Wickham," she said coldly, her voice shaking with rage, and turned her back on him.

THE RED-HAIRED CHAMBERMAID came to the door of Elizabeth's room at the inn. Elizabeth looked up from the letter she was writing, a hot blush rising in her cheeks. Did the girl know Elizabeth had seen her with Wickham? "Yes?"

The girl smirked as she bobbed a curtsey. "The young gentleman in the private parlor is asking for you, miss. Says it's urgent, if you please."

"Do you mean Mr. Andrew Darcy?" What could possibly be so urgent? Perhaps someone had found suitable clothing for him, and he wished to tell her he was leaving.

"Aye, miss."

"Very well, I will join him shortly."

Elizabeth closed the inkwell and cleaned her pen. She would try to keep this farewell brief, with no discussion of the embarrassing situation which had passed, and she could still finish her letter before dinner.

29

The maid waited for her instead of leaving. Did she think Elizabeth would become lost on the way downstairs? More likely she was hoping for a gratuity, one which would not be forthcoming.

Still, Elizabeth was grateful not to be alone when she spotted Mr. Wickham loitering in the doorway as she passed through the public dining room. His polished smile flashed as he noted her presence. She acknowledged him with a cool nod, which was more than he deserved, but she had no desire to make a scene.

At the far end of the room, the chambermaid held open the door to the private parlor. Elizabeth gave her an apologetic smile as she walked past and looked ahead into the room where Andrew Darcy lay on a sofa with its back to her, only his head visible on the armrest. "Sir, you asked to see me?"

The door clicked closed behind her.

Andrew Darcy sat up quickly on the sofa where he had been lying, clutching together the lapels of the borrowed coat he wore. Even so, it was apparent he wore nothing else above his trousers. "I did not send for you," he said sharply.

"Forgive me." Mortified at the sight of the exposed skin on his chest and neck, Elizabeth turned her back and reached blindly for the door latch, eager to escape. But nothing happened when she pushed at the door. Even a hard shove made no difference.

How humiliating! She would have to ask him for help. "The door is stuck." She kept her eyes on the floor.

"If you will turn your back, I will be happy to help." He sounded as embarrassed as she felt.

She followed his instruction and walked halfway across the room for good measure. That way, if anyone discovered them together, it would not look so very bad.

He yanked at the door, muttered something angrily under his breath, then said in a reluctant voice, "Miss Bennet, I am sorry to say we appear to be locked in."

"How could that happen? Never mind; if you will step away, I will knock at the door until someone comes to let us out."

"I would advise against that." His voice was tight.

"What do you mean? Everyone will understand it was an accident that we were locked in together, especially since I just walked in!"

"I do not believe it was just an accident. This is one of Wickham's favorite tricks, creating a compromising situation. All he needs is for someone to claim you have been in here some time."

"Mr. Wickham?" Even after all she had seen of him, she could hardly believe it. He must know how damaging an episode like this could be to a lady's reputation. It would do no more than embarrass Andrew, but it could be devastating for her. But it made too much sense, especially since it was the red-haired chambermaid who had brought her here, presumably at Wickham's behest. How could he have done this to her? "But why?" Her words came out through gritted teeth. "What could he possibly hope to accomplish by this?"

He scowled. "Presumably to embarrass me, in return for my actions earlier. You merely have the misfortune to be caught up in his petty revenge against me. Or perhaps not - you knew him in the past, too. Does he bear a grudge against you?"

Elizabeth shook her head. "None that could account for this." Her voice trembled. Wickham, whom she had so admired for months, was deliberately trying to damage her reputation. And he might well succeed, but she would not think of that now.

Andrew Darcy must have seen her distress, for he said, "We must be cleverer than him. If we call for help, any number of people will hear and become aware of our situation. If we simply wait until someone discovers the locked door on their own, only that person will know, and it may well be someone who is inclined to believe our story, or be willing to forget what they have seen in exchange for a small sum."

"But that could take hours, and it will look that much worse if we are alone in here for such a long time."

"You think so? I suspect it will make no difference if it is a matter of minutes or hours," he said heavily. "But your reputation is far more at risk than mine, so I will abide by your decision."

He was right. But to wait there helplessly as her reputation hung on a matter of chance, depending upon the person who tried the door first – why, it was intolerable! There must be another option.

Perhaps there might be another way out of the room. She hurried to the diamond-paned window, but it overlooked the street. Even if Andrew Darcy could squeeze through the narrow opening, he would certainly be seen by the passersby, and that would look even worse. There was no place in the room to hide, no handy sideboard or cupboard that he could climb into. She felt a flash of annoyance at the innkeeper for his lack of preparation for emergencies of this sort, a reaction that almost brought a smile to her face. How foolish to blame the innkeeper for this circumstance!

"I suspect you are correct that it is wiser to wait," she said reluctantly. "I will sit here by the window and watch in case my uncle and aunt return early. If I can call out to them, they will let us out with no one the wiser." It would also allow her to keep her back to him.

"An excellent idea." There was clear anger underlying his calm words.

They lapsed into silence. Elizabeth's thoughts were unhappy ones. In truth, this should matter little to her in the long run, even if there were scandal from this event; after all, apart from her aunt and uncle, no one from Meryton knew anyone here, and she could trust the Gardiners not to gossip. No shame would follow her home. But her aunt still had friends here, connections she had been so happy to restore on this visit, and any damage to Elizabeth's reputation, especially when she was supposed to be under her aunt's care, would rebound upon Mrs. Gardiner. Her friends might have to sever contact with her, and that would hurt her aunt.

With sudden fury at Mr. Wickham, she wished Andrew Darcy had struck him back. Hard. Or that Fitzwilliam Darcy had exposed Wickham's true behavior years ago, so he would not have been in a position to create this mischief.

If only she had not slipped in the mud and had to return to the inn. If only she had let her uncle walk her to the room. If only she had not tried to hide from Wickham. If only she had not believed the red-haired chambermaid. But all the if-onlys in the world could not change the position she was in, where her only real hope was the Gardiners returning early.

Chapter 4

Of course, the Gardiners were too late. By that time, Elizabeth was back in her room and physically safe, but she could not say the same for her reputation nor her spirits. Anger warred with humiliation as she related the events to Mrs. Gardiner, who had heard only the barest outline from a quietly furious Andrew Darcy before hurrying to her niece's side.

"An hour? You were locked in for over an hour? What happened then?" Mrs. Gardiner asked, her lips thinned.

"It was horrid." Elizabeth shivered at the memory. "A man pounded at the door and demanded that we open it, but of course we could not. He went for the innkeeper, who could not find the key, so they sent for the locksmith. By the time he came and opened it, there was a crowd of people including the magistrate and the mayor. The innkeeper's wife started shrieking about immorality under her roof. Wickham must have worked hard to stir up such an audience," she said bitterly.

"He seemed such a charming fellow when I met him at Christmas," said Mrs. Gardiner. "I should know better than to trust my first impression."

"He fooled me, too." Elizabeth dabbed at her eyes. "I have never been so humiliated in my life." She tried not to think of the horrid names some of the drunken men had hissed at her.

Mrs. Gardiner bit her lip. "I hate to ask you this, my dear, but did anything happen behind that locked door?"

"Nothing at all. Mr. Andrew Darcy was even more mortified by the circumstances than I was, and he would not even look at me."

Her aunt let out a breath. "Good. I am glad he, at least, did not disappoint us."

"It was my fault he went out there and confronted Wickham." The words rushed out of her. "Had I not asked his help, he would not have been injured, and would not have had to wait while his bloody clothes were being cleaned, and none of this would have happened. And he will have to live with the rumors, long after I have gone home and left them behind me."

"He does not seem to blame you. He said that if Wickham wanted revenge on him, he would get it one way or another."

"I cannot be so philosophical."

Her aunt raised her eyebrows. "Why, Lizzy, has young Mr. Darcy engaged your tender feelings?"

Elizabeth's cheeks grew hot. "Not at all. I simply dislike the unfairness of it."

"Are you certain? Because when he spoke to your uncle, he said that marriage to you would be no hardship. I think he may be taken with you. In fact, I know he is."

"Aunt, you can know no such thing!" The last thing she needed was matchmaking from Mrs. Gardiner.

"Can I not? How, then, do you explain his asking me privately when we last visited the parsonage if you had any admirers at home?" Mrs. Gardiner wore a look of puckish pleasure.

Elizabeth forced a breath out between her teeth. Not again! First Fitzwilliam Darcy, now Andrew Darcy. Why was it that the only gentlemen who showed interest in her were the ones she wished to avoid? Had she once again allowed her playful manners to mislead a man? She had tried to keep her distance because of his connection to her Mr. Darcy, or rather to the Mr. Darcy who was not hers. "Pray do not make this into a romance. He is only trying to do the proper thing. I have no interest in him in that way."

A knock came at the door. "It is I," said her uncle.

"Come in," said Elizabeth wearily.

Mr. Gardiner's brow was furrowed. "I hope you are not too shaken by all this nonsense, Lizzy. Darcy has requested that you join us briefly."

For a horrifying moment, Elizabeth thought he was referring to Mr. Darcy of Pemberley, as she had made such a point of thinking of the young clergyman as Andrew Darcy, but then good sense prevailed. "Very well." She would much rather crawl into bed.

Mrs. Gardiner insisted on fussing with Elizabeth's hair a little, as if even the finest hairstyle could make her look anything other than weary and angry, but it was easier to permit her to do it than to fight about it. "Now pinch your cheeks to put a little color in them."

Elizabeth sighed, but obeyed. "Pray let us get this over and done," she said. Trying to lighten the moment, she added, "Uncle, I promise that I will never again refuse your escort to my room!"

She was relieved to discover Andrew Darcy was waiting for them in the small sitting area in the Gardiners' room. At least that meant she did not have to go downstairs into the public areas of the inn again. The bruise on his cheek was more prominent now, but he was fully dressed.

He rose with a slight wince and bowed to her. "Thank you for seeing me, Miss Bennet. I wish to express my regret over the scene you were exposed to earlier."

"I thank you for your concern, though the fault was not yours. And I must apologize again for dragging you into this entire mess. If I had simply not said anything to you about what I had overheard, none of this would have happened."

"You were correct to tell me about it. I would not have wished Wickham's behavior to go unchecked, even if I paid a price for it."

Elizabeth bit her lip. "I am very sorry if his petty revenge causes anyone to think ill of you. I hope people will believe you when you tell them the truth."

The corners of his mouth turned down. "It may not be that simple. I assume he is still well-liked here. Most people see only his charm until it is too late. But that is my problem, not yours, and I am more concerned about a stain on your reputation. Even if this episode was not my fault, it would never have happened had I not accepted your aunt's generous help. But before I say more, I must ask you a question which you may find odd and seemingly unrelated to this matter."

Taken aback by his serious expression, Elizabeth pulled her shawl around her more tightly. "What is that?"

He took a deep breath and exhaled slowly. "What are your views on the slave trade?"

Elizabeth stared at him. "The slave trade? You wish to discuss politics now?" she asked in disbelief.

"I told you it would seem unrelated, but I beg of you to have patience with me," he said evenly.

"Oh, very well," she said crossly. "I believe it is wrong to buy and sell human beings, and the slave trade has been a stain on England's good name."

"I thank you." He rubbed his forehead. "In that case, I propose we amend this slight to your honor with marriage."

Had she not had enough shocks for one day already? "Good God, there is no reason to consider marriage as a remedy! I am leaving here next week, and as long as my aunt and uncle say nothing, no one in my life will be any the wiser that anything has happened. And I fail to see what slavery has to do with it!" Oh, bother her temper! The man was trying to do the decent thing by offering for her, even if it was unnecessary, and he was not to blame for any of this. "Forgive me; I am distraught. Your offer is most generous, but unnecessary."

He exhaled slowly. "Slavery is important because I have dedicated myself to the cause of abolitionism, so much so that I spent several years in my youth working for the great abolitionist Mr. Wilberforce. I would be honor-bound to offer for you even if you supported slavery, but in that case, my offer would have been for marriage in name only, since anything more would make us both bitterly unhappy." He held his chin high, as if expecting a disagreement. "I hope you are correct that word will not reach your home, but Wickham has been known to cause mischief for mischief's sake, and I assume he knows people there."

Mrs. Gardiner protested, "But why would he do that? He was a frequent visitor at Lizzy's family's house."

The young clergyman sighed. "I do not trust Wickham, but perhaps I am worrying about nothing."

Mrs. Gardiner said briskly, "I suspect that is the case, and that we will hear no more from him. Mr. Darcy, I will make a point of telling everyone I know here that my niece absolves you of any inappropriate behavior."

"I thank you." He bowed, looking relieved. "I will leave you now. Miss Bennet, pray accept my most sincere apologies for this unfortunate occurrence, and should any difficulties arise from it, I remain prepared to make amends."

Elizabeth tried to sound dignified, as if she still had any dignity left. "I thank you, sir."

After he left the room, her aunt heaved a sigh. "My poor Lizzy! I am so sorry this happened. I must say young Mr. Darcy handled himself very well, though. He seems an upright young man, and I do not say that only because I am an abolitionist myself."

Elizabeth's breathing slowed as the world seemed to shift back to normal. "He is clearly a man of strong beliefs, and a definite improvement over the last clergyman who proposed to me." She managed to put on a teasing intonation. "He is a little too serious for my taste, though. What a pity it was not my sister Mary in my place! They would have suited each other admirably."

"Mary? Not at all! He is an idealist, not a sermonizer. He does not moralize, nor does he wear his piety on his sleeve as she does. You have no reason to feel obligated to marry him, but were it to become necessary, I think you could make a good match of it. But let us hope it does not come to that."

"It will not," said Elizabeth with absolute certainty. Mr. Andrew Darcy might be a good match, but she had no intention of having any connection to the Darcy family. Just imagine if her Mr. Darcy came home to Pemberley and found her married to his cousin! She would rather have a ruined reputation.

Almost.

Chapter 5

Mr. Andrew Darcy called at the White Hart the following day to inquire after Elizabeth's health and to once again express his appreciation to Mrs. Gardiner for her assistance with the parsonage. Given his bruised face and somewhat stiff gait, Elizabeth felt she should be asking about his well-being instead, but she knew it would not be appreciated, and she was determined to avoid any playfulness that might give him the incorrect idea about her interest. He seemed a bit stilted at the beginning, but after the first uncomfortable minutes, he relaxed into his earlier affable manner. Mrs. Gardiner promised they would stop by Kympton once more before they left Derbyshire, and they parted on easy terms.

The following day the Gardiners and Elizabeth were away from the inn all day, visiting the Heights of Abraham and not returning until it was nearly dark. Even Elizabeth was tired by the long walk through the park, and she looked forward to a quiet dinner and an early night.

Instead they found a grim-looking Andrew Darcy awaiting their return. After paying his respects to the ladies, he asked to speak privately to Mr. Gardiner. Elizabeth's heart sank as they disappeared into the parlor. The two gentlemen had not spent any particular time together in company, so clearly something was wrong.

Her aunt was watching her with concern. "It could have nothing to do with you, Lizzy."

Elizabeth attempted to laugh, but it came out flat. "What are the chances of that? Can you think of anything else that would bring him to speak to my uncle rather than to you?"

Mrs. Gardiner hesitated. "Not immediately, but I also do not see what could have gone amiss to bring him here. If word had spread, how would he know?"

"I suppose he could not." Even if someone had ridden straight to Meryton with the news, they could not yet have returned. Perhaps she was worrying unnecessarily.

"Should it come to that, at least he would be a good match for you," Mrs. Gardiner said with forced cheerfulness. "He is a good man, and his living is a valuable one. That parsonage will make a fine home once it has a woman's presence in it, and you have often said how much you like the scenery here."

But his last name would still be Darcy, and he owed that valuable living to the generosity of the Master of Pemberley, a man she never wished to see again. She could hardly tell her aunt any of that, though. "I do not wish to be forced into marriage with a man I hardly know, and I would hate to be so far from my family."

Her aunt gave her a quick hug. "Of course, and I hope it will not come to pass. But if you have to live in that lovely parsonage, I assure you that we will come to visit you!"

A quarter of an hour later Mr. Gardiner joined them, closing the door behind him. His expression was grave.

"What is it, my love?" asked Mrs. Gardiner.

He sat down with a heavy sigh. "He has received a letter from Mr. Wickham, who says he is on his way to Meryton with the intention of sharing the news, but he could be convinced to change his mind in exchange for the sum of five thousand pounds. I am sorry, Lizzy."

"Five thousand pounds!" cried Mrs. Gardiner. "Why, that is utterly absurd. How could that poor young man possibly obtain such a sum?"

"Young Mr. Darcy tells me he cannot raise that amount, nor would he pay it if he could, for Wickham would just keep asking for more. I could not argue the point; blackmailers rarely settle for one payment."

Her mouth dry, Elizabeth said, "And if he had it, why would he pay it to protect the reputation of a girl he barely knows? It makes no sense."

"That is a very good question," said her uncle. "He believes that Wickham's motive is to damage his reputation rather than yours, going back to some old conflict, and that it has already had an effect. He was very frank with me, saying he was a difficult child, sent down from two schools before being educated at home by Mr. Morris, whom he credits with teaching him right from wrong. He says he has led a blameless life in London since then, but people here still remember him as a troublemaker. His parishioners in Kympton seem inclined to believe Wickham over him."

Mrs. Gardiner took Elizabeth's hand. "Will people in Meryton listen to Wickham? Surely they will trust you if you say nothing happened."

Elizabeth stared at the floor. "I do not know. His manners are appealing, and he appears so very trustworthy... I believed his lies without a second thought, even when people suggested I should reconsider. And when I learned what he truly was, I said nothing. He was leaving for Brighton, and Jane convinced me it was better to let sleeping dogs lie. What a mistake! Had I exposed him then, this could not have happened now."

"No point in rehashing the past," Mr. Gardiner said. "The question is what to do next. Mr. Andrew Darcy is willing to marry you, and seems to think that is the best solution for him. Whether or not it is the best for you is for you to decide. Obviously, the impact of a scandal on your sisters' prospects is a matter of concern."

A matter of concern? It was a disaster. She already had good cause to be worried for her family's future. With this scandal, her family would be shunned. Not even a tradesman would be willing to marry Jane, and her mother and sisters would be destitute and alone after her father's death. "I see."

"For what it is worth, he went over his finances with me, and you could do much worse, Lizzy. His living brings in six hundred pounds a year."

No matter how eligible he might be, his name was still Darcy. A lead weight settled in her stomach. She needed to know more about his connection to Pemberley and to Mr. Fitzwilliam Darcy. Not that it would make a real difference, since she could not put her pride ahead of her family's well-being, but she could not bear to be ignorant of it. "I suppose I must speak to him," she said.

"I think you must," Mr. Gardiner said gently. "He is waiting for you."

Elizabeth trudged downstairs, conscious of blushing as she stepped into the private parlor and shut the door behind her. Just two days ago, she had been locked in this very room, betrayed by a man she had once cared for, and with humiliation in the offing. Now she had to face an unwanted proposal, just as she had with Mr. Collins, but that had been quite different.

Then she had been embarrassed for his sake and quite certain of her own answer, with little to lose. Andrew Darcy was a gentleman she respected, even if she had no wish to marry him, and she had a great deal to lose.

He bowed. "Miss Bennet, I thank you for joining me. You are no doubt aware of why I am here, but as I have no wish to embarrass either of us, I will not pose the question I came here to ask, unless you indicate you wish to hear it."

"That is most considerate. I do not know how much choice I have, but there are some questions I would like answered before I come to a conclusion."

"Of course." He gestured to a chair by the fire. "I will be happy to tell you whatever I may."

"Forgive me. My nerves are too agitated for me to sit still." She stood beside the chimneypiece instead, running her fingertips along the mantle. "You said once that you preferred not to have anything to do with Pemberley, yet I am told that Kympton is a Pemberley living, so I assume you received it from the current Master of Pemberley."

He raised his eyebrows. "You are observant, and I suppose it is only right that I explain some of my situation to you. I was a dependent of the late Master of Pemberley, old Mr. Darcy, as they call him now, who disliked me intensely. When I was sixteen, he disowned any connection to me and ordered me never to set foot on Pemberley land again."

"How horrible!" She had never heard anything but praise of old Mr. Darcy, first from Wickham, and then from the Pemberley housekeeper. But Wickham had proven his word was not to be trusted, and it was natural for a servant to praise her master. "Yet the current Mr. Darcy of Pemberley gave you a valuable living."

The young clergyman spread his hands. "He seems to feel some sort of responsibility towards me. I have hardly seen him since we were children, but he does not appear to bear me ill will. As far as I know, he had no part in his father's decision."

"You are not close to him, then?" she hazarded. That would make it easier.

41

"No. After his father died, he made an effort to reach out to me, but my unhappy memories of Pemberley left me hesitant to have any more connection than necessary." His shoulders looked stiff.

"I can understand that, and I have no wish to remind you of past unpleasantness." Still, it did not sound as if she would be expected to socialize frequently with Mr. Darcy should she marry him. But sooner or later, Mr. Andrew Darcy would discover that Elizabeth knew the Master of Pemberley, so she might as well admit it now. "I have a confession to make. I am acquainted with Mr. Fitzwilliam Darcy."

"You are?" She had surprised him; she could see that in his widened eyes, and he did not appear pleased. "How do you know him?"

"I met him when he was visiting a friend who had taken a house near mine. We saw each other at social occasions, and later we were in company again when I was visiting my cousin." It was true, so why did it feel like a lie? "But I must be honest with you. I think it possible he would not be best pleased by a marriage between us."

"Is there a reason he would oppose it?" he asked warily.

She could not tell him the truth, but perhaps part of it would do. "He disapproves of my family. His friend wished to marry my sister, and Mr. Darcy advised him strongly against it."

Now he looked worried. "What was his objection to your family?"

She dug her fingernails into her palm. Under the circumstances, he had the right to ask. "My father is a gentleman, but my mother's family is from trade. Mr. Darcy also objected to what he saw as a want of propriety in my mother's behavior and that of my youngest sisters, who can be outrageous flirts. He did at least allow that my conduct avoided such censure." She could not keep the bitterness out of her voice.

He blinked in surprise. "He told you that? I had not thought his manners so poor."

"No, not at all." But how could she explain the extraordinary situation of Mr. Darcy's letter to her without telling him of the proposal? "I overheard him say it to someone else. But it made me somewhat wary of being in his company, hence my questions about your connection with him. But perhaps you are a distant enough relation that he would not object to your marriage to someone with my disadvantages."

He looked puzzled. "We are estranged, perhaps, but even I can hardly call my brother a distant relation."

"Your brother?" she asked blankly. "Who is your brother?"

"Fitzwilliam, of course. Mr. Darcy of Pemberley. Did you not know?"

An awful pit opened in her stomach. "Your brother? How can he be your brother? He never mentioned a brother to me, only a sister."

Andrew Darcy paled. "I should not be surprised. As I said, we have had little contact. I apologize; I assumed you knew who I was. It is not a secret. Everyone here knows who I am."

Disbelief flooded her. "I did not. I thought you were a cousin of some sort. You do not look like him."

"No," he said grimly. "I do not."

This was a nightmare. "When I visited Pemberley, there were portraits of him and his sister, and even one of Mr. Wickham, but none of you."

"I expect my miniature was destroyed long ago," he said evenly.

"And when you spoke of old Mr. Darcy, you did not call him your father." She was babbling, but she could not stop herself. How could this have happened? She was all but engaged to Mr. Darcy's brother. Good God, what would he think? She sank down into a chair, fighting the urge to bury her face in her hands.

"According to law, the late Mr. Darcy was my father," he said icily. "That day when I was sixteen, he informed me he had purchased a commission for me. He was well aware of my pacifist beliefs. When I refused it, he said I could either take the commission or leave Pemberley forever that very day with nothing but the clothes on my back. As I was leaving, he disowned me as his son. I paid him the same courtesy, and I have not called him my father since that day."

Even through the haze of her own shock and dismay, she could hardly miss that he was also distressed, his pallor now quite remarkable. "I am sorry that you were placed in such a position," she said.

"I was not bereft; Mr. Morris was, in every way that mattered, a true father to me. But I cannot help but wonder at the strength of your reaction if my brother is no more than a casual acquaintance of yours."

Now she did put her face in her hands. This was hopeless. Her sisters' future depended on Elizabeth marrying this man, but she did not wish to lie to her future husband, nor to expose the intimate secrets of his brother. There was enough standing between them without Andrew knowing she had humiliated his brother by refusing his proposal.

Perhaps she could still find a way to be truthful. "There was more, but it will not reflect well on either me or your brother. The last time I spoke to him, we quarreled bitterly. I had just discovered he had stopped his friend from proposing to my sister, who suffered grievously from his abandonment. I confronted him about it. He admitted it and criticized my family. I then taxed him about his supposed misdeeds towards Mr. Wickham – I can explain later how Mr. Wickham came to tell me lies about your brother – and he retorted quite strongly. We were both in high temper and decidedly uncivil. It is not an occasion I look back on with pride, and I daresay he most likely feels the same. I saw him briefly in passing the following day, and that was the end of my acquaintance with him. I had hoped never to see him again after making such a fool of myself."

It was even true. It simply was not complete.

"I see," said Andrew Darcy slowly. "Marrying me likely would mean meeting him on occasion, although I cannot think it would be frequent. Could you do that?"

She managed a laugh, although it sounded hollow. "I could certainly manage it. It is only an embarrassing moment in the past, and I would like to believe I have grown in understanding since then. I do not believe your brother and I will ever be friends, but I can be civil to him. I assure you my behavior on that day was not typical of me. I am quite ashamed of it, and I would wish to forget it myself. No obligation less than the present would induce me to unfold it to any human being." She was painfully aware she was echoing Mr. Darcy's own words from his letter to her.

The young clergyman was frowning, as well he might, no doubt questioning his decision to offer marriage to a woman who had behaved in such a manner. "Does Wickham know you quarreled with my brother?"

"No. He knew of our acquaintance, but not the quarrel."

He nodded. "That explains one mystery at least. I could not understand why Wickham thought I could pay him a sum that is far beyond my means. He must have assumed you were here as my brother's guest, and that I would appeal to him for the money. He said something about Fitzwilliam, but I paid no particular attention to it."

Had Wickham targeted her because of her supposed connection to Mr. Darcy? That would be the final irony. "I assure you your brother would not pay a penny to protect my reputation," she said with complete sincerity. Why would he help her after the way she had treated him?

"I hope that is not true, but in any case, I am in no position to ask him for a substantial sum of money on your behalf."

"I would not wish you to!" she exclaimed. "If Mr. Wickham thought he could profit from my acquaintance with your brother while revenging himself on you, that is my misfortune, not your problem."

"And for holding the living he still seems to feel he has some right to," he said darkly. "As if it were my fault my brother gave it to me instead of him."

Did he know the history of why Mr. Darcy had not given the living to Wickham? Elizabeth had already revealed altogether too much knowledge of his brother's private affairs, so she chose to say no more on the matter.

The door opened, revealing her aunt and uncle. Mr. Gardiner said, "You have been in here quite some time. Have you reached a decision?"

Elizabeth exchanged a glance with Andrew Darcy. Had they? "We encountered a stumbling block when I learned he is the brother of Mr. Fitzwilliam Darcy of Pemberley, who did not wish Mr. Bingley to marry my sister Jane, and I suspect he will like the idea of his brother marrying me even less." For more than one reason.

Mr. Gardiner frowned. "Does this affect your willingness to marry my niece?" he asked.

To his credit, Andrew Darcy did not hesitate. "No. It has no impact upon my responsibility to protect Miss Bennet's good name, and I do not need my brother's approval to marry."

Relief for her family's sake warred with trepidation for her own, but she made herself smile as she said, "It is decided, then." Elizabeth Bennet of Longbourn would become Mrs. Andrew Darcy of Kympton, sister-in-law of Mr. Fitzwilliam Darcy of Pemberley. Her heart twisted at the idea of seeing him again, but there was nothing to be done for it.

Chapter 6

Of course, that was not the end of it. There was no such mercy in the world. She had to keep a cheerful countenance through the Gardiners' congratulations, to smile at Andrew Darcy who was, after all, doing her a great kindness by agreeing to save her family from disgrace, and try to pretend she did not feel the walls of the room closing in around her. She numbly allowed her uncle to handle the debate over how best to seek Mr. Bennet's consent to the engagement, given the urgency of proceeding with it before Wickham could spread his poison.

Finally it was resolved Andrew would write to Mr. Bennet that very night. Elizabeth could almost hear the key turning in the lock of her future, but she kept the dutiful smile on her face as Andrew bowed over her hand before he left.

Somehow she managed to say, "I will do my best to make certain you never regret your decision today."

"As will I," he said warmly. "Regardless of how our engagement began, I believe we will have a good life together."

As he left, she felt as if her lips were exhausted with the effort of maintaining that smile. "I must write to my parents, too," she said. "Otherwise it will be quite a shock when my father receives a letter from a total stranger asking for his permission to marry me."

"I will also write to Bennet to explain the situation," said her uncle. "I must say that, despite the circumstances, it is a relief to know that you will be well married. It will improve your sisters' chances of catching husbands, too. No man is anxious to marry a woman with so many single sisters as potential dependents. You may be sure I avoided mentioning your sisters to your young suitor, even though I told him we intended to care for your mother, should she be widowed."

"You are very good to be so concerned for my family's future," Elizabeth said. And how unfair that the burden of worry had landed on the Gardiners when it should have been her father's task to set aside money to care for his daughters after his death!

"And you will be living in one of the most beautiful parts of England," said Mrs. Gardiner with determined cheer. "If only it were not so far from London! I will miss you so."

"On that I may offer you some comfort," said Elizabeth. "Mr. Andrew Darcy says he would expect us to travel to London every year or two for his abolition work, and with Longbourn only ten miles from the Great North Road, I will be able to see both you and my family." It was some comfort at least.

IT WAS MIDNIGHT BY the time she had written, re-written, and re-re-written her letter to her parents, and penned a much longer, if less coherent, missive to her sister Jane, and Elizabeth's eyes ached from her close labor by dim candlelight. She made a perfunctory effort to scrub the ink from her fingers before falling into bed exhausted, having forgotten to draw the curtains.

Dawn light awoke her the next morning, and with it, the events of the previous day came rushing back. Now the stark realization came to her that she had agreed to marry a man she barely knew. Mr. Wickham had fooled her with his agreeable manners and flattery; what if Andrew Darcy had done the same? The warning signs were there: he had been disowned by his father, had little to do with the rest of his family, and had been sent down from two schools. What was she thinking, to put herself into the power of a man when she did not know what he was capable of? Being a pacifist towards other men did not guarantee that he would not beat his wife, or prove to be cruel or a drunkard.

Panic tightened her throat. Her breathing shallow, she dressed herself with trembling fingers. What had she done? Had she saved herself from the frying pan of scandal only to jump into the fire of a life of misery?

She had to find out more about him. She had judged George Wickham by his appearance of goodness and asked no questions. This time she would do better. But whom could she ask? His servants, perhaps, but they might be reluctant to be honest about his faults. Mr. Morris, the clergyman who had introduced them, would be a better bet.

Just the thought of the amiable old gentleman steadied her. He had known Andrew Darcy most of his life and seemed fond of him. That was a good sign, was it not? If he believed the younger man was dangerous or unstable, surely he would not be on such warm terms with him. Unless, of course, he was keeping an eye on him because he feared what Andrew might do otherwise.

He could tell her more. She would speak to Mr. Morris and try to understand her future husband better. If the old rector could not reassure her, she could break off the engagement before it was formally announced.

It was much too early to go out, but she could not bear to wait, especially knowing that her aunt and uncle would likely have other plans for her later in the day. No, if she was going to break the rules and call on a widowed gentleman by herself, she might as well ignore the expectations about an appropriate time for it as well.

She waited only long enough for the townsfolk to be about in the streets. Leaving a note for her aunt, she set off without even stopping to break her fast.

To her relief, she found the old gentleman puttering in his garden, saving her the embarrassment of facing a servant at the door. He greeted her cheerfully, holding the gate open so she could enter through the archway of climbing roses.

Elizabeth folded her hands so tightly that her knuckles hurt. "Pray forgive me for calling on you at such an early hour."

"Not at all. You are always welcome, and I do not imagine this is a social visit purely for the charm of my company," Mr. Morris said with a twinkle in his eye. "How may I be of service to you, Miss Bennet?"

She carefully unclasped her hands. "You may already be aware that yesterday I agreed to marry Mr. Andrew Darcy." She still could not bring herself to call him simply Mr. Darcy. That name belonged to another man.

"Yes, he stopped by last evening after leaving you, and I was very pleased to hear the news, even if the circumstances left something to be desired."

"Well, that is why I am here. I am not as well acquainted with him as I ought to be to undertake a decision of this magnitude." Her words came out in a rush. "My instincts tell me he is a decent and honest man, but those same instincts have misled me before when it comes to a young man's character, and I have also heard things about Mr. Andrew Darcy which concern me. I came today to ask you, as someone who has known him for years, how I am to make sense of the two Andrew Darcys I have heard about. One is an upright abolitionist who is concerned for the sensibilities of his parishioners, and the other was a young hellion who was sent down from two schools and disowned by his father. I fear to find myself in the power of that Andrew Darcy."

Mr. Morris pursed his lips. "I am sorry to hear people are still repeating those old stories. One would wish that they would look at the man he is, rather than the boy he once was. But that does not answer your question, does it? This much I can tell you: he is a good man, one who has known troubles and not allowed them to defeat him. Have you spoken to Drew about your concerns?"

Elizabeth hesitated. "He told me the outline of the problems, but it is clearly painful for him to discuss his past. I thought the view of someone less involved might be clearer."

"I cannot call myself uninvolved; I was his tutor from the time he was a young boy."

"And was he an ill-tempered child?" She held her breath.

"Not ill-tempered, no. He was strong-willed about certain things, and he could not abide unfairness, something which caused him no small difficulty. Most of us learn early that if we disapprove of someone's behavior, it can be wisest to say nothing. Andrew insisted on tilting at every windmill, and he made enemies that way."

"Including his father?" Elizabeth could not imagine what would lead a father to disown his son.

The elderly clergyman removed his spectacles and placed them in his pocket. "That was a difficult situation, and most of what I know about it was told to me in confidence, but I can say this much. While Drew certainly exacerbated the situation with his lack of tact and angry outbursts, the bulk of the blame must rest with his father, who had already conceived an implacable dislike for him by the time I first met him at the age of five. Even then, Drew could do nothing right in his father's eyes and took the blame for anything that went amiss."

Elizabeth wondered how much of this she could trust, and what he might be leaving out. "But the problems were not just in his father's eyes, if he was sent down from two schools."

The old gentleman laughed. "No, for that you must blame me as much as Drew. He was sent down for his refusal to disavow the moral beliefs I had taught him. His schoolmasters did not take kindly to being lectured by a sanctimonious child about their failure to confront the evils of slavery. There was also a question of his safety. You may be aware that physical bullying is the rule, rather than the exception, at boarding schools; it is thought to build character. But a boy who refuses to defend himself while provoking the bullies by quoting Scripture at them – well, bullying can go too far, and it was easier to expel young Andrew than all the bullies."

"He held those beliefs even as a schoolboy?"

"That is where I must take the responsibility, or perhaps the credit. Lady Anne Darcy hired me as his tutor specifically to encourage his moral development, owing to her concerns about certain influences he was exposed to, and she particularly wished him to share her abolitionist beliefs."

A light dawned. "Permit me to guess; his father did not share those abolitionist views."

"Indeed, no. He had a large, very profitable plantation in Jamaica."

Apparently the Darcy family had hidden complexities. The only thing she had known about Mr. Fitzwilliam Darcy when she met him was the size of his fortune. She might have understood him better if she had learned some of this sooner. She could not resist asking, "Did you also teach the older Darcy boy?"

"Briefly. He left for school a few months after I arrived."

She would have liked to ask more about him, but could not justify that curiosity. "But you remained in contact with Mr. Andrew Darcy after he went to school."

"When he was sent down, I offered to take him on as a private student who would live with me. I knew he should not remain in his father's house."

"Did he give you any difficulties?"

"No more than any other boy in the difficult years and less than most. That moralistic streak, you know. Drew is not perfect by any means. He can be stubborn, and he does not easily let go of resentments. If it is an issue to you, his theology is somewhat Non-Conformist, so if you are hoping for a high church clergyman, you may be disappointed."

She shook her head. "Although I grew up with a traditionalist rector, I am open-minded. I had guessed he might be Non-Conformist, given his strong moral views on society's ills." If she had to marry a clergyman, it was a relief he would be encouraging her to strive for equality and justice rather than forcing her to read Fordyce's Sermons.

"I am glad you will not judge him for that, not least because he is again following my own leadings. And I must say, unlike most younger sons who enter the clergy because it is an easier life than the Army or Navy, I believe Drew has a true calling."

"I sense there is a 'but' in there somewhere."

"Not regarding his character, if that is your concern. Merely an old teacher's regret that, while I succeeded in instilling a sense of morality and duty in Drew, I do not believe he has learned to feel the joyous side of God's love. Someday I would like to see him more familiar with happiness. Perhaps your marriage will bring him that."

"I will try to make him happy," she said dully.

He gazed at her and said gently, "I wish it could bring you happiness, too, but I can see your engagement does not. Is this a poor match for you? I know little of your background. Or is there someone else you hoped to marry?"

She shook her head. "No. I just dislike being forced into it. I am well aware he is doing me a favor by offering for me. He seems to feel obligated to do it, which makes me worry he will someday resent me for it."

He chuckled. "Drew does have a tendency to attempt to rescue people, but in this case, you have no reason to fret. He is quite satisfied to marry you. In fact, I would venture to guess he is pleased it turned out this way."

Her hands curled into fists. "Pleased?" For some reason, it made her furious.

"Only with the outcome, not the method. The day we met, I had just advised Drew that he would be wise to start looking for a bride, now that he could finally afford to marry. He agreed, but did not want to court a local girl who would have heard gossip about him all her life. He planned to wait until he returned to London and could look for a bride there. I told him I thought a country girl might be better suited to life in Kympton, but he was determined. Stubborn, as I said. Then you arrived with your aunt and uncle, a pretty country girl of good birth who knew nothing of his past, and I can assure you that it crossed both his mind and mine that you might be a perfect solution to his problem."

Her mouth twisted. "I suppose I should be glad he is pleased, and that I meet his criteria so well."

"He likes you, too. How can I explain this? Most young men are always chasing after girls. Drew has never been like that. He holds in abhorrence the idea of leading on a young woman with no expectation of marriage. As a result, he is unskilled at flirtation and courting. When I said he was pleased at the outcome, it was because he was struggling with how to tell you that he found you charming and would like to know you better, especially since your time here was so short. Like any of us faced with a task we feel unequipped for, he is happy it has been taken out of his hands."

They talked a short while longer. When Elizabeth set off once again for the inn, she felt oddly discontented. What was wrong with her? She should have been reassured by Mr. Morris' words, but instead she felt almost angry. He had given her no reason to be concerned. Or was that the problem? Had she hoped he would give her an excuse to break off the engagement, some reason it would be better for her to face disgrace than to marry Andrew Darcy?

She was not ready to return to the inn and face the Gardiners and their enthusiasm for her forced engagement, so she dawdled in front of a shop window, admiring the fabrics and ribbons on display. It was a different selection than she usually saw in Meryton, and she felt a wave of nostalgia for the time when her biggest worry was choosing the perfect color of shoe-roses for the Netherfield ball.

On impulse she went inside, the bells on the door tinkling behind her. Perhaps the distraction of shopping was just what she needed right now. Her future might be out of her hands, but she could still buy a nice silk flower to add to her bonnet.

"May I help you, miss?" A neatly dressed woman, slightly stooped with age, came from behind the counter.

Elizabeth looked up from the ribbon display. "Do you have any wider ribbons? I managed to stain my favorite dress when I fell in the mud, and I am looking for ideas on how to cover the stain."

The woman looked her up and down, judging her attire and appearance. "Where is the stain located?"

She bent down and pointed to a spot near her left ankle. "The worst part is here, about three fingers wide. And then there is a discolored area along the side and a small rip over there. I suppose I should just make a new skirt, but I am particularly fond of the fabric and have no more of it." That dress had always earned her compliments. Even Mr. Darcy once said it suited her. Mr. Darcy, who was still overshadowing her life.

"What sort of dress is it?"

"A fairly simple day dress, sky-blue with a pattern of pale yellow flowers."

The woman pursed her lips. "I have a thought."

She bustled to the back and returned with a well-worn copy of Ackermann's Repository. She thumbed through it and stopped at a page. "Here we are. What if you remade it like this skirt, scalloping the bottom to remove the stain and adding a strip of fabric below it, and then a layer of netting at the top to disguise the discoloration?"

Elizabeth studied the illustration. "The rosettes might be too much for this dress, but yes, that could work." Excitement trickled through her at the thought of how stylish it would look. The milliner in Meryton never had such clever ideas!

"Perhaps some braid in place of the rosettes?" The woman sounded pleased. "I have a selection you could look at here. Or, if you wish, you could bring the dress in and see what matches best."

For the first time since her fall in the mud and all that had followed it, Elizabeth actually felt hopeful about something. "That would be lovely. I am only here for a few days, but I would greatly appreciate your advice. You seem to have an excellent eye."

The woman chuckled. "I enjoy making over old dresses, even more than new ones. Not the best business sense, I suppose, but more practical for my customers, and I do like adding a little beauty to the world."

Elizabeth could not help smiling at her enthusiasm. "I will fetch it now. It will be just a few minutes, as I am staying at the White Hart."

The woman's eyes brightened. "Aye, then, are you the young lady who is newly engaged to young Mr. Darcy? I had heard she was a Southerner."

"That is I." Elizabeth's smile faltered. At least it was "newly engaged" instead of "disgraced." Rather like making over a torn, stained dress.

"Well, my best wishes to you. It has been years since I saw him last, but I thought him a good lad when he lived here with Mr. Morris."

Elizabeth raised an eyebrow. "You did not think him a troublemaker?"

She snorted. "Perhaps he was once, but what child was not, at some point? Always courteous to me, he was, and once he stopped the other boys from stealing apples from my tree. If he learned the error of his earlier ways, then I think the better of him for it."

Just what her sister Jane would have said, to look at the bright side. There was no reason to be so distressed at the idea of this marriage. She disliked being forced into it, of course, but Andrew was a decent man, educated, and able to support her. If he had not been related to Mr. Darcy, and had chosen to court her, she might well have been pleased to marry him.

If he had not been related to Mr. Darcy.

That was the core of her trouble, was it not? Marrying Andrew meant the humiliation of being in company again with Mr. Darcy after having been so foolish and unfair to him in the past. She would have to face his disgust over her engagement to his brother. Still, why should she allow his shadow to hang over her, to destroy any hope she might feel for the match? Yes, she would have some uncomfortable interactions with Mr. Darcy from time to time, there was no doubt of it. That was no reason to refuse Andrew, not when the price of doing so was disgrace for her whole family.

She straightened her shoulders, determined to remake her attitude towards Andrew along with her stained dress. She would not give Mr.

Darcy's inevitable disapproval the power to harm her. She would banish him from her mind.

Chapter 7

Elizabeth returned to the milliner shortly afterwards accompanied by Mrs. Gardiner. Her aunt was clearly so relieved to see her niece smiling again that she would happily have ordered her a dozen new dresses. She convinced Elizabeth to allow the milliner to do the alterations for her, and enjoyed a long chat with her about current fashions in London.

When they returned to the inn, Andrew Darcy was waiting for them. Elizabeth was able to greet him with equanimity, but still felt surprisingly shy of him. Had he truly been interested in courting her for her own sake?

After exchanging greetings, he said, "I made a copy of my letter to your father, thinking you might wish to know what I had said."

"That was thoughtful of you. This will be quite a surprise to him."

"I imagine it will be. I can only hope it is not a completely unpleasant one."

Elizabeth was fairly certain her father would not be pleased by any marriage that took her so far from Longbourn, but saw no point in saying so. Instead she said lightly, "You are a great improvement over the last clergyman who asked for my hand. You, for example, seem to think my opinion of the match has some bearing on the matter."

"Of course it does," he said seriously. "You are a person, not a slave."

It was the correct answer, but also a reminder that Andrew did not share her taste for banter. Perhaps he could learn to tease with time. She would have to hope so. No, she *would* hope so, because she was determined to be optimistic about their future, to make the stained, ripped dress of their forced engagement into a fashionable gown she could be proud of.

They made arrangements to meet again the next day. "If the weather is fair, I will take you out in the gig and show you more of the countryside," the young clergyman said. "Until your father gives his permission for the engagement, we should not be alone in private, but I think driving in an open carriage alone would be unobjectionable. Perhaps we could go to Peveril Castle, since you missed the chance to see it."

"An excellent idea," said Elizabeth, who had no wish to follow her aunt's plans to visit with her Lambton friends, the ones who had made excuses not to see her after Elizabeth was compromised, but were happy to call on her aunt again now that she was engaged. Besides, she needed to know Andrew better.

WHEN ANDREW APPEARED the next morning, he said, "I had the opportunity to share our news with my brother last night. I received word he had returned to Pemberley earlier than expected, so I stopped there to tell him."

Elizabeth's heart began to pound, nausea curling inside her. "Your brother is here?" So much for not thinking about the shame of meeting Mr. Darcy again!

"Yes, and I thought it best not to delay in giving him our tidings. While I have no need of his blessing nor his approval, I did not wish to appear to be hiding our engagement."

"May I ask how he responded to the news?" Elizabeth's mouth was dry.

"He was surprised, indubitably, but he said the proper things."

Of course he would have said the proper things; what other choice did he have? "Did he speak about his past acquaintance with me?"

Andrew's expression grew shuttered. "He acknowledged it, but said nothing about the substance of it." But she was sure there was something he was not telling her, and it did not help the knot in her stomach.

Mrs. Gardiner, when she heard this news, said, "If your brother is now aware of the engagement, would it not be proper for you to take Lizzy to call on him?"

No! Calling on Mr. Darcy, facing his disgust and dislike, was the last thing she wanted to do. But her aunt was correct. If she avoided meeting him now, it would simply remain hanging over her head until she did.

Good heavens, what if the first time she saw him again was at her wedding? No, it would be better to do it now, even if she did not like it.

Andrew looked as unenthusiastic about the idea as she felt. "I suppose that is good advice, and we could put off Peveril Castle until another time."

Elizabeth glanced down at the dress she was wearing, a plain brown muslin of a serviceable appearance which she had chosen to avoid showing road dust. Should she change into her pretty green flowered dress with lace and a low neckline? That might be more suitable for a call, but she would not want to give the appearance of trying to attract Mr. Darcy's admiration. No, it was better to look plain; no one could accuse her of using arts and allurements dressed like this.

She fetched her bonnet and gloves, and Andrew handed her into the gig before swinging up to the driver's seat and setting the horses in motion. He seemed more solemn than he had earlier.

Once they left the village, she said, "I apologize if this call is an inconvenience for you."

His mouth twisted, but he said, "No, it is the proper thing to do. You will have to forgive my lack of enthusiasm. It is not about your company or even the errand, merely my dislike of going to Pemberley. I would be happy never to set foot there again."

"I am relieved that your reluctance is not about presenting me to your brother," she said.

"Not at all," he responded with a dry smile. "I am merely chasing old ghosts."

His warmth encouraged her to say, "I do wish to make a confession. I sought a character reference for you from Mr. Morris yesterday. After a long night of worrying about the wisdom of agreeing to marry a man I hardly knew, especially one who had once been disowned and sent down from school, I felt a need for some reassurance, which he was able to provide."

"What did he tell you about my father?" His voice was tight.

"Mostly that he had taken an unreasonable dislike to you and treated you unfairly, and that your political convictions, which I can only support, were the source of your problems at school."

"That, and a childish inability to keep those opinions to myself," he said self-deprecatingly. His hands tightened on the reins, and he added stiffly,

"I can understand your concern based on the bare-bones version of my history, and if you have other questions, I will do my best to answer them." It clearly cost him some pride to make the offer.

"I thank you, but I was fully reassured by Mr. Morris' answers. I can see for myself the gentleman you are today, and that is the important thing." It was the right thing to say, even if she still had some qualms.

"I am glad of that," he said wryly. "I suppose I have a confession of my own, too. When I told my brother of our engagement, I left George Wickham out of the story. He has been the source of enough family quarrels already, and I did not see any advantage in complaining of his involvement when there is nothing to be done about it."

How had he explained their compromising situation, then? But it could as easily have been an accident that they were locked in, and Mr. Darcy's hatred of Wickham was fierce enough without further feeding the flames. "Thank you for warning me. I cannot see how the subject would arise, but I will not mention him."

"Good." They reached the top of the hill where the woods ceased, and Elizabeth's eye was once more caught by the impressive view of the grand house, of which she once might have been mistress.

DARCY FELT DEAD INSIDE as he went through the motions of welcoming Georgiana, Bingley, and Bingley's sisters to Pemberley. Somehow he managed to suppress the urge to shout at them to go away, to leave him alone in his misery. Instead he politely asked the servants to show them to their rooms and paced the gallery for half an hour wishing he could be galloping over the countryside instead. Perhaps the wind whistling past his face could bring him back to life for a few minutes.

Miss Bingley was the first to present herself, no doubt hoping to find him alone, but the housekeeper had followed his instructions to have servants in whatever room Miss Bingley occupied. She had become increasingly desperate in her pursuit of him of late, and Darcy had no desire to be entrapped by her. But he could not invite Bingley without his sisters, and Georgiana needed time to get to know Bingley better before he suggested a potential match between them, so he perforce had to tolerate Miss Bingley's pretensions.

If only Elizabeth had agreed to marry him! But the thought of Elizabeth was like glass shards ripping through his skin. Elizabeth and Andrew, a punishment from a vindictive God for his sin of pride.

But he made polite conversation with Miss Bingley, listening with an effort to her gushing, obsequious praise of Pemberley, until Bingley joined them, reporting that Mr. and Mrs. Hurst had elected to rest after their long journey. Georgiana did not appear for nearly an hour, but that was hardly surprising. His sister always found Miss Bingley's attentions to be trying, and they had been traveling together for days. No doubt she had needed the time alone

Georgiana took the seat next to him, a faint air of concern on her brow. "Has something displeased you, brother?" she asked in a low voice.

Sometimes Georgiana could be a little too perceptive. From experience, Darcy knew she would not believe a flat denial. "I did not sleep well, but that is all." He had lain awake for hours, haunted by the specter of Elizabeth in his brother's arms.

His sister nodded, seeming to accept his explanation, and began to pour tea for their guests in the teacups his mother had carefully chosen to match the rose silk on the walls. Had Darcy been able to care about anything, he would have been proud to see her taking on her hostess duties with such aplomb.

The butler appeared in the doorway and intoned, "Mr. Andrew Darcy and Miss Bennet."

Elizabeth. The unexpected sight of her caught him by the throat. The familiar angle at which she held her head, the curve of her neck, her light and pleasing figure that now belonged to his brother. Darcy swallowed bile as he rose and bowed.

A crash broke into his consciousness. A shattered teacup leaked tea onto the floor at Georgiana's feet as she gaped at Drew, her face bleached of all color. Seemingly oblivious of the spill, she took a few shaky steps forward. "Drew, is that truly you?" She cast herself into his arms and began to cry.

"Oh, Georgie," Drew said in a low voice, and there were tears in his eyes as well as he embraced her.

Darcy froze at the sight of the tableau before him. Elizabeth, whom he had loved and lost. Georgiana, distraught. Drew, lost for so many years. What should he do?

Elizabeth's low, melodious voice echoed through him. "Miss Bingley, Mr. Bingley, what an unexpected pleasure it is to see you again! I noticed a lovely rose garden outside that I am longing to explore. Since you are more familiar with Pemberley than I, will you not do me the very great kindness of showing it to me?"

Darcy cast her a look of helpless gratitude.

Bingley rose to the occasion. "Ah, rose garden. Yes. What an excellent idea, Miss Bennet! Let us go this instant, Caroline." He hurried them out of the room, leaving Darcy alone with his brother and sister for the first time in nearly a decade.

Georgiana was still sobbing audibly. Darcy forced his feet forward, stepping around the maid who was picking up pieces of the broken teacup and saucer, and told her quietly to leave it until later.

The maid bobbed a quick curtsey and hurried out. Darcy gestured to the footman to follow her and waited until he closed the doors to approach Georgiana and place a comforting hand on her shoulder. "Everyone is gone," he said quietly. "It is just us now."

Pulling back a few inches, but still gripping Drew's arms, Georgiana made a visible effort to control herself. "Promise me you will not disappear again! Promise me, Drew!"

With a slight wobble in his voice, Drew said, "I promise not to disappear if that is what you truly wish. But look at you! You have grown into a beautiful young lady."

"No, I have not! I am a little girl who has been missing her brother for years and years!" Georgiana cried.

Darcy said soothingly, "Drew lives in Kympton now. You can see him at the parsonage there any time you wish."

"Kympton?" Georgiana blotted her eyes.

"Yes, Fitzwilliam gave me the living there in May," said Drew. "You are always welcome to visit me."

Darcy added, "I was going to tell you today, but there has been no opportunity."

"I am so glad!" said Georgiana. "I hate our father for chasing you away. Why did you not come back when he died?"

Drew looked helpless. "He ordered me to stay away from you and never to set foot at Pemberley again."

"But he is gone, and we want you here," Georgiana declared.

Feelings were running too high. Darcy quickly poured three glasses of wine and gave one to Georgiana. "It is true, Drew, and I wish you would feel welcome here, but I also understand the past cannot be erased so easily." He held out a wineglass to Drew.

Drew held up his hand. "Not for me, I thank you," he said coldly.

Now what had he done wrong? Then it struck him. "Drew, I freed the slaves in Jamaica as soon as Father died. Nothing here is purchased with money from the slave trade."

The lines of tension under Drew's eyes eased and he accepted the wineglass. "In that case, I thank you for the wine and, more importantly, for the freedom of the slaves."

"It was the right thing to do," Darcy said.

Georgiana added eagerly, "We do not eat sugar from slave plantations, either. The kitchens only have sugar from the East Indies, where there are no slaves. And when I left school, I joined a ladies' benevolent society where we sew clothes for freed slaves."

Drew's eyes widened in surprise. "I am proud of you, Georgie."

Georgiana beamed. "If I could not see you, I wanted to help your cause. Pray, tell me everything you have been doing these last years!"

"There is not much to tell," Drew said cautiously. "I worked for Mr. Wilberforce until I went to Oxford, and then I became a curate in Lincolnshire until Fitzwilliam offered me this living."

Taking Drew's hand, Georgiana pulled him down to sit next to her. "I want to hear every detail."

Chapter 8

In a daze, Elizabeth retraced her steps out of Pemberley, accompanied by Mr. Bingley and his sister. She had prepared herself to face Mr. Darcy's hostility, his haughty anger, or even a direct snub. She had not expected the look of naked pain as he met her eyes. And the shock of discovering the presence of the Bingleys had not helped.

Mr. Bingley ushered them from the house, pausing on the portico. "Miss Elizabeth, I must say what a delightful surprise this is. I had no expectation in the world of seeing you today. Is your family here as well?"

She struggled to collect herself. "Just my aunt and uncle, who invited me to join them on their tour of Derbyshire. I am equally surprised to see you. I expected only Mr. Darcy." Had Andrew known of their presence? She could not recall if she had mentioned Mr. Bingley's name when she told him Darcy had interfered in her sister's romance. What a tangled web this had proved to be!

"Is your family in good health?" asked Mr. Bingley. Was he thinking of Jane? If there was any chance of something good coming out of this debacle, Elizabeth would seize it.

"They are, I thank you." She decided to take pity on him. "My youngest sister, Lydia, is visiting a friend in Brighton, but all the others are at home."

He brightened visibly. "I pray you to give them my best regards."

Miss Bingley, having had enough of being ignored, said pointedly, "I do not believe I have ever heard of Mr. Andrew Darcy."

Elizabeth hesitated. Her first instinct was to avoid the question, but Darcy's look of agony when he had seen her in the doorway gave her pause. If answering Miss Bingley's impertinent inquisitiveness would take the onus of explanation from Mr. Darcy, she would do it. "He is Mr. Darcy's younger brother." She bit back the temptation of adding how surprising it was that such a dear friend of the family was unaware of his existence.

Miss Bingley looked down her nose at Elizabeth and declared haughtily, "Mr. Darcy has no brother."

"I encourage you to take up the question with him," Elizabeth said obligingly.

"No, he told me once that his brother had been disowned," said Bingley, then looked suddenly stricken. "Forgive me; I should not have said that."

Poor Mr. Bingley! "I am well aware that their father disowned Mr. Andrew Darcy for his political views, and I am glad he and his brother have reconciled." There; that should save some embarrassing questions later.

Miss Bingley's face was white. She must detest Elizabeth's apparent intimacy with the Darcy family secrets. "How did you come to make his acquaintance?"

Elizabeth gave her sweetest smile. "We met through a mutual friend."

"You must know him well, to pay a call with him alone." Miss Bingley lofted her nose in the air. "An unmarried lady can never be too careful."

Oh, yes, the knives were out!

DARCY COULD FEEL HIS skin prickling before Elizabeth even reached the drawing room, the sound of her light laugh a lure he could not resist. She came in with Bingley and his sister, but she was the only one he saw. The others might as well have been ghosts.

Drew, damn him, went immediately to stand next to her. "Miss Bennet, will you do me the great honor of introducing me to your friends?"

"I would be most happy to," said Elizabeth, with the barest glance at Darcy. "Miss Bingley, Mr. Bingley, pray permit me to present to your acquaintance Mr. Andrew Darcy, the vicar of Kympton and Mr. Darcy's brother. Andrew, Mr. Bingley holds the lease on a country house not far from my home where I first met your brother."

Darcy flushed. It was his obligation to make the introductions, but once again, Elizabeth's presence had turned him to stone. If she had thought him ungentlemanly before, this would confirm the opinion.

Somehow he managed to say, "Miss Elizabeth, welcome to Pemberley. May I be permitted the honor of introducing you to my sister, Miss Darcy?"

Elizabeth avoided his eyes but curtsied to Georgiana. "It is a great pleasure, Miss Darcy."

Georgiana blushed. "I beg of you to forgive my inappropriate display earlier," she said in a small voice.

Elizabeth said warmly, "My dear Miss Darcy, if you had not shed a tear when you saw your brother for the first time in years, I would think much the less of your familial affection. I am very grateful that Mr. Andrew Darcy has a sister who loves him so much."

The girl's eyes welled with tears again, but she blinked them back. "You are most kind."

Drew said to Georgiana, "In addition to regaining a brother, you will also soon have a new sister. Miss Bennet has done me the very great honor of agreeing to become my wife."

Georgiana's brows drew together. "*You* are marrying Miss Bennet?" She cast a confused look at Darcy.

Devil take it! Darcy had forgotten he had hinted to Georgiana of his own hopes, back when he had been certain Elizabeth would accept his proposal. She knew. And he had to stop her from saying anything. "Drew came to me last night with the glad news that he had met the companion of his future life, and I am certain you will join me in wishing them both all the happiness in the world."

Miss Bingley cried, "Eliza Bennet, you sly thing! You did not say a word! I cannot begin to tell you how pleased I am to learn of this. I could not be prouder and more overjoyed if you were my own sister!"

Darcy's lip curled. Naturally, Miss Bingley was overjoyed. In a stroke, Elizabeth had been turned from an obstacle to her pursuit of him into a potential ally.

Elizabeth seemed taken aback by this effusion of pleasure from Miss Bingley, but she recovered enough to receive Bingley's hearty congratulations. "I thank you, but I must warn you it has not yet been announced. Mr. Andrew Darcy has only just written to my father for his permission."

"Still, it is excellent news!" exclaimed Bingley.

One might almost think it an ordinary announcement of an engagement, were it not for the worried glances Georgiana kept casting in Darcy's direction. And apart from the aching hole where his heart should be.

THEY HAD ALREADY STAYED over the half-hour prescribed for calls when Andrew said stiffly, "I thank you for your kind hospitality. It has been a pleasure to meet your guests."

Miss Darcy cried, "Oh, must you leave already? Could you not stay to dine with us?"

Even knowing Andrew as little as she did, Elizabeth had no doubt he was near his limit. "I wish we could, but we are otherwise engaged for tonight," she said. It had only been an informal plan for Andrew to dine with the Gardiners and Elizabeth, but it would do for an excuse.

Looking bereft, Miss Darcy asked, "Tomorrow, perhaps?" She appeared on the verge of tears again.

Had Darcy winced at her words? But he said, "We would be delighted to have you join us, and Miss Bennet's aunt and uncle as well, if they are willing." At least he was making an attempt.

If a brief call had been this painful, a long dinner party would be agonizing. "I am honored by your invitation, but I cannot speak for my aunt and uncle's plans, and I am at their disposal," Elizabeth said.

"Where are you staying, Miss Bennet?" Darcy's dark eyes were so intent that she had to look away.

"At the White Hart in Lambton," she said uncomfortably.

He nodded. "My sister and I will call there tomorrow to deliver the invitation personally. With your permission, Drew, of course."

"Of course," said Andrew dryly. Did he resent having been left so little choice?

Miss Darcy darted forward and kissed Andrew's cheek. "Thank you so much for coming today. I cannot tell you how much it means to me!"

The young clergyman clasped her hands and whispered something in her ear. She smiled tremulously in response.

Elizabeth curtsied and bade the party good day. As she left the room on Andrew's arm, she was certain Darcy's eyes were boring holes into her back.

In the entrance hall, they encountered Mrs. Reynolds, the housekeeper who had led Elizabeth's tour of Pemberley a fortnight earlier. To Elizabeth's surprise, she took Andrew's hands and said, "Mr. Drew, I cannot tell you how happy it makes me to see you within these walls again. Your dear mother in heaven must be smiling down to see it."

"You are very kind." Andrew took a deep breath. "I have only just learned that you did indeed deliver my message to Georgiana the day I left, so pray permit me to give you my much belated thanks for placing her needs ahead of your orders."

"It was nothing, Mr. Drew. How could I have let the poor child think you had left without even a goodbye? But I must not keep you."

Outside the gig was waiting. Andrew handed her into it without a word before mounting on the other side and picking up the reins, his expression stern and forbidding, as if displeased by the warm welcome he had received.

Even if she had felt the inclination to question him, Elizabeth's own disquiet would have prompted her to silence. She could not doubt now that Mr. Darcy's tender sentiments towards her had not abated as she expected, nor that, by engaging herself to his brother, she had caused him heartache.

Learning that she had hurt him was painful enough. Worse, far worse, was the discovery that she herself was no longer indifferent to him. How had that happened? Before coming to Derbyshire, she had lived in the fervent hope of never seeing him again. After hearing the housekeeper's praise of him during her tour of Pemberley, Elizabeth had felt a certain warming of her regard, but still felt no desire to renew the acquaintance. Why, then, did she suddenly feel a connection to him, now that all hope must be in vain?

Somehow she needed to put these thoughts from her mind forever. Mr. Darcy was to be her brother-in-law. She was to marry the stranger beside her, a man whom she respected, but for whom she had no tender feelings. Looking at him did not kindle a fire inside her, not like—

No. She would not even think it. Not now, not ever. She would focus on learning to love Andrew Darcy. Her mouth tasted of ashes.

Andrew seemed to unbend a little after they passed the gatehouse. "Forgive me; I have not thanked you for your timely effort to remove Mr. Bingley and his family when my sister became distraught. That task should not have fallen to you, but since no one else acted on it, it was well done."

"I am glad you think so. My excuse was very clumsy, but it was all I could think of quickly. Mr. Bingley's presence was a shock to me."

He turned briefly to look at her. "You told me my brother had interfered in a romance between your sister and one of his friends. Was that perchance Mr. Bingley?"

She sighed. "I fear so. He was not alone in his opposition. Mr. Bingley's sisters were also against the match, though for different reasons."

"Why did they oppose the match?" Was that a hint of suspicion in his voice? Perhaps he was starting to wonder what sort of family he was marrying into.

"They wish to see their brother marry Miss Darcy."

"Good God! Georgiana is not old enough to be considering marriage." He frowned. "What sort of family is he from?" Andrew might not have seen his sister in years, but that clearly did not stop him from feeling protective of her.

"They are respectable, although their fortune is from trade."

"I see." He did not sound pleased.

She decided to take a risk. "Regarding the invitation to dinner tomorrow night, if you wish it, I will ask my aunt to say we are otherwise engaged."

He considered this. "Although I admit it is tempting to avoid another visit to Pemberley, I think it wiser to accept. Afterwards I will speak to Fitzwilliam and inform him that I would prefer to limit my presence at Pemberley. It is clear he does not want me there any more than I wish to be there."

"Why do you say that? He showed you every attention."

"And looked displeased and dyspeptic during the entire visit," he said flatly.

Elizabeth's heart sank. It was true, but how could she tell Andrew that his brother's displeasure had nothing to do with him? "He did not seem in good spirits, but there were other reasons for that. It was an uncomfortable situation, given that he and I quarreled over Mr. Bingley at our last meeting, and your sister's reaction to your arrival put all of us on a less than comfortable footing."

"That might perhaps account for some of it, but I doubt it is all."

"You said he seemed pleased to see you yesterday, and I do not know how much more welcoming he could be than to offer you the living in the first place. If he did not wish to see you, why would he have done that?"

"I suppose there is some truth to that," he said grudgingly.

"If he was disapproving of anyone, it was me. But you were received like the prodigal son! I was waiting for the fatted calf to be slain."

"No," he snapped. "I am not the prodigal son. I was cast off."

She winced. How unimaginably painful it must have been, to live in a place as beautiful as Pemberley, and to lose both it and his family at once? But she had also seen the pain his absence had caused his sister, and suspected it was true for his brother, too. And for some reason, she could not bear the idea of hurting Mr. Darcy any more. "True, but not by your brother or your sister. And from what I saw, they are both eager to welcome you back. Your sister has clearly missed you terribly, and, while your brother is not my favorite person in the world, I cannot deny he offered you quite an olive branch in the form of your living. I hope you will give them a chance."

He sighed. "You are right. I should not hold the past against them, in any case. Perhaps I will see how tomorrow night's dinner goes before making a decision."

She smiled, despite feelings that were at best mixed. Why was she encouraging further engagement with his family when it caused her nothing but pain?

Chapter 9

E lizabeth's unexpected presence at Pemberley had thrown Darcy completely off-balance. Once Drew and Elizabeth had left, Darcy had all but fled from his guests in the drawing room, unable to tolerate the conversation as Bingley kept rattling on in praise of the people they had known in Hertfordshire and his sister inserted stinging set-downs of those same provincials. Manufacturing a meeting with his steward had seemed his wisest option.

Now he exited his steward's office almost surreptitiously, hoping to reach the privacy of his room without Bingley and his sisters discovering he was free.

In his mind, all Darcy could see was Elizabeth, with her hand tucked into Drew's arm.

There was no escape this time, though, because Georgiana was hovering in the yard outside the steward's office, obviously waiting for him. Precisely what he did not need.

She hurried to his side. "Fitzwilliam, may I speak to you for a few minutes? Privately?"

He glanced back at the house, wondering whether their guests were lying in wait. "Shall we walk in the rose garden?" As soon as the words left his mouth, he regretted them. Elizabeth had asked Bingley to show her the rose garden. Not two hours ago, her feet had trod the same paths he was entering. Had she been pleased by what she saw? Had her fingers reached out to brush the leaves of these rosebushes, as he had so often seen her do when out walking, as if touching the plants around her brought her closer to nature? Had she leaned in close to sniff the flowers, her eyes closing with pleasure at the delicate aroma?

Elizabeth.

He offered Georgiana his arm. Duty. He had a duty to his sister, no matter how much he longed to be alone with his misery.

"I am so sorry for the ill-bred scene I enacted," Georgiana said in a rush. "I promise it will never happen again. I hope you can forgive me."

For a moment he could not understand what she meant. "Do you mean when Drew arrived? There is nothing to forgive. It was a natural reaction. I should never have permitted you to be taken by surprise like that. I had not expected him to make an appearance so soon, or I would have tried to find a way to warn you or to arrange for a private reunion. The fault is mine."

"I did not realize you had given him the living in Kympton." Was there a hint of accusation in her voice?

"I should have told you, but I feared raising your hopes when they might be disappointed. I thought it possible he would remain where he was and hire a curate to work at Kympton. I was not certain he would live there himself until he appeared unexpectedly last night to tell me of his engagement." He had wondered and worried about it, but had been too proud to ask his steward for news of his brother. It would have meant admitting that he feared asking Andrew about his plans himself.

"But why would he stay away? It is a good living, is it not?"

Why must she always ask the questions he least wanted to answer? "It has been difficult been us. My meetings with him after our father's apoplexy did not go well." To say the least. Darcy, distraught over his own losses and barely comprehending that Drew had truly been disowned, had appeared on his brother's doorstep and informed Drew that it was time to come home and make peace with their father. In hindsight, it had been a masterpiece of tactlessness. Drew had told him that he hoped the old man would rot in hell. "Giving him the living was my first step to earning his trust, but it will take time."

"Perhaps his engagement will help," Georgiana said. "But I do not understand that, either. When you wrote to me of Miss Bennet and said you hoped she would be a sister to me, I thought you meant to marry her yourself, not that you had her in mind for Drew. The way you spoke of her, I thought you admired her."

Of course, Georgiana had thought that, because it had been true. Because he had never dreamed that Elizabeth might refuse his offer of marriage. Perhaps he should grasp at the straw Georgiana was offering him and claim that he had been thinking of Drew marrying Elizabeth, but all it would take was a word from Drew for Georgiana to learn it was untrue. "I did admire her," he said reluctantly, humiliation burning inside him. "I realized she did not return my regard. Now I understand why."

Had Elizabeth been thinking of Drew when she had thrown those bitter words of refusal in his face? Had her anger towards him been not just about Wickham's lies and her sister's loss, but also indignation on behalf of his supposed mistreatment of Drew? Not that he had ever done anything to Drew, but his brother might have blamed him for their father's decision to disown him.

"But..." Georgiana's voice trailed off, and her cheeks grew pink. Would she put together the pieces, his dark mood after returning from Kent and his interest in Elizabeth? "And now she is marrying Drew. I hope you do not mind."

How much more punishment must he undergo for his sins? "Drew has not had an easy life, and I wish to see him happy. If Miss Bennet can bring him happiness, I am glad for them both." And because he could not keep from pouring salt in his wounds, he added, "Drew told me he loves her very much."

Georgiana bit her lip. Had she sensed the bitterness in him? "Would he have come here today, if it were not for her, do you think?"

"I do not know. I did not realize she was in the area." Drew had omitted that detail when he told him about the engagement, leaving Darcy to be scalded by the shock of her unexpected presence.

"I hope she will want him to remain connected to us," Georgiana said wistfully. "If her acquaintance with you can help to bring Drew back into the fold, that would be good."

Nausea rippled through Darcy's stomach. "Perhaps."

"I am going to do my best to become her friend," Georgiana said. "Then we may see more of Drew."

"I hope she will be a good sister to you," he said flatly. He had always thought Elizabeth would be a beneficial influence on Georgiana, one who could help her overcome her shyness and fears. But not like this. Not like this.

Elizabeth was supposed to be his. Now he was losing both her and Drew, for how could he ever enjoy his brother's company when Elizabeth stood between them? How had he found himself in this hell of pain and jealousy?

Georgiana plucked a rose and buried her face in it for a long moment. Then she handed it to him. "The scent is beautiful."

The color was the palest peach, like Elizabeth's complexion. He could not resist stroking one of the petals. Would her cheek feel as soft and delicate? He would never know.

AS PROMISED, MR. DARCY and his sister appeared at the White Hart the following morning with a formal invitation to the Gardiners to dine at Pemberley, but this was a different Mr. Darcy than the wounded man Elizabeth had seen the previous day.

This Mr. Darcy seemed to think she was invisible. He avoided looking in her direction, and when forced by politeness to speak to her, he did so with a minimum of words. He said everything that was proper, and not one word more.

Elizabeth felt sick. It was a relief when the Darcys departed once the momentous invitation had been duly delivered and graciously accepted.

Mrs. Gardiner said, "How exciting! Dining at Pemberley is a dream come true for me. How often I used to ride past Pemberley as a girl, wishing I could live in that elegant place. To be received there by the family! I cannot say I found Mr. Darcy to be quite as warm a gentleman as his housekeeper described, but I did quite like that shy sister of his. It was most gracious of them to extend the invitation."

For some reason, Elizabeth could not bear for her aunt to think ill of Mr. Darcy, even if his present haughty behavior might have deserved her censure. "I think Mr. Darcy is often uncomfortable when meeting strangers. He was perfectly welcoming to me yesterday." Or at least he had not acted as if she did not exist.

"Such great men are often a little whimsical in their civilities," said Mr. Gardiner.

Elizabeth was not so easily comforted. Yesterday she had expected to meet implacable resentment from Darcy, only to catch a glimpse of his suffering soul. Today he seemed completely disinterested in her. What had changed?

Perhaps, on reflection, he had been angered by her forwardness in taking the Bingleys away when Miss Darcy was upset, and then making introductions afterwards. Or he might be worried about whether she had said anything about her sister to Mr. Bingley. Or, more likely, he had seen her as dowdy, over-forward, and difficult, and decided she had never been worth his attention.

It hurt, far more than she thought it should.

WHEN THEY ARRIVED BACK at Pemberley after calling at the White Hart, Georgiana asked Darcy, "Will you come upstairs with me? I have something to show you."

"If you wish." Darcy could not bring himself to care about anything, but he followed her to her small private sitting room. Would this sick ache in the pit of his stomach never fade?

"Just a moment; I will fetch it from my trunk." His sister disappeared into her bedroom.

No. He did not want to be alone with his thoughts. He crossed to the window, staring out at the rising hills where the trees were in full leaf, unlike the barren winter inside him. How was he to survive this? How could God be so cruel as to let Elizabeth love Drew? It had been his one consolation after losing her, that he would somehow manage to use the lessons she had taught him to rebuild a relationship with his brother, and now this.

Georgiana returned carrying a framed miniature. "Now that Drew is back, could we hang this with the others again?" She held it out to him.

He took the gilded frame in his hands and the familiar image of Drew's face looked back at him, his cleft chin and stubborn jawline already prominent. It had once been part of the set that hung in the rose drawing room. The disappearance of this miniature should have been his first clue that there was something more to Drew's absence from Pemberley than simply visiting a friend. When he had asked a servant where it had gone, he had been told it was being cleaned, but in hindsight, that had obviously been untrue, since the other portraits had been rehung to disguise its absence. "How did you come to have this? I thought it had been destroyed."

"Father ordered it burned, but Mrs. Reynolds hid it away instead. She knew our father would never look through my belongings."

He turned shocked eyes on his sister's face. The housekeeper had not only disobeyed a direct order, but involved his sister in it? "But you were just a child."

"I was ten years old, and she knew how much I loved Drew, and that I could keep a secret. When Drew lived with Mr. Morris in Lambton and came to call on me every week, he would come through the servants' entrance, and no one ever said anything. I lived for those times."

"I do not understand. Why would he hide his presence? It was still his home." This did not sound like the Pemberley of his childhood.

"Whenever our father saw him, he would be in a bad mood for days. Drew knew that frightened me, so he kept his visits quiet."

"Why were you frightened? Surely he never punished you."

"No. I was always so careful to stay out of trouble. If I had ever broken one of Mama's rose teacups, he would have shouted and shouted at me, yet you never said a word about it yesterday. What happened to Drew – it terrified me."

"What happened to Drew?" he asked heavily. He was not certain he wished know the answer.

Georgiana's eyes widened. "He could not do anything right. He was always being punished, half the time for things he had never done."

Now he was on more solid ground. "He may have preferred to tell you he did not do those things."

She shook her head. "He never talked to me about it. I heard what the servants said. They all loved him because of the time Jenny broke a vase by accident. Drew heard her crying about it because she knew she would lose her position and her family needed her wages, and he told her not to worry; he would say he had done it since he was overdue for a beating anyway, and he would rather be beaten while saving her pain than for something

75

imaginary. I do not know why our father hated him so much, but I did not want him to start hitting me like that."

No. His father had never been unreasonable or petty. Well, almost never, but Drew had been a difficult child. He spoke out of turn, was resentful, and was sent down from Eton. He must have deserved punishing. Georgiana had just been too young and innocent to understand that the brother who was kind to her could also misbehave. But Darcy had never known how the situation had frightened her, because he had always been away at school and university. Until his father became ill, Georgiana had been almost a stranger to Darcy.

But his father had disowned Drew and hidden his actions from Darcy until he had stumbled on the truth by the absence of the miniature now in his hands. It had been Mrs. Reynolds who had hidden the portrait, who had broken his father's command not to speak of Drew's departure, and finally told him the truth, that Drew had been disowned. And then she had begged him not to tell his father that she had done so.

He raked his hand through his hair. Why had all of this been kept hidden?

Georgiana bit her lip. "Could we hang it back with the others?"

"Yes. I will have them rehung to include it." It was the right thing to do.

"Perhaps it could go in place of George's picture," she offered hesitantly.

George. It took a moment to realize his sister was speaking of Wickham. Of course his portrait was still there; they had all been painted at the same time, six-year-old Georgiana, thirteen-year-old Andrew, and Wickham and Darcy, both at eighteen. A shiver went down his spine. He never considered how inappropriate it had been for his father to hang Wickham's picture with his own children's. How had his mother felt when she saw them every day? "Most certainly. We will put Drew's picture there." And before dinner. George Wickham's miniature had polluted Pemberley long enough.

Chapter 10

Elizabeth breathed a sigh of relief when dinner at Pemberley finally ended and Miss Darcy gave the signal for the ladies to withdraw, leaving the gentlemen to enjoy their port. So far the evening had gone as well as she could have hoped, which was to say that it had been tolerable. Just as Darcy had once described her appearance at that fateful assembly where she had first seen him.

Yes, tolerable, apart from the food, which had been delicious. She had been seated between Andrew and Mr. Bingley, so the conversation had been pleasant. Most importantly, a large epergne blocked her view of Mr. Darcy, so she could pretend he was not there, or at least try to. She kept telling herself to enjoy the company, the fine dinner, and the unmatched elegance of Pemberley, but talking to Mr. Bingley only reminded her of Jane's grief. Did Darcy now suffer as Jane had? A pang settled deep inside her. Elizabeth would not wish that on anyone.

After the ladies had settled in the drawing room, Miss Darcy said, "Mrs. Gardiner, we will be having a picnic by the lake on Friday, and, if you are not otherwise engaged, it would give me great pleasure if you and Miss Bennet would agree to be our guests." She had clearly been practicing the invitation in her head.

"A picnic!" cried Miss Bingley. "What a charming idea, Georgiana."

"A charming idea, indeed," said Mrs. Gardiner regretfully, "but I fear we must decline. Tomorrow is our last day here, and we will be leaving Derbyshire early Friday morning."

"So soon?" The girl looked stricken. "Could you not stay a little longer?"

"I wish we could, but we have already overstayed our plans owing to Lizzy's engagement. My husband is needed in London, and our children are awaiting our return." Mrs. Gardiner smiled. "Or so I would like to think; but from everything I have heard, they are having such a delightful time with their Aunt Jane that they would not care if I did not return until Christmas!"

"I am certain that is not the case," Elizabeth firmly. "But I thank you for the invitation, Miss Darcy. Perhaps next summer." When she would be Mrs. Andrew Darcy. Suddenly she wished she had eaten less dinner.

"Oh, yes, I suppose we could do that," said Miss Darcy, clearly disappointed. "Have you and Drew discussed when you will marry?"

She could hardly say that it depended on how far Wickham had spread his gossip. "I have yet to hear from my father on the subject, but we have spoken of marrying after Christmas." Andrew had favored a wedding as soon as the banns could be read, but Elizabeth wanted more time to say her goodbyes to her life at Longbourn. Her breath caught in her throat at the thought of all she would be leaving behind, and she stuffed down a flare of resentful fury towards Wickham. How could he have forced her into this position?

"So long? Then, apart from your wedding, I shall not see you again until next summer, for we will be at Matlock for Christmas and then in London for the Season." Miss Darcy looked distressed.

Elizabeth was growing a little weary of Miss Darcy's neediness. "Fortunately, we will have many years to become better friends. May I write to you while we are apart?"

"Oh, yes!" the girl exclaimed. "I hope we will be great correspondents."

"A year is not so very long," said Miss Bingley. "It will pass before you know it."

A shadow crossed Miss Darcy's eyes. "I thank you for the advice." It was a different voice than she used with Elizabeth, more brittle and less lively.

Mrs. Gardiner smiled at the girl. "Miss Darcy, I am certain Lizzy would be much reassured if you were to call regularly at Mr. Andrew Darcy's parsonage during her absence and give him a feminine perspective on his restorations."

Elizabeth thought this an odd thing to say until she saw how remarkably Miss Darcy's countenance brightened at her aunt's suggestion. Of course; the girl's true worry about her departure was losing a conduit to her estranged brother. She said warmly, "I shall tell Andrew that I am depending upon you to write me with updates on the parsonage. "

"Oh, would you?" cried the girl, as if Elizabeth had done her a great favor by demanding this service of her. "I would be so happy to do that. You must tell me what you particularly wish to see done there."

"That would be a great relief to me," said Elizabeth, who had no concerns whatsoever about Andrew's ability to manage the renovations. "I will be paying a last visit there tomorrow and I will make a list." And come up with some way to explain to Andrew why his sister would be sticking her nose into his affairs.

"Perhaps I can join you there," said Miss Darcy. "I have not seen his parsonage yet."

Of course she had not seen it yet, since she had only learned the previous afternoon that Andrew now lived there. "We would both be happy to see you. Have you visited Kympton before? I find it a charming village."

"I have ridden through it," said the girl. "The church is most picturesquely situated, and there is a fine distant view of the village from the hills."

Miss Bingley, clearly tired of the focus of the conversation being taken away from herself, said, "You must take me there someday, Georgiana. I shall not rest until I have seen it! But you know how I adore your countryside here." She launched into a long description of rides they had taken in the past, all centered on the great pleasure her dear Georgiana had given her.

When the gentlemen rejoined them, Miss Darcy tugged at her eldest brother's sleeve and whispered something to him. He nodded and they both stepped out of the room for a few minutes. On their return, Elizabeth's pulses fluttered as Mr. Darcy crossed to speak directly to the Gardiners. "My sister and I regret that our further acquaintance is to be interrupted by your imminent departure. I understand Mr. Gardiner is expected in London, but we would like to extend an invitation to Miss Bennet and Mrs. Gardiner to remain here at Pemberley for as long as they wish, and we would be happy to provide our carriage for their return to Longbourn and London afterwards." He spoke calmly, but with no particular warmth, almost absently. It was a continuation of how stiff he had been all evening, more like a paper cutout of a gentleman bobbing along in a toy theatre than a living, breathing man.

"That is a very generous offer." Mrs. Gardiner, startled but clearly pleased, glanced at her husband.

Elizabeth's heart sank. She longed to return home, and the last thing she wanted was to spend any more time in Mr. Darcy's company, but her aunt's look of bright excitement boded ill for refusing the invitation. How often had her aunt said since this morning that dining at Pemberley would be a dream come true for her? Now she had the opportunity to be a houseguest at the grand estate she had admired all her life. "I thank you for the generous invitation, but I am completely at my aunt and uncle's disposal, and their plans are set."

"Nonsense," said her uncle jovially. "I think it is a fine idea, and no doubt Mr. Andrew Darcy will be happy to have more time with you, Lizzy."

"But the children are expecting me," Mrs. Gardiner said hesitantly.

"Yes, and they will be a little disappointed, but they have their beloved Aunt Jane, their nurse, and all the countryside at Longbourn to explore. They can easily spare you for another week or two."

Elizabeth dared not look at Andrew. She suspected it was a matter of perfect indifference to him whether or not she was nearby, but he would be displeased to be forced to spend more time at Pemberley. That was no doubt the precise reason Miss Darcy wished her to stay. Was this what the rope felt like during a tug-of-war? "My parents are eager to speak to me about my engagement." A very weak argument, since there had been no response yet from her father.

Mrs. Gardiner patted her hand. "We will write them long, newsy letters until they are heartily sick of the subject."

Miss Darcy hurried forward. "I beg of you to consider it. It would mean so much to me to have the chance to know you better."

Mr. Bingley had finally noticed the discussion. "You would be a most delightful and welcome addition to the party, and I have many more questions about our mutual acquaintance in Hertfordshire to ask you." He beamed, as his sisters looked sour.

Mr. Darcy's expression was unreadable. "Does this mean we will have the pleasure of your company?" His gaze seemed fixed at a point just over Elizabeth's shoulder.

God help her. "I must defer to the wishes of my aunt and uncle, and those of Mr. Andrew Darcy." Perhaps he could rescue her.

Andrew's smile was a little forced. "I cannot but be glad at the prospect of more time in your company, my dear, and I will try not to take too much advantage of Mrs. Gardiner's helpful advice."

"I am always happy to help you in any way, dear boy!" exclaimed Mrs. Gardiner. "We would be honored to accept your gracious invitation, Mr. Darcy."

Miss Bingley exchanged a scornful glance with her sister, but Miss Darcy looked radiant. "There is so much I cannot wait to show you!"

Elizabeth swallowed hard, feeling the trap close around her. "I thank you both for the kind invitation."

There had to be a way out. She could not bear to spend days on end confined with this frightening Mr. Darcy who seemed to have decided she did not exist. Why had he agreed to this invitation, when it was perfectly clear he wanted as little to do with her as possible?

Feeling sick, she waited until he walked away from the others and took a station by the window, gazing out into the darkness. Somehow, she gathered the courage to approach him and said quietly, "Mr. Darcy, I am aware your sister put you in an awkward position. If you wish, I will speak to my aunt and uncle and convince them I must return to Longbourn immediately."

He turned a cold glare on her. "Why would I wish such a thing? It is important to me that my brother feel welcome at Pemberley and retain his connection to my sister and me. For the moment, that seems to require your presence."

Of course. He did not want her there, only her ability to provide a link to Andrew. She raised her chin. "I see."

"You must be aware of the estrangement between us dating from his quarrel with my father. Perhaps you even know more of it than I do, since Andrew declines to speak to me of that time, but whatever happened between him and my father is part of the past. I wish to see the breach mended, and my sister is desperate for it." Now his eyes bored into her.

What did he want from her? "The breach seems well on its way to being healed."

"I hope so. I..." His face suddenly darkened. It was as if he wanted to say more, but then changed his mind. "Good night, Miss Bennet." He turned and walked away.

So she was Miss Bennet again. He always called her Miss Elizabeth in Kent, even though her eldest sister was not there and everyone else called her Miss Bennet. She had been Miss Elizabeth yesterday when he had been surprised by her presence, but now she was firmly and coldly Miss Bennet. And it hurt.

ELIZABETH'S UNCLE DELAYED his departure on Friday morning until the arrival of the first post, hoping for a letter from Mr. Bennet, since none had arrived the previous day. "I know your father hates to bestir himself to write, but one would think he could make an exception in a case of this sort," Mr. Gardiner grumbled.

"Yes," sighed Mrs. Gardiner. "It is hardly courteous to poor Andrew. He deserves a prompt response to his request for Elizabeth's hand."

"Indeed. I will tell Bennet as much when I stop there to see the children, and if nothing else, I will write to you myself and tell you what he says," Mr. Gardiner replied.

Then Andrew himself arrived to drive Elizabeth and Mrs. Gardiner to Pemberley, and no more could be said on the matter.

Chapter 11

E lizabeth awoke early on her first morning at Pemberley, firm in her resolution not to allow Mr. Darcy's grim visage to affect her enjoyment of this visit to his beautiful estate. Besides, if his behavior on her arrival the previous day was anything to judge by, he intended to stay as far away from her as he could. She had seen him only at dinner, and then from across the room. Miss Bingley's constant attentions to him made it easy.

She decided to wear her newly-remade dress, both because it was now the most fashionable of her day dresses and as a reminder of her resolution not to allow Mr. Darcy's attitude to impose any unpleasantness on her engagement. The dress had turned out even more flattering than she had dared to hope, and she twirled around to admire the new netting over the skirt. A good way to start her first day as a houseguest at Pemberley.

Outside the sun was shining. Mrs. Gardiner would not awaken for another hour or two, and Elizabeth gazed longingly at the parterre outside her window. Surely there would be time for a walk before breakfast.

She gathered her bonnet and gloves before setting off towards the rose garden, less out of a desire to see it than because the path there would take her past the mysterious orangery. When she had toured Pemberley with the Gardiners, in those long-ago days before she had met Andrew – had it truly been only a fortnight ago? – she had thought little of it when the housekeeper had said the orangery was private. But her curiosity had been roused when the maid who had shown her to her room yesterday had, while informing her of the necessary workings of the household, made a point of mentioning that visits to the orangery could only be undertaken with the express permission of Mr. Darcy.

What could possibly be so special about an orangery? Certainly nothing valuable could be stored there; the large, multi-paned windows would make it an easy target for thieves. Darcy could hardly worry over his guests stealing the fruit growing inside, especially since it was clear that the already spacious building had been expanded recently. Even a large estate like Pemberley was unlikely to require that much hothouse fruit!

She slowed her pace as she passed the building, eyeing the windows. The bottom halves of the glass panes were fogged over, and it was hard to see in through the clear portions, especially with the sun still low in the sky. But it looked darker than she would have expected. The orangeries she had seen on her travels had mostly contained undersized trees in pots, with plenty of open space between the trunks. Whatever was inside was much bushier than those fruit trees.

The door to the orangery opened. Elizabeth quickly turned her face away, not wishing to appear to be snooping, as Mr. Bingley came bounding out. Did he have the necessary permission from Mr. Darcy to go into the mysterious orangery?

"Miss Elizabeth!" Bingley sounded delighted to see her. "You are up early."

"I could not resist the sunny day and the beautiful grounds." Perhaps she could gain some answers to her questions from him. "What an impressive orangery this is! Why, I believe it is even larger than the one at Blenheim."

He grinned. "Yes, it is Darcy's special project. He has been expanding it."

Darcy's special project was an orangery? She was tempted to laugh. "I had not realized he had a particular interest in cultivating fruit."

Bingley laughed. "Not fruit. It is his scientific research. He grows plants from tropical climes in there. It is a veritable jungle magically transported to England."

"A jungle!" Oh, now she desperately wanted to go inside.

Her longing must have shown in her voice, for he said, "Would you like to see it? I can give you a tour."

"I would love nothing more! I have always wished to see a jungle. But I was told most clearly that no visitors were permitted," said Elizabeth, hoping to be contradicted.

Bingley waved his hand as if to brush aside her objection. "That is only to protect the plants, and I know you will not harm them. I help him with the project, so I go in every day."

"If you are certain..." Elizabeth's misgiving warred with her curiosity to see what Mr. Darcy had hidden away. "I do not wish to pry."

"It is hardly a secret, just Darcy's investigations." Bingley opened the glass-paned door. "Pray come in quickly so none of the heat escapes."

As Elizabeth stepped inside, she was struck by a wave of humid air, hotter than the warmest summer day she had known, and an overwhelming scent of rich earth, greenery, and something exotic she could not place.

A narrow flagstone path led between plants with enormous leaves, some as big as dinner plates, quite unlike the spindly fruit trees one typically found in orangeries. Instead there were strangely shaped trees and vines. She reached out to a curling tendril, then remembered these were special plants and snatched her hand back before she touched it. Oh, but it was all astonishing, everything she had ached to see when she was a child and had wandered the countryside pretending to be an explorer in a strange land.

A dark-skinned gardener crossed the path ahead of them, pushing a wheelbarrow overloaded with green and brown fronds.

Bingley said, "See that? These plants grow so quickly that they always need cutting back. If you come this way, some of the best ones are over here."

He indicated to Elizabeth that she should follow a side path, past a stove with a large pot of boiling water atop it. That explained the humidity, she supposed. Passing a woven screen, she reached another room where the ceiling had been replaced by glass panes. The plants grew even larger and thicker here.

Another gardener bent over the base of a tree, unwrapping a leather strip from the trunk, and then studying it. His shirtsleeves were rolled up to his elbows, no doubt due to the heat. Then he straightened, and Elizabeth realized he was no gardener.

"Mr. Darcy!" she exclaimed, her cheeks burning at the sight of his bare forearms and neck. An odd feeling built inside her, as if her insides were melting. What was wrong with her? True, for a gentleman to appear without proper covering was considered indecent, but she had seen workmen in shirtsleeves often enough. She could understand why it was thought to be indecent, though; the lines of his broad shoulders so clearly delineated under the fine linen sent flutters through her.

"Miss Elizabeth!" Darcy's cheeks overspread with the deepest blush, and for a moment he seemed frozen in surprise.

"Forgive me for interrupting you." Deeply embarrassed, she glanced back over her shoulder. Where had Bingley gone? She had thought he was right behind her. No, he was several yards back along the path, talking animatedly to the man with the wheelbarrow. "Mr. Bingley brought me in and said you would not mind. I did not realize you would be here so early. I can leave now."

"You are welcome to look around." He glanced down at himself and frowned. "Excuse me." He strode away without another word.

Oh, how mortifying! What must Mr. Darcy think of her, intruding in his private spot? Elizabeth fanned her face with her hand, but the slight breeze it created did nothing to cool her hot cheeks in this humid air. Perspiration was already breaking out on the back of her neck, and her hands were sticky inside her gloves.

Darcy reappeared as quickly as he disappeared, having now donned a loose housecoat over his shirt. He must have worn it to walk to the orangery. He was more covered now, but without his cravat, she could still see the notch at the base of his neck and all the skin above it. The sight made her lips tingle.

She bit her lip and gestured to the tree. "I am sorry to have interrupted you."

"It is nothing, just taking some measurements." He glanced at an open ledger sitting on a small wrought iron table, a pen and inkwell beside it.

"What sort of measurements?" she asked, it intrigued despite herself.

"Different things on different plants. In this case, the circumference of the stalk, the number of new shoots, and the length of the fruit."

He pointed to an oddly shaped appendage dangling from the top of the plant.

She tilted her head to stare at it. "That is a fruit?"

He half-smiled. "Many of them. Do you see those rows of small protuberances sticking out from the stem? Each one of those will develop into a banana."

"A banana! I had no idea they grew like that." Nor had she ever tasted the exotic fruit, but she had seen pictures of them, and once Lady Lucas had made a centerpiece with a pineapple and two bananas. "I never thought to see a banana tree."

"A plant, not a tree," he corrected. "It grows quickly, produces fruit once, and then is cut back to the ground to be replaced by the sprouts at the bottom."

She gaped in astonishment. "Does it take long to grow?"

"In the tropics, a little over a year. This one has taken almost 4 years, but our conditions are less than ideal."

Bingley appeared beside her. "Darcy is undervaluing his achievements here. He is having greater success than the botanists in Cambridge and Oxford, despite starting only five years ago. And the information he has collected is invaluable."

Darcy frowned. "My success is only because I can afford to keep the conservatory heated all year. Adding the glass roof has helped. My staff do all the measurements when I am away; I just like to keep my hand in when I am here."

"You guide the studies," retorted Bingley.

Seeing that Darcy looked uncomfortable with Bingley's praise, Elizabeth said quickly, "I had not realized you had such an interest in tropical botany."

Darcy shrugged. "I was always interested in plants. My tutor at Cambridge specialized in the tropics, and one thing led to another."

And unlike most student scientists, he had kept up his interest.

"You were his best pupil," Bingley said. "When I first arrived at Cambridge, Burton was already grieving your impending graduation and losing you to a life of frivolity. And how pleased he was when you returned and said that life in London was not to your taste!"

"You exaggerate, Bingley." But Darcy did not look displeased.

"No, I do not! Miss Elizabeth, Darcy was invited to go on a major expedition to Peru when he was only twenty-two. It was an unheard-of honor. Now deny that if you dare, Darcy! Had he gone, he would now be a world expert in the field."

As Darcy's smile turned bitter, Elizabeth said hastily, "It sounds like a fascinating adventure, but I suppose many people would not wish to leave England for so long, on what must be a dangerous journey." It did not sound convincing, which was hardly surprising, since she herself would have traded anything for such an opportunity.

"My father agreed with you," said Darcy with a slight twist of his mouth. "What of you, Miss Elizabeth? Would the dangers of the voyage put you off?" There was a challenge in his voice.

"I would go in an instant," she exclaimed. "The chance to see a new, unexplored world? I can imagine nothing better. If ladies could be explorers, I would certainly volunteer. Since I cannot, I am very glad of this opportunity to see a little of the wild jungle here."

Now Darcy's slight smile looked genuine again. "As I found consolation in planting my own jungle for the benefit of other botanists. I have some new plants that came back with that expedition, too; would you care to see them?"

"I would like that," she said. "I am all amazement at these specimens! I have never seen anything like the leaves on this banana tree – I mean, plant. So long that you hardly realize how very wide they are, too." Her hand crept out again, but she pulled it back quickly.

"You may touch them if you wish," said Darcy. "I am told banana plants can survive hurricanes."

"Truly?" She ought to demur, but when would she ever have such a chance again? She stripped off her gloves and ran her fingertips along the nearest frond. It was thicker and more flexible than she expected. She flashed a smile at Mr. Darcy, who was eyeing her with a certain hunger. "I thank you. This is such a wonderful surprise!"

HE SHOULD NOT BE DOING this. Darcy knew that. Elizabeth was marrying Drew, and he should keep his distance. But he had dreamed of showing her his conservatory, of watching the curiosity come alive in her fine eyes. It was just as he had imagined, as she asked intelligent questions about the plants in his studies, showing an interest no one but Bingley had ever done.

What a contrast to the one time he had allowed Caroline Bingley into his sanctum, and she had been full of suggestions about adding flowers and topiaries to make it more picturesque! Elizabeth understood his thirst for pure knowledge, and he craved more of her intoxicating attention.

"Look at this." He parted the leaves on a heliamphora to reveal the pitcher-shaped flower at the center. "This plant eats insects. Rain collects inside it, and when insects drink from it, the plant traps them. It has not thrived indoors, unfortunately. We have brought in bees to fertilize the plants, but even though my gardener puts water in the flower to simulate rain, the bees leave it alone. We have been trying to feed it flies, but it is not thriving."

"A plant that eats insects? Astonishing!"

"Here is another, a sundew. Do you see what looks like a drop of dew on the end of each tentacle? Try touching it."

"But it looks so delicate." Nonetheless she reached out and gently set her fingertip on it. "It is sticky – oh!" She snatched her fingers away, the back of her hand brushing against his. "It moved!"

"That is how it traps insects. My apologies; I should have warned you."

"No, it is amazing." She stared at the moving tentacles. "I never knew plants could move like that. Well, except to follow the sun, of course, but we cannot see that as it happens." She turned her attention to the mucilage that clung to her fingertip. "Is it poisonous?"

"No, just sticky, enough so that insects cannot easily escape it." He could not resist. Greatly daring, he took her hand in his – stolen pleasure! – and wiped the plant secretion away with his handkerchief. A surge of desire raced through him. If only he could press his lips to that fingertip, to the fragile blue veins of her wrist! Surely she would respond. As it was, her lips parted slightly and her eyes were darkening.

And Drew loved her.

His mouth suddenly tasted of ashes. He dropped her hand and took a step back. The excitement of her presence had trapped him, just as the sundew trapped insects to devour, but she could never be his.

She stuffed her hands into her gloves without any of her usual grace. "I... I thank you for the tour," she said shakily. "Your plants are most impressive."

"They are not yet fully established. This was a traditional orangery until I took over the estate, so the oldest jungle plants are barely five years old."

She looked puzzled. "I thought you only inherited two years ago."

"Yes, but my father was quite ill for his last three years and unable to speak, so I acted in his name."

"Oh." She glanced away, as if uncertain what to say. "I am sorry. That must have been a difficult time for your family."

He should just nod and thank her for her sympathy, but he could not. He wanted her to know the truth. "My plan to go on the Peru expedition caused his apoplexy. He forbade me to go, fearing that I would die of yellow fever, as his own brother had done in Jamaica. I told him I was of age and would go anyway. He became livid, insisting he could not afford to lose his heir. It became quite heated." The image of his father's choleric visage swam before him, still vivid after all these years.

But that had only been the beginning. Then Darcy had said it did not matter if he caught yellow fever because Drew could inherit. That was when he had discovered the truth about Drew's absence. And his father, his cool, reasonable father, had spouted horrible words about Drew, vilifying his character and everything about him, swearing he would see Pemberley burned to the ground before he let Drew set one foot there again. His eyes had bulged, spittle collecting at the corner of his mouth.

When Darcy, shocked to his core, insisted he would be leaving for Peru, his father had called him a whoreson and told him to get out, throwing an inkwell at his head. Darcy, furious, had gone to his room and stewed in his fury, until a frantic footman had rushed in to fetch him back to the study, where his father had lain crumpled on the floor, unable to speak or to move the right side of his body.

Now he was the one who could barely breathe, but gradually he regained the awareness of the present moment, and of Elizabeth staring at him. He straightened. He should not have said any of that.

Her eyes were dark with concern. "The apothecary in Meryton says anger may bring on an apoplexy, but only when it would have likely happened soon in any case."

The doctor had told him the same thing, but it had been no comfort to him, especially when facing his father's silent, accusing gaze from his bed. Until that day, Darcy had expected years of freedom before he would have to settle into his role as Master of Pemberley. Instead, he had abandoned his preparations for his scientific journey for a new, circumscribed life with his timid sister and his silent father. Instead of discovering new species, he had learned estate management. He had found Drew, told him of their father's apoplexy, and urged him to make his peace with the old man. It had not gone well. The next time he had seen Drew was when he offered him the Kympton living, hoping to regain one part of his family.

And because of that offer, Drew was able to marry Elizabeth. He said harshly, "Tell me, do you plan to see Drew today?"

"Andrew?" She sounded confused, and did not look at him. "No, he said he needed to work on his sermon."

"Will you go to hear him preach?" Why was he punishing himself this way? But that moment of closeness had fled, leaving him nothing but emptiness and anger.

Elizabeth drew in a sharp breath. "As I am your guest, I imagine I will be attending the same service you and your sister do. But I should return to the house. Pray excuse me." She bobbed a curtsey and hurried away.

He could not tear his eyes from her retreating figure.

Elizabeth.

ELIZABETH HURRIED BETWEEN rows of dense plantings, no longer entranced by their exotic nature, only seeking to put more distance between herself and Mr. Darcy. What had happened? At first she had been pleased that he was speaking to her naturally again, and then there was that strange moment when he had taken her hand to clean it. She could still feel his touch, the warmth and pressure of it, and the odd tingling that had shot up her arm, settling in as heat deep inside her, with a longing to be closer to him. No, she could not lie to herself. She had wanted him to kiss her.

What horrid wantonness was this? She was marrying his brother! She should not be having such feelings. And Darcy was the one to draw back from that intense moment – Darcy, when it should have been her. What he must think of her! And then he had made that strange confession about causing his father's apoplexy, and she had felt so close to him, as if he needed something from her. She had been wrong about that, though, for his face had suddenly hardened and his voice became cruel.

Where was the door? Somehow she had lost her way, lost in Darcy's jungle. She turned a corner blindly, but it only led to more giant plants. She needed to calm herself. The orangery was not that large. If she simply went in a straight line, she would find a wall she could follow to the door. But the paths kept twisting and turning back upon themselves.

The sight of a man's figure through the fronds halted her, her pulse racing. Had she turned herself around so far as to return to the same spot where Darcy stood? No, this man was not as tall as Darcy. Her breathing slowed as she recognized Bingley's stance, and she hurried towards him.

"Mr. Bingley, I fear I am lost. Could you point me to the door?" Her voice came out sounding breathless.

"Of course. I'll show you." He gestured with his hand. "This way."

She followed him along a narrow path, and there was the glass door. It had only been a few feet away, after all that. He held the door open for her, and she went out into a summer day that suddenly felt cold after the heat of the orangery, into thin, dry air. The freedom of escape warred with a sense of having left something precious behind. Mr. Darcy was unlikely to invite her into his slice of paradise again; and even if he did, she should refuse. She needed to see him as her future brother, not a man to whom she felt a strange, potent connection. And a deep attraction, if she were honest with herself.

But she could not allow Mr. Bingley to see how distressed she was. "I thank you for coming to my rescue," she said.

"It is my pleasure. What did you think of it?"

With her mind so full of Darcy, it took her a moment to realize he meant the orangery. "It is impressive. I have never seen anything like it.

It was like travelling to a different country." One where she could never return, no matter how much she wished to.

He looked puzzled. "Is something the matter?"

"No. Not at all," she said hurriedly. But if her discomposure was so obvious, she should provide some explanation, lest he guess at the truth. "It is nothing, truly, simply that Mr. Darcy did not seem best pleased to see me there. I will not go in again."

"I cannot imagine he objects to your presence there. He was likely just involved in his work." Bingley's open, sweet smile showed his certainty that all was right with the world.

"I think he does object. I think he does not want me here at Pemberley at all, nor to be marrying his brother." The words came out before she could stop them.

Now Bingley's expression showed sudden understanding. He drew closer, as if to tell her a secret, and said in a low voice, "It is not you, Miss Elizabeth. I can imagine how it would look that way, when you see how different he seems from how he was when you knew him in Hertfordshire. He has been in poor spirits for months, not himself at all, and it shows. I have been concerned about him. I had hoped being at Pemberley would cheer him, but if anything, it seems to have made matters worse. But I beg you to believe that it has nothing to do with you."

Elizabeth's throat grew tight. "Did... did something happen to him?"

"No, or at least nothing he will admit to. That is what worries me most. I have known Darcy for years, and I have never seen him like this. I do not know how to help him."

Her palms tingled. Could it be, or was she dreaming to think her refusal might have had a lasting impact on him? Did she even wish to know? "When did it start?"

"In the spring. He seemed fine, perhaps a little quieter than usual, and then he went away for a few weeks, and when he came back, well, he was different. Dark moods, withdrawn. He stopped caring about anything. Didn't want to do anything. Kept saying there was no point."

Elizabeth's mouth grew dry. "Perhaps it might give you a clue if you knew where he went."

"That part is easy. He was visiting his aunt in Kent. He goes there every year for Easter, but usually he doesn't stay as long. But even if something happened there, if he quarreled with his aunt, why would it have affected him so powerfully? It would not have troubled him this long."

She had always assumed that Darcy would have forgotten about her quickly, that his feelings for her ran no deeper than the sort of urgent physical desire men seemed so prone to. That he would have been angry with her and dismissed her from his thoughts. But she had been wrong, so wrong. She had assumed, without any grounds, that he was shallow and careless. No wonder he had looked so hurt when she appeared, engaged to his brother!

If he still harbored tender sentiments towards her, this situation must be dreadfully painful for him. How she had misunderstood him! Misunderstood and underestimated him.

Bingley said reflectively, "I wonder if his brother might know something about it. It must have been around that time that Darcy offered him the living. If he says anything to you, anything that might help me understand what is wrong, I hope you will feel able to tell me."

At least that much she could answer honestly. "All Andrew has told me is that his brother appeared one day, quite unexpectedly, determined to repair the breach between them. He was baffled by it." Poor Andrew, not knowing his brother well enough to perceive his unusual black humor, and then he had offered marriage to the very woman who had caused Darcy's unhappiness.

What had she done? They were trapped now, she and Darcy and Andrew. And there was no way out.

Chapter 12

B y mid-afternoon, Darcy was hot, sweaty, and tired of hiding in the orangery. Usually his work gave him a sense of peace, but today it was contaminated by his craving for Elizabeth. That brief moment, touching her hand, seeing her response, had roused all his deepest longings for her, and an even deeper confusion. He could not make sense of what she thought of him. If she felt something for him, why had she agreed to marry Drew? And why, if she hated him, had she responded so kindly when he confided about his father's apoplexy?

He skulked back to the main house, going in the back entrance, past the kitchen, and towards the servants' stairs. He told himself that it was because he looked disheveled after hours working in the dirt, but in truth he did not feel capable of conversing with anyone, not when all he wanted was to drag Elizabeth back to the orangery and make her explain herself. And kiss her until she forgot Drew's existence.

As he was passing the servants' entrance to the main hall, Miss Bingley's sharp voice pierced his ears. He quickened his pace, halting suddenly as he took in her words.

"Do you wonder if Eliza Bennet had an ulterior motive in accepting Mr. Darcy's brother?" Miss Bingley's tone was arch.

A giggle that sounded like Mrs. Hurst. "I have not, but now I am most curious why you would think so. It is an eligible marriage for her, not least since it will take her so far from that horrid family of hers."

"True, but it also offers her a delightful soupçon of revenge. When Mr. Darcy singled her out so notably at that ill-fated ball at Netherfield, it must have raised her expectations. The poor dear likely had no clue that a gentleman of Mr. Darcy's standing would never consider offering for a girl like her, but I daresay she was crushed when he left her behind without a word. Now she can have her vengeance by forcing him to see constantly what he cannot have."

Bingley's voice, sounding offended. "You might think that way, Caroline, but I cannot believe a sweet girl like Miss Elizabeth would. I do not recall her ever showing any interest in Darcy, either."

"She was cleverer than that. She saw he was tired of women fawning over him, so she decided to be different and push him away. It certainly caught his attention, and I give her credit for that." Miss Bingley sounded regretful, perhaps that she had not considered the option herself. "Fortunately, Mr. Darcy is too intelligent to be taken in for long by such a trick. But I do not think the worse of her for wanting a little revenge; on the contrary, it makes me admire her."

Darcy had to stop himself from snorting. Once again, Miss Bingley was wrong in every possible way. Wrong that Elizabeth had tried to excite his attention. Wrong that he would never deign to propose to her. Wrong that Elizabeth would seek to hurt him. She was not a vengeful person – or so he had thought, though he had been wrong about so many things when it came to Elizabeth.

No, if she wanted revenge, it would have to be for something far larger than a slight to her vanity. He swallowed hard. Something like destroying the happiness of a most beloved sister.

Ice slid through his veins. Elizabeth had reason to hate him. She had despised him for his role in separating Bingley from her sister Jane. If she did want him to suffer for that, what better way than by engaging herself to Drew, so she could flaunt in his face that she had chosen his relatively impoverished brother over all the advantages he had to offer? She must have known her engagement would pain him. Had she delighted in it, vindictively hoping to teach him a lesson?

He would not have thought it of her, but he would never have believed she could refuse him so bitterly, either. And it would make sense of her behavior in the orangery, seeking out his company, but only to make him realize what he had missed.

How could he have shown such poor judgment? He had been wrong about her from the very beginning. Charmed by her liveliness and the intelligence in her looks, he had created the imaginary woman of his dreams in her image. But the real Elizabeth Bennet was not the woman he had dreamed of, and he needed to accept that. She wanted to punish him, and she had succeeded beyond her wildest dreams.

His thoughts tortured him as he returned to his room to bathe. Wilkins, his valet, took one look at his face and said nothing, only poured a glass of brandy and held it out to him. As Darcy sipped it, hardly tasting the delicate flavor, a new, stabbing doubt struck him. Elizabeth might have deliberately set out to hurt him, but what of Drew? Was Drew simply a pawn in Elizabeth's game of revenge, or had he known all along that Darcy loved her? Had Drew, too, entered into the engagement with the goal of causing Darcy pain?

He covered his face with his hands, but hiding his eyes could not chase away the brutal thought that Drew might have conspired with Elizabeth to punish him. Surely God could not be so unjust. Losing Elizabeth had been nothing compared to discovering her treachery, but if it meant that Drew hated him, too...that would be too much.

There was no choice. He had to find out what Drew knew about his past with Elizabeth.

ELIZABETH'S ENCOUNTER with Mr. Darcy in the orangery still lingered in her mind that afternoon as she walked the grounds with the other ladies. Georgiana and Mrs. Gardiner had been deep in conversation, leaving her with Miss Bingley and Mrs. Hurst, but Elizabeth had managed to keep up the appearance of good spirits as they had strolled down the lane by the lake. When they reached the formal gardens, the paths became narrow, allowing only two abreast, and Elizabeth gratefully took advantage of the change to fall back from the others. It was not as if she had any desire to converse with them, not while she was still haunted by the revelation of how badly hurt Mr. Darcy had been by her rejection. She, who prided herself on her judgment, had misled herself, never even considering that he might have been deeply injured by her behavior!

Not that it made a difference in the end. She had no choice but to marry Andrew. It was unfair that Mr. Darcy must suffer for it, but she could not afford to sacrifice her reputation and her family's future so that he need not see them together. Her logic told her that much, but her heart whispered that she had been cruel to agree to the engagement. Or was she grieving the marriage she might have had, if she had not so badly misjudged Darcy?

That thought was too frightening to pursue.

As if she had conjured him, Darcy's deep voice sounded beside her. "May I join you?"

The unexpected sound made her jump. "Of course." She quickly clasped her hands behind her back before he could offer her his arm. She did not trust herself to touch him, even in a perfectly proper, impersonal way, with her gloved hand on his coat sleeve. It would not feel impersonal. She had to deny herself. "Your gardens are among the most beautiful I have visited." She winced as she said it, realizing how odd praise for Pemberley must sound coming from her.

His breathing sounded harsh over the birdsong. "You are always welcome to visit, when you are living in Kympton."

Embarrassed, she turned her face away, looking down at the patchwork of red and yellow flowers beside her. Each slow step revealed new textures and scents. It was easier when she avoided looking at him, but the physicality of his presence beside her still drew her to him, engendering longings she could not fulfill. "You are very generous."

"It is important to me that Drew feel welcome at Pemberley," he said abruptly.

So he wanted to welcome Andrew, and that meant he was forced to welcome her, whether he wished to or not. A bitter taste filled the back of her mouth, tainting the sunlight that warmed her skin. But she needed to say something. "I would think granting him the living demonstrates that you welcome him."

Darcy did not reply immediately. When he did, he seemed to be weighing each word carefully. "When he told me of your engagement, he was already aware that I was acquainted with you and expected me to be displeased by the connection."

Her cheeks grew hot. That was why he had sought her out, not out of a desire for company, but to discover how much she told his brother.

Suddenly the flowers were drained of their beauty. "I told him you disapproved of my family's behavior, and that we quarreled at our last meeting," she said flatly.

"Quarreled?" The word was packed with bitterness and disbelief.

Stung, she said, "Yes. That I accused you of coming between Bingley and my sister and of mistreating Wickham, before I learned that was false." When he did not respond, she added coldly, "You need not worry; I told him my behavior towards you was at fault."

His mouth twisted. "Is that all you told him?"

She could barely breathe. Did he truly think so badly of her, that she would betray his secrets to Andrew? "Yes. I have no desire to come between the two of you, and it would only have caused him discomfort if I told him the context of our discussion. I am not in the habit of hurting people for no reason."

"You will forgive me if I see it differently," he said icily.

Brilliant poppies, blue hollyhocks, fragrant lavender. She struggled to focus on them to rein in her temper, fighting the urge to defend herself. It would be pointless. Darcy would think the worst of her, no matter what she said. "I am doing the best I can in an unfortunate situation," she said through gritted teeth.

He drew in an uneven breath. "As are we all."

She turned her head away sharply, staring down at the flower border. When she could trust herself to speak without rancor, she said in a strained voice, "I agreed to remain at Pemberley against my better judgment because you and your sister pressed me to do so. Perhaps it is now time for me to leave."

"That would only serve to make Drew wonder what I had done to chase you away. I thought you did not wish to come between him and me." It was almost a sneer.

She squeezed her eyes shut, fighting back tears. A deep breath, and then another. "Excuse me, I believe my aunt is calling for me." It was an obvious falsehood; Mrs. Gardiner was deep in conversation with Georgiana, but Elizabeth picked up her skirts and hurried forward until she was so close to the others as to preclude private conversation.

Darcy did not follow her.

THE NEXT DAY, PRIOR to dinner, Miss Bingley asked Elizabeth, "Will you be attending the ball at Allston Hall on Friday?"

Elizabeth, already tired of Miss Bingley's pointed comments, said, "It seems unlikely, as I am not in the habit of attending events to which I have not been invited."

"Oh, but you are invited!" cried Miss Darcy. "The invitation included our guests. I apologize that I did not think to mention it to you earlier. The card was delivered last week."

"It will no doubt be a pleasant occasion, but I fear I must decline." Elizabeth gestured at her dress. "I have nothing suitable to wear, having packed for a tour, not a country house visit." It went without saying that the other ladies could not assist her. Miss Bingley was thinner and taller; Mrs. Hurst heavier, and, while something of Miss Darcy's might be shortened to fit her, the girl was not yet out and was unlikely to have anything suitable in her wardrobe. "I will enjoy a quiet evening here with you and my aunt."

Flustered, Miss Darcy said, "Actually, Fitzwilliam has given me permission to attend, as long as I stay with my chaperone and do not dance. He thinks it will be good practice for my Season."

Elizabeth had no desire to embarrass the poor girl, so she said, "That sounds eminently sensible. No need to worry about me; I will enjoy a little peace." This seemed to be accepted by the ladies, and if Elizabeth, who dearly loved to dance, felt a little regret, she was capable of hiding it.

She was taken aback later when the housekeeper, Mrs. Reynolds, came to her room with a dress in a style perhaps a decade old. "Miss Georgiana asked me to find something for you to wear to the ball. I believe we can make this over to fit you and bring it up-to-date in the time we have."

Elizabeth eyed the dress, a gorgeous scalloped cream silk elaborately embroidered with a design of peacock feathers. "There is no need to put yourself to the trouble. I am happy to remain here with my aunt." She could not resist touching the sleeve, the fabric soft and delicate under her fingertips.

Mrs. Reynolds ducked her head. "If you will forgive an old family servitor, if you do not go, Mr. Drew will not attend either. We all wish to see him take his place in society again. You have done so much already to bring him back into the fold."

Elizabeth blew out a breath between her teeth. Would Andrew have agreed to marry her if he had realized it would mean being dragged back into the family he had left behind? "I suppose I must, then."

The housekeeper's wrinkled face was lit by her smile. "How good you are, Miss Bennet! Will you not try this on so I can see what adjustments need to be made? If we remove the sash and add an embroidered waistband, it will look quite the style."

Elizabeth obediently stood still as the maid undressed her and lowered the silk gown over her head. "Whose dress is this?"

"It belonged to the late Mrs. Darcy. It was a favorite of hers, and Miss Georgiana loved the peacock design, so I saved it at her request."

"It is lovely." The delicate silk folds settled around her like a cloud. She had never worn such fine fabric, nor such elegant embroidery. It made her skin glow, and she felt it suited her remarkably well.

The housekeeper pinched the fabric at her shoulder. "The length is perfect on you. It will be simple enough to take in a little here and a little there. We can add some lace at the sleeves, I think, and perhaps a ruffle."

"No lace or ruffle," Elizabeth said impulsively. "It would only draw attention away from the beautiful lines and embroidery. Perhaps a little ribbon instead."

The housekeeper cocked her head. "Yes, that will work. The late Mrs. Darcy loved the simplicity of it, too."

"What was she like?" Elizabeth had been wondering about Andrew's mother, who had watched her son be disowned.

The housekeeper smiled. "Oh, she was the loveliest lady, with the finest manners! And so generous to everyone, even to the servants. She always thought of what would make people happy. She loved her children dearly – *all* of them – but as often as not there was sadness in her eyes."

"Sadness?" She was certain the housekeeper was trying to tell her something.

"Oh, she had her share of tragedy, poor lady. So many of her babies died, and the old master never quite understood her tender nature." Mrs. Reynolds seemed to shake off the mood of reminiscence. "But it is not for me to say. You will look a picture in this, Miss Bennet! Mr. Drew will fall in love with you all over again."

But it was not Andrew's reaction she had thought of when she saw herself in the mirror.

Chapter 13

"Good heavens, Lizzy, I have never seen you look so lovely!" exclaimed Mrs. Gardiner when she stopped by Elizabeth's room before the ball.

Elizabeth twirled around to display her dress to the greatest advantage. "Is it not splendid? I feel like a queen in it. I do not know what Georgiana's maid did to my hair, but I wish I could do it every night!" It was an elaborate hairstyle with many tiny braids, delicate flowers, and sapphire-studded hairpins, courtesy of the jewels Miss Darcy had inherited.

"Most flattering," her aunt agreed.

"I wish you were coming, too," Elizabeth said.

"Not I," Mrs. Gardiner laughed. "A long evening among company where I know no one and will never see any of them again has little appeal for me, and I would hardly be a sought-after dance partner. I will be happier catching up on my correspondence. I want all of my friends to know I am staying at Pemberley! But come, let us go downstairs. I want to see your betrothed's face when he lays eyes on you."

In the drawing room where the others were gathering, Georgiana clasped her hands together in delight when she saw Elizabeth. "How beautiful you look!" she exclaimed.

Andrew's clothing was elegant enough that Elizabeth wondered if his brother had provided it, but he wore it well and looked handsome. His eyes grew warm at the sight of her, and he held her hand for a moment longer than was proper as he bowed over it. "I will be the most envied man at Allston Hall tonight."

"You are very kind." She tried to match his warmth, but her stomach had filled with knots at the sight of Darcy standing behind him, his face frozen in an unreadable expression. Was he displeased to see her wearing his mother's dress? In the three days since their discussion in the garden, he had barely looked at her, much less spoken to her. Apart from this moment, his eyes had always moved straight past her, as if he had decided she was invisible. Even if it were true that he had loved her and regretted her refusal for months, now he had dismissed her from his life.

ELIZABETH WAS GLAD to escape from the carriage at Allston Hall. Sitting for an hour across from a gentleman who ignored her presence could not but be uncomfortable, but somehow it was much worse when it was Darcy, who had once loved her. She had spent most of the journey feeling ill, and she could not attribute it to traveling in the well-sprung Darcy carriage. At least it was over for now.

Allston Hall was a sprawling red brick Jacobean manor. Elizabeth entered on Andrew's arm, following behind Darcy and his sister as they were announced into the large, wood paneled ballroom. The decor was old-fashioned, with larger-than-life portraits of people in antique dress and heavy wooden furniture lining the walls, but it exuded a warmth and historic charm.

Andrew partnered her for the first set, proving himself to be a more graceful dancer than she had expected, and she enjoyed the lively country dance once she was certain Darcy was in the other line of dancers. Towards the end of the second dance, as she and Andrew stood out at one end of the set, she saw him stiffen and frown.

"Is something the matter?"

He shook his head. "Someone whom I prefer not to meet is here. That is all."

Then the dance caught up to them again, and there was no further time to speak. She had seen that look of distaste on his face before when he was speaking of slavery. Was there a slaveholder here? Probably more than one, given how common it was to hold lucrative overseas plantations.

Mr. Bingley claimed her for the second set. This time she could not avoid Darcy as she danced. When he took her hands across the line, a ripple of pleasure went up her arms, but as she took in the cold expression on his face, a hollow feeling in her stomach replaced it. What was wrong with her, that she could feel attracted to a man who was not only her future brother, but also hated her? Somehow she must learn to defeat this.

After that set ended, a footman approached her. "Miss Bennet?" he asked with a bow.

"That is I."

"Mr. Andrew Darcy asked me to give you a message. He was called away urgently and will not be returning tonight."

Elizabeth stared at him. Why would Andrew leave without speaking to her directly? Had he taken ill? But if so, would he not have said so? She could not imagine what would have called him away. His parishioners were not wealthy; if something had happened to one of them, they could not have afforded to send to Allston Hall for him. All his relatives, or at least the ones he was speaking to, were here.

She chewed on her lip. No, more likely someone had behaved offensively to him, perhaps the person he had preferred not to meet. He might have felt his only choices were to make a scene or to leave, and he would not want to embarrass his brother. But she wished he had not abandoned her. It made no real difference in practice, since she would be riding back to Pemberley in the Darcy carriage in any case, but she disliked it. "I thank you for the message."

It left her feeling oddly off balance in this room full of strangers, so she decided to sit out the next dance with Georgiana. But when she reached the chaperone's seating area, she discovered Mrs. Hurst was no longer beside the girl. Instead, the altogether too familiar figure of George Wickham leaned intimately towards Georgiana, whose head was bowed.

Rage pounded in Elizabeth's ears. All the misery that man had caused her, turning her life upside down – and how dare he endanger Georgiana's reputation by approaching her publicly? She had to get him away from the girl, quickly, and without drawing anyone's notice.

She hurried up to him. "Why, Mr. Wickham," she crooned with an excess of honey. "Did you forget that you promised me this dance? The set is already forming," she said loudly enough for people nearby to hear.

He looked up at her in astonishment and only fleeting embarrassment. For a moment she thought he might refuse, but too many people had overheard her words. His teeth flashed in that familiar ingratiating smile. "Miss Elizabeth, I have been looking forward to it all evening. Forgive me, Georgiana. I hope to have the pleasure of speaking to you later."

The girl did not look up, but mumbled something Elizabeth could not hear.

Seething, Elizabeth allowed Wickham to lead her toward the set.

Wickham smiled again. "I am astonished, Miss Elizabeth," he said in a tone of great affability. "I would have thought I deserved no special attention from you."

How had she ever thought him sincere? But she was among the friends and neighbors of the Darcys, and she could not afford to create a scene. She fluttered her eyelashes at him. "Why, how could you think such a thing, dear Mr. Wickham? I was so delighted to see you in Miss Darcy's company."

His eyelids drooped. "Dearest Georgiana! I was always a great favorite of hers. She was a sweet child, and I could not resist the urge to pay my respects."

Elizabeth tilted her head. "I would have sworn you told me in Meryton that she was proud and unpleasant, but perhaps becoming engaged so suddenly has caused my memory to fail me."

"Ah, yes, I must give you my congratulations," he said smoothly. "You will no doubt enjoy that fine parsonage. How I would have liked to live there myself! It is nothing to Pemberley, of course, and I can hardly blame you for resenting me for that."

"What has Pemberley to do with it?" she exclaimed irritably, but then the music started and she could thankfully turn to the gentleman below her. She had no desire to talk to Wickham, only to keep him away from Georgiana.

But he was not done speaking to her. As soon as they were at the end of the set, he said, "I truly do owe you a most sincere apology, Miss Elizabeth. You have always been kind to me, and it was utterly wrong of me to involve you in my quarrel with the Darcys. If I had thought for even a moment, if I had not been in the heat of anger, I would never have done such a thing to you. I was always very fond of you."

She gave him a sidelong look, astonished that he would think any apology in his power. "I will take your words with all the sincerity with which you meant them," she said icily. "I am dancing with you for one reason only, to keep you away from Miss Darcy."

"I mean her no harm," he protested.

"No more harm than you meant her at Ramsgate?"

That caught his attention. "I fear you have been given some misinformation, Miss Elizabeth," he said in a tone of such wounded righteousness that she almost hesitated.

"You have been kind enough to give me a great education in misinformation, Mr. Wickham. If I see you within a dozen feet of Miss Darcy again, I will march straight into the card room and fetch Mr. Darcy, who will show his displeasure in a far less pleasant manner than dragging you off to dance. You may be certain I will have my eye on Miss Darcy every minute."

His upper lip curled. How had she ever believed him handsome? "I regret that you feel that way."

When the dance ended, he sketched her the merest shadow of a bow before walking quickly away from her. She watched after him, her eyes narrowed, until he left the ballroom, and then she headed towards Georgiana.

She was still some distance from the girl when her hostess stopped her. "Miss Bennet, I have been requested to make an introduction. May I present to you Mr. Hadley, cousin to the Earl of Matlock? He is most particularly eager to meet you."

Mr. Hadley was a heavyset man of perhaps fifty or sixty with an old-fashioned full beard. Elizabeth was in no mood to dance with an old lecher, but at least this gentleman's eyes were on her face, not her neckline, and he, after all, was a Darcy connection, since the Earl of Matlock was Lady Anne Darcy's brother. "It is a pleasure, Mr. Hadley."

He bowed stiffly. "I was delighted to hear of Mr. Andrew Darcy's engagement, and wanted to give you my very best wishes."

"You are most kind," Elizabeth murmured, hoping that would be the end of it.

He cleared his throat. "I understand that your intended has been called away, and wondered if, in his absence, you might be free for the supper dance."

She longed to say no, her nerves still frayed by her encounter with Wickham, but she could hardly refuse one of Andrew's relations. "I would be honored, sir."

Mr. Hadley kept the conversation to light subjects, such as her enjoyment of the evening, until the end of the dance, but afterwards he steered her towards one of the small, two-person tables set up on the garden terrace, and she began to worry. It was hardly secluded; there was no more than three feet between the tiny, wrought-iron tables, but it suggested an inappropriate desire for intimacy. He had kept a respectful distance during the dancing, but she intended to remain on her guard, and she was still concerned about Georgiana. Hopefully her threats would be enough to keep Wickham away from the girl.

The old gentleman started safely enough by asking her about her impressions of Derbyshire, and then said, "It was a fine thing that Darcy gave your intended a living. He has been away for a long time."

Was he fishing for gossip? Or might Mr. Hadley be the slaveholder whom Andrew had been eager to avoid? If that was the case, she would leave him with no doubt about her own position. "Yes; he spent some years in London as part of Mr. Wilberforce's household before going up to Oxford. He did admirable work for the abolitionist cause."

He did not seem offended, but his eyes seemed to focus off in the distance. "His mother would have been proud of him. She could never bear to see any human being suffer, no matter how mean their situation."

For the first time she felt a spark of interest. Andrew had told her almost nothing about his mother, so all she knew was the little bit that the housekeeper had let slip. "I know very little about the late Lady Anne Darcy."

A shadow crossed over his face. "Oh, she was a very fine lady. Gentle and kind, too good for this world, and always laughing, at least when she was a girl. I saw very little of her after her marriage. You have no doubt seen the portrait of her at Pemberley."

"There is not one there that I have noticed, certainly not in the portrait gallery. Perhaps it is in Darcy House in London. I have never visited there."

"You do not know what she looked like, then?" He reached into his pocket, pulled out his watch, and detached a small locket from the fob. He opened it, holding the cover between his thumb and forefinger, and then held it over the table in front of her. "This is Lady Anne."

Curious, she peered at the image of a young lady with laughing eyes, her dark hair piled high on her head. She could see a little resemblance to Andrew, mostly around the eyes, although more to Georgiana. Then the incongruity of it struck her. "You carry a portrait of Lady Anne Darcy with you?"

He smiled sadly. "She and I were childhood sweethearts. It is not a secret; anyone here could tell you. It created a bit of a scandal when she told her father she would not marry Darcy or anyone but me. I told her not to; there was no possibility her father would permit Lady Anne Fitzwilliam to marry the son of a country squire with no connections to offer, but she would speak her truth." He gazed at the portrait, a sad half-smile hovering over his lips. "This was her last gift to me before her father forced her to marry Darcy."

So Lady Anne Darcy had no choice in her marriage, either. Had she tried to make the best of it, as Elizabeth hoped to do for herself? If so, her success must have been limited, since the Pemberley housekeeper had told her of Lady Anne's grief. Had it been due only to the babies she had lost, or was she unhappy with her husband? "It is a sad story. I hope she was able to find some happiness at Pemberley."

"I know only a little of that time. At her request, I stayed away. I believe she took great comfort in her children, though."

What had Lady Anne thought when her husband had disowned Andrew? Was she in favor of it as well, or did it break her heart? But Andrew had already been living with Mr. Morris for two years by then, so apparently she did not mind being separated from him. Perhaps Mr. Hadley saw what he wished to see rather than the truth of the matter. "I think she would be proud of her children if she were to see them today." Or would she worry over her second son's forced engagement?

"I am glad to hear it. Thank you for listening to an old man prattle on about the distant past. I still take comfort in speaking of her and hearing about the part of her that lives on in her children."

Elizabeth's heart went out to this odd, old-fashioned gentleman who was so clearly still in love with Lady Anne. There could be no real harm in speaking to him of Lady Anne's children, so she shared a story or two about each of them. It was heartwarming to see how much a few words seemed to please him.

AFTER SUPPER, ELIZABETH danced another set with Mr. Bingley, and then sat the last out with Georgiana, weary after the long evening. When their party finally left Allston Hall, she was surprised to discover Andrew already inside the carriage. It must not have been a true emergency, which only made his departure more puzzling. Had he been sitting there waiting for them all these hours? She supposed it was more sensible than trying to make his way back to Kympton on foot in the dark, an easy target for any thief or footpad.

She was longing to ask why he had left, but having his brother, sister, Bingley, and Miss Bingley sharing the spacious Darcy carriage meant a delay of any serious discussion until there was greater privacy. She hoped the others would permit her to be silent; she had no desire to relate her experiences of the evening.

Mr. Darcy did not oblige her. He asked Andrew harshly, "Why did you leave without a word?"

Andrew stared straight ahead, not looking at his brother. "I saw the potential for an unpleasant scene, and wished to avoid gossip." His voice had an edge to it.

Elizabeth could guess how much criticism from Darcy would hurt Andrew. "I am glad you did so," she said firmly. "I overheard a most offensive conversation about slavery. How could you have kept both your silence and your honor among certain members of that company? If you knew those men from London, you were right to leave."

Andrew shot her a look of mixed gratitude and puzzlement. "I am sorry you were exposed to such talk."

Darcy did not appear satisfied by this explanation, but Miss Bingley, sensing an opportunity, said, "Everyone I met was uniformly charming. You are most fortunate in your neighbors, Mr. Darcy. I would be happy to spend more time in their company."

Feeling Miss Bingley's flattery was a much safer topic than Andrew's disappearance, slavery, or Mr. Wickham, Elizabeth remarked on the excellence of the entertainment and encouraged Miss Bingley to comment on every moment of her evening.

Chapter 14

As soon as they reached Pemberley, Darcy retired to his study, a wounded animal seeking refuge in his lair to lick his wounds and suffer in privacy. God above, what a nightmare of an evening! He had thought he could control himself on the subject of Elizabeth marrying Drew, but that was before watching them dance together as everyone exclaimed what a handsome couple they made, seeing their bodies move in perfect concert, Elizabeth's eyes bright with pleasure. Their bodies would move together in a different dance once they were married, and the idea made him physically ill.

Unable to bear his thoughts, he had escaped to the Allston Hall gardens, walking out into a little wilderness where no one would see him casting up his accounts. He remained there, hiding in the dark, until he feared his absence would be noted. He forced himself back to the ball he had never wished to attend, only to find Elizabeth dancing with none other than George Wickham, flirting and smiling sweetly at him.

How could he have fallen in love with a woman who would torture him in this way, who would encourage a blackguard like Wickham and still behave as if she had done nothing wrong? But the woman he had believed her to be would never have engaged herself to his brother. How could she have turned out to be such a duplicitous, deceptive woman... and why could he not stop loving her?

He poured a large brandy and drank it too quickly, especially after imbibing heavily at the ball to settle his nerves. He studied his glass for a moment, and then refilled it. How was he to live like this?

A knock sounded at the door. "Come," he barked. It had better be someone he could get rid of quickly.

But the door opened to reveal Elizabeth, still wearing that silky, scalloped gown that clung to her body like a waterfall of fabric. The dress she had worn while dancing in Wickham's arms and with Andrew. He hated it, and he wanted to rip it off her and make love to her.

He rubbed his forehead. What was she doing here? She should not be here alone, especially not so late at night. She knew it, too, because her fingers twisted together and she chewed on her bottom lip. No, he must not think about her lips, or he would go mad.

Why had he drunk all that brandy? He needed his wits about him, and instead he was more than half foxed. "Is there something you require?" he blurted out, harsh even to his own ears.

"Forgive me for disturbing you." Her eyes darted around the room, as if afraid to settle anywhere. "Something happened at the ball, and... and I felt I should inform you of it."

That damned ball. Fury rose in him. "Did you ever bother to read my letter?"

Now she looked at him, surprise in her fine eyes. "Your letter? The one you gave me at Hunsford?"

"That was the only letter I ever wrote you." Apart from the dozens he had burnt instead of sending to her. "Did you read it?"

Her brow furrowed nervously. "Yes."

"Why did you not believe me?" he demanded in angry disgust.

She appeared to muster courage. "I believed you."

"Yet you danced with that blackguard Wickham anyway. Are you fool enough to think he will treat you differently? Has his charm made you lose your mind?" What was wrong with him? He should not be saying these things. No wonder she hated him. He hated himself.

"I despise Mr. Wickham, sir," she said in a tight, small voice. "I danced with him for one reason only, which was to separate him from your sister without making a scene. He was trying to impose himself on her. Because I did believe your letter, I insisted he dance with me instead, in order to keep her safe. I came here now because I thought you ought to know he had approached your sister. If I had been certain Andrew knew of his history with Georgiana, I would have gone to him instead of you. Now I have accomplished that task, and I shall leave you in peace." She curtsied stiffly and turned away.

She had not wanted to dance with Wickham? God, how he ached to believe it! He darted to stand between her and the door. "No. Do not go. I..." He raked his hand through his hair. "I am sorry. I misunderstood."

She kept her eyes down. "It is nothing. Pray excuse me."

"It is not nothing." He tried to wrangle his brandy-fuddled brain into submission. If he had been wrong about that, what else had he been wrong about? "Do you love my brother?"

She spread her hands in front of her, examining her fingers as if she might find the answer there. "I have the greatest respect for Andrew, and I believe I can learn to love him." Her voice trembled.

"Why, then? Why are you marrying him? Are you so desperate to punish me?"

"Punish you?" She stared at him, seemingly uncomprehending. "Why would I do that?"

"Revenge. For interfering between Bingley and your sister. For insulting your family. For..." He could not remember what he was going to say, not when her eyes were full of pain and shining with unshed tears.

She wrapped her arms around herself and turned away. "I have no desire for revenge. I was at fault for believing Wickham's lies, and I hold nothing against you. I did not know Andrew was your brother when I agreed to marry him. I was under the impression he was a distant cousin of yours." She sounded defeated.

Darcy's laugh cracked with disbelief. "Not know he was my brother? How could you fail to know?"

Now she glared at him. "How could I know? You never mentioned a brother, only a sister. Nor did Miss Bingley, who could not stop talking about how intimate she was with your family. Nor did your aunt, Lady Catherine, nor your cousin, Colonel Fitzwilliam. When I toured Pemberley, I saw portraits of you, your sister, and even of Mr. Wickham, but none of another boy. Andrew was introduced to me as Mr. Darcy of Kympton. He told me more than once that he never visited Pemberley. Why should I have thought him your brother rather than a distant relation?"

A red haze swam in Darcy's vision. It was impossible. How could she fail to know? That Drew himself would have said nothing, yes, since he did not want the connection; but everyone knew Drew was his brother. Someone would have told her. True, Lady Catherine would not speak Drew's name, not after he had gone to work for Wilberforce and the abolitionists, since all of her late husband's money came from the West Indies. Andrew was dead to her. And his father had removed Drew's miniature from Pemberley years ago, but still, everyone knew. Everyone.

But for years no one apart from Georgiana had mentioned Drew to Darcy. No one would risk opening that wound, not when Drew refused Darcy's olive branches and continued to blame him for their father's rejection.

If only he had learned the truth of why Drew had left Pemberley sooner! Why should Drew believe he cared when it had taken over a year for Darcy to track down his missing brother? But he had not known, not until the night of his father's apoplexy. He had believed his father when he had said Drew was away visiting friends.

Just as Elizabeth had believed he had no brother, because no one had told her otherwise.

But she had, by her own confession, agreed to marry a man she thought to be a cousin of his, to whom he had given a valuable family living – and without asking him anything about his family. No woman would agree to an engagement knowing so little about their prospective husband! And only three months after he himself had offered her his hand and his heart.

His mind might be muddled with alcohol, but that was clearly ridiculous. "You agreed to marry him without asking any questions about his family? I do not believe it."

"It is not as if I had an excess of time, or much choice in the matter," she retorted, her nostrils flaring.

No time or choice? "What do you mean?" he asked thickly.

"I —" She broke off abruptly, swallowed hard, and appeared to collect herself. "If you wish to know more about the circumstances of my engagement, I suggest you apply to your brother." She tried to dodge around him.

"I am asking you. Why did you agree to marry him, if not to revenge yourself on me?" Let her have a reason, any reason!

"It had nothing to do with you, and it was certainly not revenge," she said tiredly, but then a look of apprehension spread over her face, and she clapped her hand to her mouth. "Oh, dear God!"

"What is the matter?" Somehow his hands were on her arms.

"Wickham," she said brokenly. "He used me to hurt you."

"Wickham? What did he do?"

She opened her mouth as if to respond, but then shook her head instead. In a trembling voice, she said, "Nothing. Nothing at all. I misspoke. Pray disregard it."

"No. You must tell me!"

She looked away. "There is nothing to tell," she said dully. "He approached your sister, and I danced with him for the reasons I told you. That is all."

She knew, then. She knew that seeing her dance with Wickham would hurt him. But could he trust her? Could Andrew trust her? "I will speak to Andrew about it."

"No! I beg of you, say nothing to him!" She swiped her hand across her eyes. "He most particularly asked me not to speak of that to you. I would never have mentioned it, had I not been in such a disturbance of spirits. Can you not simply forget I said anything?" Her fine eyes shone with tears as she pleaded with him.

He could not refuse her, even if she had deliberately set out to hurt him. But she had said that was not true, had she not? And yet she had still agreed to marry Drew, even without loving him. It made no sense, or at least none that his drink-fuddled mind could find. But he could not bear her tears. "I will not speak to Drew," he said softly.

She bowed her head. "I thank you."

He could not help it. He wrapped his arms around her and held her to him gently, as if she might break, as if she were the most precious thing in the universe, as if somehow he could protect her from this pain.

For a moment she laid her head on his shoulder, but then she stiffened and pushed him away. "No!" she cried. "I cannot."

Of course. Why would she want comfort from the man she hated? He stumbled back a step. "Forgive me." There was nothing more he could say or do. It was finished.

She shook her head and ran from the room, leaving behind only desolation.

Chapter 15

The following morning, Elizabeth knew her first task had to be to speak with Andrew. If Darcy had misunderstood her dancing with Wickham, so would Andrew if he ever learned of it. Better to tell him herself and give her reasons. And if visiting the parsonage at Kympton gave her an excuse to avoid Darcy after that mortifying scene the previous night, so much the better.

In vino veritas, they said, and too much to drink had certainly shown a different side of Darcy from the one who ignored her. How could he possibly think she was marrying Andrew to punish him? That was a cruel blow, but not as hard as that moment when his older affections had emerged and he had taken her into his arms. Oh, how she had longed to stay there! But she was engaged to his brother, and she owed Andrew her loyalty. As it was, she had almost revealed Wickham's part in her engagement, which Andrew had specifically asked her not to do. Two near-betrayals in a matter of minutes. Thankfully Darcy had seemed to think she was speaking about Wickham's behavior at the ball. Perhaps, if she were very fortunate, the drink would have wiped it all from his memory.

She wished she could wipe one particular moment from her own memory, the one where she had realized just how deep Wickham's perfidy ran. Somehow he must have guessed at Darcy's feelings for her. When she looked back on his comments at the ball, and even a vaguely remembered statement at their first Derbyshire meeting in the parsonage garden, it was now clear that he thought her presence indicated a forthcoming marriage to Darcy. What better way to injure his old enemy than to make it appear that his brother had compromised the woman Darcy loved? Andrew had never been Wickham's target, or only a distant second. It had been Darcy all along he had sought to hurt. And he had succeeded brilliantly, using Elizabeth as a weapon. The cruelty of it was breathtaking.

She had not thought she could feel any worse about the circumstances of her engagement, but she had been wrong. Even if Darcy wanted nothing to do with her now, how could she ever forget that she had been the instrument to cause him such pain?

And she could not forget how it had felt when he had held her close to him. A moment stolen in time, when it had seemed that he forgave her and still cared. But his look of horror as she left the room had told her that it had only been a fleeting weakness, brought on by too much wine.

It could never happen again.

At least she was likely free of him this morning, when he was no doubt sleeping off the effects of the late night and the strong drink. She was feeling the lack of sleep herself, since her thoughts had woken her earlier than she would like after being up half the night. Her aunt had been the only one at the breakfast table, and Elizabeth had entertained her with tales of the ball.

Georgiana had caught her just as she was about to leave for Kympton. "Are you going to see Drew?"

Elizabeth tilted her head as she eyed the girl, wondering why she was asking a question to which she already knew the answer. "Yes, I am."

In a small voice, Georgiana asked, "Do you plan to tell him Mr. Wickham spoke to me?"

Ah. That explained her concern. Elizabeth said carefully, "Mr. Wickham has caused trouble for Andrew in the past. I must explain why I danced with him before he hears that detail from anyone else, but I will make certain he understands you were giving Wickham no encouragement and that you were unhappy about his presence. No one can blame you for his behavior."

"I hope not. But I should thank you for helping me. You did not truly wish to dance with him, did you?"

"Mr. Wickham? I would sooner waltz with a cobra."

The girl's look of shock at her words quickly gave way to an astonished smile. "Good. He is a cobra."

ANDREW WELCOMED HER with a warm smile. "Just in time! I was planning to call on you shortly." He hesitated, the smile fading. "I finally received a response from your father."

"Oh, dear. What did he say?" If her father had chosen this moment to display his sense of humor, she was going to be seriously displeased. "Pray tell me he did not refuse his consent."

"Not as such, no, but he says he cannot decide without meeting me first. A hard point to argue, I suppose." It was obvious Andrew was making an effort to be fair, but she sensed he was displeased. Understandably. After all, it would take him two full days traveling to get there and then another two days back, to say nothing of the expense.

"Oh, dear, I am sorry," she said. "As if it is not enough that you are rescuing our family from scandal, now he demands that you make a long journey! It is quite unreasonable, and I will tell him so." How dare her father make this already difficult situation more fraught?

He shook his head. "I can understand his position, and, under normal circumstances, I would have made such an application in person. I will honor his request. My question for you was whether you would prefer me to go immediately or if I should wait and escort you and your aunt when you return home next week."

"If you must be put to such an inconvenience, I suppose it would make more sense to wait." She would rather not throw Andrew into the lion's den of her family alone. At least she could hope to mitigate some of her parents' worst behavior.

"It would be easier, certainly. The only question is whether Wickham might see the delay in formally announcing our engagement as an opportunity to make mischief. I suppose it would not make much difference in the end, as long as we do announce it eventually."

She sighed. "I think it is unlikely to be a problem, as my mother has no doubt already informed the entire neighborhood of your offer for me, so that should provide protection. But Wickham is why I am here. He was at the ball last night." After a brief explanation of how she had come to dance with him, she added, "Threatening him with your brother seemed to work, so I feel no great concern that he will cause more trouble for us."

He nodded. "It was good thinking to make him dance with you. I thank you for keeping Georgiana safe from him."

"I had to do something. I was shocked to see him there; I had not expected your neighbors to include him in their invitations."

He scowled. "He has many friends among the local gentry, thanks to his time as an accepted member of the Pemberley household."

Before she could reply, the maid entered and bobbed a curtsey, wringing her hands nervously. "Sir, you said I should ask you if I didn't know what to do about something. There's a lady here to see you, but she wouldn't give her name. Should I send her away?"

"No, show her in," said Andrew. "A gentleman who refuses to give you his name should not be admitted, but there are times when a woman may wish to see a clergyman without anyone's knowledge."

"Yes, sir. Thank you, sir," said the girl hastily, and retreated from the room.

"Indeed?" Elizabeth asked Andrew archly.

He shrugged. "Women who find themselves in a difficult situation have been known to turn to a clergyman for assistance."

"I see. Should I leave you, then?"

"No need. If this were one of my parishioners, Betty would have recognized her. If she is a stranger, it is better if I am not alone."

Betty reappeared and showed in a slender lady dressed in a staid black dress, a dark veil hiding her face.

Andrew bowed. "Pray come in, madam. How may I be of assistance to you?"

"So formal, Drew?" Her accent was elegant. She tossed back her veil, revealing a young woman's face.

Andrew's eyebrows shot up. "Lady Frederica, this is indeed a surprise. Clearly I must offer my sympathies on your loss."

"My loss? What – oh, this?" She gestured down at her black skirts. "Merely a disguise. No one has died."

He blinked. "I see." It was clear he did not see at all. "Would you care to sit down? Betty, a tea tray, if you please."

His visitor glanced at Elizabeth. "Might I speak to you alone, Drew?"

Stiffening, Andrew said, "Forgive me. May I present to your acquaintance my betrothed, Miss Elizabeth Bennet? Elizabeth, I have the honor of presenting —"

"Better to avoid my name," the newcomer interrupted. "She might wish to be able to plead ignorance of my visit someday."

Elizabeth already had a very good idea of their visitor's identity, but had no intention of interfering, so she merely curtsied and tried to hide her intense curiosity. Why would the Earl of Matlock's daughter be paying a secret visit to Andrew?

Lady Frederica said, "Still, my congratulations to you both. How is it that I have heard nothing of this?"

"It has not yet been announced," said Andrew with a chill in his voice.

"I was not criticizing, merely surprised," said Lady Frederica with unusual directness. "Forgive me; I am not at my best today, or I would not be here."

Elizabeth turned to Andrew. There was no reason for her to stay, especially after Lady Frederica had refused to be introduced to her. "If you will be so kind as to excuse me, I feel an unaccountable urge to stroll about the garden."

Andrew's face tightened. "Perhaps we should all go." Apparently he did not wish to be left alone with Lady Frederica.

Well, this was uncomfortable! Especially when Elizabeth was trying to be on her best behavior. There was no simple way out of this sticky situation without violating at least one rule of etiquette, so she might as well choose the most honest approach. She smiled at Lady Frederica. "Perhaps we should begin again. If I am to be privy to this conversation, I should explain that several months ago, I made the acquaintance of Andrew's cousin Colonel Fitzwilliam, who mentioned his sister Frederica more than once."

"And I look like him," said Lady Frederica ruefully. "Oh, well, so much for my attempt at anonymity. But my business today is something I wish to keep from my family. If either of you are not in a position to honor that, I would ask you to be generous enough to say so straight out, and I will drink my tea and speak only of unimportant matters before returning home."

Andrew snorted. "No one in your family ever talks to me. I suppose that if I happened to see one of them about to be run down by a galloping horse, I would pull them out of the way, but that is the extent of my goodwill towards your family. I have no idea what you might wish to discuss with me, but I will not betray your secrets."

Elizabeth tried not to stare. Another set of family problems? What had Andrew done to anger his mother's family? She said stiffly, "Apart from having met Colonel Fitzwilliam when we were by coincidence visiting the same location, I do not even know your family, and certainly have no reason to tell anyone your secrets. My loyalty is to Andrew."

Lady Frederica studied her for a moment. "I suppose that is all I can ask. Drew, Evan says I can trust you."

Andrew tilted his head. "Evan Farleigh?" He sounded surprised.

"Of course. Who else?"

"Farleigh is a member of Parliament," Andrew told Elizabeth. "We moved in the same circles in London."

Lady Frederica tossed her head. "He thinks I do not understand the ramifications of my current plans. He told me to ask you what it is truly like to be disowned by your family."

Andrew's jaw dropped. "Why? Surely you are not expecting to be disowned."

"In fact, it is quite likely," she said coolly, as if such a thing were a matter of little import. "I intend to marry Evan, you see."

"Ah," said Andrew. "I cannot imagine your father would approve of that. But would he actually disown you for it? I know he despises abolitionists, but he may be more reluctant to disown his only daughter than an already disgraced nephew."

Poor Andrew! His father had disowned him for refusing to fight, and his uncle had done so because he was an abolitionist. No wonder Andrew expected so little from his family!

Lady Frederica wrinkled her nose. "He would overlook Evan's politics if he had a title or riches, but, sadly, he does not, or at least not enough wealth to meet my father's standards. As it is, my father has refused to give his consent, and he will never forgive me for marrying against his wishes."

"I am sorry," said Andrew, and it sounded as if he meant it. "Farleigh is a good man, and for what little it is worth, you have my best wishes."

Lady Frederica blinked rapidly. "Wait. You do not, then, advise me to leave off this plan because it will cost me my family?"

Andrew studied his hands. "Being disowned is...unspeakable. Losing everyone, losing your home. But at a certain point, there is no choice. If keeping your family means giving up your very self, then there is no decision to make. And I suspect you would not be here today, had you not already reached that point where it is impossible to stay."

She exhaled sharply, and then relaxed back in her chair. "You are correct, of course. I wish I had spoken to you long ago."

Andrew hesitated. "I am sorry you are facing this. If there is any way in which I may be of assistance to you, you need only ask."

"That is kind of you, especially given how poorly my family has treated you."

"You have never ill-treated me, Lady Frederica. We may not have crossed paths frequently in recent years, but on the occasions when we have, you have always been pleasant and never cut me. I have appreciated that."

"Well, you never did anything to hurt me, either," she said. "But there is one thing you could do, if you are willing, and that is to attend my wedding. It is more for Evan's sake than my own; his father is worried about facing hostility from my family, and showing that even one relative is willing to support me would help."

Andrew smiled. "Even the very least among your relations, with no wealth or influence? Of course. I would be happy to do so."

The image of Darcy the previous night suddenly rose before Elizabeth, his hair disheveled and his eyes full of pain. He had told her how much he wanted to heal the breach with Andrew. Yet neither Andrew nor Lady Frederica seemed to see a reason to speak to him about this situation. How would he feel when discovered his brother had known about Lady Frederica's dilemma and kept it from him? Impulsively she said, "What of Mr. Darcy? Mr. Fitzwilliam Darcy, that is. Would his presence make a difference?"

Lady Frederica exchanged a glance with Andrew before saying tactfully, "I expect he would take my father's side and insist Evan is not my equal."

Elizabeth shook her head. "As long as the gentleman is respectable, I believe he would have sympathy for your position, from things I have heard him say about love matches. He has also been trying hard to make amends to Andrew, and I imagine he would find it uncomfortable if this were kept secret from him."

"Drew?" asked Lady Frederica.

"I cannot say," Andrew said heavily. "My instinct is always to keep my distance, but Elizabeth knows Darcy – the man he is today – better than I do. I will grant he has given me no cause for distrust."

Lady Frederica tapped her gloved fingertips together. "It would be a risk, but his support would help a great deal with Evan's family. But if Darcy were to tell my father my plans, it could make my life more difficult."

"I do not believe Fitzwilliam would reveal it if I asked him not to," said Andrew. "He holds his honor close."

And so it was resolved that Andrew would speak to Darcy that very day, as Lady Frederica waited with Elizabeth at the parsonage.

Chapter 16

The worst of the pounding in Darcy's head had begun to diminish by the time Drew arrived, asking to speak to him privately. More trouble, no doubt. Exactly what he did not need after last night. It was hard enough to face his brother, knowing that he had betrayed him by holding Drew's betrothed in his arms, and that even now he only wished he could do it again.

Why did Drew wish to speak to him alone, anyway? Please God let it be nothing to do with Elizabeth! If she had told him of the previous evening, this could be the end of everything. Once the door was closed behind them, he said formally, with a heavy heart, "How may I be of service to you?"

Andrew took a deep breath. "I would like to seek your advice regarding a mutual acquaintance of ours who is facing a difficult situation, but first I would ask your word that what I tell you will go no further."

Relief flooded him. "Of course." If Drew was actually willing to come to him with a problem, Darcy would promise far more than that.

"Our cousin Frederica called on me this morning asking for my help. She intends to marry against her father's wishes, and expects to be disowned for it." One corner of his mouth turned up in a wry half-smile. "She came to me as the family expert on being disinherited."

Darcy winced inwardly. "Unfortunate, but hardly surprising. Frederica has always had a will of her own. Is the gentleman in question inappropriate, or simply not to Lord Matlock's liking?"

Drew seemed to consider the question. "He is a gentleman, one I know and respect, but his family is a notch, perhaps two notches, below Matlock in both fortune and connections. He is also a Whig. I daresay he will make a good husband, but I doubt they will move in the highest circles as she does now."

"She loves him, then?"

"I did not ask. I assume so, since it seems unlikely she would lack for suitors, given her dowry and connections."

"No, she does not. Still, she is of age, and can marry whomever she chooses." But why was Andrew asking his help about this? "Are you concerned that Matlock may seek vengeance on you for helping her?"

Drew snorted. "Matlock, having already disowned me, has no further power over me. No, in truth I am here on Frederica's behalf. She asked me to come to her wedding so she will not be completely without family in attendance. Since I have been outside the family for so long, she barely knows me, and I imagine it would mean rather more to her if you were there. She did not dare ask you because she thought you would side with her father. Perhaps you do; I do not know. But I thought you should have the opportunity to decide for yourself."

Good God, was Drew actually starting to trust him? A bit of warmth kindled in the emptiness of his heart. "I thank you for that consideration. I would like to speak to Frederica myself before making a decision, but, if her intended is a respectable and decent gentleman, I see no reason why I would not be willing to do so, even if her father opposes the match. I do not approve of his treatment of you, either, and have told him as much."

Drew looked startled. "That was good of you." He appeared to struggle for a moment. "If you wish to speak to Frederica, she is still at the parsonage. She did not wish to accompany me here; she was concerned word would get back to her father. She says there are servants here who are in his pay."

"Devil take it," groaned Darcy. "I suppose I should not be surprised. He always has to have a finger in every pie." And now that he knew of it, he could put a stop to it, unlike so many other problems that had no solutions.

ELIZABETH HAD NEVER met anyone like Lady Frederica Fitzwilliam before. She had heard enough stories about decadent behavior among the aristocracy to know better than to assume an earl's daughter would be meek and biddable, but Lady Frederica's open and forthright manner was still a shock. After spending an hour in her company, Elizabeth knew far more about the Fitzwilliam family and Lady Frederica's life than she had learned in a month's acquaintance with her ladyship's more reticent and proper brother, Colonel Fitzwilliam.

Surprisingly, Elizabeth found that she liked her. And it was a good distraction from the thoughts of last night with Darcy that insisted on inserting themselves into her mind.

By the time Andrew returned with Darcy, Elizabeth was answering Lady Frederica's equally forthright questions about her own family, and was pleased to discover that her ladyship seemed completely unconcerned about her mother's trade connections.

The sight of Darcy left her with that too familiar pang of pain and shame. Apart from a brief bow in her general direction, Darcy ignored her as he greeted Lady Frederica. Last night had changed nothing. Why did it have to hurt so much? She could not bear it, so she said, "If you will excuse me, I will leave you to your conversation."

Lady Frederica reached out and took her hand. "Do not go, I pray you! I would appreciate having another woman here."

She could hardly refuse so direct a plea without making a scene, so Elizabeth resumed her seat, making an effort to avoid looking in Darcy's direction. Not that it made any difference. She was invisible to him again. That brief moment of painful connection the previous evening was over. Did he even remember it, or was that memory hers alone to suffer through?

Darcy said, "Frederica, Drew has explained your situation to me. You do not need me to tell you that you can marry whomever you wish, since you are of age. Since Drew says he is a respectable gentleman, you have my blessing."

Her ladyship tilted her head to one side. "I thank you."

"That is the simple part," Darcy continued. "If I am to take a public stand on the matter, though, and potentially face a break with your father over it, I would need to know a little more. You are obviously under no obligation to answer my questions, but it might help me to make a decision."

Lady Frederica's smile was almost feline. "If you are willing to consider braving my father's displeasure, the least I can do is to answer your questions."

Darcy nodded. "How long have you known the gentleman? Drew did not tell me his name."

"Mr. Evan Farleigh. A little over three years. We have been waiting in the hope my father would give up on a grand match for me as I get closer to being on the shelf, but I have realized that will not happen. He would rather see me a spinster."

"Unfortunately, I cannot say I am surprised," Darcy said. "Now, with your connections and your dowry, you could have your pick of husbands."

"I would not go that far. Many men prefer wives who are submissive and obedient, and everyone knows I am not."

"May I ask why you have chosen this one?"

"Why him?" Lady Frederica chewed her lip, as if pondering the question, and then she burst out, "Because he listens to me when I speak. Truly listens, not just pretends to do so. We often do not agree, but he cares about my opinion."

Darcy raised an eyebrow. "A good reason. I understand his politics displease your father. Have you become more political, then?"

She shook her head. "In truth, no. I will support Evan's positions when we are married. His interest in political reform is admirable, but to me the most important thing is that he cares about something of importance, something more than the next card game or horse race or prize fight. I am sick to death of men who care about nothing but their own pleasures."

"Well said," Andrew remarked. "He will suit you well, then. I am glad to learn of this side of you; it is something we share."

That was another thing Elizabeth should be grateful for in her future husband – that he chose serious concerns over a life of meaningless pleasures. If only Andrew's admirable qualities could stop her from thinking about his brother!

Darcy studied Lady Frederica. "Given your reasons, I would be happy to offer you my support. When is the wedding?"

Lady Frederica grimaced. "Not for some months, as Evan insisted that I consider the matter over the summer. He worries I will regret being disowned. Now I will not see him until the Season begins, as my father will not allow me to return to London until then. Six months is a very long time to have no contact." She looked away, blinking rapidly.

Darcy said slowly, "Frederica, if I told your father that Georgiana could benefit from your company, would he permit you to visit Pemberley? And perhaps Drew might consider inviting his friend Farleigh to visit here at the parsonage."

"I would be happy to do so," Andrew declared. "Is he in London at present? I will be there in a fortnight and could stop by to invite him. It might be easier to explain matters in person."

Lady Frederica made no reply, and Elizabeth realized that, despite her calm façade, she was struggling to keep her composure. Finally she said shakily, "You are both very good to me. I am accustomed to being alone with this." She fished out a handkerchief and dabbed at the corners of her eyes. "And you hardly know me, Drew."

Andrew gave a ghost of a smile. "It is not difficult to do the right thing, and I do understand, none better, the magnitude of the risk you are taking. I may not know you well, but you will always be part of my family."

"And mine," added Darcy.

For a minute Lady Frederica pressed her handkerchief across her eyes. "I will have you know I never cry," she said with some annoyance.

Elizabeth was near tears herself. How could Darcy be so gentle to his cousin after his coldness and anger towards her, his efforts to ignore her very existence? He was so kind to Lady Frederica, yet could not bring himself even to look directly at Elizabeth. And it was her own fault. It ached deep inside to watch this side of Darcy that was lost to her forever. This was the generous, loyal gentleman the Pemberley housekeeper had described to her; the one whose good opinion she had lost forever. And now, when it was too late, she knew just how much she wanted that good opinion.

Andrew's one-eared cat jumped on her lap and curled up, purring rhythmically. Oh, dear, now she was truly at risk of crying! In desperation, she began silently counting backwards from a hundred to distract herself from those dangerous sentiments.

"What of Richard?" Darcy asked Frederica. "Will he not stand with you?"

"My brother? I have not asked him, nor do I intend to. I think he would, but he needs the allowance our father gives him, not to mention those connections that keep him out of the worst battles. I dearly hope he will stay in contact with me after I am married, but how could I ask him to pay such a high price merely to attend my wedding?"

"Understandable," Andrew said with a nod.

Lady Frederica said, "It was much easier to ask you, Drew, since my father has no more power over you, having already disowned you. Darcy, I hope it will not make any difficulties for you."

Darcy shrugged. "He can do little besides complaining about me. I am glad you trusted me enough to ask."

"I deserve no credit for that," Lady Frederica declared. "It was Miss Bennet's idea. I am embarrassed to admit I thought you would oppose my little mésalliance. She was the one who spoke up for you and convinced Drew to tell you."

For the first time since his initial greeting when he entered the room, Darcy slowly turned to look at Elizabeth, his dark, unreadable eyes boring into her. In a voice devoid of its earlier warmth and ease, he said, "Then I must thank you, Miss Bennet, for giving me this opportunity to be of service to my cousin."

She had wanted so badly for him to look at her, to truly see her, and now that she finally had his attention, she only wanted to escape from it. With a sick feeling at the pit of her stomach, she somehow forced out the words, "You have told me how important family ties are to you." She truly could not bear this. Before the tears gathering in her eyes could leak out, she added, "Pray excuse me." She nudged the cat gently from her lap and hurried from the room before he could acknowledge her.

She headed out into the gardens, tears now flowing down her cheeks. But the others might still be able to see her through the sitting room windows, so she hastened to the protection of the small kitchen yard, where she leaned back against the rough stone wall, closed her eyes, and tried to still her racing pulse.

"Is something the matter, miss?" It was the accented, musical tones of the Antiguan servant, Myrtilla.

Elizabeth's eyes flew open to discover Myrtilla sitting on a bench, a small bundle on her lap. With an embarrassed half-laugh, Elizabeth said, "No, I am quite well." And she realized how foolish this must sound when her distress was easily visible, and added dismissively, "Just something someone said. Nothing of importance."

The young woman's scarf-wrapped head bobbed as she nodded. "Words, they can be cruel things." She slid to one side of the bench. "Come, sit here and you can help me."

No servant had ever spoken to Elizabeth in such a familiar manner before, but it was done in such a warm and friendly voice that she was reluctant to criticize her for it. More importantly, the shock of being told to help in a servant's work had chased away her tears and replaced them with a desire to giggle.

Her mother would have told her to give Myrtilla a set-down to establish her place as her future mistress, but that felt wrong. What would Lady Frederica do in this circumstance? Probably whatever she liked.

Elizabeth sat down next to Myrtilla. "What are you doing?"

"Trying to feed this little one." Myrtilla lifted the cloth to reveal a tiny puppy, his eyes still closed. "He is the runt, and his mother has not enough milk for him. There was an herb we used in Antigua to help mothers produce more milk, but I cannot find it here, so we must make do. Let him smell your hand." She took Elizabeth's hand in hers and held it in front of the puppy's face.

A small damp nose moved against her palm, nuzzling and tickling her skin. "What is his name?"

"He has no name. He is little more than a week old and cannot hear yet." Myrtilla scooped up the puppy, wrappings and all, and held him out to Elizabeth. "Hold him against you, so he can feel the warmth of your body and your heartbeat."

Feeling a little foolish, Elizabeth cradled the tiny creature to her, watching in fascination his snuffling head movements. He had a charmingly lopsided look, with a circle of dark fur around one eye in an otherwise white face. A rush of warmth rose in her at the sight of a waving paw.

"He likes you." Myrtilla held out a tiny scrap of toweling. "Let me wrap this around your little finger, with a bit dangling off the end, just so. Now we will dip it in the milk." She took Elizabeth's hand and guided it to a small bowl of milk.

Her fingertip grew wet under the fabric, and she dripped milk on her skirt as she lifted her hand to wave it in front of the puppy's nose. Nothing happened. "How do I get him to take it?" she asked Myrtilla.

The girl shrugged lightly. "Try putting it in his mouth and rubbing his tongue. I could only get him to take a very little, but perhaps it will be enough to keep him from starving. If he eats nothing, he will die, and that will be God's will, but we must do our best to keep him alive, yes?"

"We most certainly will!" Elizabeth shifted the puppy into her lap so she could wiggle her finger between his jaws. His tiny toothless gums pressed into her fingertip through the fabric. "Still nothing, but perhaps he will swallow a drop or two by accident."

"Be patient." Myrtilla reached over and stroked the puppy's neck under his chin.

Elizabeth felt the slightest tug on her finger. "I think he is taking it." She spoke just above a whisper.

"I knew he would like you," Myrtilla announced. She stood and moved the milk bowl closer to Elizabeth. "You may bring him to me in the kitchen when you like. I must start on dinner."

Truly the strangest interaction with a servant she had ever had!

The tugging on her finger grew stronger, as two tiny puppy paws began to press rhythmically against her arm. No, this puppy would not starve, not if she had to sit here all day and night feeding him. She let him suckle her finger for a time before dipping it back in the milk and returning it to his eager mouth.

It was utterly engrossing. She whispered encouragement and endearments to the puppy, even if he was too young to be able to hear them. It was still important. She was so focused on her efforts that she only looked up when she realized something was blocking the sunlight.

It was Mr. Darcy, staring down at her with an inscrutable look. "Why?" he asked harshly.

She stared at him in confusion for a moment until she realized what he meant. "Why did I tell them to speak to you?"

He frowned. "Yes."

The puppy gave a tiny whimper, no doubt sensing her distraction. Slowly she dipped her finger in the milk and replaced it in his mouth, letting his suckling soothe her. She should say something polite and meaningless, but if Lady Frederica could be forthright, so could she. "You would have learned eventually that Lady Frederica had sought Andrew's help, and it occurred to me that you would dislike having been excluded. And I thought you might wish to help her. Nothing more than that." Now her voice was trembling again, her new sense of peace lost. She bent down to kiss the puppy's head, heedless of how inappropriate her behavior might seem.

"What is that animal?"

"A puppy. Andrew can tell you his story." She did not look at him. Why could he not leave her be?

"Why are you feeding him? Has Drew no servants?"

She glared at him. "Because, although you may not believe it, I want to be of use. And he needs me." She gazed down at the puppy, determined not to let Darcy upset her again.

After a minute, the light grew brighter again, and Elizabeth looked up to see Mr. Darcy's back disappearing around the corner of the kitchen yard. A lump filled her throat.

Chapter 17

I *need you.* The thought pounded in Darcy's head as he rode back to Pemberley from the Kympton parsonage, haunted by the sight of Elizabeth's swollen, reddened eyes. How could she respond to that puppy's need, and not his own?

His heart had twisted in his chest when Frederica had said that Elizabeth had spoken up for him. Was he so desperate for the least bit of caring from her? But that had been nothing to seeing her cradling that puppy, as once he had dreamed she would cradle his child. Now it would be Drew's baby she would hold to her breast, not his.

Good God, he was going to be sick.

Hurricane tossed his head in protest, and Darcy realized he had tightened the reins involuntarily. Damn it, what was wrong with him? He could ride better than this by instinct alone, and now he was making Hurricane suffer for his sins. He loosened the reins.

His mind would not stop whirling, even when he reached Pemberley and made his way to his study, pausing only to send a message to the housekeeper that he wished to see her. He might not be able to solve the mystery of Elizabeth, but at least he could stop Matlock from spying on his household.

But as soon as he reached the safety of his study, the image of Elizabeth's tearful expression presented itself before him again. It made no sense. There had to be something he was missing. Why had Elizabeth drawn him into this? Perhaps she had hoped to create a rift between him and Matlock. Or more likely, she thought he would reject the idea entirely and provoke a fight with Drew. She knew that would hurt him. That must be it.

But her eyes had been red. Why would any of this have made her cry? Even if she had been disappointed at the lack of conflict between him and

Drew, she would hardly have wept over it. He slammed his fist on his desk, then rubbed the aching flesh. Damn it.

The housekeeper chose that unfortunate moment to appear, raising an eyebrow at his expression. "You wished to see me, sir?"

He tried to collect his usual Master of Pemberley demeanor, but it was unlikely to fool the woman who had known him since birth. "Yes, Mrs. Reynolds. I learned today that someone on our staff has been sending information about the family to the Earl of Matlock. I wish this person to be found immediately and dismissed."

Now both her eyebrows went up. "As you wish, sir, but first I must inform you that I am the person you are seeking."

"*You?*" He stared at her in shock. Of all the staff in both his houses, Mrs. Reynolds was the one he most relied on, the one he trusted, the one who had been almost a second mother to him. Then he realized what she must mean. "I do not believe you. Whom are you protecting?"

"No one. It is I, truly it is. When I first came here with your mother, her brother insisted that I send secret reports to him. Naturally, I informed Lady Anne, hoping she could protect me from him, but she said that if I refused, he would simply find someone else to spy on her, and at least she could trust me to keep the most important things private. While she was alive, she herself told me what to write, telling him just enough secrets to make him think he knew it all. After Lady Anne's death, I sent the reports on my own. It seemed preferable to the alternative, but I will certainly stop if you wish."

Now he felt truly off-balance. His uncle, spying on his mother? Darcy studied the housekeeper. "Why did you never mention this to me?"

She turned her palms up. "I should have done so, I suppose, when your father died, but it seemed easier to simply continue than to explain to you that your uncle had been attempting to interfere for years."

"You should have informed me. What have you told him?"

"Of late? There has been little to report since you are rarely here. I try to adjust what I say to allow for what he might have heard elsewhere. For example, last autumn I told him Miss Georgiana was moping over a horse who had died rather than that she was in a decline after her visit to Ramsgate. Just last week I sent him a report on Mr. Drew's engagement, giving my impression of Miss Bennet's background, but not mentioning the questionable beginning of it."

He nodded, and then her words sank in. "What do you mean by that – the questionable beginning of it?" A sense of foreboding gripped his throat.

"Oh, the ridiculous rumor that he compromised her. I did not see any advantage in giving his lordship further ammunition against Mr. Drew, especially as I am certain that boy would never have done anything improper. Goodness knows there has been no sign of improper behavior between them since."

Darcy's heart threatened to pound out of his chest. "What question of compromise?" He forced the words out.

Mrs. Reynolds fingered her apron. "Why, I do not know all the details, but I understand they were locked in a room together at the White Hart."

Elizabeth had been compromised? Being locked in together was not the sort of thing that happened by accident. Were her aunt and uncle that desperate to marry her off, or had Drew done it to win her? He rubbed the back of his hand against his mouth. "Who did it? Who locked them in?"

The housekeeper frowned. "According to the gossip, everyone has denied it. That is why some people are blaming Mr. Drew."

He tapped his fingers impatiently on the desk. "Tell me everything you know of this."

"That is really all, except that Mr. Drew proposed to her when they were discovered. Miss Bennet refused, but later thought better of it. This is only what I have heard, and I asked no questions."

"Elizabeth did not want to marry him?" His mind seized on this key point as if it were a floating spar and he a drowning man.

"Not then, but she could hardly have known him a week at that point. They say he was quite taken with her, but she had shown no interest in him before. From what I have seen, though, she takes her duties seriously, and I believe she will make him a good wife."

Elizabeth had not wanted to marry Drew. What was that she had said, that she had not known Drew was his brother because there had not been time to find out? And he had disbelieved her, because it made no sense. But if Elizabeth had not betrayed him voluntarily, that made all the difference. The relief overwhelmed him.

"What else?" he demanded.

"That is all I know, sir. I may overhear gossip at times, but I do not ask questions, not about the family." She wrung her hands. "Would you like my resignation, then, sir?"

"No, of course not. Why?"

"Because of Lord Matlock. You said the person who made the report should be dismissed."

Darcy waved his hand. He cared nothing for Lord Matlock, not now. "No. But you should speak to me before you make reports, as you did with my mother."

"Yes, sir." Mrs. Reynolds dipped a quick curtsey and left.

Darcy's mind spun. What had Elizabeth said, that night after the ball? That she had neither time nor choice in the matter? He had thought it meant that she had felt rushed, that she needed to make a decision before she left Derbyshire since she would not see Drew again after that, but that did not explain having no choice. If she had been afraid of scandal, that was different.

Who had been responsible for locking them in? It had to have been her aunt or uncle, eager to prevent her from ending up a spinster. He could not, would not believe that Drew had created a compromising situation to force her hand. Not his brother. And Elizabeth showed none of the resentment towards Drew that he would expect if she felt he had forced her into the engagement. But the same argument could be made for her aunt and uncle. Could it have been merely an accident, or someone making mischief?

He needed to know what had happened, every detail. He could not bear not knowing. But he could not ask Drew, not without his brother becoming defensive and angry.

He jumped to his feet and hurried upstairs, taking the steps of the grand staircase two at a time in his haste, and found his valet laying out his clothes for dinner. "Wilkins, I need some questions asked, very discreetly."

Wilkins straightened, a gleam of interest in his eye. "I am at your service, sir." It was not the first time he had assisted Darcy in this manner.

"It appears my brother's engagement is the result of a compromising situation where he and Miss Bennet were locked into a room at the White

Hart. I want to know the details, but no one must suspect me of having an interest in this matter."

Wilkins' upper lip curled. "Compromise, is it? If you would not mind giving me a few free days, perhaps so I can visit my old mother and friends here, I can find you some answers."

"Take as much time as you need. Ask Mrs. Reynolds to assign another servant to your regular duties."

And then he would have some answers, but not to the question that hung before him. Why had Elizabeth spoken up for him, and what had made her cry? Dare he let himself hope that she might care for him even a little?

ELIZABETH WAS GLADDENED by the news that Andrew had agreed to dine at Pemberley after Lady Frederica's departure, less out of a desire for his company than because his presence would make it easier for her to avoid another private conversation with Mr. Darcy. She only wished she could bring the puppy, too. Anything to distract her attention from the Master of Pemberley and his anger at her.

It was still a struggle to keep her composure. Too much had happened in the last day; encountering Wickham at the ball, the late-night discussion with the half-drunken Darcy, meeting Lady Frederica, and crying over Darcy. She needed some quiet time, preferably a long walk alone in the countryside, and instead she would have a long evening in stressful company. She did not trust herself when she was so much on edge. Andrew would provide a useful distraction.

With her late return from Kympton, she hurried through dressing for dinner, but she still arrived downstairs to find the entire party gathered in the saloon, chatting amicably. Georgiana had claimed the nearest chair to Andrew, of course, and Miss Bingley was attempting to monopolize Darcy's attention. That suited Elizabeth perfectly.

After greeting her, Andrew said to the assembled group, "I have had a minor change in plans. When Elizabeth returns to Hertfordshire, I plan to go with her and spend a few days becoming acquainted with her family, perhaps with a brief stop in London to attend to some business."

"An excellent idea," said Mrs. Gardiner. "We will be glad to have your company on our journey."

Georgiana bit her lip. "Might I be permitted to join the party?"

Elizabeth suppressed a groan. She should have anticipated that. Not that the girl's presence by itself was a problem, but having her stay at Longbourn and be exposed to her ill-mannered mother and younger sisters might be. "You would be welcome at Longbourn, but I must caution you that it is by no means as fine a home as you are accustomed to, and it is filled with a large and sometimes boisterous family. Privacy is not always easy to come by."

"I think your family is delightful," said Bingley stoutly, although he could not have missed some of the same behavior which had so troubled Mr. Darcy. "But if Mr. Andrew Darcy and Miss Darcy wish, they would be most welcome to stay at my house, Netherfield, which is but three miles from Longbourn."

"You are very generous," said Andrew, "but I would not wish to put your staff to the trouble of opening up the house simply for a short visit."

Elizabeth, whose hopes had been momentarily raised by the idea of limiting Andrew's and Georgiana's exposure to her family, could say nothing.

"It would be no trouble." Bingley's expression suddenly brightened. "Perhaps I will go there, too, after my stay here."

Miss Bingley immediately protested, "Nonsense. We are expected in Scarborough."

Bingley said firmly, "You can go to Scarborough without me. You are the one Aunt Emily wishes to see, not me."

His sister looked down her nose at him. "There is no cause for you to go running off to Netherfield simply because Mr. Andrew Darcy, whom you barely know, wishes to meet his future in-laws."

Bingley jumped to his feet. "Caroline, that is quite enough. You will go to Scarborough, and I will go to Netherfield. I would like to see my friends there, and that is that."

His sister's eyes narrowed. "You know perfectly well there is no one there who is worthy of your attention. Do not let yourself be led astray by the memory of a pretty face. I admit she was a sweet girl, but unworthy of you."

Elizabeth tried to bite her tongue, but anger on her sister's behalf prevailed. "I wonder that you would say that in front of me." Somehow she managed to keep her voice level.

Miss Bingley's mouth opened and shut. Clearly she had not considered Elizabeth's presence. "I fear you misunderstood me," she said icily.

Bright flags of color flew in Mrs. Gardiner's cheeks. "She misunderstood nothing, Miss Bingley. I saw your attitude to my dearest niece Jane when you called on her during her stay in London last winter." She threw a pointed glance in Mr. Bingley's direction.

Miss Bingley looked down her nose at her. "I have no idea what you mean."

Mrs. Gardiner delicately pressed her hand to her chest in a parody of disbelief. "How foolish of me! Of course your social life must be so busy that you have completely forgotten how Jane called on you in London, and it took three weeks before you returned her call at my house, and even then you could only stay a few minutes."

Bingley straightened abruptly. "Miss Bennet was in London?" he demanded.

With a telling smile, Mrs. Gardiner said, "Oh, yes. She came to us after Christmas and stayed until April. She was so looking forward to continuing her friendship with your dear sisters. What a pity they had no time for her."

Bingley's face paled. "Caroline, I wonder that you never mentioned it to me."

With a toss of her head, Miss Bingley exclaimed, "But I did! I am certain I told you of it. Perhaps you were not listening."

"Or were too foxed to remember," added Mrs. Hurst.

"I would not have forgotten any mention of Miss Bennet!" stormed Bingley.

"Charles!" cried Miss Bingley. "Remember where you are!"

Bingley jumped to his feet. "No, Caroline, you should remember where you are, and who pays your allowance!"

Darcy laid his hand on Bingley's arm. "Come, will you join me in my study? There is something I wish to show you."

Bingley glared at him, but then his opposition seemed to melt. "Oh, very well. But this is not over, Caroline!"

An uncomfortable silence fell as Darcy and Bingley exited the room. Then Caroline Bingley shot a poisonous glance at Mrs. Gardiner. "What a tempest in a teapot! It is a pity some people cannot understand the ways of their betters."

Mrs. Hurst frowned. "Caroline, I feel the need to refresh myself. Will you not join me?"

"If you say so, Louisa." With only the barest hint of a curtsey, Miss Bingley flounced out, followed by Mrs. Hurst.

Mrs. Gardiner covered her face with her hands. "Oh, my temper, my terrible temper! I am so sorry, Lizzy."

"It is nothing, Aunt," Elizabeth said uncomfortably. "I confess I was longing to give her a set-down myself."

Andrew added, "You are not alone in that. I can understand your discomfort, Mrs. Gardiner, but at the same time I cannot think it an altogether bad thing for Bingley to know that his sisters have been deceiving him. Secrets can be poisonous."

Elizabeth nodded. "What is more, I doubt there will be any lasting harm. Mr. Bingley is a most forgiving gentleman." And altogether too easily led. Would Darcy tell Bingley the truth of his own part in the deception? Not that it mattered. In any case, this scene would only confirm his ill opinion of her and her family.

IT MADE NO SENSE FOR Darcy to be in good spirits the following day. His explanation to Bingley about why he had hidden Jane Bennet's presence in London had turned into a bitter quarrel. Bingley had decamped for Hertfordshire early this morning without a word of farewell to anyone, with the possible exception of Elizabeth. But if Bingley had said anything to Elizabeth, Darcy knew nothing of it, since Elizabeth had been successfully avoiding him all day. He should feel miserable, not happier than he had in weeks.

But his spirits were, if not high, better than they had been since he had learned of Elizabeth's engagement. He was worried about Bingley, yes, but Bingley could not hold a grudge for long, and would eventually accept that Darcy truly regretted his past behavior. And Elizabeth... well, she was still engaged to Drew, but it made all the difference to know it was not by her choice. It was as if a huge abscess inside him had been lanced. The injury still ached, and he knew the pain would be worse before it improved, but it was such an enormous relief to know that she had not deliberately betrayed him.

He knew it would not last. Nothing had changed; Elizabeth was still engaged to Drew, and if their marriage went forward, it would torture Darcy for the rest of his days. But now there was a faint hope, an irrational one, perhaps, that somehow their marriage might be prevented. If Drew had not chosen to enter the engagement, perhaps he could be persuaded to let her go. And even if he did not, at least Darcy knew Elizabeth did not hate him, and that by itself was enough to make the sun shine a little brighter.

He tried to forget that Drew had claimed to love Elizabeth.

When he retired for the night, he was surprised to find Wilkins was waiting for him. His heart began to pound faster at the expectation of finally getting some answers. "That was quick," he said. "What have you discovered?"

"It was simpler than I had anticipated," the valet said. "I found a milliner who was in Mrs. Gardiner's confidence, and she related most of it to me."

Darcy drew in a sharp breath. "So it was the Gardiners who locked them in?"

"No, sir." Wilkins clasped his hands. "They were away when Mr. Drew and Miss Bennet were locked into a private parlor together, and the word was deliberately spread so that a large crowd, including the magistrate, was there to see them released. No one has confessed to locking the door, but I found the circumstances somewhat suspicious." He stopped and took a deep breath. "Immediately prior to the incident, Mr. Drew had quarreled publicly with George Wickham, who struck him several times, causing some minor injury. Wickham was also the one who fetched the magistrate."

A moment of disbelief, and then sick fury exploded inside him. "Wickham?" he cried. "*Wickham* did this?" He had an unaccountable, almost overpowering urge to grab Wilkins by his shoulders and shake him. Or to hit something. Or someone. "How *dare* he?" But, of course, Wickham always dared. He would dare anything, if it was to his benefit.

But how would he profit from forcing Drew to marry Elizabeth? He had never particularly cared about Drew. The puzzle suddenly snapped into place. Wickham only cared about hurting Darcy, and Andrew had suddenly, mysteriously entered into an engagement that had cut Darcy to the quick. There were no coincidences where Wickham was concerned, especially when it came to hurting Darcy.

And this time, he had hit home, cut straight to Darcy's heart and twisted the knife, taking both Elizabeth and Drew away from him. It would have been more merciful to kill him.

Wilkins silently poured a glass of port and handed it to him. Wilkins, who had been with him for years, who would have certainly guessed at his interest in Elizabeth and knew all of Wickham's sins. "There is more, sir. Miss Bennet initially refused to marry Mr. Drew, but changed her mind after he received a letter threatening to expose her dishonor in Meryton. The milliner did not know who had sent it, but the culprit is obvious."

"Damn him!" Darcy could not think, could hardly see for the rage enveloping him. Why was the port sloshing in his glass? His hand was trembling. He gulped half of it down, oblivious to the burning sensation. Nausea roiled his stomach. This was his own doing, for showing Wickham mercy once too often. Never again. This would stop now. He would free Elizabeth from Wickham's threats, and then....

No. It was too soon to think that far ahead. "I need you to find out where Wickham is."

With a dry, half-smile, Wilkins said, "I have the address he is staying at in Grimsby, but he is unlikely to be there more than a day or two more. Rumor has it that he is in trouble with a moneylender and does not want to remain in any one place for long."

"Then we cannot let him get away. We leave for Grimsby at first light." Darcy's free hand tightened into a fist. Wickham would suffer for this.

"I have already requested to have your trunk brought down. Will you wish to bring Mr. Wickham's paperwork?" He meant his debts, all the IOUs Darcy had bought up over the years, for the sake of Wickham's victims.

"Yes," Darcy growled. He set down the glass before he threw it at something. He would save his rage for Wickham.

Chapter 18

The servants were still busy at their work when Elizabeth came downstairs early the next morning; a maid was polishing a table in the drawing room while another scrubbed the hearth. A little boy carrying a bucket of ashes dodged past her, clearly taken aback to see a guest up and about so soon after daybreak. Perhaps she was overly optimistic to think there would be breakfast available already. Well, she could always ask for tea and toast if there was not.

Surprisingly, the butler was already by the front door, so she approached him directly. "I would like to go to Kympton in an hour. Would the gig be available?" It was a rather forward request for a guest to make, but she had no intention of hiding in her room from Mr. Darcy's ill temper when there was a hungry puppy who needed her at the parsonage. If the servants thought her too demanding as a result, it was nothing to her.

Hobbes bowed. "It will be ready for you, Miss Bennet."

"I thank you." She turned towards the east wing where the breakfast room was located, but before she took more than a few steps, two burly footmen came through the entrance hall carrying a trunk. The butler held open the front door, revealing a waiting curricle with four harnessed horses. What was all this activity?

She turned at the sound of footsteps on the main stairs and cursed her luck. Darcy and his valet, both dressed for travel, were coming purposefully down the stairs, Darcy snapping on his gloves as he strode forward. She had successfully avoided him almost all of the previous day, but her luck was at an end.

Then he saw her and stopped abruptly. "Miss Elizabeth." His voice was hoarse, and he bowed belatedly, his dark eyes firmly fixed on her.

Apparently she was no longer invisible, and she was Miss Elizabeth again. What had changed? "Good morning, Mr. Darcy."

"I..." He reached up and tugged at his cravat. The butler stood behind him, holding up a many-caped driving coat.

"Fitzwilliam!" Georgiana came tripping down the stairs, in a dressing gown with her hair still plaited, clearly just arisen from bed. "What has happened? My maid said you were leaving."

Darcy tore his gaze from Elizabeth. "It is nothing. A business matter of some urgency has arisen unexpectedly. I will only be gone a few days."

Mr. Darcy was leaving Pemberley? Elizabeth felt it like a blow to her stomach. Was it because of her?

His sister plucked at his sleeve. "But you said nothing about it yesterday! Is it something dangerous?"

His laugh sounded forced. "Not at all. I received word late last night that...a friend requires my assistance."

The girl's eyes widened. "A duel? You are going to be his second? But that is illegal!

"No." Darcy, seeming stricken, glanced at Elizabeth. Somehow she could tell he felt trapped, unable to either tell the truth or lie. Well, she would help him, for his sister's sake if nothing else.

She linked her arm with Georgiana's. "Your brother doing something illegal? I think not! I would venture to guess that his friend got himself in some sort of awkward mess, probably involving drink, cards, horses, or all of them put together, and your brother is riding to his rescue. He does not want to embarrass our delicate female sensibilities with the details, but I doubt there is any reason to fret."

"Is that what it is?" Georgiana asked timidly.

He rubbed his hand over his chin, looking abashed. "Something not unlike that."

The girl gave a sigh of relief. "You should have said so! Of course you must help your friend."

"Yes, he must," said Elizabeth warmly. "And you and I will have the great pleasure of allowing our thoughts to run wild about what difficulties your brother's friend may have run into. I am certain we can create a story more interesting than the boring truth. Mr. Darcy, I wish you an easy journey, and you may tell your friend on our behalf that Georgiana and I are quite cross with him and he must improve his behavior in the future."

Darcy almost smiled. She might have missed it, as his lips hardly moved, but there was a warmth in his eyes that Elizabeth had not seen since the days before his proposal. "I will do that. Now I must be off." He bowed and headed out the door.

Why did that look of pleasure in his dark eyes make her throat seize up and tears swim in her eyes?

Georgiana stared after him, still looking bereft.

Elizabeth collected herself. This girl was to be her sister. "Come, Georgiana dear. You must get dressed, and then you can breakfast with me. I am required to visit Andrew this morning, or rather, to visit that poor puppy whose mother has rejected him. Would you like to accompany me? As long as you do not object to puppy messes, I would be glad of your company, and Andrew will be happy to see you."

Outside the door, Darcy swung up into the curricle and picked up the reins. Elizabeth forced herself to look away, but her throat tightened as she heard the jangling of the harness and the hoofbeats of the horses on the gravel drive. He was gone.

WITH DARCY AWAY ON his mysterious business, Elizabeth's last two days at Pemberley should have felt more peaceful, but somehow the very walls of his home were so imbued with his presence that she seemed unable to forget him for more than a few minutes at a time. If only she could make sense of his behavior! One moment she was certain he had left Pemberley solely to avoid her; the next she recalled the warmth in his eyes when she had seen him in the entrance hall, and her chest would grow tight as she remembered what Bingley had said about how changed Darcy was after she refused his proposal.

She had more free time, too, after Miss Bingley and the Hursts also left the following morning, and took advantage of it to haunt the orangery, spending hours among the jungle which had been calling to her ever since she had first seen it. Darcy's spirit was even more present there, though.

Would she ever be able to daydream about exploring a jungle again without thinking of him taking her hand and cleaning off the sundew sap? Sitting by the banana plant he had shown her almost brought tears to her eyes.

The only time she felt truly at ease was when she went to Andrew's parsonage to care for the puppy, whom she had christened Sir Galahad. Andrew had laughed heartily when he heard the name, saying that he thought it quite fitting that a common mongrel should have such an aristocratic name. Elizabeth, with mock dignity, had replied that Sir Galahad was quite an uncommon mongrel, and Andrew's amusement had given her hope that perhaps someday he could learn to tease. But she never told him that she had chosen the name because the puppy, like a true knight, had saved her when she was a damsel in distress. She was utterly determined to save him in return.

Unfortunately, Sir Galahad's mother rejected him completely the day after Elizabeth had first met him, leaving him totally dependent on hand-feeding from Myrtilla, Andrew, and Elizabeth. At least Myrtilla had managed to find an old feeding bottle which made it a simpler and substantially less damp process, but still time-consuming.

The following day, as Elizabeth was coaxing the puppy to drink, Myrtilla said, "Perhaps you should take him back to your home when you leave. There will be no one here but the maid when we are gone, and she will not take the time. He likes you best, in any case."

"You are not staying here?"

Myrtilla shook her head. "No. Since the master is bound for London after visiting your home, he says I can go, too, so I can see my family."

Elizabeth bit her lip as she gazed down at the fluffy puppy. In truth, she had been feeling wistful about leaving him, knowing that he would not remember her when she returned to Kympton as Andrew's wife. "It is such a long journey, though, and he is so small. What if he does not survive it?"

Myrtilla shrugged, with her startlingly matter-of-fact approach to life and death. "Likely he will not survive if he stays here."

Traveling with a puppy would be messy and would slow them down, all for an unwanted mongrel Andrew could not bear to see drowned. But she loved the little scrap of fur, and if she took him home, he would be hers. "I will speak to Andrew, then."

DEALING WITH WICKHAM always meant unexpected problems, so it was hardly a surprise to discover he had already left Grimsby. Darcy had hoped to be back at Pemberley within three days, but it took nearly a week to track him down to a run-down inn in Hull. By then, Darcy was in no temper for his games.

The innkeeper was more than willing to lead Darcy to Wickham's room in exchange for a few coins, or perhaps it was the pair of burly Bow Street Runners looming behind him. "Right away, sir. I'll have you know I don't allow no lawlessness here."

"Naturally." Darcy had no doubt that half of the rough-looking men drinking in the taproom were smugglers, nor that the innkeeper used the illegal goods they brought in.

The man nodded in satisfaction. "Up the stairs, then left at the landing, third door on the right."

Once they reached the room, Darcy instructed the Runners to wait on the landing until he called them, but kept Wilkins beside him. Wickham would not be above attacking him physically if he thought Darcy was alone. With a grimace, he pounded on the dingy door that hung unevenly on its hinges.

"What d'you want?" It was Wickham's voice, his words slurring. Just the sound of it made Darcy's neck stiffen. How many times had he fallen for Wickham's tricks before he had learned his lesson?

"Let me in and I will tell you."

Shuffling footsteps sounded before the door opened, revealing Wickham in his shirtsleeves, the neck falling open. He gave his lazy smile. "Why, Darcy, to what do I owe the pleasure?"

"Do you truly wish me to tell you out here where everyone can hear?"

Wickham stepped back and held the door open. "By all means, do come in," he drawled. "I would offer you a drink, but it would not be up to your standards."

"I will pass." Darcy wrinkled his nose at the state of the room. Dirty clothes littered the floor, and the smell of sweat pervaded the small space. The sooner he was done with this, the sooner he could leave. All he needed was one answer. "I understand I have you to thank for my brother's engagement." His voice dripped irony.

Wickham smirked. "Ah, yes, one of my best efforts! I did hope you would find out about that. Which one of them told you?"

So it was true. He had been so sure, but now he knew. "It matters not. But this is the last straw. I have let you run free too long for my father's sake."

Wickham curled his lip. "Are you going to offer me a commission in India again, as you did after my little affair with Georgiana? Perhaps I will take you up on it this time."

"You accepted the offer last time and then broke your word. This time it is debtor's prison, and you may be grateful that I am sparing your life. You can come quietly or not. Your choice."

With an incredulous grin, Wickham draped himself into a chair, hooking his leg over one sidearm. "Sorry, Darcy. I have other plans."

Darcy gestured to Wilkins, who opened the door and called out, "Now, if you please!" The two Bow Street Runners elbowed their way into the room. Each grabbed one of Wickham's arms and jerked him to his feet.

"Let me go!" shouted Wickham. "He has no right!"

"I bought up your debts," Darcy said coldly. "You should have gone to India." He stood and walked away.

"Wait, Fitzwilliam!" Wickham's voice rose in desperation. "You cannot do this! Your father – what would he say? We are cousins!"

Darcy looked back over his shoulder, a bitter taste in his mouth. "So your mother convinced my father, and since my uncle had conveniently died in Jamaica, no one could prove otherwise. I have never believed it, and God knows you have never acted the part, always striking out at my family. I have given you every chance, but no more. From now on I will show you the same mercy you have shown me, which is to say, none."

Wickham's cries were still ringing in his ears as he left the inn.

Chapter 19

Any other man would consider taking a tiny puppy on a coach journey of several days a ridiculous concept, but Andrew, of course, thought bringing Sir Galahad rather than leaving him to die was a splendid idea. Elizabeth was just beginning to comprehend how much her betrothed thrived on helping those in need, be they animals or people. Fortunately, Myrtilla and her brother were accompanying them to wait on Andrew, so they had assistance with Sir Galahad's needs.

At least the puppy's presence solved the question of the pace of their travel. Without him, they could have made the journey to Longbourn in two long days, but with the frequent stops the puppy would require, they had to take an easier pace and spend two nights on the road. Elizabeth did not mind the change; that way they might arrive at Longbourn earlier in the day and relatively fresh. Her chief concern was the damage that Sir Galahad might do to the elegant Darcy carriage, but no matter his messes, the coach was spotless again each morning, no doubt thanks to Myrtilla's efforts.

The journey proved more tolerable than she had anticipated. Mrs. Gardiner was, as always, a cheerful, pleasant traveling companion, and Georgiana, no longer in constant fear of separation from Andrew, seemed more at ease than Elizabeth had ever seen her. Andrew took less part in the conversation than the others, but he listened attentively. He seemed happier, more like the man she had first met before his brother had returned to Pemberley. And Sir Galahad made them all laugh as he tried to crawl from one person's lap to the next on his little belly.

Her mood lightened as they drew closer to Longbourn, or rather as they grew farther from Mr. Darcy. He was never far from her thoughts, but now that she no longer had to fear meeting his implacable gaze at any moment, some of her pain slipped away.

At Longbourn, the entire family came outside to meet the carriage, a pleasing honor she had never before received on her return home. The sight of Bingley by her sister Jane's side, looking as enamored of her as ever, made Elizabeth beam. If her own forced engagement to Andrew accomplished nothing apart from bringing Jane and Bingley back together, it was well worth it. She and Jane had always talked of their desire to marry for love. At least Jane had a chance to achieve it. Elizabeth would have to learn to be satisfied with marrying for respect.

The pleasure she took from the glow on Jane's face made it easier to tolerate her mother's irrepressible and tasteless raptures over Elizabeth's engagement, along with her broad hints that she hoped Jane would not be far behind. Fortunately, Elizabeth had forewarned Andrew and Georgiana about her mother's manners. Georgiana still seemed taken aback, as well she might, but Elizabeth already had a plan for that.

As soon as introductions were made, she caught at her sister Mary's sleeve and drew her over to where Georgiana stood, Sir Galahad's basket on the ground next to her. "Mary, we are in dire need of your assistance," Elizabeth said. "We have a puppy who is terribly hungry and is too young to eat on his own. Could you help Georgiana find some milk for him?" She flipped back the lid of the basket, lifted out the sleeping puppy, and handed him to Georgiana. "He was the runt, and his mother rejected him."

Mary's eyes softened. "Oh, the sweet thing! Of course. Come this way, Miss Darcy, and we will get him settled straight away." She led Georgiana towards the kitchen, her head bending close to the newcomer's as she asked, "How old is he? Does he have a name?"

Elizabeth smiled after them, then turned to rescue Andrew from her mother's adoring clutches.

Finally, after a great deal of excited babble from Mrs. Bennet, the entire party was invited in for refreshments, but as soon as they reached the sitting room, Andrew requested the honor of a private conversation with Mr. Bennet. Elizabeth's mother announced her approval, perfectly willing to allow the already hooked fish out of her sight in favor of casting further lures to Mr. Bingley.

Despite having no real doubts about the outcome, Elizabeth had to make an effort not to watch after him, and her stomach churned. This was it. Her father would give his permission, and her engagement would be official. There could be no backing out now. In truth, there never had been another option, not with Wickham lurking in the background, ready to spread his rumors that she had already been intimate with Andrew, but after today, it would be final. Her future with Andrew would be sealed. Any other dreams would have to be locked up and put away forever.

She yanked her mind back to her homecoming. She needed to be grateful for what she had instead of focusing on what she had lost. And there was much to be grateful for, starting with Jane and Bingley's undeniable happiness together. And in the absence of her disruptive youngest sister Lydia, who was fortunately still away in Brighton, Kitty was well behaved and seemed pleased to have Elizabeth back. When Mary and Georgiana finally appeared, Sir Galahad was asleep in Mary's arms, and the two girls were happily chatting together. Apparently a puppy in need could overcome even Georgiana's shyness and Mary's tendency to moralize.

Andrew returned after a quarter of an hour with her father, looking unruffled, if slightly puzzled. Elizabeth, who doubted he had ever met anyone with her father's odd sense of humor, greeted him warmly and encouraged him to sit with her.

After a few minutes, Mary came to join them, still cuddling the sleeping puppy. "I wished to give you a particular welcome," she said shyly to Andrew. "I am very glad we will have a clergyman in the family. I am a great reader of sermons. Perhaps you could recommend some for me."

"Mary is the most pious among us," Elizabeth agreed.

Andrew looked pleased by her interest. "I would be happy to do so, though, from what Elizabeth has told me of your rector, my religious views may differ somewhat from those you have been exposed to."

"Andrew is a bit of a Non-Conformist," Elizabeth said gently, not certain how Mary would receive this shocking fact. It would not matter to her parents; her father mocked their doddering traditional clergyman after every sermon, and her mother would not care if Andrew preached devil worship as long as his living was valuable.

Her betrothed grinned unapologetically. "Not quite a Methodist, though, despite what some would say. I remain firmly inside the Church, dedicated to reforming it from within."

Mary gulped. "I would still be glad of your opinions."

"And I would like to hear yours," Andrew said politely. "Perhaps we can speak more tomorrow."

As soon as Andrew and Georgiana departed for Netherfield, accompanied by Bingley, Mrs. Bennet's voice rose in her usual complaints of ill-usage. "Mary, take that creature to the stables this minute! You have no compassion on my poor nerves. You know I cannot bear your ragged animals in this house."

Elizabeth's time at Pemberley had strengthened her own resistance. "Sir Galahad is mine, Mama, a gift from my husband-to-be. He is delicate and needs frequent care, and Andrew would be most displeased if I were to leave him in the stables. He will stay with me in my room, but for your sake I will keep him out of the public rooms."

Two months ago, her mother would have taken to her bed in a fit of nerves at such defiance from her least favorite daughter, but either Elizabeth's newly-betrothed status protected her, or her mother feared antagonizing the man who was foolish enough to wish to marry her. "Oh, very well," Mrs. Bennet said crossly. "Keep him away from me, though."

Mr. Bennet cleared his throat. "Lizzy, perhaps you could join me in the library. Without the puppy, if you please."

Elizabeth sighed. "Mary, would you be so kind as to look after him for me?"

"Naturally. I am always happy to help." Mary's sanctimonious words were belied by how tightly she held Sir Galahad. Elizabeth suspected she might have had to tear him away otherwise.

"I thank you." With a sigh, she followed her father, hoping whatever teasing he had in store for her would not have a hurtful edge. She did not want to lose the happiness this homecoming had brought her.

"So, Lizzy," her father said as she sat down across from his desk. "Most travelers bring back a petrified spar or a pretty watercolor, not a young man."

155

"Not to mention a puppy. I have always striven to be something beyond the commonplace," she said lightly. "But I confess he is a most unusual souvenir."

"Perhaps you like the idea of being the first among your sisters to marry."

"Not I. Did not my uncle explain the situation to you?" It was an unnecessary question. Mr. Gardiner had shown her the letter before sending it.

"He did, but I could not help wondering if vanity might have played a role. After all, what better riposte to Mr. Darcy of Pemberley, who did not find you handsome enough to dance with, than to marry his brother?"

She tightened her lips as a sudden wave of pain rippled through her. She had managed to put Mr. Darcy from her mind for a few minutes. "I assure you, Andrew's connections had nothing to do with my decision, such as it was." How little her father understood of her situation!

Mr. Bennet drummed his fingers on the polished surface of his desk. "Why has his brother excluded him from his will?"

She blinked in surprise. "I did not know he had. Andrew's father disowned him, but his brother never did." It was an unpleasant shock. Why would Darcy have done such a thing, especially given how eager he was to welcome Andrew? Had she misjudged Darcy yet again? No, she could not believe that. It was likely an old will, one that predated their reconciliation. That would make more sense.

"Your oh-so-worthy young man felt the need to inform me that his brother's estate, should he die without children, would go to their sister, not to him."

For some reason, his humor rankled. "Is it not the job of the suitor to state his prospects openly?"

"Ah, Lizzy, has exposure to that dull fellow already dampened your sense of humor? For shame."

"I have had a long, tiring journey, and have no desire to hear anyone disparage the man I have no choice but to marry. He may not laugh as often as I would like, but he is honorable, clever, and well educated."

He frowned. "I do not see why you must marry him. What is a little scandal? If it scares off a few suitors, then they were not worth having in the first place. I would rather have your company at the cost of gossip. As it is, I will be left with no sensible conversation."

"I am sorry for that, but I am not sorry I will have a home and an income after you die, rather than live the rest of my life as someone's charity case." There was no point in saying the rest; he had never shown any real concern for what would happen to them after he died. He left that worry for the Gardiners, so she said in a cheerier voice, "And my mind is quite fixed on remaining respectable, so I can only hope you will visit us often."

"Well, I suppose there is nothing for it, then," he said grumpily.

WHEN SHE WAS FINALLY alone with Jane that evening, Elizabeth teased, "Mr. Bingley seems very much at home here."

Jane colored prettily. "Oh, dearest Lizzy! I have so much to tell you. He has asked me to marry him!"

Elizabeth clasped her hands together in delight. "Pray tell me you said yes!"

"Of course I did! We decided not to inform anyone until after your return, though, lest we steal the thunder of your engagement. Now you are the first to know! Exactly as it should be, for had you not met him again at Pemberley, it would never have happened. I owe all my happiness to you!"

"Or to our aunt, who was the one who actually told him you had been in London," said Elizabeth, determined to be fair. "But I had been busy dropping hints that you would be glad to see him again."

Jane embraced her. "I still thank you for it, again and again! I cannot wait until tomorrow, when my dear Bingley will speak to our father." Her expression sobered. "But what of you? I should not be speaking of my happiness when you did not choose your engagement. I hope you are not terribly unhappy."

"I would not describe myself as unhappy," Elizabeth said carefully. "I am rather stunned by the speed with which everything has occurred, and I do not feel fully settled about it yet, but Andrew is a good man. He will make a fine husband, and I am determined to make the best of it."

"Do you mean that? Aunt said you showed no interest in him before...before it happened." Apparently her compromising situation was too painful to mention.

"No, it is true. I avoided him, and you are the only person I can tell why! It was not because I disliked Andrew, but because I found the idea of spending time with one of Mr. Darcy's relatives uncomfortable."

"And instead you ended up as Mr. Darcy's houseguest! Was it very difficult?"

If only she could tell Jane the truth! But Jane was marrying Bingley, and, no matter how much Elizabeth trusted Jane, it would be all too natural for her sister to confide in her lover, who was also Darcy's friend. Darcy did not deserve to have his pain exposed, and so she could not tell Jane the hardest part, how much it hurt to know she had injured him. Instead she said, "It was embarrassing, of course, but we seem to have each decided that the past between us is to be forgotten. Andrew knows nothing of his brother's proposal, and it shall stay that way. We must all forget it ever happened."

"You may depend upon me. I will never breathe a word of it to anyone." But Jane still looked troubled.

BINGLEY, ANDREW, AND Georgiana arrived at Longbourn the next morning, proposing a walk through the countryside with the Bennet daughters. Elizabeth was not surprised when Bingley and Jane fell behind the others, and she quietly informed Andrew of Jane's news.

"So quickly! Well, that explains his excitement last night. He did not tell us anything about it, but he seemed unusually exuberant, even for Bingley, and he certainly could not return here swiftly enough this morning," said Andrew, who also seemed in unusually good spirits.

"The resolution may have been quick, but their connection was resumed after a long interruption," Elizabeth replied. "I am very happy for them, and hope only that your brother will not be disappointed by the news."

"I think not. He told me his only objection to your sister was a belief that she did not care for Bingley, and you have said that is untrue," Andrew said confidently.

How much Andrew's attitude towards Darcy had changed in the few weeks she had known him! At least she could take some small credit for that healing, even if it made her own life more difficult. "Oh, one other thing. I spoke with Cook, and she has promised to use only honey and no sugar while you are here, apart from the sugar bowl, of course. My mother will not agree to pay extra for sugar not produced by slaves, so this is the best I can do."

"I thank you. That will make it easier. I would hate to anger your parents by refusing to eat their food," he said with an apologetic smile.

Because, of course, Andrew would never violate his principles. Given a choice between being rude or eating sugar produced by slaves, he would choose rudeness every time, even if he were dining with royalty. The idea almost made her giggle, until she recalled that King George and his family also refused to eat West Indian sugar in support of the abolitionist campaign.

On their return to Longbourn, Bingley disappeared into Mr. Bennet's library, and returned a few minutes later, wreathed with smiles. Mrs. Bennet received the news with an excitement that embarrassed Elizabeth, but Andrew seemed to take it in good humor, even when she announced that there must be a party to celebrate the engagements of her two eldest daughters. He went so far as to voluntarily sit beside her mother and talked to her for a quarter of an hour.

Later, when the younger people went outside to sit in the garden, Andrew exerted himself to entertain Mary and Kitty, answering Mary's questions about his religious beliefs and going so far as to offer to loan her his copy of Mr. Wilberforce's *Practical View of Christianity*. Elizabeth, playing tug-of-war with Sir Galahad in the grass, smiled to see Mary happily accept the offer of a book which their staid minister had preached was heretical, and decided exposure to Andrew would be good for her moralistic sister.

And then there was the pleasure of seeing Jane and Bingley sitting together on a bench, their fingers entwined. Jane's lovely face looked somehow softer, and she exuded a delighted contentment such as Elizabeth had never seen in her before. Dearest Jane! She deserved this happiness after all she had suffered and for all the goodness of her nature. Still, a wave of sadness rose in Elizabeth. Once she had wished to experience that kind of heartfelt love herself.

She glanced over at Andrew, who was laughing at something Mary had said. Had Mary actually made a joke? He was trying so hard to please her family, and doing it well, unlike his brother, who had scorned the Bennets as ill-mannered and beneath him. Why could she not love him as Jane loved Bingley?

Because of a pair of intent dark eyes that she could not forget. She ruffled her fingers in Sir Galahad's soft fur and hugged him close to her chest, as if the puppy could soothe the ache inside her.

MARY TRIPPED DOWNSTAIRS the next morning, Andrew's book in her hand, and then sat reading it at the breakfast table. Fortunately, Mrs. Bennet was still abed after being up late celebrating having two daughters engaged, or Mary would have been scolded for it.

"Do you find it interesting?" Jane asked.

Mary did not even look up from the book. "I stayed awake reading it until my eyes ached. It is so different..." And then she was lost in the book again. She did not look up again until Elizabeth arose at the end of her meal, when she said, "Lizzy, Jane, may I go with you to Netherfield today? There are things I do not understand, things I must ask him." There was no question as to whom she referred.

Elizabeth hid a smile. Clearly she would have to get used to her future husband being a great favorite among her family. "I would be pleased to have your company. Kitty, do you wish to come? Georgiana would be glad to see you both."

"I suppose I might as well," yawned Kitty. "I would like a closer look at her bonnet. I wish I could find such fine silk flowers!"

When they arrived at Netherfield, Elizabeth took a moment to whisper to Andrew, "I believe you have charmed my family. My mother keeps telling me I do not deserve such a man as you. I have no idea what you said to her, but she thinks you are marvelous."

The corner of his mouth turned up. "I only listened to her and told her I understood her worries. I have found it works marvels with nervous ladies."

Then Mary captured him with her questions, and Jane insisted that Elizabeth serve as chaperone while she and Bingley walked in the garden.

"If you insist," said Elizabeth. "Though I thought one of the advantages of being engaged was not having to worry about being alone together."

Jane blushed prettily. "Once it is formally announced, yes, but we must be careful until then."

Elizabeth shrugged at Andrew and followed Jane and Bingley into the garden. She stayed a dozen paces behind them, ostensibly to give them privacy, but the time alone was a balm to her soul, too. She had not realized how tense she had been about her return and how Andrew would react to her family, but now she knew he could handle himself with them, and it was a relief to simply walk and enjoy the flowers.

Half an hour later, a few drops of rain began to fall, so they returned to the drawing room. Instead of the happy discussion Elizabeth had expected, Kitty was crying quietly into a handkerchief, Georgiana's arm around her shoulders. Mary sat hunched with her hands clenched around her book, her knuckles white.

"Good God!" Bingley turned to Andrew. "What have you done?"

"Nothing," said Georgiana hurriedly. "We were only talking."

Kitty dabbed at her eyes. "It is my fault," she said shakily. "We were talking about abolition. I told him what Mama had said, about how the slaves would not feel their mistreatment as we would, and Mr. Andrew said we should ask one of them."

Elizabeth had not noticed Myrtilla standing beside the door. Andrew nodded to the Antiguan woman. "That will be all, I thank you."

Bingley said with an uncharacteristic sternness, "This is hardly a suitable subject for gently bred young ladies."

Andrew rose slowly to his feet, his eyes hooded, a look he had often worn at Pemberley, so unlike his easy-going air at Longbourn. "Forgive me, ladies."

Mary paled. "I do not like it at all, but it is something we need to know," she said steadily.

Andrew sketched her a bow. "That may be true, but it behooves me to remember what a shock the truth can be to those who have been protected from it. I am too accustomed to the company of my fellow abolitionists, and I ought to have been gentler."

Elizabeth found it difficult to believe Andrew had been harsh, but clearly the discussion had put him at odds with Bingley, his host. Bingley had always disliked conflict, and likely would prefer not to think too hard about the suffering of slaves. Perhaps his fortune, like so many these days, had some connections to slave trade. That would explain his sudden anger.

Jane said brightly. "We had the loveliest walk in the garden. I would insist that you come out to admire the hollyhocks, but since it is raining, perhaps Mary would favor us with some piano music."

It should have worked, since Mary was always eager to display her abilities, but this time she shook her head. "You must forgive me. I cannot go from such thoughts to playing pretty music. Those people need help!"

Elizabeth, torn between changing the subject to reduce Jane's tension and acknowledging Mary's distress, said, "Shall I play? Georgiana, I wonder if Mary might like to see the project you are working on for your charitable society."

"Oh, yes!" cried Georgiana. "Miss Mary, would you care to come upstairs with me? I would very much like to show it to you. Miss Kitty, too, if you wish."

As the girls went upstairs, Elizabeth sat down at the keyboard and played some country airs for Andrew, Jane, and Bingley, hoping the storm had passed.

Nothing more was said about it, apart from a private apology from Andrew for upsetting her sisters, but both Mary and Kitty were clearly still mulling over what they had learned. They were unusually quiet on the way home. And the next day, when Mrs. Bennet insisted that Mary put down her book, she started a new sewing project that looked suspiciously like the aprons Georgiana had been making.

When Andrew, Georgiana, and Bingley arrived, Mrs. Bennet ordered the tea tray. Kitty tossed her head and said, "No sugar for me. I have decided I dislike it." That was a sacrifice indeed, since Kitty was known for her sweet tooth. Myrtilla's words must have made an impression to convince her to stop eating sugar grown by slaves.

Elizabeth reached over and squeezed her hand. "Aunt and Uncle Gardiner will be proud of you, as am I."

She had not expected the sacrifice from flighty Kitty, but Kitty had always followed Lydia's poor example. If she and Mary had now decided to emulate Andrew and Georgiana, it was a definite improvement, one that made Elizabeth wish Lydia would stay in Brighton for a long time.

Chapter 20

After a week at Netherfield, Andrew and Georgiana set off to spend several days in London. On their return, they stopped at Longbourn for a brief call. Both seemed in good spirits, Andrew reporting that he had been able to speak to several of his abolitionist friends, while Georgiana was full of news of the new bonnets and sheet music she had purchased.

Just as they were preparing to leave for Netherfield, where they were to spend one more night before returning to Derbyshire, Georgiana cried, "Oh, I almost forgot! I have something for you, Elizabeth."

Elizabeth followed the girl as she hurried out to their carriage and spoke to her maid. After rummaging in a trunk tied to the back of the carriage, the maid produced a small enameled box and handed it to Georgiana with a curtsey.

Georgiana held it out to her. "This is for you. It was in the back of my wardrobe at Darcy House, where it has sat for years. I had almost forgotten about it. My mother gave it to me before she died and told me it was for Drew's wife."

Surprised, Elizabeth took the box. It was only a few inches across and perhaps six inches long. Given its light weight, it presumably contained some piece of jewelry. She lifted the lid to disclose a silk-wrapped bundle with a wax seal labeled, "To be opened privately."

Her eyebrows shot up, and she carefully lowered the lid. "Thank you," she told Georgiana. "It says to open it privately, so I shall." What could be such a secret?

"I know." The girl giggled. "I peeked inside the box once, when I was too young to know better, but I stopped when I saw the seal."

Andrew joined them then, having stayed inside speaking to Mrs. Bennet, and promised to call again in the morning before they left.

Curious, Elizabeth went straight to her room. Behind the closed door, she opened the box again, broke the seal, and unwrapped the silk to reveal a silver pendant engraved with a heart. No, not a pendant, but a locket, and somehow familiar.

She brought it close to her eyes and fiddled with the latch until it opened to display two portraits. On the right was a young Lady Anne Darcy, a copy of the portrait that the old gentleman at the ball in Derbyshire had shown Elizabeth. On the left was Andrew, wearing an elaborately decorated coat of the sort fashionable thirty years earlier. How odd! According to Andrew, he had never seen his mother after he turned sixteen, yet she had a portrait of him as a young man. Not a very accurate one, though, since the man in the portrait had brown eyes, whereas Andrew's were green. And the cheekbones were not quite right.

She frowned, puzzled. It could not be Andrew. This gentleman looked very much like him, sharing that distinctive jawline and cleft chin, but his hair was powdered, and she had never seen Andrew choose foppish clothes, much less those of a generation past. But his face was the image of Andrew's. Except for the green eyes.

A sharp, disbelieving breath tore through her.

Andrew, who looked nothing like his father nor any of the Darcy forebears whose portraits lined the Long Gallery at Pemberley. Andrew, whose father had despised and eventually disowned him. Andrew, whose mother had loved another man before her marriage, the same man who had shown her a locket that matched this one, and claimed he was Lady Anne Darcy's childhood sweetheart.

She dredged up her memories of the ball in Derbyshire. What had his name been? Headley? No, Hadley, that was it. When Mr. Hadley had shown her the locket, he had carefully covered the picture on the left so she could not see it, and could not connect that young man who looked so much like Andrew to him. And she had not seen his telltale cleft chin because of the unfashionable full beard he sported, despite his otherwise stylish attire.

Mr. Hadley had hidden his face behind that beard to protect Lady Anne Darcy's secret. And Andrew knew it. He had walked out of that ball to avoid seeing his true father.

Her mind raced. Oh, so much made sense now! Why old Mr. Darcy, who was otherwise held to be generous and decent, had hated Andrew so. Why Andrew wanted nothing to do with Pemberley or the Darcy heritage. He was not simply being stubborn and refusing to let go of the past as she had thought. Now it was clear he saw himself as an imposter.

She sank into a chair, her legs suddenly weak from the shock. It should not matter, at least in the most public way. By law, Andrew was old Mr. Darcy's son, even if he was the precise image of Mr. Hadley. Nothing could change that. Another man might not be troubled by it, but Andrew, with his strict moral code, must feel like a pretender whenever he set foot at Pemberley.

An imposter. Her mind froze on the image of Andrew standing with his brother and sister. Andrew clearly knew the truth, but did they? She suspected Georgiana did not, or she would not have given her this box so innocently. Mr. Darcy was a more difficult question.

Oh, how Andrew must hate being the product of adultery! He had paid an enormous price for his mother's sins.

She cradled the locket in her hand, examining the miniature of Mr. Hadley. What of him, the man who had seduced Lady Anne Darcy? He had seemed so anxious for any word of the boy he had fathered. Andrew clearly wanted nothing to do with him, but Hadley had deliberately sought her out. He wanted a connection.

What was the truth of it? Had Hadley and Lady Anne been lovers throughout her marriage? And what of Georgiana's parentage? Darcy bore a distinct resemblance to old Mr. Darcy, but if Mr. Hadley was Andrew's father, perhaps he was Georgiana's, too. Darcy's father had never rejected Georgiana as he had Andrew, though. Perhaps he did not care about a girl child being a cuckoo in his nest.

An unpleasant shiver went down Elizabeth's spine at the thought, and she closed the locket. As she started to set it back in the box, she noticed a folded paper, almost hidden by another piece of silk.

Her heart beating faster, she pried the paper out and unfolded it to reveal a small piece of lady's stationary written in a shaky hand.

Be not alarmed, madam, on receiving this posthumous letter. As my illness overtakes me, there are some last confessions I must make, and this is one of them.

It is my dearest hope that you, whoever you may be, feel a true affection for my son. It is likely you already know why my husband holds him in such distaste, but Andrew is only aware of part of the story. If you are to understand him, you must understand the truth, and I hope you can share it with him.

When my husband first turned against Andrew, I tried to defend him to the best of my ability, for my dearest boy was innocent of my sins. But the more I protected him, the angrier my husband grew, and Andrew suffered even more for it. I learned that any attention I paid to Andrew would be repaid to him in the form of a beating. After much reflection, I realized the kindest thing I could do was to avoid provoking my husband by showing no affection to Andrew. I chose a caring tutor and governess for him, and left him completely to their care. When attempts to send him to school failed, his tutor took him into his home and gave him the affection I wished I could have.

I hoped that could continue until it was time for him to go to university, but it was not to be. He came to Pemberley every week to visit his sister, who was most attached to him, and while he was sensible enough to stay out of his father's way on these visits, Georgiana was too young to understand that she should not mention them, and more particularly not defend Andrew when her father criticized him. Soon my husband's wrath began to turn to her, and she needed my protection in a way Andrew no longer did.

Thus I made my cowardly decision to encourage my husband to send Andrew away. I did not anticipate how harshly he would do so, nor that he would send my dearest boy off without a penny to his name, but I did agree to it. My punishment is the suffering I have endured in not knowing where he is or what he is doing, for my husband has forbidden me from contacting him or even mentioning his name. It breaks my heart that Andrew will forever believe I wished him to go away. I cannot ask anyone I know to tell him otherwise without my husband becoming aware of it, so my only hope is that you, a young lady I will never meet, will bear this message to him. I hope it may bring him understanding and peace.

I pray you will give my dearest boy all the affection he so deserves, the love I wish I could have shown him. I have paid a harsh price for my sins, but

Andrew should never have done so. There is so much more I wish I could tell you, but my strength is fading.

It was unsigned.

Elizabeth stared at the letter, reread it, put it aside, then picked it up and read it again. The evident despair of Lady Anne Darcy caught at her, yet it was almost as if she felt her infidelity should have no consequences. Or perhaps she had simply been too ill to write about that part.

Poor Andrew! How he had suffered for something that had happened before he was born. Was this common knowledge? Had people at the Allston House ball been laughing into their sleeves when she had spent so much time with Andrew's father? Wickham had said something to Andrew about his father, something that had struck her as odd at the time, but now it made her suspect that he knew.

Who else? Mr. Morris, the kind old clergyman, had said there were things about Andrew's relationship with old Mr. Darcy that he could not reveal. And the younger Mr. Darcy must know as well. He must have thought her impossibly naïve. Oh, how mortifying to discover that everyone had known her future husband's secret except her!

A flicker of irritation burned inside her. Andrew ought to have told her the truth. She was his future wife, after all. Why had he not trusted her with it? Why had he allowed her to stumble blindly at Pemberley around a truth everyone else could see?

No. She should not condemn him unheard. But it was a struggle to keep her mind open until she could ask Andrew for an explanation of his silence, when her mind kept leaping ahead to possible explanations, each angering her more than the last.

She tried to quell her agitation and to collect herself, but as soon as she went downstairs, her mother called her over. "What was it Miss Darcy gave you? Hill said she heard her say it was from her mother."

Oh, no. "Just a little trinket and a note welcoming me to the family, nothing more."

Mrs. Bennet waved her handkerchief. "Well, bring it here so we can all see it!"

She was trapped. Showing them the locket would reveal the truth, and, if her mother learned about his parentage, all of Meryton would know by tomorrow. But what excuse could she possibly give for refusing to show her family the gift from Andrew's mother? "Hill no doubt also overheard that it was to be opened privately, and the note from Lady Anne Darcy said it was only for my eyes. Surely you would not wish for me to disregard her wishes."

"Whyever not? She is dead and unable to complain about it, and we all wish to see it. Why must you always be so difficult?"

Elizabeth drew herself up as straight as she could. "Andrew would be furious with me if I showed it to you, and I owe him my loyalty," she said icily. "And now I am going to take a walk." She stalked out before she said anything worse.

On returning to her room to fetch her bonnet and gloves, she spotted the enameled box on her dressing table. She could not leave the contents there; her mother was not above searching her room while she was out. Quickly she stuffed the locket and the letter into her pocket.

She set off down a footpath, paying little attention to where her feet were leading her until some of her distress was spent in exertion. She had already traveled a mile or so before realizing this was the same route she had taken nearly a year ago to visit Jane when she lay ill at Netherfield.

Yes, that was the answer – she would walk to Netherfield and speak to Andrew about her discovery. It was far better than waiting until their brief meeting tomorrow morning, after which she would not see him for months. No, best to settle this now. Newly energized, she clambered over a wooden stile into the next pasture where last time she had landed in a mud puddle. At least now it was dry. She would not arrive at Netherfield with her petticoat six inches deep in mud.

Andrew and Georgiana seemed startled to see her, as well they might since they had only left her a few hours previously. Andrew said, "You walked all this way alone?"

"Not for the first time," she said, with a bit of an edge to her voice. "Forgive me, Georgiana, but I would like to speak to your brother privately."

The girl's eyes rounded. "Of course," she said nervously.

"Perhaps we could go to the library," Andrew suggested, gesturing to the room behind the double doors.

"I thank you." Elizabeth allowed him to lead her there.

When he had closed the doors behind him, Andrew asked mildly, "Is something the matter?"

"Yes, something is the matter!" cried Elizabeth. "I learned something about your past today, and I would much rather have heard it from you." It was not how she had intended to tell him, but his distant calmness had somehow enraged her.

His lips grew white as he pressed them together. "Who told you?" He had not even asked what she had discovered.

"A voice from beyond the grave," she snapped. She opened the locket and thrust it at him.

Frowning, he looked down at it, and then dropped it on a side table as if it had burnt him. "Where did you get that...that thing?"

"Your mother had left a package for your future bride. Georgiana gave it to me today."

He stared at the floor for a minute, and then looked up at her with dilated pupils. "Do you wish to break our engagement, then?" he asked woodenly.

She stared at him. "What? No, of course not. This changes nothing."

"Then why are you so angry?"

She forced herself to straighten her fingers, which seemed to want to form into fists. "I am angry because you did not tell me yourself, and instead left me floundering in an attempt to understand why you were estranged from your family and why everyone tiptoed around it!"

He exhaled slowly and bowed his head. "On that I cannot defend myself. You are quite correct. I should have told you the truth." He sounded defeated.

His behavior took the wind from her sails, leaving her feeling vaguely guilty and frustrated. "I accept your apology. I am sorry to have been so harsh to you."

Andrew did not look up. "I deserve it. It was wrong of me to take advantage of your ignorance."

"I think you misunderstand. It is not that you took advantage, but that you left me in a difficult position where I did not understand your behavior. That is all."

Now he did meet her eyes, but his were pained. "I did take advantage. After returning to Derbyshire, where everyone knew, I enjoyed being with someone who saw me as a person rather than my mother's great mistake. And I knew you would not have agreed to marry me had you known, so I selfishly kept my secret. You have every right to be furious with me."

"I...what? It would have made no difference in my decision to marry you." At least she thought it would not have. After all, she had little choice in the matter, but it was probably just as well that she had not realized precisely how difficult a situation existed between Andrew and his family.

His lip curled. "You would have agreed to marry a man who is illegitimate?" His voice flattened on the last word.

"You are not illegitimate! The law says you are the son of Mr. George Darcy and Lady Anne Darcy, and nothing can change that."

"Yes, in the eyes of the law, I am legitimate. The eyes of God are another question." His mouth held a bitter twist.

Now her outrage took a different direction. Who had taught him that an innocent child was to blame for the sins of his parents? It could not have been the kind Mr. Morris. "I cannot speak for the divine, but you committed no sin."

He snorted. "That did not stop my father – my legal father – from blaming me for it. Repeatedly."

She winced. "I am sorry he took his anger out on you, but it was still not your fault."

"Even my mother blamed me. When I was very young, she was warm and generous to me, but once my parentage was known, she wanted nothing further to do with me. She still acted the role of mother to Georgiana and Fitzwilliam, but not to me. I was her failure, and she never forgave me for it." His hands clenched into fists.

Elizabeth shook her head, horrified. "No. You are wrong. Your mother loved you."

The words kept pouring out of him. "The day my father threw me out, she stood at the top of the stairs and watched me walk away. She said nothing, and did not even raise her hand to bid me farewell. She was glad to see me gone. And you want me to believe there is nothing wrong with me, when even my own mother wanted to be rid of me?"

171

"No! That is not true, and I can prove it." She fished in her pocket and brought out the letter from his mother. She pushed the folded paper towards him. "This was with the locket."

He held his hand up to stop her. "No. I do not want it, whatever it is. I want nothing of hers." It was the same ringing voice of utter certainty that he used when speaking of slavery.

"You must read this. Truly."

He shook his head decisively. "I have spent years learning to put my parents behind me, and I have accomplished it by refusing to allow thoughts of them into my life." He pointed at the letter. "Reading that thing would ruin all of it."

She took a deep breath. "I believe you may be choosing to be overly inflexible in this case. I have read it, and you need to know what it contains. You would not refuse to hear out any other suffering human soul, would you? Why start with your mother?"

"Suffering? My mother? Hardly! I am the one who suffered for her pleasures." His mouth twisted with distaste on the last word.

"You did not suffer alone." She tried to keep her voice even. "Andrew, I am asking you to trust me that this letter is important for you to read."

He stared at her in frustration, his desire to refuse evident in his very stance. "I would prefer not to," he said through gritted teeth.

They had never truly disagreed about anything, and she was hesitant to change that, but these stakes were too high, and it was past time that she learned what would happen if she pressed him. "I am sorry, but nonetheless, I am asking you to do so."

His eyes narrowed, and, with a hissing sound, he snatched the letter from her hand. He did not say a word as he unfolded it, his hands trembling with suppressed anger.

With trepidation, Elizabeth watched him, hoping to see the stony lines of his face soften, but there was nothing, only his eyes moving across the page. What would happen when he finished? Would he turn that anger on her? Well, if he did, she would stand up for herself. After all, it could not be worse than quarreling with Mr. Darcy, and she had survived that more than once.

THE PRICE OF PRIDE

When he reached the end of the page, he appeared to start again at the beginning. Part way through, he pressed his fist against his mouth. He kept staring at the paper, as if more words might appear on it, seemingly having forgotten Elizabeth's presence.

Finally he looked up, his eyes haunted. "What else?" he asked heavily.

"There is nothing else," she said gently. "Except that you should know that I met him once, at the Allston House ball. I was his partner for the supper dance." Somehow it felt wiser not to mention Mr. Hadley's name.

His lip curled. "And he did not tell you himself?"

"No. I had no idea until I saw that locket. He congratulated me on my engagement and mentioned that he was your mother's childhood sweetheart. Mostly he encouraged me to talk about you."

"What did you tell him?"

"The truth, as far as I knew it, about your time in London and taking the Kympton living. Nothing about your quarrel with your father, since that was a private family matter. I hardly knew you then myself. He asked about your brother and sister, too."

"I do not wish to have any contact with him, nor for you to do so."

Since they seemed hardly likely to cross paths, she said, "Very well, but I would value your insight into who else might be aware of your situation and how you would like me to handle it."

He seemed to relax, or at least stop looking as if he expected her to pull out a horse whip at any moment. "It was common knowledge at Pemberley from the time I was six, which was when my father discovered it. Wickham knows, of course, and my brother certainly must, though he has never said anything. My parishioners have been whispering about it since Wickham's visit, so he must have said something. Mr. Morris knows, too."

"What of the other guests at the ball? It did not seem as if anyone was paying any particular attention to my discussion with him. But perhaps it was such old news no one cared any longer."

He frowned. "I cannot say. No one has ever said anything to me, but I was still a child when I left. I should not have returned. The gossip would have died a natural death."

"Whom are you trying to protect? Your mother? She is beyond the knives of the gossips' tongue. The Darcy family name? Forgive me, but I think your good works do more credit to your family than any scandal about your parentage." But now she understood why he held such strong moral beliefs and felt his behavior had to be above reproach.

To her surprise, he smiled slightly. "For someone who is angry at me, you are very fierce in my defense."

"When someone is badly wronged, as you have been, yes, I am fierce. Your mother may have been at fault, but you are not."

His eyes widened. "May have been at fault? *May have*?"

She hesitated, squirming inside. "It appears that way, but I have lived long enough in this world to know nothing is a simple question. Perhaps it was merely for her own pleasure, in which case she deserves full blame, or perhaps it happened in a moment of weakness when she was desperate for any affection because she was bitterly unhappy in her marriage and her husband mistreated her. Or perhaps the other man took advantage of her and she never consented to it. I do not wish to condemn too harshly when I do not know the circumstances. But infidelity is never acceptable in my mind."

"I am relieved to hear that, since I do expect fidelity in marriage, both for husband and wife."

"I can promise you that." But the flash of pain in Darcy's dark eyes rose before her.

A hesitant knock sounded. Andrew said wearily, "Yes?"

The door cracked open and Georgiana peered in, her face drawn. "May I come in just for a minute?" she asked in a small voice.

"Of course you may," Elizabeth said.

But Georgiana's eyes were only on Andrew as she entered and her words poured out in a rush. "I am so sorry. I did not mean to cause difficulties. I should have told you what I was bringing her, but I was afraid you might tell me not to. I had promised our mother on her deathbed that I would give it to your wife someday, so I had to, you see. I hope you can forgive me."

Andrew took a moment to collect himself. "There is nothing to forgive. You were right to keep your promise, and it is likely just as well I knew nothing of it until afterwards."

"You are not angry at me?"

He reached over and tugged one of her ringlets. "When have I ever been angry at you, poppet?"

She gave a little, hiccoughing giggle. "But I made trouble for you and Elizabeth."

"Not trouble," Elizabeth said firmly. "The package just raised some questions, and Andrew has been kind enough to answer them for me."

Andrew put his arm around Elizabeth's shoulders. "See? All is well."

It was the most physically intimate he had ever been with her. It felt strange to have a man's body so close to hers, but not unpleasant. At least it did not seem to bother him. She had begun to wonder why he took none of the usual liberties an engaged man might with his betrothed. "Yes, all is well, and I thank you for bringing me the box from your mother."

"Oh. Then I will leave you, and I apologize for interrupting." She turned to the door.

"No, a moment, please," said Andrew. "I have a question for you, if you do not object. What did our mother say when she gave that to you?"

"Just that I should hide it away where no one could find it and give it to your wife if you married, and that it was important. I asked if I should give it to you, and she said no, because she had promised our father on her honor that she would not try to contact you, and she would not break her word. Well, she did not exactly say that; she was too ill to express herself well, but that was the gist of it. But I was glad she told me, for I had always wondered."

"What had you wondered?" Andrew's voice was not completely steady.

"Why she did not talk to you herself. Every time you visited me, she would send for me and ask me how you looked and to repeat everything you had said, and then she would cry and cry. She always said it was because her fire smoked so badly, but it did not, of course."

Andrew had gone nearly as white as his shirt collar, and, if Elizabeth was not mistaken, would soon be in danger himself of having to blame the library fire for smoking. Quickly she took Georgiana's arm and said, "Since I am here, will you not show me the new bonnets you bought in London? I am dying to see them."

"Of course," Georgiana said, with a confused glance at Andrew.

175

As Elizabeth was nudging the girl towards the door, Andrew said firmly, "I will drive you back to Longbourn. There is no need for you to walk alone."

This was not the moment to argue with him. "That is very kind of you."

Chapter 21

Andrew had little to say for himself as he took Elizabeth home. He had borrowed Bingley's curricle for the trip, and appeared unusually preoccupied by the business of driving the horses. His countenance was more thoughtful than angry, though, so the silence was not too uncomfortable.

He seemed in better spirits the next morning when he and Georgiana stopped by Longbourn to say their farewells. She had felt a little trepidation that he might have, on reflection, been angry at her initiative, but when he took her aside for a private adieu, he said, "I should thank you for what you did yesterday. You were right to insist that I read that letter. It has given me a great deal to think about."

"I am glad. I have been a little worried for Georgiana, since she seemed quite upset."

He glanced back at his sister. "She is better now. I expect we will have some long talks on the journey home."

He kissed her hand before he left, but it did not send a tingle up her arm as Darcy's every touch could do. "I will see you in December, then." They had resolved that he would come to Longbourn for Christmas, with the wedding to follow afterwards.

She waved as they drove away. Perhaps now her life could return to normal for a little while, and she could learn to accept her future with Andrew. How odd it was that only two months ago she had not even known of his existence! And she had thought she would never see Darcy again. Now she could not even be free of him in her most private thoughts.

Mary came up beside her. "Will you miss him very much?" she asked.

Elizabeth smiled at her. "It will seem strange not to be tripping over members of the Darcy family right and left, but I think I shall manage."

TO DARCY'S SURPRISE, Drew called at Pemberley on the very morning after his return from Hertfordshire. Darcy had expected to have to hunt him down at the parsonage, given how much Drew seemed to dislike coming to his old home, and always wanted to leave as soon as possible.

He looked different today, too. Usually when he came to Pemberley he seemed stiff and kept his eyes down, but today his gaze traveled around the room as if he had never seen it before, seeming to pause on the paintings and even the elaborate plastered ceiling.

"Welcome back," Darcy said. "Georgiana has been telling me every detail of your journey, which she seems to have enjoyed immensely. It sounds as if you took prodigious care of her."

Drew smiled. "It is not difficult to be good to Georgiana. I was glad of the chance to get to know her better. I hope you have been doing well, and that you were able to resolve your business successfully."

It took a moment for Darcy to recall his own departure to chase down George Wickham. Drew would have known nothing of that, only that he had left unexpectedly. "It was satisfactory, I thank you."

His brother shifted from one foot to another. "I have been wondering what happened to the portrait of our mother. I noticed it was no longer in the gallery."

"It is in Georgiana's private sitting room, at her request. Would you like to see it? Georgiana is out riding, but I know she would not mind." If Drew was willing to even mention one of their parents without that ferocious scowl, Darcy would happily break into a locked vault to show him the portrait.

Drew hesitated. "Yes, I would."

As they headed up the stairs, Darcy said, "Georgiana tells me Bingley and Miss Bennet are to be wed." Of course, Bingley had not entrusted him with that information, and Darcy could hardly blame him.

"Yes. From all appearances, they are deeply in love."

"I had thought something like that might happen. It is good news. I imagine the Bennets are very pleased." It was as close as he could come to asking about Elizabeth's reaction.

"They seemed to be."

Darcy tried again. "What did you think of the Bennets?"

"We rubbed along well enough. Mr. Bennet would rather Elizabeth remained closer to home, but he gave his permission anyway, not that he had much choice in the matter. Mrs. Bennet's pleasure in our engagement was so fervent as to make up for any deficit. I liked her sisters, especially Miss Mary. She has a good mind, although she has had little opportunity to develop it."

Darcy blinked. "I never had the pleasure of conversing with her beyond a few words." Nor had he wished to do so.

They had reached Georgiana's rooms, and Darcy opened the door to the sitting room for Drew. "You will find the room very much unchanged. Georgiana wished it so, since it had been our mother's favorite. She says she feels closer to her here."

"I hardly remember it, to tell you the truth. I stayed away from this part of the house." Of course he had. Drew would have had to pass their father's rooms, now Darcy's, to get here.

Darcy had spent hours sitting beside his mother in this room. He had to remember how different Drew's life at Pemberley had been. "She was very fond of the view from the window."

Drew stepped inside and looked about him. His air of relaxation seemed to have disappeared; now the tendons were sticking out on his neck. He took several deep breaths before turning to the painting.

In the full-length portrait, Lady Anne stood in the Pemberley gardens, her hand resting gently on a carved stone balustrade, every inch the regal earl's daughter. The painter had flattered her and made her look happy; Darcy recalled when it was painted, shortly after another child had been still-born. In reality, his mother had appeared pale and wan. Not as pale, though, as the final time he had seen her, a fortnight before her death, when she had clasped his hand and begged him to take care of Drew if anything happened to her.

The ghost of that past scene suddenly rose in his mind. His protestation that of course he would take care of Drew and Georgiana, and his mother's weak insistence that no, it was Drew who needed him. He had paid little attention beyond reassuring her, since Drew was then seventeen and therefore, in Darcy's mind, would doubtless not appreciate oversight by his elder brother. But she had known, as he had not, that Drew had been disowned, sent off without a penny, and most likely desperately in need of his assistance. But she had been too weak to talk for more than a few minutes, and he had forgotten it until now.

Why had he not taken her more seriously and asked more questions? Because he had been too certain of his own beliefs, trusting his father to know what was best for his brother and sister. And Drew had suffered for it.

Now his brother studied their mother's portrait closely, his expression withdrawn. "There was another one, was there not, from when we were children, with you standing beside her?"

"And you were on her lap, yes." Darcy licked his lips, but there was no point in pretending. "Father had that one destroyed after you left. Mrs. Reynolds managed to save your miniature, but she could hardly smuggle away a painting of that size. Had I been here, I would have tried to stop it, but Father carefully hid all that from me. I did not even learn he had disowned you until the night of his apoplexy, after Mother's death. He had forbidden everyone here to speak of it to me." It was a relief to get the words out. He had wanted to tell Drew this for years, but there had never been an opportunity when it would not have felt like an attempt to defend his own failings.

A crease appeared between Drew's brows. "How unsurprising."

"I imagine Mother was unhappy about it, too. It was her favorite painting."

Tilting his head to one side, Drew said, "It looked more like her than this one does. But I am glad to see it, anyway." He turned to the door.

Darcy decided to seize his opportunity while Drew was in what seemed to be an unusually receptive mood. "Will you come to my... to the library? I would like to tell you about the business that called me away so suddenly." He only remembered at the last minute that Drew had bad memories of his study.

Drew looked surprised by this invitation, but not displeased. "I would be happy to."

He waited until they were safely inside the library and the door shut behind them. This was not business he wanted the servants overhearing. "I hope there was no unpleasantness in Meryton owing to the little scandal Wickham tried to create."

Drew looked up at him in surprise. "You heard about that?" He did not sound troubled by it.

"That is the business that called me away. I have reached the end of my tolerance for Wickham's mischief. He is now in debtors' prison, and since I hold thousands of pounds of his debts, there he will remain."

"I cannot say I am sorry to hear it. At least he will not harm anyone there."

"I would hope not, in any case. I wish I had done it sooner, rather than giving him so many chances. Too many people have been hurt because I could not bring myself to put an end to his freedom."

Drew nodded. "Understandable, though. He was your friend for many years, and the old man doted on him."

"Because he thought Wickham was his late brother's natural son. I doubt it myself, but it is possible. There is little resemblance except in their characters. Uncle Charles was quite the profligate himself, which is why Father sent him off to Jamaica to manage the plantation, thinking he could get into less trouble there."

Drew stiffened. "Wickham always claimed it was true, but he would, of course, even if he knew otherwise."

"Wickham delights in any lie that can reflect well upon himself." Darcy chose his words carefully. "But now he is in my power. Under the circumstances, he would doubtless be persuasible to informing the good people of Meryton that he was mistaken about your compromising situation."

Drew considered this for a moment. "I see no need for that. No one mentioned any talk, so either he did not say anything, or if he did, there is no point reminding people about it. The Bennets have been through enough."

Darcy's mouth grew dry. "What of you? Perhaps you would like your freedom from an engagement you were forced into."

Drew gave him a puzzled look. "I was hurried into it, perhaps, but I was already close to offering for Elizabeth. Wickham's antics simply made matters progress more quickly."

Darcy's heart sank. It had only been a slight chance, but now it was gone. "You want to marry her, then."

His brother swiveled towards him with a fierce expression. "Is it so surprising to you? I had no family at all for six years, and now I want one of my own, one from which I cannot be ejected on any man's whim. Elizabeth is a perfectly acceptable match for me, even if you did not think her sister good enough for Bingley."

"I meant no criticism of Miss Elizabeth. Any man would be fortunate to have her." The words tore at his throat. But there was more he had to say. "But you need never fear losing your place in this family. Our father was wrong. I deeply regret all that you suffered for it. If it were in my power to undo what he did, I would do so, no matter what it cost me."

How strange that he should even need to say that. His father had drilled the lesson into his head again and again. Family came first. His primary duty as head of the family would be to protect them, even before caring for Pemberley. And yet his father had cast Drew off as if he were rubbish.

Drew poured himself a glass of brandy and took a sip of it before answering. "I am what I am, and the past cannot be changed. I appreciate what you have done to welcome me here, including inviting Elizabeth to stay despite your quarrels in the past. I want for nothing except for you to stop trying to interfere with my marriage plans."

It was like a blow to the chest, because of course that was exactly what he had been trying to do, though not for the reason Drew thought. He had to say something, though, or he would lose all the progress he had made with Drew. "My apologies. It was a misunderstanding, nothing more. When I heard of Wickham's deceit, I thought perhaps you had felt obligated to offer for her against your wishes. You say that is not the case, and I believe you and am glad of it." Even if his mouth tasted of ashes.

"Yes. I want to marry her."

"Then so you shall." He had to call on all his strength to continue. "Did you set a wedding date while you were in Hertfordshire?"

"Just after Christmas. I will go to Longbourn for the holiday, while you and Georgiana are at Matlock." He cracked a slight smile. "Not an invitation that would include me."

Darcy seized at the change of subject as if he were drowning and it were a raft. "Yes, I must decide what to do about that. Those plans were made before I learned of Frederica's situation – even before you took the living here – and I suspect I may not be welcome there by Christmastime either, if Lord Matlock learns I have helped her. Were you able to speak to her future husband while you were in London?"

"Yes, and he is delighted to know that I, and most particularly you, will attend the wedding, whenever it may be. I am to write him as soon as we know when Frederica will be at Pemberley, and he will come here."

"Very good. I will write to Lord Matlock, then, and invite Frederica to stay."

A smile broke out on Drew's face. "While I am doing this to help Frederica, I have to admit that I find a certain pleasure in knowing that doing so will also give her father a figurative black eye. He deserves it, and more."

Chapter 22

Despite the preparations for Jane and Bingley's wedding, Longbourn seemed quiet to Elizabeth after Andrew and Georgiana departed for Pemberley. She had grown accustomed to greater companionship traveling with the Gardiners and then at Pemberley. With Jane often preoccupied with her wedding clothes and planning, Elizabeth spent more time taking long walks alone or chatting with Mary and Kitty.

Nothing felt the same as it had been before her trip to Derbyshire. Or perhaps everything was the same, but she was different. Then she had been heart-whole and carefree; now she was bound to Andrew and struggling with her hopeless obsession with his brother. The more she tried to put him out of her head, the more he filled her thoughts.

After a fortnight passed in this manner, she was working on her embroidery as Kitty read aloud from the latest novel from the circulating library when the sound of hoofbeats and wheels on gravel came from the lane outside. Mary set her work aside and hurried to the window.

"Who is it?" Jane asked.

Mary turned a surprised look on Elizabeth. "Why, it is Andrew's brother! Mr. Darcy himself! What could bring him here? I hope nothing has happened to Andrew."

Her heart in her throat, Elizabeth hurried to stand behind her sister. It was him, and she had lost none of her exquisite awareness of him. "I cannot imagine why he is here. He is not in mourning, nor does he appear distressed, so it cannot be anything too terrible." But her pulses fluttered. What could possibly have brought Darcy away from Pemberley? Andrew had not mentioned anything in his last letter about it.

Darcy did not seem in a hurry, stopping to speak at some length with his coachman before turning to the house. He paused, then, catching sight of them in the window, and bowed. Elizabeth curtsied in return, although he could likely not even make out her action, but studied his face. He seemed to be smiling at her, not the sort of expression he had usually worn during her time in Pemberley, but perhaps that was just the distortion through the wavy glass. Whether or not it was a true smile, he did not look angry or distressed, and she breathed a little easier.

He came up and knocked at the front door, and Elizabeth hurriedly sat down and picked up her work again, a little embarrassed to have been caught staring at him. The sound of the front door opening and the butler's gravelly voice drifted in, followed by footsteps. But they did not stop at the drawing room, and she glanced up to see his figure striding past the open door.

"He must be going to our father," said Mary. "That sounds serious."

Elizabeth chewed her lip. What on earth could Darcy want to speak to her father about? It made no sense. Darcy had no say over Andrew's ability to marry her. She did not think he would have appeared so much at ease outside if something terrible happened to Andrew, but how could she know for certain?

Or could he have discovered something so awful about Andrew that he felt Mr. Bennet should be informed? She could not imagine Andrew would have committed any shocking sin, and the question of his mother's infidelity was irrelevant, given the law. Yet something had made Mr. Darcy come so far out of his way. "Jane, is it possible he is visiting Mr. Bingley?"

"Bingley did not mention anything of the sort to me, but I suppose it is possible," Jane said. "He would be glad to see him, I am certain."

Given Bingley's apparent quarrel with Darcy just before he left Pemberley, Elizabeth was less certain of that, but she said nothing, just returned to her embroidery, her mind abuzz. By the time Darcy and Mr. Bennet emerged from the library and into the drawing room, seeming on the best of terms, she had worked herself up into a fine state of anxiety.

Darcy greeted them all properly, reporting that Andrew was in excellent health when he had left Pemberley the previous week. Elizabeth was too embarrassed to do more than glance at him and to say a few words in response, but the glass in the window had not lied. He was still smiling and seemed in good spirits, even when Mrs. Bennet entered and began to fuss at him.

After a few minutes of this, but with perfect civility, Darcy turned to Elizabeth. "Miss Elizabeth, I wonder if you might do me the honor of joining me on a walk outside? Drew asked me to give you a few messages."

Should she believe in this new affability? Oh, how she wanted to, but at the same time, she could not imagine Drew giving any messages to his brother, not out of a lack of trust, but because he would despise being in Darcy's debt. If he had wanted to contact her, he would have written her a letter, as he had already done twice. So why did Darcy wish to speak to her alone?

"I would be happy to do so." She did not know whether to hope this amiability on Darcy's part would last, giving her even more memories to break her heart over, or whether his coldness would return. But she could not resist the opportunity to spend even a few minutes with him, and she wanted to discover what he had said to her father, so she hurried off to fetch her bonnet and gloves.

Once they were outside, strolling along the lane, Darcy seemed disinclined to speak. She walked beside him in silence for several minutes, the tension of uncertainty winding tighter inside her. Finally, in some desperation, she said, "I hope your sister is in good health."

He looked surprised. "Georgiana? Yes, she is quite well."

"I am glad to hear it. I enjoyed her company while she was staying at Netherfield."

He hesitated, and then said, "I owe you an apology for my behavior towards you at Pemberley, a profound apology. You must have thought me most uncivil, and you would have been correct."

She blinked in surprise. This was the last thing she had expected from him. Carefully she said, "I did not expect any particular attention from you, as I was an intruder to your family party." It was impossible to say what she truly meant without breaking the silence about their past connection.

"I invited you, yet I did not show you the welcome a host should. I can only plead in my defense a mistaken understanding of the nature of your engagement to my brother; but while that might explain my sentiments, it is no excuse for my want of manners. For that, I must humbly apologize."

A mistaken understanding? What could he mean? "I accept your apology, and am most grateful that your opinion of me seems to have improved, but I am puzzled by what understanding you might have had." She held her breath. She desperately did not want a return of his anger, but she could not forever be treading on thin ice with him.

"It is only fair to tell you, although it embarrasses me that I even temporarily attributed such motives to you. When I saw that you did not appear to be enamored of my brother, I could establish no better explanation for your engagement than that you wished to revenge yourself against me for the harm I did to your sister, knowing that your marriage to Drew would be —" He broke off abruptly, as if biting his tongue. Then he continued in a quieter voice, "I should have known better. I did know better than to think that sort of bitter vengefulness was in your character, but it was easier to believe I had been sadly mistaken in my judgment of you than that — well, no matter."

"No," she said in a small voice. "I have no desire to hurt you in any way."

He flushed. "I am glad of that. Once I knew Wickham was somehow involved, it was only a matter of time before I discovered the truth."

Her mouth went dry. "The truth?"

"That he forced you into this engagement. That you did not wish to marry Drew. That you are paying the price for Wickham's hatred of me. I am very, very sorry for that."

Tears filled her eyes, but she blinked them back. "You are not responsible for his behavior."

"No. If I were, matters would be quite different. But I have done what little I can to compensate for what it has cost you."

"What do you mean?" There was nothing to be done for the opportunity she had lost, and no one to blame for that but herself. If she had not been so blind, if she had only seen earlier who Darcy truly was...

"You are no doubt aware that my father disowned Drew. I have just written a new will, making him my heir, and I also made a settlement on you. Your father has all the details."

"A settlement on me? That is a generous thought, but completely unnecessary. Andrew's living will support us quite well."

"But you deserve better, and your children must lack nothing. Your eldest son will inherit Pemberley someday, so your children must be raised as befits that expectation, which would be impossible on a clergyman's income."

She stared at him. "That is ridiculous! You will marry and have children of your own."

He stopped, gazing intently at her. "No, Elizabeth. I will not marry." His words hung with certainty and meaning.

In shock, she shook her head. "You must marry and have a family." Even if the very thought tore at her insides and made her want sob like an infant.

"I cannot. And this is the right thing to do. Drew was ill-treated by my father, and you have been cheated of a future of your choice by Wickham. It is proper that your son should have Pemberley."

A thread of hysteria wrapped itself around her throat. "No, it is not proper! And Andrew does not want Pemberley, not for himself and not for his children! He can hardly bear to cross the threshold. He would hate it!"

Darcy raised his chin. "It has been the scene of unpleasant memories for him, but that can be forgotten with time."

"No! You do not understand. He would not want to inherit any Darcy property. He hates even bearing the name, which he feels he has no right to."

"Of course he has a right to it, and to Pemberley." Darcy sounded puzzled.

"By law, yes, but that is not enough for him when he feels it is not his by moral right." How had she come to be arguing the very position she had criticized in Andrew?

"My father's disowning of him does not make him any less of a Darcy. He needs to leave that in the past."

She caught her breath in sudden realization. Was it possible they were talking at cross purposes? She could hardly believe it. "You do not know, do you?" she murmured. "He said you did, but you do not."

"What do I not know?"

Horrified, she pressed her gloved hands to her mouth. She did not want to be the one to tell him. Perhaps she should ask him to speak to Andrew, but the very idea of how Andrew might respond to Darcy's questions was worrisome. Surely it would be easier for Darcy to hear the truth from her than from his defensive and possibly hostile brother.

"What is it?" Darcy demanded. "Are you ill? You look pale. Do you wish to sit down?"

"No." She squeezed her eyes shut for a moment. It was easier when she could not see his face. "I am merely taken aback. I thought you were aware of a certain painful circumstance. Andrew told me you already knew. And I am somewhat nervous about being the one to inform you of it."

He frowned. "You need not fear me. Not ever."

"It is not that." She rubbed her forehead beneath the brim of her bonnet. How could she be the one to tell him? It was hardly her place, and what if he hated her for it? "There is no proper way to say this. Andrew is not your father's son."

To her astonishment, he laughed. "That old canard? Are people still whispering that nonsense after all these years? It is a lie, I assure you. Surely Drew cannot believe it."

"He does believe it." She swallowed hard. This was worse than she imagined. "He believes it because it is true."

"It is not true, and I am sorry Drew repeated those old lies to you. You may be certain I will have words with him about it."

"He was not the one who told me. I learned the truth from a letter your mother left behind. I am sorry. I wish I could believe it was a lie."

He shook his head. "How could you have a letter from my mother?"

"She left it with your sister, to be given to Andrew's bride."

"This sounds more like another of Wickham's tricks. It must be a forgery. I assure you, my mother was a true and faithful wife." His voice was harsh.

Oh, how she hated to be the one to disillusion him! If he had been denying the truth his whole life, the idea of it must be excessively painful to him. "If you wish, I will show you the letter, and you may determine for yourself if it is her hand. But it is not only that. Andrew acknowledged it, and I have met the man who...fathered him and saw the resemblance." Her entire body felt tight. Would he be angry at her?

His jaw worked. That he was distressed was clear to see, that he was angry, she guessed, but the hardest part for Elizabeth was fighting back the urge to offer him comfort or at the very least to tell him it was not true. But the cat was out of the bag; she could not unsay what she had said. And she owed it to Andrew to stand for the truth.

Darcy stretched his hand, spreading his fingers and then bringing them back together, again and again, as if the feelings inside him could not be contained. "Are you certain?" The words burst out of his mouth.

Suddenly the terrible tension seemed to leech away. "Yes. I am sorry for it."

He released an explosive breath. "It is not as if no one has ever tried to tell me. But my mother was such a gentle soul, and even now I cannot believe she would —"

Elizabeth could not fight her longing to ease his distress. "We do not know the circumstances. Perhaps it was only the one time."

His mouth twisted. "Even that is difficult to imagine. And you say Drew knows this?"

This was safer territory. "He has always known, ever since he was a child. He said it was common knowledge at Pemberley, but I cannot speak to the truth of that. Something Mr. Wickham said, in hindsight, makes me think he knows."

"Hardly a surprise. If there is a disgraceful secret to be known, Wickham is always the first to discover it," Darcy said with disgust. "So Drew knows this man?" Clearly the word 'father' stuck on his tongue.

Time to tread carefully. "He knows his identity, but refuses to have any contact with him."

"Who is he?" he asked harshly.

She battled with herself. "I do not think Andrew would want me to reveal that. He has paid a high enough price for these secrets from the past."

An arrested expression took over Darcy's face. "Good God, so he has. This explains a great deal. Our father – my father – must have known."

"He never forgave poor Andrew for a sin not of his making."

His countenance darkened. "Will you show me the letter?" he asked tautly.

What had changed? Something had upset him again. "Of course. As soon as we are back at the house."

BREATHE. ALL HE NEEDED to do was to breathe and put one foot in front of the other. Simple, really, apart from the knives in his gut. One knife was the knowledge that his mother had been unfaithful, his parents' perfect marriage anything but. Then there was the knife of humiliation. How many times had people tried to tell him this, and he had refused to listen? How often had he threatened to beat another boy for telling such an arrantly false tale? How pathetic they must have thought him, to be unable to face the truth!

But not as pathetic as the third knife had made him, the biggest, sharpest knife, that Elizabeth's concern had been for *poor Andrew*. Darcy was the one whose family she had just ripped away. Without a moment's notice, she destroyed his memories of his mother and his father, and her thoughts were only for *poor Andrew*.

One foot in front of the other. Breathe in, breathe out.

It had been such a profound, soul-searing relief to learn that Elizabeth had not wanted to marry Drew. Even if Darcy still could never have her, he no longer had to torture himself with wondering if she loved Drew or just despised him. She was only marrying Drew because she had to. He could forgive her for that, and even imagine a future where he could have a special, if platonic, bond with Elizabeth, an acknowledgment of the spiritual connection he had always felt with her. She could be Drew's wife, but her heart could belong to Darcy, and her children could be Darcy's heirs. It was something.

Until she mentioned *poor Andrew* and shattered his fantasies. Blood pounded sickeningly in his ears.

Breathe. Walk. Breathe again. Think of anything except the future where Elizabeth focused her attention and affection on *poor Andrew*.

Chapter 23

Darcy waited in the Longbourn garden while Elizabeth fetched his mother's letter and the locket, his heart aching. Reading the letter tore away the last of his disbelief; he knew his mother's hand too well. He could not let himself consider her words yet, though, not when he still had to face Elizabeth.

When he finally refolded the paper and held it out to her, Elizabeth said hesitantly, "Mr. Bingley is inside, and Jane already told him you were out walking with me. He did not see me when I went inside, but I think he may be hoping to see you."

Just what he did not need – another quarrel with Bingley after all these shocks. But he had survived apologizing to Elizabeth, and she did not appear to hold a grudge, so perhaps Bingley would forgive him, too. More than he would ever forgive himself, since by separating Jane and Bingley, he had doomed his own hopes with Elizabeth. "Shall we go in, then?"

She looked pleased, so at least that was something. "Very well." She tucked the damning letter and locket in her pocket.

Inside, Bingley seemed happy enough to see him, but moved nervously from one foot to another. "I say, Darcy. Are you staying long?"

"No. I merely stopped by to speak with Mr. Bennet, and I hope to reach Cambridge tonight."

"Are you expected there? Because, if not, I would be honored, uh, pleased if you were to join me at Netherfield. You can thrash me at billiards and tell me how your research is coming along." Behind Bingley, Jane Bennet clasped and unclasped her hands.

Darcy wanted nothing more than to run off and hide in his lair to lick his wounds, but he could hardly refuse such an obvious olive branch. "I would be happy to accept your invitation. I am in no particular hurry to reach Cambridge. And I would like to hear more about your upcoming nuptials. I am very happy for both of you."

Jane Bennet gave an obvious, if silent, sigh of relief, and beamed at him.

"I thank you," Bingley said. "I am, of course, the happiest man in the world."

LATER, IN THE CARRIAGE returning to Netherfield, Bingley said, "Is it not odd that it has turned out that Miss Elizabeth will be a sister to both of us?"

Odd was not the word Darcy would use. Tragic, perhaps. "You seem very content with your Miss Bennet."

"Oh, I could not be happier! I know you had some concerns about the connection initially, but since you approved of your own brother marrying Miss Elizabeth, I assume you changed your mind." Bingley sounded nervous. Was he afraid Darcy would disapprove of his engagement?

As if he would not give everything he owned to call Elizabeth his wife! "I did, but that was only when I thought your Miss Bennet was indifferent to you. When there is true affection on both sides, some difference in rank and fortune can be overlooked." If only he had learned that sooner!

Of course, if Lord Matlock had held that position, Darcy's mother would have married her childhood sweetheart, and Darcy might never have been born. At the moment, that felt as if it would have been a mercy, compared to the agony he felt now. He had adored his mother, and it turned out he had never even known her. He had respected his father, who had mistreated Drew. He had fallen hopelessly in love with Elizabeth, discovering her presence was the one thing that lit up his world, and lost her to his brother. Yes, he would rather never have been born.

And during that awful moment when Elizabeth had shown him his mother's locket and the letter, when the shock of the image of his mother's beloved face next to a second Drew shot through him like a musket ball, and he lost the last vestige of hope that somehow, somehow this was all a terrible mistake – just then, as Elizabeth had laid her hand on his arm to comfort him, a current of connection and recognition had reverberated between them. It was real, this bond between the two of them, and she was going to be Drew's wife.

"Are you even listening to me?" Bingley sounded aggrieved.

Darcy passed his hand over his forehead. "Forgive me. I was preoccupied by something Miss Elizabeth told me. It was inexcusably rude of me. Pray, what were you saying?" A year ago he would have given Bingley a set-down instead of admitting his fault. That had been before his pride had cost him Elizabeth.

Mollified, Bingley sat back on the carriage bench. "It was not important. Did everything go well with Miss Elizabeth? You seem very serious, but you were like that at Pemberley, too, as if you no longer enjoyed her company."

Damn it. Bingley was too perceptive. Darcy had best tell just enough of the truth or Bingley would keep picking at him like a terrier. Somehow he managed a light laugh. "You know that I admired her, and not in the way one thinks of one's future sister. My relationship with Drew is tricky enough. I need to find a new way to think about Miss Elizabeth."

"Hah, yes, I see your difficulty," said Bingley with a sage nod. "At least it never went further than admiration. What was that about your business with Mr. Bennet?"

"Just finalizing settlements," Darcy said firmly. Bingley might hear that much from Jane Bennet, anyway. "No, what disturbed me was something else entirely, something about my brother."

"I hope nothing has happened to him."

Suddenly Darcy could not bear to keep it inside. "Nothing new. It appears the reason my father disowned him is because he was another man's child. I never knew."

"Oh, I say, that must have been a surprise," Bingley said. "My mother had several lovers after I was born, and I always wondered who Caroline's true father was. Not that it mattered; no one ever said anything about it. Rather bad form for your father to make a fuss over it."

Darcy gaped at his friend, snapping his mouth shut before the words spilled out. Bingley's parents were not the Darcys of Pemberley. How dare he compare them? Bingley's parents had kept their children at an arm's distance, and Darcy had never heard his friend express the slightest affection for either of them.

But his own parents were different. He had never supposed their marriage to be a love match, that rarity of rarities for their generation, though he had always assumed it was one of mutual respect. But what did that mean? His father did have a mistress, but he never flaunted her in his wife's face, so it had never shocked Darcy. Not as much as learning that his mother had loved another man.

Just as he loved Elizabeth, even after resolving that she was to marry Drew.

It was intolerable.

WHEN THE TWO ELDEST Bennet daughters were finally alone at bedtime, Jane said, "You looked sad at dinner. I hope Mr. Darcy was not difficult with you today."

"We did not quarrel," Elizabeth replied wearily. "In fact, he was much friendlier to me than he was at Pemberley, where it seemed he could not bear to be in my presence."

"The poor man! It must have been so hard for him to tolerate seeing you engaged to his brother. But perhaps his attachment to you has already begun to wane. I hope so, for both of your sakes."

Why had she ever told Jane about Mr. Darcy's proposal at Hunsford? "No, I fear his attachment is as strong as ever. His new amiability is because he has forgiven me for my engagement after learning I was forced into it. Oh, Jane, I hate that my marriage is causing him so much distress!" Her own pain was something she could never admit to Jane or to anyone. Andrew deserved better than that.

"It is sad, Lizzy dearest, but it is not your fault. You did not ask him to fall in love with you."

"No, but I could prevent his misery by breaking my engagement to Andrew." It was the first time she allowed herself even to think of it.

"Oh, no, Lizzy! You would be foolish to give up Andrew. You like him and respect him, and he is a good match for you. And think of the scandal! You would never get a respectable offer again if you jilt him."

Elizabeth's throat tightened. "When I agreed to the engagement, my primary reason was for our family. If I did not marry Andrew, all of you would suffer, especially when our father dies. Now you are engaged, and my scandal would not matter as much."

"But it would matter, and you would end up alone, with no husband or children. You deserve more." Jane lowered her voice. "Besides, Mr. Darcy will recover from his disappointment soon enough. Men always do. In a year or two, it will be behind him and he will fall in love with someone else, but you would have sacrificed your entire future for him. Promise me you will not do it."

"I promise not to do anything without thinking it through, but your point is a good one. He may well recover." But Mr. Hadley still carried Lady Anne Darcy's miniature thirty years after losing her.

And then there were her own feelings. Would she ever recover?

ELIZABETH LOOKED SURPRISED to see him when Darcy arrived at Longbourn the following morning. Or perhaps she was simply shocked at his appearance, the dark circles under his eyes that had been so evident in his mirror. But she still agreed to walk out with him.

As they started down the lane, he said gravely, "Thank you for agreeing to see me."

"Of course. Is there some way I can be of assistance to you?"

Oh, how he wanted to tell her the truth of what he wanted! That he longed to take her hands and have her rest her head on his shoulder as she once had so briefly, at Pemberley. But it could not be. It could never be. Instead, he cleared his throat. "I am in need of advice. I have long known that Drew does not feel he is a part of our family, but I thought it was simply a reaction to being disowned. What you told me yesterday changes my understanding, but not my goal, which is for Drew to rejoin the family and accept his role as a Darcy. The question is how to accomplish that."

Elizabeth seemed to choose her words carefully. "Then this does not alter your view of him?"

"Of course not. He is my brother, and I want him to stop running from his heritage."

She bit her lip. "I hope you can accomplish that. I will support your efforts to the extent that I can."

He turned an intent look on her. "I need your help. How can I get him to leave his resentment behind? You know him better than I do, much as it shames me to admit it."

"I do not know him well."

"And I know him hardly at all. I knew the little boy I played with, but after that, he avoided me. We barely spoke for years until he took the living, and even now he seems very careful of what he says to me. I do not know how to earn his trust."

Elizabeth brushed her fingers against the pointy leaves of the holly bush. Did they prick her delicate fingers through her thin gloves? "Andrew is driven by the desire to help people who are suffering. He likes to be of service. If he felt you needed his assistance or his advice, that might help."

But he did not need Drew's help. And what could he possibly turn to him for advice about? Still, he suspected she was right. "I will see what I can do."

She must have heard the doubt in his voice. "Perhaps you could tell him about the dilemmas you face at Pemberley or with your sister. Do you have concerns about her first Season? Tell him about them. Let him see you as human and uncertain."

He had spent his whole life learning to hide his uncertainties, to be a proper Master of Pemberley, and now she wanted him to admit to them? "It will not come naturally to me." To say the least.

She gave him an arch look. "No, I suppose not. Let me think – you have a plantation in the Indies, do you not, where you freed the slaves? Could you ask his advice on how to, oh, set up a school for the former slaves, or how to encourage them to improve their lot?"

"That is an excellent idea," he said slowly. "It would certainly appeal to Drew. And it would allow us to work together."

"It would also show him how his connection to you could help with his cause."

"That is true. It is a good idea." He paused. Would his next question break this fragile new understanding between them? "I have another question for you, and I fear you will not be pleased with me about it. Yesterday you declined to identify...that man, for understandable reasons. But I am selfishly going to request that you reconsider. There are others I could ask, any of the servants at Pemberley, for example, but I want this entire story left in the past. If word gets out that I am questioning my servants about it, the tale will be on everyone's lips again."

Elizabeth hesitated. "I suppose that is true. May I ask what you plan to do with the information?"

A fair question, and one he had no good answer for, apart from his own desperate need to know the answer. "In all likelihood, nothing. I do not intend to confront the man or anything of the sort. But I assume he and I travel in similar social circles, and I do not wish to somehow draw attention to him because I did not know better."

She nodded. "When I learned the truth, I felt a pretty fool for having had a long conversation with him in complete ignorance. Not that it made the slightest difference, but it is an unpleasant sensation."

"I thank you for your understanding. That is why I am asking you once more if you will reveal his identity, but one word from you will silence me on the subject. I do not wish to make you uncomfortable."

Elizabeth swallowed hard. "I can see your point, but I would not wish Andrew to think I betrayed his secrets."

Darcy dipped his chin in acknowledgment. "I will not tell him you were involved. I think it best if he continues to believe I have known this all along."

"Very well, then," she said slowly. "His name is Hadley. He is a Fitzwilliam cousin."

Darcy's eyebrows shot up. "The barrister? The one with that ridiculous beard?" he asked disbelievingly.

She scowled at him. "That ridiculous beard covers a chin which looks exactly like Andrew's. You saw his portrait."

He blinked. "I had not thought of that. I have met him, of course, but I cannot claim to know him well."

"He wishes he could know you. I spoke to him at the ball at Allston House, before I knew any of this, and he was eager to hear about all of Lady Anne's children. Poor, lonely man." She plucked a leaf from a passing bush. "And poor Andrew."

Her words, which had echoed in his ears the previous night, stung anew. "Poor Andrew! You seem to feel very sorry for him."

Elizabeth began to shred the leaf in sharp, abrupt movements. "I do," she said in a low voice. "He has been cheated again and again. First of his parents' love, then of his home, and now..."

Darcy could feel no pity for Andrew. "And now what? He is marrying you."

She bent her head so he could see nothing but the brim of her bonnet. "He deserves a wife who loves him, one who wants nothing more than to make her life with him, to make him happy. Instead, he is getting me." Her voice was choked.

For a moment he did not understand, and then his breath caught in his throat. Could she possibly be saying what he longed to hear? Dear God, his heart might burst with joy! "Elizabeth," he whispered.

"I know," she cried. "I know I should not. I should never have said anything. Pray forget it, every word of it, I beg you."

"Elizabeth," he said again, his voice stronger now, and replete with all the ardent love that filled him. "Do not ask me to forget this. Whatever else may happen, give me this one moment before I must return to face reality."

She sniffled. "I *hate* reality. And I know, I am the most spoiled, horrible person in the world, weeping and wailing because I cannot have the one particular thing I want more than anything, when in fact I have so much to be thankful for."

She loved him. It was true. And he could do nothing to heal the pain it caused her. "You are the most exquisitely wonderful creature in the world," he said in a low voice, wishing he could pour out his love to her. But she was too loyal to welcome such a thing when she was betrothed to another man, and he loved her even more for that honesty.

Elizabeth took two gasping breaths, and then she turned to gaze at him, her fine eyes shimmering with unshed tears. "We should return to the house."

"Yes, of course." The words came out automatically, but he knew his expression was giving him away. But they both owed Drew better than this, so he tore his eyes away from her and began to walk.

Finally she broke the silence to ask, "When will you be leaving for Pemberley?" Her voice only quavered a little.

At least it was a question he could answer. "Not until after Bingley's wedding. He has asked me to stand up with him."

A sad smile creased her rosy lips. "Then I shall see you there. Perhaps I will write a letter to your sister that you could deliver."

"I would be happy to, though I will be stopping for several days at Cambridge while I am in the vicinity, taking the opportunity to collect new specimens and to discuss my plant research with the natural scientists there."

"That reminds me; I have a confession to make. After you left Pemberley, I took every opportunity to steal into your orangery and visit your jungle. I hope you do not mind. It is the closest I will ever come to my ridiculous childhood dream of exploring unmapped lands." She said it lightly, almost teasingly, but he could sense the sorrow behind her words.

"You are always welcome in the orangery. Had I known you liked it so much, I would have encouraged you to go there. I hope you will return often when you are in Kympton." He only just stopped himself from saying that anything that belonged to him was hers. It was another level of grief, discovering that she was interested in the research no one else cared about. She would have been perfect for him.

"I fear I shall not be able to resist, now that I know such a wondrous place exists, to tap into my childish dreams. My mother would never forgive you if she knew, after all the years she spent convincing me that young ladies should never hold such ideas. Did you know that I used to sneak into my father's library to read the journals of Captain Cook? Now, are you not shocked, sir?" This time she was definitely teasing.

"I am shocked and dismayed, but only that I have missed the opportunity to discuss his explorations with you." How could he have failed to know this side of Elizabeth? She was perfect for him. Perfect. Except that she was marrying Andrew. "Someday I will have to show you my other favorite travel journals in the library at Pemberley." He was pretending, of course, as if some day they could be great friends, despite Andrew. But for the moment, he could not give up the dream.

Chapter 24

"Come along, Darcy! We must not be late to the church!" cried Bingley.

There was still enough time before the wedding was due to start that they could have crawled on their hands and knees the entire way and still been on time, but Darcy allowed himself to be hurried into the carriage.

Bingley was all but bouncing on the bench in anticipation. "I cannot believe this is finally happening! Is my cravat straight?"

"Perfectly. And your wedding will be flawless, as will be your bride." Darcy did not allow the hollowness he felt creep into his voice. It was not Bingley's fault that Darcy had ruined his own chance of experiencing the joy and fulfillment of marrying the woman he loved.

They reached the church with over half an hour to spare. Darcy resigned himself to spending the time keeping Bingley's anxiety under control, but all he could think of was that Elizabeth would soon be there.

He had somehow forced himself to stay away from Longbourn yesterday, knowing it would be too easy to fall back into banter with Elizabeth, and from there to yearning looks and weighted phrases full of hidden longing. He ached for that moment of closeness to her, to once again hear her all but admit her feelings for him, yet it was wrong. It was beyond wrong. Drew was his brother. It would be easy to pretend he and Elizabeth were behaving properly as long as they did not touch each other, but it was untrue.

Was this what his mother had felt for Andrew's father? Had they, too, thought that they could keep their distance while still allowing each other to see their feelings? The very thought made him ill.

And at the same time, he gloried in knowing he would see Elizabeth again soon, and that his body and spirit would come alive in her presence. And it was wrong, wrong, wrong.

It was exactly as he had foreseen when Elizabeth floated down the church aisle towards him. A vague awareness told him that her sister, the true bride, walked on her father's arm behind her. All he could see was Elizabeth, in her finest dress, walking to meet him at the altar, and his heart pounded in protest because it was only a shadow of the reality he longed for.

Bingley stood directly in front of the altar, in the place that should be Darcy's. Jane Bennet would be beside him soon, and the clergyman would read the marriage lines over them, not for Elizabeth and Darcy. The marriage he had once sought to prevent would be consummated tonight, but he would never have the woman he loved. Instead Drew would forever stand between them.

But now Elizabeth took her place opposite him, her eyes lowered and her cheeks becomingly flushed. Was it due to being in front of the congregation or because of his presence?

For a moment she was hidden behind her father and sister as they passed. Then he drank in the sight of her like a man dying of thirst, so caught up in her presence that the Rector's voice startled him as he intoned, "Dearly beloved, we are gathered together in the sight of God..."

The familiar words of the wedding ceremony washed over him, but all he was conscious of was the woman opposite him.

Elizabeth, a lacy handkerchief clutched in her hand, had turned her attention to the bridegroom. Darcy, captivated by a chestnut ringlet that danced over her cheekbone in the sunlight streaming through the tall church windows, was barely aware of them. Would that ringlet be silky to his touch? Would it spring back if he tugged it? The oft-imagined image of Elizabeth with her dark hair loose around her shoulders and a teasing light in her eyes rose before him, leading to a fierce pulse of desire.

Damn it, what was wrong with him? He was in church, and she was engaged to his brother, but he could not bring himself to stop believing that she was his.

The rector turned to Bingley. "Wilt thou have this woman to thy wedded wife, to live together after God's ordinance in the holy estate of matrimony? Wilt thou love her, comfort her, honor, and keep her in sickness and in health; and, forsaking all others, keep thee only unto her, so long as ye both shall live?"

Yes. Yes, he would. Forever. The thought made him half-dizzy as he stared at Elizabeth, and now she gazed back at him, her heart in her eyes, as the rector asked Jane the same question. Was she feeling what he was?

He could not look away from her, even as the minister had Bingley and Jane Bennet take hands. The bond tying him to Elizabeth felt so real that it was astonishing that the congregation could not see it.

Then Bingley spoke, and the words echoed in Darcy's head, but the names were changed. *I, Fitzwilliam, take thee, Elizabeth, to my wedded wife, to have and to hold from this day forward, for better, for worse, for richer, for poorer, in sickness and in health, to love and to cherish, till death us do part, according to God's holy ordinance; and thereto I plight thee my troth.* Yes. Yes.

And she continued to watch him, tears spilling out of her fine eyes, as Jane made her response, and Darcy heard in his heart Elizabeth's musical tones saying the same to him.

He could not reach out to her, could never reach out and put a ring upon her finger, never, not ever. But he said the words in his heart. *With this ring I thee wed, with my body I thee worship, and with all my worldly goods I thee endow: in the name of the Father, and of the Son, and of the Holy Ghost. Amen.*

The rector intoned, "Let us pray."

A frantic madness seemed to fill his mind. Darcy needed all the prayers in the world, far more than that old man holding the Book of Common Prayer and his congregation could provide. What had he done? Pledging himself to Elizabeth in his heart, right there in the sight of God in front of the altar? She was not his, would never be his. Yet he knew, down to his very bones, that the vows he had silently made were true, and that he could never forget them. How could something that was so very, very wrong feel so right?

Had his mother once made silent vows to Hadley, even as she married Darcy's father?

For a moment, he feared he would be ill, right there in the church, beside the newlywed couple. He was supposed to be celebrating the most joyous day of their lives, and instead he was sinning grievously in his heart.

Elizabeth was the one who broke the gaze between them, and it was almost a relief. Almost. He had to close his own eyes, to look into himself and remember who he was, and who he needed to be.

There could be no repetition of history. He had to stop this, and he had to do it now.

How could Elizabeth have a chance to learn to love Drew when Darcy was always in the background, his heart at her feet? He knew better than to think he could learn to stop loving her; he had tried with all his might after Hunsford, and today his love for her was even deeper than it had been that night, when he had thought it the most powerful feeling he had ever experienced.

He was the Master of Pemberley, damn it, and he had a responsibility to his family, to the people he loved. If he truly cared for Drew, if he truly loved Elizabeth, then there was only one solution. He had to leave.

Yes, leave Pemberley, leave Elizabeth, leave Drew. Give them a chance to grow together in affection, a chance for this unspoken, illicit passion to fade. If there was a shred of decency still left in him, it was the only thing to do.

Would London be far enough? He would still see them periodically then. They would expect him at Pemberley for Christmas, and Drew had spoken of visiting his London friends. No, moving to London would not fix anything. It would just mean allowing his feelings to build for months as he waited to see her again. It had to be a complete separation. He did not know how, but he had to find a way.

HURRICANE TOSSED HIS head when Darcy turned off the main road to Pemberley. He had gone ahead of the carriage carrying Wilkins and his luggage, and the ride had been long enough to tire even the stalwart Hurricane. Darcy leaned forward to pat his neck. "Not long now," he told the horse. "Just a brief stop in Kympton, and then home to your stable."

Drew would not be expecting him, but Darcy needed to have this conversation before he reached Pemberley and had to explain his new plans to Georgiana. He hoped Drew would not be out. He had been dreading this conversation since leaving Cambridge, and having to wait for his brother to return would not help. Fortunately, the maid said he was at home and showed him into Drew's study.

His brother's immediate reaction to his arrival was to look wary, an expression Darcy was altogether too familiar with. "Fitzwilliam, I had not heard you were back."

"Just now arriving. I have not yet been to Pemberley. I stopped here on the way in the hope of speaking to you about my plans."

"Plans?" The wary look redoubled into a flat-out distrustful expression.

"Yes. You may know that years ago, I was going to take part in a scientific expedition to Peru, but I had to withdraw because our father refused his permission, and then because of his apoplexy. When I stopped by Cambridge to visit my old tutor on my way home, I learned they are planning a second voyage to depart in the spring, this one to Surinam, and they have asked me to join them." He tried to sound enthusiastic. And he was, in a way; he knew he would enjoy being among fellow naturalists and the discoveries he would make, and it was preferable to hiding out on the continent or any of the other options for taking himself out of the way for a long period of time. But it was hard to feel excited about anything when it meant leaving Elizabeth behind.

Drew furrowed his brows. "How long would you be gone?"

"Three years, which is why I could not do it without your support." Three years away from Pemberley, but it was the right thing to do. Three years should be long enough for Elizabeth to learn to love Drew, and for Darcy to learn to live without her.

"My support? What have I to do with it?"

"Would you be willing to act as Georgiana's guardian while I am gone?" He had planned this discussion carefully, and this was the part he thought Drew would agree to most easily.

Drew considered this. "I suppose I could, if you are certain you wish me to."

"Who else but her brother? I doubt it would be an onerous task, especially since Georgiana is so fond of Miss Elizabeth Bennet. Richard Fitzwilliam is also her guardian, but I would feel better if she were directly under your care, and I am certain she would far prefer it."

"You will need to tell me more of what would be involved. Would you want her to live with me?"

"That would be up to you. She had her own household in London, and there is no reason she could not continue that if you choose."

"You do not have a preference?" Drew sounded surprised.

"If you are to be her guardian, it must be your choice. Also, your situation is different from mine, since you will be married by the time I leave." A sharp pang tightened his chest. "People can look askance at a young girl living alone with her much older unmarried brother, hence her current situation. But you should decide what works best for you."

Drew examined this comment as if looking for a trap in it. "Very well. I am willing to take on that role if it will assist you."

"I appreciate it." Darcy drew in a deep breath. This was the difficult part, but if he wanted Drew to move past his distaste for Pemberley, it was crucial. "There is one more thing. My steward at Pemberley is competent for the day-to-day management of the estate, but he must have someone to oversee him for unusual situations where time may be of the essence. May I tell him he can approach you with any urgent questions?"

Drew's eyes narrowed. "I know nothing about estate management or Pemberley's needs."

"This would require mostly common sense and the ability to speak for me. He can write to me with long-term questions, but if, say, there should be an epidemic in the village, or an unusually bad harvest, he would need permission to offer assistance to those in need." That should appeal to Drew's desire to relieve suffering.

His brother looked tempted, but he bit his lip. "It would not be appropriate for me to make decisions at Pemberley."

Now. It was time. "Is this because of all that foolishness about our mother?"

Drew scowled and jerked his head in an approximation of a nod, but he did not meet Darcy's eyes.

"Forgive me, but it is past time to let go of all that nonsense," Darcy said. "My father was irrational and shortsighted to allow it to affect his behavior rather than ignoring it."

"It is the truth," Drew half-snarled, his shoulders hunched.

"The truth is that you are my brother, and the law says you are a Darcy. If you refuse to play the role of a Darcy, you will keep the scandal alive. For the sake of your future children, if nothing else, we must let it remain in the past."

"My children? What have they to do with it?"

"Everything. If you continue to remind people of the scandal, how will that affect the marriage prospects of your daughters? Do you want your sons to be not-quite-Darcys? Whereas if you stand in for me when I am away, accepting the mantle of being a Darcy, it will all be forgotten soon enough. My father is dead. You have nothing to gain by continuing to insist you want nothing to do with the Darcy heritage, and a great deal to lose."

"But the Darcy heritage is not mine by right."

"I beg to differ. Thirty years ago, Pemberley was encumbered with debt and in poor condition. My father married our mother for her enormous dowry. All that money was spent paying off Pemberley's debts and investing in the estate. Surely you would not deny that heritage is yours. And your children's."

"No," Drew said slowly, drawing out the word. "But why do you care?"

"Because you are my brother, and, just as you wish to right the wrongs of the slave trade, I wish to right the wrongs my father committed. And, yes, it would be of benefit to me to be able to rely on you to handle Pemberley while I am away, but beyond that, I want our family back the way it was before my father used you as a weapon to punish our mother. Do you remember when we would run around the halls at Pemberley and laugh? I want your children to be part of my family. Our mother made a mistake one night many years ago, and I want that night to stop ruling our present." He had not meant to say that much, but it had burst out.

"If it was only one night, and I have no reason to believe that. It was still adultery, no matter how little it troubles you."

"Oh, it troubles me. I hate the thought of it. But it was not your fault. Why should I reject you for it when my father always kept a mistress, even when he was a newlywed? When he had his own brother's supposed bastard educated alongside me? My father had no right to throw stones."

"I suppose not." But he looked unconvinced.

Recalling the letter Elizabeth had shown him, he plunged on. "Not to mention his cruelty to our mother. Do you remember how heartbroken she was after every still-birth or baby who died after a month or two? Eight of them, one after another, and only you and Georgiana survived. And then, because of him, she lost you, too. She would want you to move forward. Let me honor her memory by bringing you back into the family where you have always deserved to be."

Drew slowly rubbed his forehead. "I will consider it," he said reluctantly.

"I hope you will, for my own sake. The expedition five years ago would have been the culmination of everything I had worked for, and I had to give it up because our father refused to allow it. I have always regretted it. This is my second chance, but I cannot do it without your help." If that did not convince him, nothing would.

His brother finally looked up. "Very well. I will do it, for your sake."

Chapter 25

A fortnight later, a letter from Andrew arrived for Elizabeth. It was hardly a surprise; he had written weekly since his return to Derbyshire. Usually his missives were relatively brief descriptions of local events, his sermon, and the restoration of the house. This letter, though, was three pages long and closely written.

Elizabeth's eyebrows rose as she finished the first page, and she reread the last paragraph twice.

Mary said, "I hope nothing is the matter."

She shook her head slowly. "Not at all; only a surprise. His aunt in Bath wishes to meet me, so I am invited to go there for a fortnight." It would be odd enough, given that he had never so much as mentioned this aunt to her, but that was only part of the strangeness in the letter. Particularly odd was the final section:

The importance of this journey, though, lies in another matter, one which I am reluctant to commit to paper. You may perchance recall an unexpected caller at the parsonage, a young lady dressed in mourning; and should you be willing to undertake this journey, it would suffice to resolve some of the problems which beset her.

Well, that was mysterious, but she loved to travel and had always wished to see Bath, and if it would help Lady Frederica, Elizabeth would be happy to take that as an excuse. "Mama, may I go? He says he will send a carriage for me, and he suggests I bring Mary as my chaperone. We would be lodging at his aunt's house in Bath, along with Miss Darcy and their cousin, Lady Frederica Fitzwilliam. Andrew will stay at a hotel for propriety's sake." There was no mention of Darcy in the letter, so it should be safe enough for her.

"Of course you should go," cried Mrs. Bennet, "and you must take very great care to put Mary in the way of some of the wealthy gentlemen in Bath. Why, it could be an excellent place to catch a husband!"

Mary said primly, "I have no interest in husband-hunting, but I would be very glad of the opportunity to see Georgiana and Andrew again."

"Foolish girl, there is no reason you cannot do both!" Mrs. Bennet fanned herself furiously.

Elizabeth said soothingly, "I imagine we will have many opportunities to make new acquaintances in Bath. What a happy thing that Jane gave Mary so many of her old dresses when she purchased her wedding clothes! Mary will certainly look her best."

Mrs. Bennet's eyes widened. "Quite right, Lizzy! I will check them this minute. Perhaps a little extra lace might help, or some fresh ribbons to bring them up to the latest fashions." She bustled from the room.

"But I do not care about looking fashionable," Mary called after her.

Elizabeth ostentatiously put a finger to her lips. "Shh. Let her have her dreams. This way she will allow you to go with me, whereas if she thinks you will not make the most of the opportunity to find a husband, she will insist on sending Kitty in your place."

Mary's eyes grew round. "But would you not rather have Kitty?"

Shaking her head with a smile, Elizabeth said, "Have you not noticed that I am spending more time in your company now? I admit that I was less than fond of your Fordyce's Sermons stage, but I enjoy hearing about what you are learning from the books Andrew recommended for you. And he did particularly request you as my chaperone."

Her sister's cheeks flushed. "You are so fortunate to have caught the interest of such an excellent man. Jane's husband has wealth and good humor, but he is nothing to Andrew, who is so wise, good, and generous. And thoughtful – it was very kind of him to think of me."

It had indeed been considerate of Andrew to invite Mary, who would never otherwise have received such an opportunity. Elizabeth needed to remember Andrew's virtues rather than focus on his occasional testiness and rigidity. But deep inside, she knew that the real problem lay with her, not him. She could have learned to be happy with Andrew if she had never seen Darcy again. Somehow she needed to drown those inappropriate feelings he induced in her.

Perhaps this journey to Bath would be her chance to draw closer to Andrew. A fortnight in his company without Darcy's presence might be just what she needed to convince her recalcitrant heart to cleave to Andrew.

ELIZABETH'S DETERMINATION not to think of Darcy on her journey to Bath did not outlast the arrival of the carriage at Longbourn. One look at the elegant lines of it and the liveried coachman and footman was enough to convince her that Darcy, rather than Andrew, was footing the bill for this private transportation. No wonder Andrew had refused her offer that she and Mary could travel by public stagecoach!

Darcy would no doubt say this was his way of helping Lady Frederica, although Elizabeth was still baffled as to how her travels could be of assistance to that lady's dilemma. But she could not dismiss the thought that he had done it for her.

There was altogether too much time to think during the two days' journey. The scenery of the Berkshire Downs was a pleasant novelty, and stopping at a coaching inn for the night was a reminder of her journey to Derbyshire with the Gardiners. Still, she found Darcy's dark eyes rising before her imagination far more often than Andrew's green ones.

They reached Bath late on the second day, traveling down a steep hill into a confection of modern buildings built of matching, honey-colored stone. Elizabeth and Mary both gaped out the windows at the sights moving past them until the carriage climbed another hill and pulled to a halt outside a terraced townhouse overlooking a circular common garden.

As the footman handed them out, Elizabeth shaded her eyes as she looked up at the tall buildings forming a circle around her. "Oh, my. I do believe we are in the fashionable part of town."

"Indeed you are!" It was Andrew's voice, with a laugh underneath it. "This is the Royal Circus, one of the finest addresses. Welcome to Bath, my dear."

"Good heavens, where did you spring from?" Elizabeth exclaimed.

"I was loitering in the garden, hoping to catch you before you arrived." He took the hand she belatedly offered and kissed it lightly. "I hope your journey went well. Miss Mary, I am so glad you could join us."

"I thank you for the invitation," Mary said gravely.

Elizabeth smiled at Andrew, pleased to see him in such good spirits despite the difficulty of their last meeting. "The carriage you sent was very comfortable, and the roads were good."

"It was Darcy's doing. The carriage, not the roads, that is," he said. "If you are not too fatigued, there is, er, something nearby I would very much like to show you before we go inside." Andrew was as poor at making excuses as his brother.

"I would be happy for a little exercise after sitting in the carriage all day. Do you not agree, Mary?"

"Indeed so," Mary said with an air of confusion.

"Very good." Andrew instructed the footman to carry their trunks inside, and then offered Elizabeth his arm. "If you will be so kind as to join me, I will show you the most fashionable address of all, the Royal Crescent."

"I have seen an engraving of it," said Elizabeth, trying to hide her curiosity at his unusual behavior.

As he steered her down one of the other streets leading into the Circus, Mary trailing behind them, he said quietly, "Thank you for indulging me. There are certain explanations I must make where the servants cannot overhear, as several of them are in the pay of Lord Matlock."

"Just as at Pemberley?" Elizabeth asked.

"It is a habit of his, and it is important that no word of Lady Frederica's ulterior motives in coming here should reach him."

"That is something I am quite curious about myself! How does my presence in Bath help Lady Frederica?"

"Ah, yes. It is rather complicated, but Matlock suspected Frederica was planning something and would not let her go to Pemberley because he does not trust my brother. He said that if she wished a change of scene, her only option was to stay with our aunt, Lady Margaret, here in Bath. She is a veritable Gorgon when it comes to propriety. Frederica concocted the plan of marrying secretly here. She still wants me to attend her wedding, though, so I needed an excuse to come to Bath. That was where you came into it, since my aunt had already insisted on an introduction when she heard of my engagement. I had planned to ignore it, as I have ignored every other demand she has made of me for years, but in this case, it served my purpose. But the wedding must remain a secret from Lady Margaret."

"I see. I assume, then, that I should pretend never to have met Lady Frederica?"

He pursed his lips. "I had not thought of it, but your acquaintance would be hard to explain. Not that you are likely to have much opportunity to explain anything; Lady Margaret dominates every conversation. Fortunately, she is unable to leave the house owing to her gout, and we have planned outings for every day. I hope she will not prove too difficult a hostess."

Elizabeth said, "I was able to tolerate her sister, Lady Catherine de Bourgh, well enough, so I imagine I can manage Lady Margaret."

Nodding, he said, "You know what you are facing, then. They are two peas in a pod."

"When is Lady Frederica's wedding to take place?"

"That is uncertain. Farleigh's family was supposed to meet us here, but his father took a chill and has been delayed." He glanced back at Mary, still following behind them to give them privacy, and said in a lower voice, "There is another matter of which you should be aware. This one is not secret, but I would not wish you to be taken by surprise should Georgiana mention it."

Tilting her head in curiosity, Elizabeth asked, "What is that?"

"I will be taking over as her guardian while my brother is away, and she has asked if she could live with us during that time. Naturally, I told her I would have to discuss it with you, especially as it will be for some years. She is anxious for an answer and may press you on it, although I have asked her not to do so."

Elizabeth's breath caught in her throat. "Your brother is leaving?"

"On a scientific expedition to South America, of all things! At first I thought it was just a whim and he would change his mind, but it seems he is determined," Andrew said with a laugh. "Do not ask me why; I would never wish to do such a thing!"

The terraced houses on each side of the street seemed to crowd in on Elizabeth, her vision growing momentarily dark. Darcy was going away? Her heart pounded. She had no need to ask his reasons; it was because of her. Darcy was leaving his home and his family for years because she was marrying Andrew. Her stomach squeezed tight.

Andrew must have seen something in her expression. "If you object to Georgiana living with us, you need only say so. I have made no promises."

She tried to gather her wits. "No, I was simply taken by surprise, and there is much to consider." But her heart ached anew.

After they had spent a few minutes admiring the sweeping arc of Palladian townhouses that constituted the Royal Crescent, Andrew said, "Lady Margaret is likely wondering what I have done with you, so I suppose we should go back."

Elizabeth agreed, and they returned down Brock Street to the Circus where a stuffy butler showed them into an over-decorated parlor. An elderly lady swathed in a ridiculous amount of black lace sat in a large gilded chair elevated above the rest of the room as if it were a throne. "It is about time, young man!" she snapped at Andrew. "Have you no sense of proper respect?"

But Elizabeth could spare no thought for the tirade that would no doubt be directed towards her at any moment, for just behind Lady Margaret sat Fitzwilliam Darcy.

"ANYONE IN BATH WITH any pretension to fashion must go to the Pump Room each morning," Lady Frederica told Elizabeth the next morning as they walked down the steep hill into the center of Bath, accompanied by Andrew. "It is the center of Bath society."

Elizabeth decided not to mention that Darcy certainly had pretensions to fashion, and had chosen to remain behind with Georgiana and Mary. "But what does one do there?" Elizabeth asked.

Lady Frederica waved her hand. "Speak to those you are acquainted with, and be introduced to those you are not. Promenade up and down the room. In theory, drink the mineral water, but I do not advise it if you are not ill. The taste is unspeakable." She gave a little shudder.

"It is much like the fashionable hour in Hyde Park," said Andrew. "One goes to see and to be seen, rather than to do anything."

Not that she had ever been to the fashionable hour at Hyde Park, but this was not the moment to mention that. "I will try not to disgrace you," she said with a laugh.

Lady Frederica said briskly, "Fear not, you will all be very popular. Newcomers always are. We will be meeting my Evan there, and he will make a point of flirting with you. It is all part of the plan to keep anyone from suspecting my attachment to him."

Clearly Lady Frederica had it all planned out, so Elizabeth said, "How delightful! What could be better than the opportunity to flirt with a fine gentleman with absolutely no concern for any consequences. Andrew, I do hope you will not be jealous," she teased.

His mouth quirked. "I will manage to control myself. I do trust you, after all."

Elizabeth managed a smile, but it was false. She did not deserve Andrew's trust, not when her heart was full of his brother.

The Pump Room proved to be a large room lined with columns and full of elegantly dressed people, many of them elderly, some seated while others strolled up and down. A gallery at one end held musicians who played softly enough to permit conversation, and a marble vase along one wall served as a fountain for the famous waters.

A handsome, dark-haired young man strolled up to them as soon as they entered the room. From the way Lady Frederica's expression softened on spotting him, Elizabeth suspected this must be her forbidden suitor. He greeted Andrew by name and bowed to Lady Frederica before saying, "I say, dare I beg the favor of an introduction to this lovely young lady?"

Lady Frederica's lips settled in a line. "Miss Bennet, may I present Mr. Farleigh of Edington Manor? Mr. Farleigh, Miss Bennet of Longbourn in Hertfordshire."

Elizabeth offered him her hand with a smile. "A pleasure, Mr. Farleigh."

He ostentatiously kissed her hand, which would have been embarrassing had it not been for the silent amusement in his eyes. "The pleasure is all mine. Would you care to promenade the room with me?"

She gave a laughing half-glance at Andrew before assenting. As they set off down the room, leaving Andrew and Lady Frederica behind, Mr. Farleigh said softly, "I thank you. Once we have been seen together by a number of people, it will be safe to return to the others."

"I am at your disposal, sir." She fluttered her eyelashes, attempting to put on a good show of flirtation.

"You are most kind." As they walked, he nodded to a few people they passed, introduced her to an elderly gentleman who appeared to be mostly deaf and called her Miss Pennet, and pointed out the Master of Ceremonies. Then he seemed to spot someone at the side of the room and murmured, "Just the thing. One of Matlock's relations. It will be perfect for her to see you with me." He led Elizabeth to a small table where an older lady with claw-like fingers sat in a Bath chair. "Mrs. Todd, may I have the honor of presenting Miss Bennet to your acquaintance? She is a new visitor and knows almost no one."

"Charmed, Miss Bennet. Do sit down, I pray you, or I shall end up with a crick in my neck. Mr. Farleigh, I hope you are well."

"How can I be aught but well when I have the good fortune of escorting a lovely lady? Dare I hope that the waters have helped your arthritis?" asked Mr. Farleigh.

"The hot baths have provided some relief, I thank you. I am accustomed to warmer climes, and I feel the cold English air in my bones."

"Ah, yes. Miss Bennet, Mrs. Todd lived in Jamaica until recently, and never tires of telling us how much she misses the palm trees."

The older woman said, "Of course, when I was there, I missed our English chestnuts just as much. I am never satisfied!"

"I have heard Jamaica is very beautiful," said Elizabeth diplomatically, wondering how to extract herself before Andrew caught up to them. A well-to-do person from Jamaica almost certainly had connections in the slave trade, even if they were not an outright slaveowner. A relative of Lord Matlock's was most likely the latter.

"Incomparably so," said Mrs. Todd. "Were it not for the ongoing tragedy of slavery, it would be Paradise."

Elizabeth breathed a silent sigh of relief. "I can only imagine. Simply visiting Bath is a tremendous adventure for me; I have never been to this part of England before."

That gave Mrs. Todd the opportunity to ask her about Longbourn, and they chatted for several minutes until the older lady became suddenly silent, staring over Elizabeth's shoulder with an arrested expression.

Instinctively Elizabeth looked up to see Andrew standing behind her, wearing a questioning look. If Mrs. Todd was a connection of Lord Matlock's, he would already know her, unless she had been in Jamaica all his life, but it was not Elizabeth's place to offer an introduction.

Mrs. Todd, sounding a little hesitant, said, "Miss Bennet, would you be so kind as to introduce me to your friend?"

"Of course. May I present Mr. Andrew Darcy, the vicar of Kympton in Derbyshire, to your acquaintance? Andrew, this is Mrs. Todd."

"Derbyshire...Are you a connection of Mr. Darcy of Pemberley, then?" asked Mrs. Todd.

Andrew bowed. "His brother." He said it without any of the coldness she might have expected a few months ago. Perhaps they had indeed made progress.

Mrs. Todd smiled, with a sudden look of understanding. "And here is *my* brother, whom I suspect you may already know."

Elizabeth's welcoming smile faded as she recognized the familiar, bearded face as Mr. Hadley. Andrew's father. Oh, dear! No wonder Mrs. Todd had been staring at Andrew, given the strength of his resemblance to her brother in his younger days. Elizabeth ought to have realized there could be a connection when Mr. Farleigh had said Mrs. Todd was related to Lord Matlock.

Andrew blanched. Then he said abruptly, "Pray excuse me." Without even a bow, he stalked off, weaving between several strolling parties, heading towards the door.

Elizabeth forced herself not to stare after him. She had to find a way to distract them from his behavior. With a forced smile, she said, "Why, Mr. Hadley, this is a surprise!"

"You know each other?" Mr. Farleigh asked, clearly trying to smooth over Andrew's odd behavior.

"Yes, I danced with him at a ball in Derbyshire this summer. What a small world this is!"

Tension lined Mr. Hadley's eyes, and his hand gripped the back of a chair so hard that his gloves were drawn tight. "Miss Bennet, it is an unexpected pleasure. And Farleigh, good to see you again."

Mrs. Todd said slowly, "That young man, Mr. Andrew Darcy. I hope he is not unwell."

Elizabeth said lightly, "Not at all. He had mentioned earlier that he might have to leave on an urgent errand." Of course, Mr. Farleigh and Mrs. Todd knew perfectly well that Andrew would not have left without saying something, but it was the best she could do on the spur of the moment. "Mr. Hadley, I had not expected to see you in Bath." It was a rather forward demand for information, but she needed to change the conversation.

Mr. Hadley released the poor tortured chair and moved his hand to rest on Mrs. Todd's shoulder, no doubt giving a message of his own. "I had not expected to make the journey here when last we met, but when my dear sister's doctor recommended that she take the waters, I could not permit her to come alone." He leaned down and said something in Mrs. Todd's ear, but Elizabeth could not make it out over the hum of conversation and music. Then he turned to her and bowed. "Miss Bennet, dare I hope you might honor me with your company for a turn about the room?"

Surprised, Elizabeth said, "It would be my pleasure, sir." She took the arm he offered and they set off down the length of the Pump Room, following many other parading groups. Once again, he had singled her out, and this time she knew why.

"Well, Miss Bennet, I apologize if inviting you to walk with me has put you in a difficult position," he said as they reached a gap in the crowd. "Am I to understand from your reaction upon seeing me that you know rather more about me than you did when we first met?"

Conscious of the need for propriety, she said carefully, "I have learned something more about your connection to the Darcy family, yes."

"Then I can only be grateful you are willing to converse with me," he said, with a note of sadness. "I did not seek out this private conversation –

inasmuch as any conversation here can be private – in order to embarrass you, but rather to ask your assistance in preventing even more uncomfortable meetings. I am well aware that your betrothed prefers to avoid my presence. I left Derbyshire after the ball at Allston House for that very reason. Unfortunately, as I am in Bath for my sister's sake, I am unable to depart at present, but if there is some way in which I can be informed of his plans, I will do my utmost to avoid those places where he intends to be."

That was unexpected. She drew back a little. "You wish to avoid him?"

His cheeks paled. "No, not at all, but my wishes are of no importance in this matter. He wishes to avoid me, and, as that is the only thing I am permitted to do for his sake, I will do my best to honor his choice."

Her heart went out to the old man, whose adultery with Lady Anne Darcy had brought him such pain. "I see," she said carefully.

He glanced to the group of elderly ladies whose promenade was rapidly bringing them within eavesdropping distance. "I will be quick, then. He ought to be able to come and go here in Bath without having to worry about my presence. Pray tell him I will pretend to have a slight malady which will keep me indoors."

"You should not have to take such measures," she objected.

He held a finger to his lips as one of the elderly ladies approached him to inquire about his sister's health, barely disguising her curiosity about the young woman on his arm. No sooner had she left than an old gentleman took her place.

It was some time before she was alone with Mr. Hadley again, or at least as alone as two people could be in the crowded Pump Room, and now she was certain there was more to his tale than she knew. Seizing her moment, she said, "If you would be willing, I would be glad of an opportunity to discuss this further in a more private location."

His eyes widened. "I am always at your service. Always. Tell me when and where, and I will be there."

No, she was not mistaken. He was desperate for any possible connection to Andrew. "I do not know Bath well. A park, perhaps, early in the morning, before the social whirl begins?"

He nodded. "Where are you staying?"

"In the Circus."

"The Gravel Walk, then, would be convenient to you, and is relatively private. Anyone can direct you there. I can be there tomorrow morning if you wish."

Yes, an early morning walk would be the easiest time to get away. "I will join you if I can. Should something prevent me, how may I contact you?"

He pulled out a silver calling card case and gave her one. "My lodgings are on Great Pulteney Street."

She slipped the card into her reticule just as Lady Frederica and Mr. Farleigh approached them. "I thank you."

Chapter 26

"Where do you suppose Andrew went?" Lady Frederica asked as they prepared to leave the Pump Room. Elizabeth had been wondering the same thing herself.

"No doubt he walked back to his hotel," Mr. Farleigh said, but from the odd look he gave Elizabeth, she wondered how much he knew.

Returning to the hotel would have been sensible if Andrew had wanted to avoid notice, but Elizabeth remembered how he had waited in the carriage after the Allston House ball, as if to draw attention to his sudden departure. And, indeed, as she stepped outside, she spotted him sitting on a bench in the Abbey churchyard.

Andrew rose and approached them, his expression tight as if he expected trouble. "Are you done, then?"

Lady Frederica, forthright as always, asked, "Why did you leave like that, Andrew?"

He flushed. "There was someone I did not wish to see."

Lady Frederica raised her brows, as if she found this reason inadequate. Then she gave a faint shrug. "I prefer to leave old scandals in the past, where they belong."

Elizabeth winced, guessing Andrew would be hurt by her reaction. "Andrew, the Abbey looks most impressive. Might I impose upon you to explore it with me?"

After a quick glare at Lady Frederica, Andrew offered her his arm. "I would be happy to do so, my dear, if Farleigh would be kind enough to see Lady Frederica back to the house."

Mr. Farleigh cocked an amused eyebrow. "Nothing could make me happier, as you know well. Unless, of course, I can manage to lose our way en route."

Elizabeth, aware of how tense Andrew was, squeezed his arm gently as they strolled towards the towering Gothic splendor before them.

As they approached the Abbey entrance, he pointed to the sides of the archway and said flatly, "Those are the famous carvings of angels ascending to heaven. I am afraid that exhausts my knowledge of the Abbey. I have not visited Bath since I was a child, and I was more interested in running around in the Parade Grounds than in architecture, not that I was permitted to do so for long."

Oh, yes, he was deep in his grievances over the past.

"Look at the detail on those carvings!" she cried. "Each angel has a different face, and how realistic their bodies seem as they clamber up! Oh, but are some clambering down? That looks quite uncomfortable. Yes, it is just like Jacob's ladder in the Bible, but I must say I have never quite understood why some of those angels were descending, either." There, that should give him an opening to speak on the subject of theology. And the carvings truly were fascinating.

"There are many theories. Some say they were descending to help us. From the look of suffering on that one face, it looks more as if he is being punished for his sins." His voice was too even. "Speaking of sinners, did *he* approach you again?"

"He asked me to walk with him."

His lips thinned. "I hope you refused."

She took a breath. Would he be angry? "I felt it wisest to treat him as I would any other casual acquaintance. Doing otherwise risks drawing more attention to a scandal everyone has long since forgotten. So I accepted."

He scowled. "You knew I would not wish you to speak to him."

As if that should be her sole motivation! "I had guessed as much, but I have not yet vowed to obey you, and until that time, I will do what I think is right. Could you not see that Lady Frederica had forgotten you had any connection to him until you refused to be in the room with him? Someday we will have children, and I would rather not have a scandal hanging over their heads. Therefore, I will treat him exactly as I would any other distant relative of your mother's." Would he hear her silent criticism of his own behavior?

He looked furious. "It is not only a matter of gossip. He is an adulterer. I will not be in his presence, nor will I have you associate with him."

Her temper began to rise. First he had left her to smooth over his abrupt departure, and now this! "If that were your true reason, you would never go into the Pump Room or any other public place at all. You know as well as I do that half of the gentleman there are adulterers, and many of the ladies, too. Much as we may dislike it, it is a fact of our society. But you need not worry about encountering him; he told me that he knew his presence made you uncomfortable, and so he would claim an illness which would permit him to remain indoors during our stay here."

Andrew looked astonished, but then the pinched look returned to his brow. "You see, he knows full well that he is not fit company for decent people."

Elizabeth waited several seconds before deeming herself calm enough to respond. "Not at all. I think he was merely concerned for your comfort."

Her betrothed snorted his disagreement. "This is a personal matter. I will not tolerate his presence, nor for you to have any connection to him."

She dug her fingernails into her palm, trying to regain control. How she despised being told what to do without a rational explanation! This was the sort of behavior she would have expected from the proud Mr. Darcy she had first known in Meryton, not from Andrew, whom she would all too soon be vowing to love and obey.

It struck her then. Mr. Darcy had in fact done exactly the same thing, warning her to stay away from Wickham, but without giving her reason beyond that he felt she should do so. Naturally, she had disregarded his warning and prided herself in pursuing Wickham's friendship, attributing Darcy's dislike of him to snobbery. But she had been wrong, oh, so very wrong, allowing her prejudice to blind her.

In hindsight, it was perfectly clear why Darcy had not given his reasons at the time. Wickham had injured him and his sister in deeply personal ways, with behavior far worse than anything Elizabeth could have imagined then. Could this be a similar situation, where Elizabeth allowed Mr. Hadley's pleasant manners to charm her into failing to see his faults?

No. It was quite different. Wickham had maligned Darcy to her, whereas Hadley had said nothing improper about Andrew and had seemed concerned for his well-being. Still, she must remember not to trust her first impressions as she had with Wickham, or to assume his motives were good. She still had every intention of meeting Mr. Hadley privately, but it would only be to gain information, not to treat him as a friend.

ELIZABETH AROSE EARLY the next morning, anxious to leave the house before Georgiana or Lady Frederica were awake. It would not do to have them offer to join her on her walk. That left her with a dilemma, though, since she could not go out alone in a strange city, yet she could hardly take one of Lady Margaret's maids with her after Andrew's warning that some of the staff were spies for Lord Matlock. Finally she asked Myrtilla, whom Andrew had brought to act as Elizabeth and Mary's maid, to accompany her. The risk that close-mouthed Myrtilla might mention her meeting with Mr. Hadley to Andrew seemed less worrisome than Lord Matlock discovering it.

The Gravel Walk proved to be directly behind the opposite side of the Circus, so they arrived even sooner than she had anticipated. Mr. Hadley was already there, seated on a bench as if he had been there for some time.

The bearded gentleman stepped forward to meet her. "Miss Bennet, how lovely it is to see a familiar face this early in the morning." His eyes darted nervously to Myrtilla.

For Myrtilla's ears, Elizabeth said, "Lady Frederica mentioned how pleased she was to discover another relation visiting in Bath. Myrtilla, I will walk with this gentleman for a time." Oh, why had she said it so clumsily? He had not even asked to walk with her.

Myrtilla curtsied, but her expression made it obvious her sharp eyes had missed nothing. "Yes, Miss Bennet." She stepped back several yards and waited, her head bowed in apparent submission.

Elizabeth hesitated, but there was nothing she could do about Myrtilla's suspicions, which were true enough. At least she would be unlikely to think this a romantic assignation, given Mr. Hadley's age.

As they began to walk, Mr. Hadley said, "I thank you for suggesting this. I am glad of the chance to speak to you further." He looked worried, though.

She probably looked at least as anxious. "I am as well. Forgive me if I seem somewhat ill at ease. I am not in the habit of clandestine meetings."

He cleared his throat uncomfortably. "Ah, yes, of course. I assume your betrothed is unaware of this."

She eyed him thoughtfully. "I did not discuss it with him, but he has expressed a desire that the past should remain buried. He may be correct in that, but I find I must understand that past before I can bury it. You are the only person still living whom I may ask about it, so I hope to take advantage of the opportunity. However, if you find my inquiries impertinent, I will not be offended if you decline to respond."

He shook his head. "I will be happy, more than happy, to help you in any way. I would do anything in my power to contribute to Andrew's happiness. For many years, that has meant removing myself from his vicinity, but I have done so only because he has desired it, not out of any wish of my own."

As she had thought, then. "I cannot offer any hope that such a situation might change. I seek only to improve my own understanding."

His eyelids drooped. "I understand. May I ask how you discovered the truth? Did he tell you?"

She grimaced. "It was stranger than that. I received, by an indirect route, a package left by Lady Anne Darcy for Andrew's future bride. It contained the twin of the locket you once showed me, and a letter."

His expression brightened. "A letter from Lady Anne?"

She hated to disappoint him. "It concerned only Andrew and certain messages she wished me to give to him. It was a brief note from a dying woman to a complete stranger. It told me a little, but there are still things I wish to know, such as why Lady Anne Darcy, an earl's daughter, was so much in her husband's power that she had no other way to contact her son."

He winced. "I can tell you little of what happened after Andrew was six, for once Darcy discovered the truth, he clamped down on Lady Anne's freedom. No letters left Pemberley that he did not approve. She was not allowed to see visitors alone. A few times she managed to send me messages in secret, but that was all."

"Surely the *ton* had something to say about this. They are notorious for whispering secrets."

He gave her a puzzled look. "But Lady Anne was not received in the *ton*."

Elizabeth's jaw dropped. "Not received? An earl's daughter?"

His mouth twisted. "An earl's disgraced daughter. After our attempted elopement, no one would receive her."

She caught her breath. "I know nothing about this elopement."

His face flushed above his grizzled beard. "It was a terrible mistake. If I had any idea of the price she would pay – but we were young and in love, and her brother was forcing her to wed Darcy. He caught us before we reached the border, dragged her back, and married her to Darcy. But the damage to her reputation was done. Her brother had to double her dowry to get Darcy to take her, and he never spoke to her again."

"But she agreed to the marriage?"

He turned haunted eyes on her. "After her brother threatened to ruin me if she did not. God in heaven, how I wish she had told him to do his worst to me! But she was not like that. She could not bear to have harm come to anyone she loved."

She had still chosen to have an affair, but that was beyond what Elizabeth could decently ask about. "I see."

"She was determined to make the best of it. She had a letter smuggled out to me, saying that if she could not have the man she loved, she would do her best to be a good wife, and asked me to stay away from her so she could learn to forget what might have been."

"But you did not." The words jumped out of her mouth before she could pull them back.

"I did. For five years I did. Then our paths crossed at a house party. I had not known she was coming. Darcy had never been told whom she had eloped with. That had been part of the deal Lady Anne had struck with her brother to protect me. I never stopped loving her, but she thought perhaps we could be friends, and I was willing to accept anything. She told me about her sorrow, her two babies who had died, her loneliness. Of all her family and friends, only her sister still visited her. She had made few new friends, and always kept her secret from them. One thing led to another and one night we were both weak. One night!" His voice trembled and he shook his head.

So it had not been an ongoing affair. "Were you discovered?"

"Not then. It was years later, when her husband saw me again at a ball. I had wondered a little when I heard Lady Anne had given birth to a son, but it had been only the one night, and I had no idea he bore such a resemblance to me. Darcy thought nothing of it until he came face-to-face with me when I was dancing with his wife." His eyelids drooped again. "That was the last time I ever saw her."

"What happened then?"

He shrugged unhappily. "I received a letter from her through a mutual acquaintance. She asked me to stay away from anywhere she might be, for her sake and for Andrew's. I did so. I grew this beard to disguise the resemblance between us. I managed to catch a glimpse of the boy once when he was at Eton – oh, not to speak to, just across the chapel. I knew I should stay away, but I had to see him somehow. Once he left home, I tried to meet him, man-to-man, but as soon as he learned my name, he refused to have anything to do with me. I cannot blame him, yet I wish... But it does not matter what I wish. I avoid events where he might be. I would not have been at the Pump Room, had I known he was in Bath."

She had no comfort to offer him. If Andrew had his way, nothing would ever change. "You had no further contact with Lady Anne, then?"

"A few letters over the years, but she could say little in them because her sister, Lady Catherine, was the only one who would deliver them for her, and the letter always arrived opened. But I treasured them even so." He hesitated, his eyes drawn. "There is something else I would treasure, if I might ask it of you. Could you, would you, tell me something of him? Nothing private, just something anyone might know. What is he like? What makes him smile? Does he prefer to ride or to hunt? I would be happy even to know what his favorite jam might be, that I might think of him when I eat it at breakfast."

Elizabeth's heart went out to the poor old gentleman, her plan to be careful lest he prove another Mr. Wickham cast aside. "I do not yet know his favorite jam, but perhaps I can tell you a few stories. Shall I tell you how we met?"

His smile lit his face. "I would like that very much."

She told him of how Andrew had saved her from the inedible cake and bitter tea at Mr. Morris' rectory, making the tale sound droll and putting Andrew in the best light. Then, as they rounded a curve in the Gravel Walk, she caught a glimpse of Myrtilla trailing behind, and she launched into the story of visiting Andrew's parsonage with Mrs. Gardiner to help with his household management.

Mr. Hadley drank in every word. "I am happy to hear that he has such care for those in his employ. He is like his mother in that; she was always concerned about her servants, even the least of them."

What else could she tell him? "One of the things I admire about him is that he always notices who is in need of attention." She recounted how he had won over her mother and how her younger sisters had changed for the better under his influence, and Mr. Hadley seemed to glow with pride at her words, so she added, "I have known him only a brief time, but there is a great deal to admire in him."

He smiled. "You saw in him so quickly the man you wished to marry?"

She opened her mouth to agree, but the words would not come out. Somehow she could not bring herself to lie to this kind, lonely man. In a quiet voice, she said, "No. We were forced into the engagement by a man seeking revenge. He deliberately orchestrated a compromising situation."

He gaped at her. "Someone wanted revenge on Andrew?"

"No. Or yes, but that was only a small part of it. Though I did not know it at the time, another man was the true target, one who loved me, because it would hurt him to see me either ruined or married to Andrew." To her dismay, her voice shook a little.

With a look of concern, he said, "What does Andrew think of this?"

She hung her head. Why had she told him so much? "He does not know about the other man. It is better if he thinks it was only a petty revenge on him."

"I think there is more to this situation than you are telling me," he said carefully.

"Of course there is! But the important thing is that I am fond of Andrew, and I will be a good wife to him," she said fiercely.

His brow knitted, and they walked silently for several minutes. Elizabeth's heart pounded. Why had she said anything? What must he think of her?

Finally he said, "There is nothing wrong with marrying someone you do not love, as long as respect and some sort of affection are there, as you clearly feel for Andrew. But if you love this other man, I beg of you to think carefully about what you are doing, not for Andrew's sake, but for your own. Having to live with scandal or in poverty are, without question, great hardships, but they do not destroy your heart and soul the way it would to give yourself to one man while loving another."

Elizabeth stared at him in shock, her heart twisting in her chest. How dare he make such a suggestion? He barely knew her, yet he felt he had the right to recommend that she end her engagement? "I said he loved me, not that I loved him."

"If you do not love him, then I have overstepped badly. Not for the first time, for sometimes I find I must say what I feel is right and true, even when it may not meet society's approval. Forgive me."

She made a weak attempt at a smile. "Something you and Andrew have in common, then."

"He does that as well?" He gazed off into the distance for a moment. "Then I shall not feel ashamed of it, and say only this: if you do not love this man, you may ignore what I am saying. But I do not think you would be feeling such distress if you did not care for him. If Lady Anne were alive, she would tell you how bitterly she regretted choosing a forced marriage over ruination and loss of her family, despite her beautiful home, children she loved, and a decent and respectable husband."

Her throat ached with unshed tears. "Ah, but she would have had you to console her in her ruination. She might have felt differently, had her only other choice been to be alone." He had no idea what it would cost her if she broke her engagement. A life in service, away from everyone she loved, while her family faced disgrace because of her. No, it was far too much to ask.

He studied her keenly. "He could not marry you, then? I am sorry for it. I do not think she would have felt differently, though, for she considered running off even when she believed I had long since forgotten her. The only thing that stopped her was the thought of losing her children." Then he added gently, "But you are not Lady Anne, and you must do what is right for you. You need not listen to the meanderings of an old man who knows nothing of your circumstances."

She struggled to swallow. "You must think me a very odd sort of person."

"I find you a refreshingly honest and genuine young lady, and I believe you will make an excellent wife for Andrew."

"You are very kind." Her voice hardly trembled.

"And I trust Andrew is enough his mother's son that he will treat you with all kindness, even if this engagement was forced on both of you."

"You need have no concerns about that," she said with more certainty. "He is content with the match. I am told he was already considering making me an offer before his honor forced him to do so, though I was unaware of it. If your fault, sir, is to say too much when you feel strongly, mine is to be completely oblivious to gentlemen who admire me, to the point where I am utterly astonished when they propose."

That made him laugh, as she had intended. "How very disconcerting that must be!"

"You have no idea! Fortunately, thanks to Andrew, I am now immune from that particular dilemma. It is a great relief, I assure you." She managed a wry smile.

"It will spare you from unwanted proposals, perhaps, but I suspect you will still have many young gentlemen admiring you. How fortunate that you can be oblivious to them!" he teased.

They had by then gone past the end of the Gravel Walk and strolled the entire length of the lawn in front of the Royal Crescent, so Elizabeth said, "Indeed! I fear I must be turning back now, or I shall be late for breakfast, and Lady Margaret will scold me."

He chuckled. "I can believe that, for she was quite a scold even as a child! I could never understand how someone as sweet as Lady Anne could have two sisters as shrewish as Lady Catherine and Lady Margaret."

Taking with relief the opening that gave her for a harmless topic of conversation, she said, "Would you tell me more about Lady Anne's youth? Someday I would like to be able to tell my children something about their grandmother."

"Why, I would be glad to!" With that happy subject, they retraced their steps.

As they reached the end of the Gravel Walk, Elizabeth said hesitantly, "I thank you again for answering my questions. I do not hold out great hope, but I will ask Andrew if he would consider meeting with you."

He caught his breath. "I would not wish to cause any trouble between the two of you." But the longing in his voice gave him away.

She smiled. "I confess my motive is not to please you, but because I think Andrew would benefit from facing the ghosts of his past."

"I will trust you on that, and I thank you for today. Even if nothing further comes of it, this conversation has been a great gift to me. And I hope you know that I will hold the personal matters you shared with me in the strictest confidence. I am quite proficient in the keeping of secrets."

Myrtilla came up to them then, so Elizabeth merely curtsied and bade him good day.

Conscious of the late hour, they hurried back to the Circus, Elizabeth forcing his strange suggestion from her mind. When they arrived at Lady Margaret's lodgings, breakfast was already over and the gentlemen had arrived.

Darcy's eyes fixed on her immediately when she strolled into the drawing room, as had been the case since her arrival in Bath. It was as if he had decided that leaving for years gave him permission to look his fill upon her in the meantime. Heat flooded through her, and Mr. Hadley's words rushed back into her head.

Andrew, who had been conversing softly with Mary, greeted her a little stiffly. Was he still angry over her words the previous day? If so, he would be furious if he discovered she had met with Mr. Hadley. "I understand you have been out already," he said with a hint of disapproval in his voice.

"Yes. I woke early, and, as Mary can no doubt tell you, I often take a morning walk," she said.

"Alone?" He sounded a bit shocked.

Perhaps it would be better not to address the fact that she usually did walk alone, at least not in front of the others. "I took a maid with me, and went no farther than the Gravel Walk and the Royal Crescent. Hardly an outing."

Lady Frederica pronounced, "Perfectly respectable, I would say. We were just making plans for the day. The Pump Room first, for those who will, followed by a drive to Lansdown Hill. It is but a few miles away, and the views are spectacular. On a clear day like this, we may be able to see all the way to the Bristol Channel. Does that suit you?"

"Admirably." It was easier to pretend that Andrew's testiness had not disturbed her than to deny how much she was warmed by Darcy's gaze.

Chapter 27

The party divided into two groups for the journey to Lansdown Hill. Lady Frederica and Mr. Farleigh set out on horseback, while the remainder of the party traveled in the Darcy carriage. Elizabeth's mind was so caught up in her discussion with Mr. Hadley that she responded absently, if at all, to the others. Her thoughts ran in circles, stumbling from sympathy towards the lonely old man who loved the son he could never know to outrage that he had dared suggest that she break her engagement. Her eyes kept turning to Darcy, who once again was observing her with a concerned look, and her stomach would lurch.

Fortunately, her silence was less evident to the others, as Andrew gave a dramatic rendition of the history of the Battle of Lansdown, and Mary and Georgiana peppered him with questions. He seemed to thrive on their admiration, becoming more affable and livelier. Her sister was in particularly good looks today. Georgiana had wheedled her into allowing her own maid to arrange Mary's hair, and, if Elizabeth was not mistaken, to add a little subtle blush to her cheeks. Combined with the becoming gowns Jane had handed down to their younger sister, replacing her usual drab, untrimmed dresses, Mary had been transformed from the plain Bennet daughter to an attractive young lady.

After a long climb into the hills, the carriage pulled up in a wayside along a country lane. Elizabeth was not surprised to find Lady Frederica and Mr. Farleigh nowhere in sight, although they ought to have arrived first. No doubt they had gone off somewhere for a little privacy.

"We must walk the last bit of the way, but it is not far," said Mr. Darcy, gesturing at a track through the field. "This is the way towards Prospect Stile."

"Where is Sir Basil Grenville's memorial?" asked Georgiana.

Darcy consulted a small map. "It is further along, but there is a short cut across the field there."

Georgiana caught at Andrew's sleeve. "Let us go there first so you can finish the story."

Andrew smiled at his sister. "Certainly, if you wish." His head tilted towards Mary's as the three of them set off together, leaving Elizabeth to walk behind them with Mr. Darcy. Apparently her lack of interest in the battlefield made her less interesting company. Or perhaps it was that her eyes did not light up when he looked at her, as Georgiana's and Mary's did.

Now she was alone with Darcy. Even though her pulse might show a distinct tendency to race, there was nothing improper in it. Darcy would be her brother when she married Andrew, and despite what Mr. Hadley had said, that was her only choice. But he was looking at her so intently that her stomach dropped.

She needed to think of Andrew. "They do make a picturesque threesome, do they not?"

"Indeed."

"Your sister has been an excellent influence on Mary, convincing her that being accomplished does not mean one cannot also be personable and fashionable."

It had been Andrew, though, who first brought Mary out of her shell during his visit to Longbourn, talking to her and taking her ideas seriously rather than simply rolling his eyes at her as the Bennets had always done. It made Elizabeth feel ashamed to see how very little attention it had taken to change Mary for the better. Andrew was a good man who truly cared for those in need. She had to remember that.

They came to a stile overlooking the broad valley. Andrew and the others had already raced ahead, but Elizabeth paused to take in the spectacular view over the countryside and hills, the golden buildings of Bath filling the hollow behind them. "Is it not astonishing how different the world looks from above? When I am walking across a field, it seems to be the entire world, yet from here, I can see how each one fits into the next like a puzzle."

"We are fortunate to have such a clear day. Do you see that glint of reflection beyond the hills? If I am not mistaken, that is the Bristol Channel."

"Such a huge body of water, full of storms and shipwrecks, and yet it looks tiny and peaceful from here." If only her own problems could seem so tiny and far away!

Suddenly Darcy said in a quiet, tense voice, "Is something wrong? Have you and Drew quarreled?"

Taken aback, she struggled to form a response, wanting to deny it. But Darcy had been watching her so closely since her arrival, and he must have noticed the change in her after their visit to the Pump Room. Should she say it was a private matter, or something foolish that was easily resolved? That would be best. But it was already too late to say any of those things. Her silence had given her way.

And she could not lie to him.

"A situation arose which we see differently," she said reluctantly. "No doubt we will find common ground on it eventually."

He studied her. "Is it serious?"

The quarrel with Andrew after the Pump Room? Likely not. But what Mr. Hadley had said to her that morning – oh, yes, that was serious. His words kept ringing in her ears. And here she was, walking alone with Darcy while Andrew laughed with Mary and Georgiana; and she was glad of it.

"No, merely a matter of differing approaches." She should leave it at that. She knew it. But she wanted so badly to tell him, to know if she was right that he would share her outlook. "It turns out Mr. Hadley is in Bath. Andrew gave him the cut direct at the Pump Room yesterday, as he has done before. Andrew is cross with me because I spoke to Mr. Hadley, despite knowing that he would not want me to do so."

Darcy was watching her closely. "Cutting him only draws attention to a matter which we would rather everyone forgot."

Relief trickled through her. "My point exactly."

"Should I speak to Drew about it?"

"No! I pray you, do not. I should not have told you this much."

His mouth worked. "Then I shall not. But I would wish you could always tell me anything." His voice was deep and heartfelt.

Heat burned in her chest. She knew what he was saying, and it made her heart contract and her skin ache with the desire to touch him. But she belonged to his brother.

What would Darcy say if he knew Mr. Hadley had counseled her to break her engagement because of him? Or how much the prospect tempted her, foolish as it might be?

No. He was one person she could never tell, because he just might be imprudent enough to think they could have a future together, and that was impossible. That option had vanished the day she accepted Andrew's proposal. A gentleman of Darcy's stature could never marry a woman with a broken engagement, especially not one who had jilted his brother. That was reality. There could be no happy ending for them.

Determinedly she said, "Andrew is unhappy with my position, and I would not like to be the cause of conflict between you, especially when you are leaving for South America so soon. He values your good opinion more than you may realize."

"He has seemed more at ease with me of late," Darcy acknowledged, and then added in a low intense voice, "*You* know why I must leave."

She blinked hard, fighting back sudden tears. She had known, of course, but it was different to hear him say it to her. "I cannot tell you how sorry I am that you must leave your home to avoid..." She could not bring herself to finish the sentence.

"Not only that. It is my duty to my family. Drew needs to accept responsibility for Pemberley, and he will only do that in my absence. The two of you need time alone, without my presence. My father had his faults, but he taught me that my responsibility to my family comes first. He may never have counted Drew as part of our family, but I do."

"Still, it is a high price for you to pay, to be away for three years." It would be easier for her, without question, but she would miss him desperately.

He did not deny it. "There will be compensations. Seeing the tropics with my own eyes, new plants and animals, gaining scientific knowledge, expanding my horizons."

Yellow fever, malaria, risking death from illness or injury. What if he died there, and she never saw him again? Pain filled her chest, stealing

237

the words from her throat. Finally she asked, "What will happen to your collection of plants in your absence?"

"I have hired a tropical botanist to care for them." With a small, rueful smile he added, "Perhaps you would be so kind as to check in on the orangery occasionally, since you enjoy my jungle."

"If you wish it, I would be happy to do so." Even as she said it, an image rose in her mind, and she could see how it would be. She would end up escaping the parsonage as often as she dared to hide among the tropical plants and dream of Darcy, remaining faithful to Andrew in body but not in spirit, even when Darcy was on the other side of the world. What would happen when he finally returned? Would it be the same as now, when she chafed at Andrew's restrictions and only felt fully alive in Darcy's presence?

Andrew's laughter drifted back towards them, even though the threesome was now far ahead. He rarely laughed like that with Elizabeth. Mary might be the plain sister, but she aroused Andrew's tenderness and made him laugh. Andrew might have wanted to marry Elizabeth in Derbyshire when he had decided it was time to wed and a non-local girl would suit him best, but if he had the choice now, might he have chosen a different Bennet sister, one who shared his interests more closely, and adored him as Elizabeth never could? No, she was doing Andrew no favor by keeping him in an engagement he had outgrown. He would be happier with a woman who never contested his opinions and wanted nothing more in life than to be a clergyman's wife. Instead he would grow old quarreling with Elizabeth, never quite content, but unwilling to admit why, while Darcy, who loved them both, suffered alone at the sight of them together, taking their children as the heirs he would never have of his own body. For the rest of their lives.

Mr. Hadley was right. It would be better to be alone than to perpetually live a lie, helplessly watching the pain her presence caused. She could not make that sacrifice, even if her family suffered for it.

And just maybe, if Andrew could be persuaded to take Mary in her place, her family's reputation might still be salvaged, or at least not be harmed as badly.

"What is it? Is something wrong?" Darcy asked, interrupting her reverie.

She came back to herself abruptly, realizing she had suddenly stopped walking. Taking one step and then another, in a body that seemed to be awakening in a new way, she said, "No, nothing at all. Just a thought." Even her voice sounded stronger as the weight of her engagement lifted from her shoulders.

Yes. This was the right thing to do. She had no idea what she would do nor how she would find her way in the world, but she was not going to marry Andrew. For the first time in weeks, she felt free.

SHE WANDERED ON IN a daze, pacing along the footpaths beside Darcy, both acutely aware of him and in a world of her own as she tried to imagine her future. Perfunctorily she admired the view from different spots, and the monument atop the battlefield. But once it was time to return to the carriage, she knew she needed to make some plans.

It was one thing to decide to break her engagement. How and when to do so was another question, especially when she and Mary were guests of Andrew's family and far from home. Remaining in their company after she jilted Andrew would be most uncomfortable; it would be best to leave immediately after doing so.

She risked a glance at Mr. Darcy. Yes, it would not do to see him again after that. He might think she would be dangling after another offer from him, even though that was impossible. Her farewell to Andrew would also have to be her final farewell to Mr. Darcy. But, oh, how that would hurt, never to see his dear face again, never again to feel that vital connection she craved. She would never know what would become of him, never know if he and Andrew managed to maintain their relationship, never know the woman Georgiana would grow to be.

Lady Frederica and Mr. Farleigh caught up to them by the carriage. Her ladyship said, her face alight with pleasure, "Darcy, Evan tells me his family will be here Tuesday, so I thought perhaps a family dinner on Wednesday, with the wedding on Thursday. Would that suit you?"

Darcy gave a faint smile at her enthusiasm. "I have no fixed engagements."

"Capital! I cannot believe this is truly happening after all this time. Evan, will you make the arrangements at the Abbey?"

He bowed. "Gladly. I have the license already. It will be the happiest day of my life."

Elizabeth watched their interplay with a catch in her throat. She would never have that moment, and with her new decision, she would not even be present for their wedding.

Or was that fair to Lady Frederica? Breaking her engagement to Andrew mere days before the wedding would certainly cast a pall over the occasion, and perhaps add another layer of scandal to an already fraught event. Would it not be kinder to wait until after Lady Frederica's nuptials to end her engagement? It was only a matter of a few days, after all.

And it would be a blessed reprieve. A few more days before she had to bid Darcy farewell forever.

Ahead, she heard Mary laughing. Yes, and a few more days for Mary in this improving company as well. And just possibly enough for a happy ending for Andrew and Mary.

Chapter 28

Back at Lady Margaret's townhouse, Elizabeth chose to stay close to the other ladies rather than sit with Andrew. If she had to wait to break the engagement, it would be easier if she avoided Andrew as much as possible. Besides, it was distracting to listen to Georgiana's cheerful chatter about her first Season, now just over a year away. Lady Frederica had agreed to sponsor the girl, so there were many plans to be made about new gowns, balls, Venetian breakfasts, and her court presentation. It was a world away from Elizabeth's come-out, which had merely been a matter of her mother announcing she was old enough to attend the public assemblies in Meryton. It was a timely reminder of the distance that lay between her and the Darcys of Pemberley.

She hardly noticed when Andrew excused himself for a few minutes, but on his return, he was frowning and asked to speak to her privately. Nervously she rose and followed him to a small anteroom. Surely he could not have guessed what she was thinking! But her guilty conscience made her wonder. "Is something wrong?" she asked him.

He eyed her silently for a moment. Oh, yes, something was troubling him. "I just spoke to Myrtilla, to tell her that if you were to insist on walking alone, I wanted at least two maids with you. Do you know what she told me?"

Oh, dear. She had all but forgotten her other great sin of the day. Perhaps it was for the best to have it out in the open, though. She did owe him the truth about meeting Mr. Hadley, and perhaps, just perhaps, some good might come out of it. Now that she no longer needed to worry about keeping Andrew's good opinion, it could be worth a few risks. For his sake, and for Darcy's. "I imagine she told you I met Mr. Hadley. I had intended to explain that to you myself when the opportunity arose."

He grimaced. "She said you met a man with a beard and spoke to him at length."

She lifted her chin. "It is true, though I imagine you are unhappy to hear it. I know you wish me to avoid him, but there were questions I wished to have answered. What is more, I would like to tell you what I learned."

He let out an explosive breath. "As if I could believe anything that man says!"

"It is difficult to judge whether to believe a man one has never spoken with, but having done so, I think he is honest. He certainly owned his faults to me. May I tell you what he said?"

"I suppose you mean to tell me whether I agree or not," he snapped.

"No, if you prefer, I will say nothing."

He glared at her, then turned his back and went to stare out the window. "You can tell me if you wish it so much," he said reluctantly.

She almost smiled at this grudging acknowledgment of his own curiosity. Quickly she repeated the gist of her conversation with Mr. Hadley, leaving out only the parts which concerned her own feelings.

When she finally stopped, he said gruffly, still without looking at her, "What else?"

"That is all, but he offered to meet with you directly if you had questions, or for any other reason."

His hands clenched into fists by his side. "No. I will not speak to him."

A few days ago she might have left it at that, but she had nothing to lose now. "It is your choice, naturally, although I wonder about your assumptions. One of the things I admire most about you is your desire to give a voice to everyone, be they servant or slave. Anyone except this one man. You believe in forgiveness and turning the other cheek, but not for this one man. Yes, he sinned and you suffered because of it – though he himself was not the source of your suffering. It seems to me that you are blaming him for the sins of your mother's husband, and in that you may not be following your own tenets."

He stiffened. "I believe I am the best judge of my own tenets, I thank you."

She had gone too far. "Of course you are. But may I ask you to consider a different question? What advice would you give to someone else in such a position, someone with an unwanted connection to a man who had sinned long ago, but had attempted to lead an upright life since then?"

His shoulders lowered and he looked away. "I have only your word that he has not continued to sin," he grumbled.

Sensing weakness, she pushed forward. "True, and I only know what he has said, which is not proof. Still, is it enough to warrant having one conversation so you can assess his repentance for yourself? You could always choose afterwards not to continue the acquaintance."

He rubbed his hand along the mantelpiece, his head bowed. "Only God can judge him, not I," he said in a choked voice.

She caught her breath. Had she misunderstood him completely? She pressed her fingers to her forehead, all her assumptions turned upside down. Andrew *wanted* to meet his father, likely longed to meet him and to have his love, but believed he should deny himself, that he should despise the man. And Elizabeth was offering him not so much persuasion as temptation incarnate. She said carefully, "It is certainly your decision, and I will press you no further. I told him you were unlikely to agree to a meeting. He will be disappointed, but not surprised, if he hears nothing from me."

Andrew's face twisted. "Very well; I will meet him this one time, but I promise no more."

She smiled. "I thank you."

He held up his hand. "One more thing. I want Fitzwilliam to come with us."

Surprised, she asked, "Your brother?"

"Yes. I will not do this behind his back."

"A fine sentiment." She struggled to conceal her delight. If nothing else, Andrew's bond with Darcy seemed to be growing. Someday it would be a comfort for her to know that she had at least helped to heal their wounds.

"YOU WANT ME TO COME with you?" Darcy blinked in astonishment, looking from Andrew to Elizabeth and back. This was obviously her idea. "I barely know Hadley." And in truth, he had no particular desire to meet his mother's lover. The very idea made his skin itch.

"You are my brother, which comes ahead of any claim he has on me. And I wish to make it clear that in seeing him, I am not denying my Darcy ties."

Darcy twisted the signet on his little finger. "If you wish me to join you, I would be honored to do so. I confess that I do not fully understand the purpose of this meeting, but I will do my best to support you." Because Elizabeth wanted it to happen.

Andrew's mouth twisted. "Elizabeth believes I should have a connection to him."

"I do not know if there should be a connection," she said quickly. "I merely do not wish to see a lonely, sad old gentleman – your mother's cousin, no less – treated like a leper."

Darcy nodded. "It could be an advantage to be on polite terms with him, if he is willing."

"Oh, he is willing," said Elizabeth unguardedly. "He is desperately hungry not only for any detail about Andrew, from his preferences in reading material to his taste in jam, but also for a connection to any of Lady Anne's children. He still loves her memory."

Andrew rubbed the heel of his hand against his forehead as if he were in pain. Darcy hoped Elizabeth knew what she was doing. But he had to trust in her greater knowledge of Andrew, and would meet Hadley, much as the thought made his stomach churn.

THE MEETING WITH MR. Hadley had been arranged at the neutral ground of Sydney Gardens. Darcy wondered whose suggestion it had been, Elizabeth's, Andrew's, or Mr. Hadley's, and how Elizabeth had explained to the others why she needed to go out alone with Andrew and Darcy.

It had been some years since Darcy had visited the Gardens, but the memory came back to him as they entered through the Sydney Hotel. As he purchased their tickets for the pleasure garden, he spotted Mr. Hadley waiting for them just outside the hotel's tea room. Good Lord, the man did look like Drew, full beard or no.

"Oh, do let us have tea before we go into the gardens," Elizabeth said brightly. "I am parched after our walk here."

Darcy knew perfectly well Elizabeth was accustomed to far longer walks than the one they had taken to reach the gardens, but he would trust her judgment if she felt sitting down to tea would be preferable to walking. It was obvious Drew was nervous; Darcy had not seen him look so stiff since his first visits to Pemberley. "Tea would be just the thing," he said.

Elizabeth gave him a grateful look, and Darcy followed the almost imperceptible nod of her head indicating that he should sit across from her so that Drew and Hadley would not be next to one another.

She led the sort of light social chatter that was often his downfall, sharing her opinions of Bath, asking Mr. Hadley about his favorite local spots. Had he found a church he could recommend for Sunday services, as the nearest one to their lodgings seemed too traditional for her tastes?

Darcy could not but admire how she gave Hadley an opening to show knowledge of Non-Conformist ministers, before shifting the subject to his home in London and his work as a barrister.

Drew sat woodenly, barely touching his tea, despite Elizabeth's attempts to draw him out. Darcy did his best to fill in the gaps, finally thinking to ask Hadley about their common relations among the Fitzwilliam family.

Hadley said, "I was surprised to see Lady Frederica here. I would not have thought Bath to be to her taste."

"It is not," said Drew abruptly. "She wanted to get away from her father, and this was where he would permit her to go."

"Avoiding Matlock, is she? Wise girl," said Hadley.

"He is *your* cousin," Andrew said with a frown.

Hadley's lips tightened, increasing his resemblance to Andrew. "Matlock and I also go to the same tailor. I believe that is the sum of what we have in common."

The lines around Drew's eyes relaxed a little. "He disowned me years ago for my work with Wilberforce. Called me a traitor to the family."

A flash of anger crossed Hadley's face. "I am sorry for it, though I would have expected no better of him. Even as a boy, abolitionists made him livid. Couldn't stand the guilt of it. It was a bone of contention between your mother and him at one point."

Drew looked suddenly interested. "My mother fought with him about slavery?"

"Only a few times. He did not tolerate dissent, and she was punished for it. After that, she hid her beliefs from him, but donated most of her pin money to abolitionist causes. She was also forbidden to see me, since Matlock believed – quite correctly, I might add – that my influence had exposed her to those unacceptable ideas."

Elizabeth asked, "Were you interested in abolition at a young age, then?"

"It was one of my father's pet causes, and my nursemaid, whom I loved dearly, was a freed slave, so it came quite naturally to me. I was never punished for my beliefs, as Lady Anne was."

Darcy said, "It is easy to be against slavery, but it takes a particularly brave soul to make those beliefs public within a family whose fortune depends upon the trade. I am glad to know that my mother, like Drew, was bold enough to take that risk." And he had to admit that Hadley was hard to dislike, no matter what he had done in the past.

Drew flushed with pride, and Elizabeth smiled. It was enough.

AFTER THEY FINISHED their tea, the party set off down the broad avenue that bisected the pleasure garden, Drew and Mr. Hadley deep in conversation about abolition, Elizabeth and Darcy rarely contributing anything. That suited Darcy, even more so as the two other men fell back a little. Here, walking with Elizabeth, he could pretend that it was just the two of them.

Or not.

"That seems to be going well," she said quietly. "Especially given how hard I had to push Andrew to agree to come."

"You did?"

"I confess so." She laced her hands behind her back. "I prefer facing the truth rather than hiding from it."

There was nothing he could say to that. She knew his truth.

She increased her pace, and he lengthened his stride to match it. Gesturing to the lanterns along the path, she said, "This must be lovely when it is illuminated in the evenings."

"It is, though not well suited for private conversation. It can be quite crowded. Is there anything you would like to see while you are here? The labyrinth is over there, and boasts some pretty grottoes."

Elizabeth shaded her eyes. "Not today, I think. While in general I am fond of labyrinths, of late I have spent too much time trying to find my way out of the maze in my thoughts to enjoy being in a physical one."

His heart began to thump. She must be feeling it, too, that same sense of being lost, of having no way out, of turning one blind corner at a time, only to find another dead end. She understood. But she was still marrying Andrew.

And he needed to behave like an honorable gentleman, even if all he wanted was to gaze into her fine eyes. What had they been speaking of? Oh, yes, the gardens. "Perhaps the ornamental bridges over the new canal, then. They are picturesque."

She bowed her head. "I would like to see them."

After consulting with Drew and Hadley, Darcy led the way into a side path leading to the canal, past the flower borders and the shrubbery. He cast a glance at Elizabeth, but her bonnet brim shielded her expression from him. A break in the trees came into sight before the water itself, but there it was, the bridge a graceful arch over the canal. They strolled to the peak of it, where Elizabeth turned and rested her hands on the wrought iron railings. Below them, canal boats moved slowly, pulled by a draft horse on the towpath.

Elizabeth sighed. "You would scarcely know we are in the midst of the city here."

"Or that the canal is so new. It looks as if it has been here forever, rather than a modern miracle that crosses the entirety of England."

A lighterman on the narrow boat pulled off his cap and nodded admiringly at Elizabeth, making her smile and raise a hand in greeting.

"Indeed," she said to Darcy. "It must be an exciting trip, to travel all the way across England without leaving the water, although I suppose it is nothing to the journey you will be taking soon." There was something wistful in her voice.

He looked back, but Drew and Hadley were nowhere in sight. "Our friends seem to have vanished."

She smiled. "They sat down on a bench some time ago. I think we were becoming *de trop*, which is just what I would have wished."

"You sound pleased."

She considered. "I may be mistaken, but I believe Mr. Hadley is a good man, and that Andrew can benefit from knowing him better. He seems more content now, and I wonder how much that has to do with the letter from your mother."

"I agree he appears more at peace with himself," Darcy acknowledged. Then, because he could not help himself, he added "And you? You seem different somehow, as if something has changed for you as well."

She started, casting an almost frightened look at him, and then gave a rueful smile. "I have found my own peace, I suppose. I realized some battles are not worth fighting, and that I needed to accept certain truths. It has been freeing."

"What truths are those?" He had no right to ask, but he trembled with the need to know.

Curling her fingers around the railing, she gazed down into the dark water. "That you will be away for three years, and when you return, you will be a different person, one who has explored a new world and lived among a group of natural scientists rather than the *ton*. I will be a different person, too, with three years of experience that... Well, no matter. You will not have shared those experiences. We will be strangers to one another."

It hurt to hear her say it, even if it was precisely why he had decided to go away. "And that gives you peace?" There was a bitter taste in his mouth.

"No. It gives me freedom." Now she looked up at him, her eyes deep enough to drown in. "Freedom to let myself feel what I feel, instead of attempting to fight it every minute. The freedom to live in the present for this short time here in Bath, with honesty in my heart. Knowing that by the time you return from your expedition, it will no longer matter. That is what has given me peace."

His heart filled his throat. Could he believe his ears, or was he deceiving himself into hearing what he wished for? Without thought his hand moved to cover hers as it lay on the railing. And then her fingers tightened around his.

It was a miracle. A silent miracle that flooded him with emotion, making the entire world fade away except for those few inches of skin where he could feel the pressure of her hand through the gloves they both wore. It was frighteningly intimate, as if he were stripped of everything before her.

Oh, God, Elizabeth!

Even when she married Andrew, this moment would still be his. This brief moment, when she held him in her heart.

"There you are!" It was Drew's voice, sounding both pleased and energetic. Hadley stood beside him.

Darcy wanted to clutch her hand, to tell Drew that Elizabeth was his, but instead, with infinite regret, he lifted his hand, feeling the aching loss of something precious. But her magnetic draw was beyond his ability to resist, so he slid his hand close to hers until he could feel the pressure of her little finger against his. It looked innocent, but even that slight touch sent desire surging through him.

Beside him Elizabeth closed her eyes, her cheeks flushed. But she said, "Yes, here we are. I think that lighterman on the narrow boat has been flirting with me." She did not move her hand, though.

"How dare he!" But Drew said it in a teasing voice. "I suppose he could not resist you."

Darcy certainly could not resist Elizabeth.

Drew sidled up beside him and said under his breath, "I say, do you suppose we could invite Hadley and his sister to dine with us? He says she would like to meet me properly."

His duty to his family had to come first. Somehow he stepped away from Elizabeth. "Hadley, it has been a pleasure to become better acquainted with you. Dare I hope you and your sister might dine with us at the York House?"

Hadley flushed, beaming. "We would be most happy to do so. Most happy. I thank you."

Elizabeth nudged Darcy with her elbow. He looked down at her inquisitively and saw a look of concern. What was wrong? Had she not wished for Drew to be better acquainted with Hadley?

She coughed. "There is one slight matter. If you dine with us, you are likely to guess at the ulterior motive for our presence in Bath, which must remain private for now. It is of the utmost importance that Lord Matlock get no wind of our plans."

Frederica. He had forgotten all about Frederica. Their original plan to dine at the York House rather than Lady Margaret's had been to permit Farleigh to join them.

"I feel quite safe agreeing to keep secrets from Matlock, whatever they might be," Hadley said.

With an arch smile, Elizabeth stepped forward and whispered in the old gentleman's ear.

A grim look clouded his face. "You may depend upon me. Matlock stopped my elopement and sentenced Lady Anne to a life of unhappiness. He will do the same to his daughter only over my dead body."

"I hope it will not come to that," said Elizabeth lightly. "But I am glad to have you as an ally."

Chapter 29

The dinner at the York House went well. Lady Frederica and Mr. Farleigh had no eyes for anyone but each other, while Andrew, Mr. Hadley, Mrs. Todd, and Darcy spoke mostly to each other. The conversation was somewhat limited, though, owing to the presence of Georgiana and Mary, both of whom were ignorant of Andrew's parentage, so Elizabeth dedicated herself to entertaining them so well that they would be unlikely to notice anything unusual. It put her in a good position to observe the soft, warm glances Andrew occasionally sent in her sister's direction, so different from any he had ever given her.

At the end of the evening, Mr. Hadley sought her out and took her hand between both of his. "This has been one of the finest days of my life, and I have you to thank for it," he said quietly. "If there is ever anything I can do for you, anything at all, I hope you will inform me. I owe you more than I can say."

Elizabeth glanced to the side, where Georgiana was approaching her. "I am so happy you were able to join us. I hope it will be the first of many such occasions." It was true, even though she would not be present at them.

His eyes twinkled. "Well, I have been invited to a certain occasion at Bath Abbey on Thursday, so I will see you there."

THERE WERE ONLY TWO days left, and Elizabeth had a great deal to accomplish during them. She had packed and re-packed her belongings until they fitted into a small trunk and a satchel she could carry. What did not make it in would have to return to Longbourn with Mary. Fortunately, Mary had a separate bedroom, and did not notice any of her preparations.

The best course seemed to be to begin her search for employment in London. She had just enough money for coach fare, so she intended to throw herself on the mercy of the Gardiners, asking them to keep her secret and to loan her money for lodgings until she found a position. Perhaps they might even know of someone looking for a companion or a governess.

In the meantime, she had scoured the London papers that were delivered to Lady Margaret, who read nothing but the social news and was perfectly willing to allow Elizabeth to take them afterwards, although with a warning that too much news could unbalance a young lady's mind. Elizabeth made a list of employment agencies, but perusing the advertisements had showed her the great flaw in her plan. Every position seemed to ask for a letter of character from a previous employer, and she had none.

She chewed on her fingernail, an old habit, long since broken, now returned with her anxiety over what to do next. Clearly she would not be eligible for many of the better jobs with no character letter, and it was hardly surprising. Why would anyone hire a girl with no references, a runaway who could be any kind of criminal?

There must be something she could do. Perhaps her aunt would know someone who might be willing to produce a letter. But no – there was someone she could ask, someone who had offered to assist her if she ever needed it, who would be the one person to understand why she was doing this.

Suddenly decisive, she hunted through her reticule and found the card Mr. Hadley had given her at the Pump Room. Yes, there it was.

The next morning, she begged off from Lady Frederica's planned excursion to the Roman Baths, pleading a headache. Once the others had left, she crept out and made her way to Great Pulteney Street.

At the door, she told the butler she wished to speak to Mr. Hadley privately. The disdainful look he gave her was fully deserved; no woman of good birth would request to see a gentleman alone. But Elizabeth had nothing left to lose. Once she departed from Bath, she would no longer have a reputation to worry about.

After a few uncomfortable moments waiting in the entry hall, praying that Mrs. Todd would not discover her there, Elizabeth saw Mr. Hadley coming towards her, an expression of concern on his face. He must know that this call could ruin her reputation, so he assumed it must be bad news.

"My dear Miss Bennet, is something the matter? Shall I fetch my sister?"

"No, I thank you. I must ask to speak to you privately."

His eyes widened and his cheeks grew pale. "Not Andrew?" he asked, practically in a whisper.

Of course that would be his first worry, that she was bearing bad news. "Andrew is perfectly well, but I am ending my engagement to him."

"Ending your engagement? But why?" He looked devastated. "Here, come into my study."

She followed him into a small room and waited until he closed the door. "I have many reasons. Were you not the one who told me not to marry him if I loved another man? At the time, I was willing to take the risk, but it has become clear that Andrew has developed tender feelings for my sister, and she returns them. It is time for me to remove myself from the middle of this and allow them their happiness."

He blinked several times. "Your sister, Miss Mary?"

"She is better suited to Andrew than I am."

"But what of you? By ending your engagement—"

"I will be disgraced," she interrupted. "I have considered all that. I will have to leave my home and start a new life. From the time I was forced into the engagement to avoid shaming my family, there has been no other choice."

"But what will you do?"

"I intend to seek a position as a governess or a companion." She would not let herself think about how much she would dislike being in service to strangers. "But in order to do so, I must beg a small favor of you."

"Anything, of course. If you are in need of money..."

She shook her head. "I cannot accept that. All I ask is a letter of character, if you could see your way to writing one for me. Without one, I am unlikely to find a respectable position. I know you have no experience of my abilities, but I promise you I will work hard and be a credit to you."

He studied her compassionately. "I would be happy to do that service for you."

She expelled a long breath. "I thank you, again and again. It will make a great difference."

"But I would prefer to go even further. You have met my sister, who keeps house for me. As you have seen, her arthritis is crippling her, and she could benefit from a companion who could assist her. Would you consider such a position? It would give you a safe place to go, and if you find you dislike it, I would be happy to give you a character reference so you could find a position more suited to you."

Elizabeth caught her breath. "That is nothing short of charity on your part, and I cannot take advantage of you so."

He smiled. "Perhaps in part, though I have considered hiring a companion for her for some time. She does need one, even if she will not admit it. But, Miss Bennet, you gave me my son. There is nothing I could do for you that would begin to repay what you have done for me."

"I did that for Andrew's sake. Even though he denied it, I could see how much he needed to know you."

"You saw a problem that was hurting him, and you undertook to relieve it. Will you not permit me to do the same by helping you?"

Tears poured into her eyes, tears of relief. "Thank you. Thank you. I will accept your generous offer."

"Thank God!" he exclaimed. "I will feel much better knowing you are safe, especially when you have sacrificed so much for Andrew's happiness."

A home with Mr. Hadley, whom she trusted, and working for Mrs. Todd, who seemed a cheerful lady. It was more than she had possibly hoped for. "I do not intend to tell Andrew until after Lady Frederica's wedding. I made the decision several days ago, but did not wish my actions to overshadow her day of happiness."

"When do you wish to begin, then? You can come here whenever you choose."

She swallowed hard. "The day after the wedding, then. I will break the news to Andrew, and then leave directly. I think it would be better if he did not know where I have gone." Because Darcy must not know. Her voice shook, and the tears spilled over.

He offered her his handkerchief. "I understand. And, for what it is worth, you have my support."

LADY FREDERICA FARLEIGH, *née* Fitzwilliam, kissed Darcy's cheek just before they left the Abbey after her wedding. "Thank you again for stepping up to give me away, even though it will earn you my father's displeasure."

"I was proud to do it, and I am not worried about your father. There was bound to be a break with him sooner or later," Darcy said. "I am just relieved we have made it through today without any interference from him."

"Well, the fireworks will begin as soon as I tell Lady Margaret I am married. I expect it will be quite an unpleasant scene, with some memorable language."

He chuckled. "I expect you are right."

When they reached the York House, where the wedding breakfast was to be held, Darcy took Drew aside. "I think it would be wisest if we were to keep the young ladies from returning to Lady Margaret's house today. There is no point in having them witness the quarrel that is bound to ensue when she learns of Frederica's marriage."

"Quite right," said Andrew. "We could go walking on the Parades until it is time for this afternoon's concert."

"An excellent plan." And perhaps Darcy could once again manage to stroll with Elizabeth. With only two days left before they were due to leave Bath, he wanted to steal as much time with her as possible, more memories to warm his lonely years in the jungles of South America.

But Elizabeth stayed close to her sister at the wedding breakfast, looking pale and subdued. He hoped she was not unwell. She had wept a little at the Abbey, but he had not thought much of it since women so often cried at weddings.

He managed to walk beside her on the way to the Parades. The busy streets of Bath did not allow for private conversation, but still, something was different about her. He was sure of it. The warmth, the teasing, the secret glances and double meanings that had characterized the last few days had faded away.

She took his arm as they walked down the steps into the small pleasure gardens by the North Parade, sending a surge of warmth through him. One more opportunity to pretend for just a moment that he could be the man in her life rather than Drew. But still she looked somber.

"You seem quiet today," he said finally. "I hope nothing is the matter."

She gave him an anxious glance from under the brim of her bonnet, and then looked away as if admiring the flower border. "Nothing of note. I did not sleep well last night."

Was that truly all? "Were you concerned about the wedding? I must admit that I did not dare breathe until they were pronounced man and wife. I kept expecting Lord Matlock to come charging in and disrupt everything."

"That had not occurred to me as a possibility," she said. "Perhaps ignorance truly is bliss." But she had not said what was troubling her.

Georgiana came to walk on his other side, precluding any possibility of asking more personal questions. Instead, Darcy asked, "Are you looking forward to today's concert? I heard George Bridgetower play in London years ago. His talent is quite remarkable."

"I am," Georgiana said. "Is it true that his father is an African prince?"

Darcy smiled. "He has claimed so, but others say he was a slave in the West Indies. But he himself was such a prodigy on the violin that the Prince Regent took him into his household when he was but a child, and he has only improved since then."

But Elizabeth said nothing.

At the concert in the Upper Rooms, Drew and Georgiana sat between them, so Darcy could see nothing of Elizabeth beyond an occasional movement. But after Mr. Bridgetower ended the concert with a virtuoso performance of a sonata by Beethoven which could have left no one unmoved, Elizabeth joined in the general praise, her eyes alight. Darcy breathed a little easier then, content to stand back and drink in her pleasure.

She seemed happy as they mingled with the other concertgoers. Andrew had spotted a friend from London and gone off to greet him, leaving Darcy to take the coveted spot beside Elizabeth. It felt so right, to be greeting acquaintances with her by his side. If only it could always be that way!

But soon enough Andrew approached them, smiling broadly, accompanied by a dark-haired couple. "Mr. and Mrs. Genova, may I introduce Miss Elizabeth Bennet, my betrothed, of whom I told you when I visited last month, and my elder brother, Mr. Darcy of Pemberley? The Genovas are originally from Parma, but in exile since Napoleon annexed it, and are great supporters of our abolitionist community."

Mrs. Genova, a striking woman not much older than Darcy, tapped Elizabeth's arm with her fan. "What an honor this is, to meet the young lady who won the heart of the oh-so-elusive Mr. Andrew Darcy! I cannot tell you, Miss Bennet, how many girls in London admired that stern, handsome countenance of his and set their caps at him, but they might not have existed for all he noticed."

Drew laughed. "She exaggerates greatly, of course, but she does it so charmingly that I can hardly complain!"

Elizabeth's sparkling smile almost hid the fact that she had gone pale and her eyes had lost their luster. "I can well believe he had a great many admirers."

Mrs. Genova seemed well pleased by this, and expressed her hope that Elizabeth and Drew would dine with them in London on their next visit to Town. Elizabeth said all the right things, but to Darcy, it seemed as if she lacked her usual vibrancy.

Mr. Hadley and his sister joined them then, praising the music. Elizabeth smiled at them, but if anything, she grew paler.

Worried, Darcy said quietly, only for her ears, "Are you certain you are quite well?"

Elizabeth looked down. "Only a bit fatigued. Perhaps I should return to the townhouse to rest."

At least he could make that easier for her. "Shall I tell Drew? I will escort you back."

She gave him an amused, limpid glance. "It will take me all of four minutes to walk there, if I make an effort to go particularly slowly, and it is still broad daylight."

"Nonetheless, I insist. I prefer to speak to Lady Margaret myself before she has a chance to scold you about Frederica's wedding. I intend to inform her you knew nothing about it before Drew and I marched you into the Abbey." He smiled, hoping to make it seem a secret they could share.

"You will get no argument from me, sir, if you wish to take all the blame for it."

But as they reached the Circus, she was biting her lip again. Once inside the house, she turned to face him, as if about to say something, but remained silent. Finally he said quietly, "Go on up to your room, and I will distract Lady Margaret."

She nodded jerkily. "I thank you. And also..." She gazed up at him.

God, how he loved her eyes! How could he live for three years without seeing them? "Yes?"

"Thank you," she said, and then added, all in a rush, "I thank you for everything. Everything."

Was she talking about the concert? "You are most welcome," he said softly, letting his love spill into his words.

She took an uneven breath. Suddenly her eyes were filled with tears, and then she turned and ran up the stairs.

"Elizabeth!" he called after her, but she did not turn back.

Was it simply her fatigue or more of the odd mood that seemed to have plagued her all day? He could hardly follow her into her bedroom, so it would have to wait until he could speak to her in the morning. In the meantime, he still needed to face Lady Margaret.

Chapter 30

A hand shook Darcy's shoulder, tearing him roughly away from a dream of kissing Elizabeth in the moonlight. "Go away," he mumbled.

"Sir, you must wake up." It was Wilkins' voice, and his valet sounded worried. He shook Darcy's shoulder once more.

Darcy rubbed the back of his hand over his eyes. The light coming through the window was pale and gray, raindrops streaking down the panes. "What is the matter?"

"It is Miss Bennet. She left Lady Margaret's house just after dawn, alone, with a trunk and satchels. She got into a private coach."

"What?" Darcy, now fully awake, pushed himself into a sitting position. "How do you know this?"

"The man you had watching the house in case Lord Matlock arrived spotted her. He came and reported it." Wilkins hesitated. "And while he was telling me, I saw Miss Bennet come into the hotel and ask to speak to Mr. Drew, saying it was urgent and could not wait. The clerk sent for him. I watched over her until he came down, and then I came to you, sir."

What possibly could have caused Elizabeth to flee from Lady Margaret? His aunt had a cruel tongue, but Elizabeth had stood up to Lady Catherine de Bourgh with no difficulty. And why would she have taken her belongings with her?

Perhaps this was why she had been in such an odd mood yesterday. Had someone frightened her? Matlock, perhaps, but why? "At least she had the sense to come here," he said, more to himself than to Wilkins, who had already opened the wardrobe to select his clothes for the day.

Wilkins turned back to face him. "My apologies, sir; I failed to make myself clear. The clerk asked if she wanted a private parlor or some tea, and she said that she would only be here a few minutes, and her coach was waiting."

Something was very wrong.

Darcy swung his legs out of bed and stood up. "No time to dress, then. Just my housecoat and trousers."

Wilkins looked horrified. "At least let me shave you, sir."

He hesitated. He would not help Elizabeth by storming in looking like an unkempt buccaneer. "Make it quick, then. Cold water will do."

"As you wish, sir." Wilkins' tone expressed his disapproval. He believed in doing things properly.

Darcy chafed at the delay as Wilkins carefully scraped off his stubble. As soon as his valet turned away to put down the razor, Darcy jumped up, wiped his own face, and pulled his housecoat on right over his nightshirt.

A sudden tapping at the door caught his attention. Wilkins opened it, revealing a boy in the hotel's uniform. "That lady – she's leaving," he piped, with a nervous glance at Darcy. "Crying, too."

Elizabeth was crying in public? What in God's name had Drew said to her? Darcy pushed past Wilkins and the boy and raced for the stairs, hurtling down them two at a time, heedless of his stockinged feet.

He pounded to a halt on the marble floor of the lobby. Empty, except for the clerk at the desk and a maidservant carrying a tray. He rushed to the clerk. "There was a lady here, Miss Bennet," he bit out.

The clerk nodded to the door. "Just left, sir, not five minutes ago, and —"

Darcy did not wait to hear the rest. He rushed out into the street, nearly knocking over a boy standing outside. Rain dripped onto his head, and a puddle soaked through his stockings, but he did not care. He peered up and down the street, but did not see her. No, Wilkins had said her carriage was waiting. There – a modest carriage stood on the opposite side of the street. Without even stopping to look, Darcy charged across in front of it, earning an angry cry from a horseman who rode past him.

The carriage door was just closing as he reached the pavement on the opposite side. With no regard for proper behavior, he grabbed the handle and yanked it open.

A wave of relief rolled over him at the sight of Elizabeth. Her reddened eyes grew wide, and she clutched a balled-up handkerchief to her mouth as she shrank back in the seat.

"Elizabeth, what is wrong?" he asked.

"No...Nothing," she stammered, and then rolled her eyes at the obvious untruth of it. "Ask Andrew. He will tell you. I must go."

"I want you to tell me. Has someone hurt you? Frightened you?"

She wet her lips with the tip of her tongue. "No, nothing like that."

A terrible thought rocked him. "Did Drew do something to you?"

"Not at all!" Shock filled her voice. "I must leave. Andrew will explain everything."

What could he say to make her tell him what was wrong? There must be something. "Where are you going? Longbourn?"

She closed her eyes as if in pain. "Yes. Longbourn." She sounded calmer now, and more distant.

"I will escort you there, then. You should not be traveling alone." Could she not see how worried he was?

She bit her lip. "I thank you for your concern, but there is no need." Suddenly resolute, she leaned toward him. "Mr. Darcy, if you have ever cared for me, I beg of you, let me go."

Her fine eyes were full of tears, but he could not doubt that she meant it, even if the knowledge cut him like a knife. She did not want his help.

Slowly he forced his fingers to release the door latch. He could not hold her prisoner on a public street. "If that is what you wish, all I can offer you is the hope that you may soon find relief from whatever troubles you. But I beg you..."

Her voice caught as she said, "I thank you. Farewell, sir." She held out her hand, and for a moment he thought she was reaching for him, but it was only to pull the door closed.

The click of the latch sounded oddly final. As soon as Darcy stepped back, the coachman shook the reins, and the carriage lurched down the street. He stared after it, suddenly feeling the cold rain trickling down his neck and his sodden feet. But that was nothing to how the sight of her tears had cut his heart.

He had to find a way to help her, whatever the problem might be. Once Andrew told him what had happened, he would finish dressing and ride out after her, rain or no rain. Even if he missed her on the road, he would catch up to her at Longbourn.

He stopped short on the steps to the hotel. Longbourn. Elizabeth's sister was here in Bath. Why would Elizabeth be returning home while leaving Mary behind? It could not be the truth. Why had she told him that, then? Or had he assumed, and she only agreed? But if she was not heading to Longbourn, then he had no idea where she was going.

Drew must know. He raced upstairs and pounded on his brother's door.

"Not now." Drew's flat voice came through the door. "Come back later."

"I must speak to you. It is urgent, most urgent."

The door flew open, revealing his brother. Drew's hair was disordered, standing on end as if he had raked his hand through it. "What is it?" he demanded.

"I just saw Elizabeth leaving. In tears. She would not tell me why, only that I should ask you."

Drew scowled, but he stepped back. "I suppose you had better come in, then. I do not want the whole world to know. Good God, you are soaking!"

That was the least of his worries. "Do you know why she left?"

"She jilted me, that is why!" Drew snarled. "Are you satisfied now?"

Darcy's jaw dropped. "What?"

"Yes, she broke the engagement. Said it had been a mistake. A mistake!"

He felt as if he had been sucked into a whirlwind, battered by opposing feelings. Elizabeth was free – but Drew had lost the woman he loved. Somehow he managed to say, "I am very sorry. I had no idea."

Drew laughed harshly. "Nor did I. I thought she was happy, fool that I am! No, she would rather be ruined than to spend her life with me. And I thought she liked me."

Ruined. The word echoed through him. With a failed engagement behind her, that would be true, but he would put an end to that once he found her. Right now Drew needed him. "Did she give you a reason?"

"Is not my birth reason enough?" Drew threw the words at him as if they were knives. "Who would want to marry a bastard?"

Darcy blinked. "No, that I will not believe."

Drew jutted out his chin. "She was happy enough to marry me until she discovered the truth, and then everything was different. That is proof enough for me."

"It makes no sense. She was the one who wanted you to know Hadley. She must have had another reason." And he knew what it had been. But had she told Drew about him?

Drew stared at Darcy like a wild deer transfixed by a hunter, and then he collapsed onto a chair and covered his face with his hands. "No. I failed her. It is my own fault." His muffled voice reeked of despair.

Darcy stiffened. If Drew had hurt Elizabeth, he would... He had no idea what he would do. "What do you mean?"

Drew's words were barely audible. "I was disloyal to her. In my heart."

Disloyal in his heart? Sometimes Drew was completely incomprehensible. "In what way?"

"She said... She said it was one thing to be forced to marry if neither of us had another attachment, but she no longer believed that was the case for me. I denied it, of course, but then she asked me if I would swear on my honor that I had never once thought Mary would make me a better wife than she would. What could I say? Her own sister!" He picked up a pillow and pitched it across the room.

"Mary Bennet?" Darcy could not hide his disbelief. It was beyond comprehension to him that any man could prefer Mary over Elizabeth.

"Oh, I know, Lizzy is prettier and more charming, but Mary cares about the same things I do. She is excited by what I am teaching her. She seeks out my company. Lizzy will agree with me on many things, but Mary is passionate about them. But it is wrong, wrong, wrong. I should have closed my heart to her."

That was one appeal Darcy could understand all too well. "That is easier said than done. The heart follows its own rules." As he had learned, in the hardest possible way. But now, for the first time, there was hope for him. Drew could marry Mary Bennet, and then, after a decent interval passed, Darcy could approach Elizabeth, and this time she would accept him. The surge of triumph filled his chest.

"I did not know. I am not like you. I always avoided contact with young women because I would consider nothing but marriage, so Lizzy was the first young lady I ever conversed with at length. I thought it was safe to let her sisters close, but my sinful nature was too strong."

"You did nothing sinful. Perhaps this is all for the best. Now you and Miss Mary can be together." And he could have Elizabeth and a future he could rejoice in.

"Only at the cost of Lizzy's future, because of my mistake."

"There may be a little gossip, but it is hardly the end of the world."

Drew turned agonized eyes to him. "You do not understand. Lizzy is leaving her family and friends and seeking employment. She says she can never go home because of the scandal. That is the price of my mistake."

The words stabbed him. Through numb lips, he forced out, "Seeking employment?"

"She has already taken a position as a teacher in a school for girls."

Elizabeth, having to earn her keep? No. Never. "Where? What is the name of the school?"

Drew looked away. "She refused to tell me, only that it will be best for her family if she simply disappears. When I tried to insist, she said she was no longer my responsibility."

And Andrew had permitted her to leave? "No matter. We will find her."

Drew's head slowly swung to gaze at him. "But why? It is her right to refuse to marry me."

He could hardly tell Drew that his true reason was because he wanted to marry her himself. His brother was not ready to hear that. "To make certain she is safe."

"She knows she can contact me if she is in need. I told her so. She has family who can help her, too." Drew sounded exhausted.

Elizabeth would not ask for help, not unless she were desperate. "It is not as simple as that, not if she is worried about scandal touching her family."

His brother's eyes were haunted. "It is her choice, not mine. If there is one thing I have learned in my life, it is that you cannot make someone love you. She wants to be gone. Let her go."

The words knocked the breath out of Darcy. How did Drew know? And then he realized the truth. Drew was speaking of himself, not Darcy. But Elizabeth had left Darcy, too.

Had he misread all her recent gestures? No. He was certain she cared for him. Perhaps it might not be love, but she had feelings towards him. Why had she not turned to him now?

Drew might be ready to let her go, but Darcy was not. Not without a chance to ask why, at least. And there was no time to waste.

DARCY STRODE BACK INTO his room as quickly as he could manage in his dripping stockings. "Wilkins!"

"Yes, sir?" His valet stepped out of the dressing room, took one horrified look at him, and fetched a towel.

"Never mind that," Darcy snapped. "I need you to find where Elizabeth Bennet has gone. Her carriage pulled away not ten minutes ago. She has taken employment at a girls' school somewhere. Check the coaching inns to see if she has boarded a coach or is waiting for one."

Wilkins looked disapproving. "Sir, you are soaking wet. Pray permit me to assist you first."

"Now, Wilkins. There is no time to lose."

Wilkins stiffened. "Yes, sir." He disappeared back into the dressing room, reemerged in a great coat and carrying an umbrella, and started out the door.

"Hire as many people as you need. Spare no expense."

Wilkins bowed. "Yes, sir." As soon as the door closed behind him, Darcy threw off his dripping housecoat and sat down to peel his sodden stockings from his cold feet.

Why? Why had Elizabeth fled? Breaking her engagement, yes, but she must know he wanted her! Was she afraid of scandal? Or did someone disapprove of the match enough to threaten her? The only way to know would be to ask her.

Where could she have gone? How could she have found a position without anyone the wiser for it? Someone must have helped her. Or no –

there were schools here in Bath. She could have walked right into one and applied for a position. And there were agencies, were there not? If Wilkins did not find Elizabeth or where she had gone, Darcy would send him to check the agencies. He could visit the schools himself. All he needed to do was to say he was looking for a school for his young ward, listen to the headmaster drone on for a bit, and then ask to meet all the teachers.

That, and he must speak to Mary Bennet to find out if she knew anything. Surely Elizabeth must have confided in her sister.

Having the beginnings of a plan made the sickness in his stomach recede a little. Taking the towel, he vigorously dried his wet hair. Clothes. That was the next step.

ONCE HE HAD DRESSED, Darcy headed for the Circus. The rain had slowed to a drizzle, so an umbrella was sufficient protection for the short walk.

He found Drew already there, closeted with a pale, red-eyed Mary Bennet and Georgiana. When Darcy attempted to ask what Miss Mary might know, Drew interrupted him.

"We have already been through this," Drew said. "Lizzy left a letter for Mary, but said nothing more than what she told me."

"She did apologize for leaving me here, and gave me money for stage fare," said Mary quietly.

Darcy asked, "Have you any thoughts, or even guesses, of where she might have gone?"

"None. This is a complete shock to me. I cannot imagine why she would do such a terrible thing." Mary's voice trembled.

"Has she ever spoken to you about seeking employment, perhaps sometime in the past?"

Mary shook her head. "Never. We were not that close until recently. But I suppose we were not close at all, if she did this with no word to me." She dabbed furiously at her eyes.

"What about—"

Drew interrupted, "Fitzwilliam, I will not have your distressing Miss Mary with questions. She has had a bad shock."

Darcy swallowed hard. Drew had the right of it; he should not be allowing his impatience to rule over common politeness. "My apologies, Miss Mary." He bowed stiffly.

"I will be returning Miss Mary to Longbourn," Drew pronounced. "I have asked Georgiana to accompany us, as it would be improper for Miss Mary to travel alone with me, even with a maid. I must also answer to Mr. Bennet for Lizzy's disappearance."

"I should be the one to do that," Darcy said.

Drew uncoiled himself and rose to his feet, outrage outlining his features. "I am not a child. She was my betrothed and was here at my invitation. This matter has nothing to do with you. Just because Lizzy jilted me does not make me incompetent."

Nothing to do with him? Suddenly it was more than he could bear. "It has everything to do with me. The only reason Wickham forced you into this engagement was to hurt me. If it were not for me, Elizabeth would be safely at home among her family, her reputation intact."

"What is this nonsense?" demanded Drew, flushing. "I was the one Wickham wanted to embarrass."

Darcy felt his hands shaking. "Wickham did not care about you. It was all about me. He thought nothing could hurt me worse than to see the woman I loved ruined by my own brother. What he did not expect was for you to offer for her. That made it the perfect revenge."

"The woman you loved?" Drew laughed scornfully "What is wrong with you? You did not even like her. She told me about your quarrel."

"But not what preceded it, which was her refusal of my proposal of marriage." Darcy's words ricocheted around the room like a gunshot, leaving shocked silence in their wake.

"You proposed to Lizzy?" Drew's voice throbbed with disbelief. "Tell me another fairy story."

"Yes, I proposed to her," Darcy said savagely. "Before you ever met her."

Finally Drew licked his lips. "It makes no sense. Why would she have refused you and then accepted me?"

"Because she liked you better, and because Wickham had told her lies about me." Darcy could not hold back his bitterness.

"It is true, Drew." It was Georgiana, speaking in a small voice. "I knew about it. Or at least I knew Fitzwilliam intended to propose to her, back in the spring. That was why I was so shocked when you announced she was engaged to you."

Drew stared at Darcy. "Why did you never tell me?" His voice was filled with pain.

Darcy's breath was uneven in his throat. He had worked so hard to build trust with Drew, and this might ruin it all. "Because you loved her, and I wanted you to be happy. Both of you."

Oddly enough, it was Mary Bennet who reached the final conclusion. "Is this why you decided to go to South America?"

He wanted to refuse to answer, to hide his private pain, but there had been too many secrets, and now Elizabeth was gone. He gave a single sharp nod.

She pressed further. "Did Lizzy know you were leaving because of her?"

His fingernails bit into his palms. "She guessed."

Drew rubbed the bridge of his nose, as if he could not take any of this in. Finally he said, "Regardless, I must still return Miss Mary to Longbourn, and I see no advantage to your coming. You may choose to blame yourself, but Lizzy's reputation will only be damaged more if you reveal any of this."

Darcy could not dispute the point. "Then the carriage is at your disposal." And because he could not bear Drew's wounded expression another minute, he strode out without a further word. Elizabeth was gone, and Drew might never forgive him.

HE COULD NOT FACE RETURNING to the hotel only to sit alone in his room awaiting news from Wilkins. Instead he roamed aimlessly through Bath, barely noticing his whereabouts. There were too many people on the streets, too many witnesses to his agony, so eventually his feet found their way to the lesser traveled towpath of the Kennet and Avon canal. But that path led him beneath the bridge where he had stood with

Elizabeth just three days earlier, glorying in the touch of her hand and her acknowledgment of her sentiments towards him.

And now she was gone, without even a word to him. Had she thought he would not care? Somehow he must speak to her. This could not be the end for them!

Slowly he trudged back to the York House. He stopped at the desk to ask the clerk to prepare a list of schools in or near Bath. Before he could get the words out, the elderly man said, "Ah, Mr. Darcy, there was something for you." He peered into a desk drawer. "Here it is."

Recognizing at once the feminine writing he had glimpsed when she wrote letters at Pemberley, Darcy took it in a shaking hand. Elizabeth had written to him.

He hurried up to his room, and without even bothering to remove his hat or greatcoat, he broke the wax seal. The letter lacked the usual neatness he had seen in her letters, as if written in a great hurry, as it must have been, and it began without a salutation.

I have written so many letters in the last day explaining my actions, but none to you, thinking you the sole person who could need no explanation of my decision to break my engagement. But our brief conversation earlier showed me that there was still room for misinterpretation, and I would not wish to leave you with a false impression, nor do I wish to accidentally cause a new breach between you and your brother.

Andrew is in no way at fault for my decision. He has always treated me with respect and propriety. The fault lies only in me, and my own unwillingness to be a source of unhappiness. Here in Bath I have been forced to acknowledge the true cost your mother paid for making a good practical match when she held another man in her heart. Knowing that, I could not choose to follow that path, especially as it became ever clearer to me that Andrew would be much happier with my sister, whom I believe has developed tender feelings for him. That is my sole motivation; there was no mistreatment whatsoever involved.

Several lines after this were scratched out.

My one hope out of all of this is that somehow your brother and my sister will make a match of it, not only to protect my family from the worst of the scandal of my broken engagement, but because I believe it would be in the best interest of both of them. I watched their attachment grow, but I fear that somehow Andrew may decide he ought not pursue it. I did my best to convince him, but he needs you, too. Your good opinion matters a great deal to him.

As for the rest, all I can do is to hope that your expedition provides you distraction and a new focus. I will think of you often. God bless you.

E. Bennet

A round blotch stained the last paragraph.

A whirlwind of emotion tore through him; an aching relief at the indirect acknowledgment of what lay between them, gratitude for this confirmation that Drew was not at fault, and fury at the lack of answers to any of the questions that plagued him.

Devil take it! He needed to talk to her. To see her. To take her in his arms and tell her he loved her.

And that was impossible, at least for the moment.

DARCY STARED AT DREW in disbelief. "No, I am not going to waste two hours dining with Lady Margaret and listening to her attacking Elizabeth."

Drew scowled at him. "Yes, you are, because that is the price of protecting Lizzy's good name."

"What do you mean?"

"Lady Margaret does not yet know the truth. I do not want her spreading the news of my broken engagement in her own unpleasant manner, so I told her that Lizzy received news that her father was badly hurt and left on the first post, but that Mary was ill and unable to travel with her. It is easy enough to believe, since Mary is clearly upset. I think it better to wait to make an announcement ending the engagement after we have settled on the best course."

Darcy had not even considered trying to minimize the scandal. Once again, Drew was thinking more clearly than he was. "What do you believe the best course is?"

Andrew flushed. "To reduce gossip as much as possible. We cannot afford to have my scandal hanging over Georgiana's head when her Season begins. Assuming Mary is willing, we will marry quickly. That should provide the best protection for the Bennets, and it will show that I do not blame the family. I wish to prevent the worst of the damage, enough that Lizzy may eventually be able to visit her family without shame."

That Elizabeth should be reduced to the hope of not shaming her family! Then a thought struck him. "Did you ever tell her Wickham is imprisoned?"

"No. It did not seem necessary." But color rose again in Drew's cheeks.

Of course. Elizabeth had agreed to marry Drew because of the blackmail and Drew feared that, without it, Elizabeth might end the engagement. Marrying her had been so important to him, and he would not have wanted to take that risk.

But if Elizabeth did not know that Wickham was no longer a threat, then she would think the end of her engagement would mean absolute ruination. A broken engagement was scandalous enough by itself, but doing so when Wickham was ready to spread rumors that she and Drew had been intimate – that would be disastrous. She would be universally shunned in Meryton and her entire family would be shamed. She would be beyond unmarriageable. But that was not the case, and she did not know it.

He rubbed his hands over his face in sudden comprehension. That was why she had vanished. Not because she lacked faith in him or because she did not love him, but because she thought it impossible for her to have any future with him when she was seen as both unchaste and a jilt. No wonder she had fled.

But that could be fixed. He would find her, tell her that Wickham was no longer a threat, and convince her they belonged together.

Suddenly he felt able to take on the world. Starting with dinner with Lady Margaret. Then he would find Elizabeth.

Chapter 31

After over a month of hunting for Elizabeth, Darcy's confidence had fled, drained by false lead after false lead. In Bath, Wilkins had been unable to find a coaching inn that had sold a ticket to a young lady matching Elizabeth's description. Darcy's hopes had been raised by the news that a Bath employment agency had placed a dark-haired girl as a teacher, but it turned out to be a sharp-faced young woman from Devon. He visited every school within miles of Bath, pretending to be looking for a place for his fictional ward, and insisted on meeting every single teacher. None of them were Elizabeth.

He had returned to London after exhausting all the possibilities in Bath. Interviewing Elizabeth's aunt and uncle brought him no new information, and he had no reason to doubt them as they expressed their own anxiety over her disappearance. He had hired an investigator to check more distant schools.

His best hope had been to learn something when he returned to Netherfield for Drew's wedding to Mary Bennet, but his brother had quickly informed him that, for his bride's sake, he did not wish Elizabeth's name to be mentioned during the festivities. Darcy would have to wait.

After the wedding, as he stood outside the Longbourn church, Sir William Lucas approached him and said affably, "What an auspicious day it was for the Bennet family when Mr. Bingley came to Netherfield Park. Two daughters married in such a short time, and you had the privilege to stand up with both grooms! The Bennets are fortunate indeed."

Darcy gritted his teeth. He needed the goodwill of the local neighborhood if he hoped to gain their assistance in finding Elizabeth, so he forced himself to reply with a veneer of amiability. "I have been most privileged." Given the effort it took not to strangle the old fool for calling the Bennets fortunate, this qualified as beyond polite. The price of marrying off their third daughter had been losing their second one. What was Elizabeth suffering in her employment? How could her impertinent high spirits tolerate the bondage of service?

Sir William rubbed his hands together. "Capital, capital. A fine day indeed."

Darcy managed to keep an agreeable air through the tedious wedding breakfast at Longbourn, pretending not to notice that Drew and Mary's marriage did not deserve the same excessive hospitality and rich foods that had accompanied bringing Bingley into the family. Drew, lacking a fortune of his own, was less valued by Mrs. Bennet, much as she seemed to like him. It was harder to ignore the overheard whispers of amazement that plain Mary Bennet had somehow managed to displace Elizabeth. Instead he tried to focus on how happy Drew looked. If only he could share in that happiness.

As soon as Drew and Mary drove off on their wedding journey, Darcy made his way back to Netherfield and plotted how to obtain a private conversation with Jane Bingley. In the three days he had been there, in the rare moments when Mrs. Bingley had not been wrapped up in planning for her sister's wedding, her still-enamored husband had clung to her side. If need be, Darcy would present his questions to the two of them together, but he suspected Jane would give him a more sympathetic hearing. She had new lines of worry around her eyes, and he suspected she was as concerned about Elizabeth as he was.

He finally caught her the next morning as she was arranging flowers in the dining room. "Mrs. Bingley, you make a charming picture," he said with a bow. "I must thank you yet again for hosting me here."

She turned to him with an embarrassed smile. "You are most kind, but I cannot help recalling something my sister Lizzy once told me about you."

Taken aback, he asked, "What was that?"

"She said that it was easy to know when you were telling the truth, because you lack a talent for disguising your motives. Is there something you wished to say to me?"

So quiet Jane Bennet had become more confident now that she was married! He bowed again. "You are quite right, and your sister is what I wished to speak to you about. I have been trying to locate her, and I hoped you might be able to help me do so."

"I thought it might be that. I doubt I can be of much assistance to you, much as I would wish you success. I am so worried about her." She bit her lip as she tucked a pink hothouse flower into one side of her arrangement.

He expelled a slow sigh. "As am I. Might I be permitted to ask if she has been in contact with you?" Pray God, let her have told her sister something, for he was quickly running out of places to look.

Mrs. Bingley frowned. "I received a letter, as my parents did, but she asked me not to tell them of mine. The news of her broken engagement did not shock me, for she had once mentioned the idea to me. I thought she had put it aside. I was wrong."

He caught his breath. "Did she give you a reason?"

She seemed to be studying something over his shoulder, and then gradually her eyes focused on him. "At the time we discussed it, she was concerned about you," she said, almost apologetically. "Otherwise I would not be telling you any of this. Long ago, when she never expected to see you again, she had confided to me what happened in Kent."

Once it would have embarrassed him to have her know about his failed proposal, but now it was a relief not to have to explain his concern. "I am grateful that you understand my position. Dare I hope Miss Elizabeth told you something of her present situation?"

"Only that she is the companion of an older lady whom she likes, and that she feels very fortunate to have found that position, nothing about who her...employer may be or where she lives." She stuttered a little over the word, as if hesitant to admit her sister was in service.

"A companion? She told Drew that she had taken a job as a schoolteacher."

Mrs. Bingley colored delicately. "She mentioned in her letter that she was going to tell him something misleading, in case he took it into his head to search for her."

All those days he had spent visiting schools, wasted, while the trail had gone cold. Finding a lady's companion would be even harder than a schoolteacher. "Do you happen to know if she looked at any advertisements for positions while she was still here?"

"Not to my knowledge. I wish I could tell you more. I would do anything to bring her home."

"At least I have a better idea what to look for now," he said. "I do not wish to leave any stone unturned. Do you have any suggestions who might have more information about her whereabouts?"

She shook her head. "I think she would tell me if she told anyone. She did say that eventually she would give me an address where I could write to her if I wished – if I wished! – but I could not tell if she meant next month or in ten years." Her voice shook.

"I hardly need say that I would like to know if she does, but should you feel unable to tell me, if perhaps she asks you to keep it a secret, could I ask you to give her a message from me?"

Mrs. Bingley fished out a handkerchief and dabbed at the corners of her eyes. "That would depend upon the message, I suppose."

"It is twofold. First, that I would like to speak to her. And second, that George Wickham is unable to spread any gossip about her. I assume you know about his threats that led to her engagement, and I fear she has fled to avoid the possibility that he would tell people she and Drew behaved improperly. As it happens, he is in debtor's prison to prevent him from ruining anyone else's life, so she is safe. If she knows that, perhaps she will feel able to return to her family, if the scandal is nothing more than a broken engagement. But I have no way to communicate it to her."

"Oh! That would be such a relief! You may be certain I will tell her that, should I have the opportunity." She pressed her hand to her chest. "I thank you for giving me some hope."

He bowed to her and tried to smile. He knew little more than he had before, but now he needed to start his search again from the beginning.

TWO LONG MONTHS LATER, months of sleepless nights, his investigators had still found no sign of Elizabeth. Darcy forced himself to do the necessary tasks to run Pemberley and his research, though often he could barely concentrate on what was needful. Finally, he could bear waiting no longer, so he rode to the parsonage to speak to his brother.

Drew looked up from the sermon he was working on when Darcy appeared, and Mary put aside her mending. If Darcy could have been glad of anything, he would have been pleased to see how well marriage seemed to suit Drew, but instead, as always, the sight of the former Mary Bennet was a stabbing reminder of Elizabeth's absence.

His brother greeted him warmly, quite a change from the suspicion of only half a year ago. Mary quickly excused herself, leaving the two of them alone.

"I hope all is well at Pemberley," said Drew.

"Well enough," Darcy replied. But small talk was difficult these days, too, so he did not even try. "I am planning to go to London. The expedition leaves next week."

His brother looked up at him sharply. "Have you changed your mind and decided to go with them after all?"

"Of course not. But I am going to see them off and to assist them with some difficulties with their equipment."

"If you still wish to be part of it, it is not too late," Drew said carefully.

"Leave England for years when Elizabeth is still missing? I think not," Darcy snapped. But it was not Drew's fault, so he added, "Forgive me. I do not know how long I will be in Town, so would you be so kind as to keep an eye on Pemberley and Georgiana while I am gone?"

Drew studied him, his brows drawn together. "While I would be glad to help, there is no need. Your steward has managed in your absence many times in the past, and I know so little of estate management that he would do better to write to you in London than to ask me."

"Still, Georgiana would feel better if she knew you were taking charge."

His brother paused, considering. "No, she would feel better if I went to London with you, and there are people I need to see there anyway."

It was what he had wished to avoid. "Damn it, Drew, I do not need a nursemaid! I am simply going to help with the launch of the expedition."

"You do not need a nursemaid, but perhaps you may need a brother. Or can you give me your word that is the only reason you are going, and it is not because you plan to begin searching for Elizabeth yourself?" When had Drew learned that commanding tone?

He tried his best Master of Pemberley stare, but it seemed to have lost its power when Elizabeth vanished. "I plan to talk to the investigators, of course, and there are many other things I may wish to do in London."

"I am not fool enough to think you are going there for the society. You have hardly spoken to anyone in months. You only eat when you know Georgiana is watching you." Drew raked his hand through his hair. "Fitzwilliam, you might as well accept my help gracefully, since the other option is that Georgiana will cry until you agree to allow her to accompany you. This way Mary can stay with Georgiana, and, unlike our sister, at least I will not hang over you every minute."

The worst part is that Drew was right – Georgiana would do exactly that. How had he lost control of his family to the degree that they felt he could not be trusted to travel to London alone? "You would leave your new bride behind?"

Drew shrugged. "I will miss Mary, but it would do her good to be here without me for a time. She needs to gain her footing as mistress here without worrying about what I will think of every decision she makes."

Darcy ought to resent Drew's insistence on inserting himself into his business, but it was too much effort, like everything else these days. Besides, he would be glad not to be alone.

Chapter 32

Mr. Hadley entered the sitting room still wearing his greatcoat and hat, so Elizabeth put aside the novel she was reading aloud to Mrs. Todd. It was not holding her interest anyway; little could these days, and her employer's taste in books often did not match her own. But that was the reality of her new life as a companion.

"Good day, ladies," he said, and then turned to his sister. "My dear, may I borrow Elizabeth for the afternoon? I require her assistance for a mission of mercy."

"Certainly, if Lizzy has no objections," Mrs. Todd said. "What has happened?"

He held up his hand. "No time to spare now, but I promise to give you all the details later. The carriage is waiting."

Surprised, but not averse to an outing, Elizabeth fetched her pelisse and bonnet. When she met Mr. Hadley in the entry hall, she asked, "Where are we going?"

He held the front door open for her, his manner as calm and courteous as ever. "I will explain as we go."

Now curious, she ducked her head as she stepped into the carriage. Why was he hurrying her along, yet showed no signs of distress? Perhaps he simply did not wish to answer her questions, and, of course, he had no need to do so. Just because he usually treated her more like a family member than a servant did not change the fact that he was her employer, and thus able to give her orders. Well, he would explain himself when he was ready. She had learned to trust him in the months she had lived in his household.

It did not matter where they were going, after all. She needed the distraction. Ever since reading a report on the launch of the South American expedition in last week's newspaper, an odd emptiness had taken

THE PRICE OF PRIDE

over her. Darcy was gone. He was no longer breathing the same air of England that she was. It should make no difference, since she could not see him anyway, but it did. Even her food had lost its savor.

The carriage lurched into motion after he settled in across from her. She folded her hands in her lap, but raised a querying eyebrow.

He caressed the head of his walking stick. "I thank you for joining me. A rather unexpected situation has arisen. I believe I told you Andrew Darcy was in London."

She pointedly looked out the window. "Yes, and that you saw him a fortnight ago and he was doing well." He knew she wanted no involvement with Andrew, especially as his presence in London meant staying close to home lest she accidentally encounter him.

"I called on him earlier today, only to find him in some distress. An accident with a runaway horse and carriage two days ago left him with some minor injuries—"

She interrupted, "I am sorry to hear it, but Andrew is none of my business any longer. I have no desire to see him, and I do not understand why you would bring me on a mission of mercy to him!"

He held up his hand. "It is more than that. Drew would have been much more seriously hurt, had his brother not deliberately stepped between the runaway and Andrew. His injuries are much more severe."

She clapped her hands to her mouth in horror, suddenly unable to breathe. "Not Mr. Darcy? But he is on his way to South America!"

"He decided against going on the expedition. I am sorry to say he is in some danger from this accident. Naturally, Andrew is distraught, not least because his brother seems to have given up and is not complying with his doctor's orders."

"No," she whispered, tears pricking at the corner of her eyes. Suddenly she would give anything to know he was safe on a ship, even if it was carrying him away from her for years, as long as he was alive and safe.

"Andrew says Darcy has been asking for you, and becomes quite agitated when you do not appear. I know you want nothing to do with the family, but if your presence can calm him and improve the chances of his recovery, I hope you will not object to trying."

"I will do anything I can to help." Her voice quavered. "What happened to him?"

"He was trampled by the horse. I do not know his precise injuries, but he is very weak."

Her heart ached at the thought of strong, proud Darcy, lying broken and confused. And she had known nothing of it, just gone about her day as if her world had not cracked apart into tiny pieces. She sucked in a breath and released it in a silent prayer. He must live. He must! She could not bear it otherwise.

Why were the horses so slow? What if she did not get there quickly enough? She did not even know how far it was, since she had avoided going into Mayfair since her arrival in London, just on the chance he might be there. Now she could not understand why she had left him in the first place.

The carriage pulled up in front of a row of townhouses. Elizabeth let herself out as soon as the groom lowered the steps, not waiting for Mr. Hadley to hand her down, almost oblivious to her surroundings.

The butler had only just admitted them to an elegant terraced house when Andrew charged down the stairs into the hall. One of his arms was in a sling, his cravat was askew, and his hair was mussed as if he had been running his hand through it.

He skidded to a stop in front of her. "Elizabeth, thank God! He keeps asking for you."

Her heart skipped a beat. "Is his condition so bad, then?"

Andrew grimaced. "The doctor sees signs of bleeding inside, and we can only pray that it stops. But he fears for his recovery, especially because he refuses to take anything."

"May I see him?" She handed her bonnet to the waiting servant, hardly noticing the luxury surrounding her.

"Of course. This way."

He led her up the stairs and opened the door to a large bedroom. The curtains were closed, leaving the room dim, but Elizabeth sucked in her breath at the sight of the still form lying on the bed.

Andrew hurried to his bedside. "Look! We have found her."

Darcy, so pale that he barely looked alive, raised his head and shoulders, his lips moving silently.

A voice in the darkness behind him spoke. "Sir, you must lie back." It was Darcy's valet, pressing his master's shoulders until he collapsed down onto the pillow.

She did not remember moving, but somehow she was kneeling next to him, her heart pounding. "I am here," she said in a trembling voice.

He turned his head as if it pained him. "Elizabeth?" It was little more than a hoarse whisper, disbelief echoing in it.

"Yes, I am here." Without a care for who might see, she reached for his hand, which lay limp on the counterpane. His skin was cool despite the warmth of the room, and she pressed her lips to the back of it and then held it to her cheek. He could not die; she would not allow it.

His fingers tightened on hers, his mouth working for a moment before he forced out the words, "Where? How?"

Elizabeth shook her head. "I do not know what you mean."

Andrew's quiet voice came from behind her. "He has been worried about you. We all have."

She did not take her eyes from Darcy's dark ones. "I have a position as a companion to Mrs. Todd, Mr. Hadley's sister. He brought me here today after Andrew told him you had been asking for me. I am perfectly well."

He closed his eyes for a moment, and then reached out his other hand shakily and touched her hair, as if needing to prove to himself that she was real. "Stay. I beg you."

She felt his words more than she heard his barely audible whisper. Tears flooded her eyes. "I will."

His valet said, "Mr. Darcy, now that Miss Bennet is here, you must drink." He sounded exhausted. In all the time Elizabeth had been at Pemberley, she had never heard Wilkins speak apart from acknowledging an order, much less interrupting a conversation. He must have been desperate.

Darcy ignored him.

What had Andrew said? That Darcy's refusal to take anything was endangering him? Resolve filled her. "Yes, they say I can only stay if you drink something. Will you do that for me?"

His mouth twisted, but he nodded, a bare movement of his head. A servant hurried forward to stand next to Elizabeth, holding a cup of some sort. On the other side of the bed, Wilkins slid his hands under Darcy's shoulders and gently raised him a few inches. Their alacrity told Elizabeth how significant this was.

As she rose to her feet to make room for the servant, Darcy clutched at her hand. "I am not leaving," she promised. "Drink."

As Darcy took a few sips, the valet said urgently to someone, "Fetch more warm beef broth." Another servant scurried from the room.

Darcy winced as he swallowed. His eyes were sunken, and his cheekbones stood out in a way they had not when she had seen him last. She studied his hand – yes, it was thinner, too. It could not be due to his injury, if that had been but two days earlier. He had lost weight. Had his appetite deserted him, as hers had after their parting in Bath?

Her heart ached at the sight of him. It had been agonizing enough to think she would never see him again; but she had known he was still there, somewhere in the world. To think that he might die, that she might have to live knowing that he no longer existed, the flame of his life snuffed out, made her want to sink to the floor and howl like an abandoned animal.

Tears overflowed her eyes. He was still alive, his hand in hers, and she would fight to keep him that way. She whispered a prayer.

He turned away from the cup. "No more."

She squeezed his hand. "One more sip, I beg you, for my sake. Just one."

He sighed, but allowed the servant to raise the cup to his lips again.

"I thank you," she said warmly. It did not matter that there were tears running down her cheeks. He would understand.

And she could help him. One of her duties with Mrs. Todd was to coax the older woman to eat on those days when her pain was bad. Elizabeth had become rather good at it, and she could do the same for Darcy.

She would do anything for him.

A servant materialized beside her, placing a small chair next to Darcy's bed. Elizabeth sank into it gratefully.

His valet eased him back onto the pillow, and Darcy immediately turned his face to her again. "Tell me..." His strength seemed to fail him with that effort.

Tell him what? Suddenly conscious of their surroundings, of Andrew and Mr. Hadley watching her, she asked, "Shall I tell you what I have been doing?"

He nodded, his eyes sending a different message, one of longing and need that spoke all too deeply to her. What if she lost him? Icy fear tightened around her chest. She wanted to sob like a child, not to make conversation. But he wanted to know of her journey, and she could deny him nothing, not now, not when any moment might be the last.

For his sake, she forced herself to push her fear and desperation aside, and strove to speak calmly. "Well, I have been with Mrs. Todd, who quite spoils me, treating me more as a favorite niece than a companion. We stayed in Bath for nearly a month, until she finished taking the waters. Since Mrs. Todd likes nothing better than to be read to, I had the opportunity to exhaust half of the circulating library in Bath before we left." And she had desperately needed the distraction, between her grief over everything she had left behind and her fear of discovery. Now that grief seemed a tiny thing in comparison.

His eyelids had been drifting down as she spoke, but they popped up again as soon as she paused, so she resumed. "Then we went to Lyme for a month, and, oh, what a treat that was for me! I had never seen the sea before, and I fell quite in love with it, the scent of the salt, and the immensity of it. Mr. Hadley kept saying he was going to lock me up to keep me from stowing away on one of the ships – is that not right, sir?" She had never told him her secret dream, though; that one day she might sail away with Darcy by her side, away from all the gossips and scandalmongers, to a land where she could love him with her whole heart.

Mr. Hadley chuckled. "I am still amazed we managed to drag you away, though, now that I think on it, I do recall being forced into a promise to return in the summer so you could try sea bathing."

"You see?" asked Elizabeth with greater cheer than she felt. "I am quite spoiled."

"No, my sister is spoiled," Mr. Hadley retorted. "I have rarely seen her in as good spirits as she has been since you joined our household."

Darcy's mouth turned down. He must dislike hearing that Mrs. Todd needed her. This was not the time to upset him, so she added quickly,

"Since then we have been in London. Mr. Hadley's house is near Bedford Square, so I have spent several afternoons wandering through the wonders of Montagu House." She had avoided the large parks lest she meet someone she knew from before, especially any of the Darcys. And now here she was in Darcy's own home, in his bedroom. And he might be dying.

His eyes bored into hers. "So close..."

Close indeed, and had she known he was in London, it would have haunted her constantly. "I have thought of you every day," she confessed in a low voice. Every hour would have been more accurate, but she could not admit to that. She should not have said even this much in front of Andrew and the servants. For their ears, she added, "I have missed all of you – Andrew and Georgiana, too – and I have wondered how Lady Frederica and Mr. Farleigh are doing."

"Quite splendidly," drawled Andrew. "Did Hadley not tell you?"

Mr. Hadley cleared his throat. "That was a confidential meeting."

Elizabeth turned to stare at them in time to see a flush rise in Andrew's cheeks.

"I had not considered that aspect," Andrew said stiffly. "Lady Frederica speaks of it so openly. My apologies."

"No apologies needed," said Mr. Hadley easily, with his characteristic warmth. "I was simply explaining why I could not tell Miss Bennet about it. You, on the other hand, are most welcome to do so."

"Oh, I see," said Andrew. "Well, Hadley brokered a meeting between Lady Frederica and her brother, Viscount Smithfield, presenting the case that it might serve him well in the future to have familial connections among the Whigs. He told him the tide had turned on slavery, and, while Matlock could slow that tide, he could not stop it. He convinced Smithfield that, when he inherits, he might appreciate having allies who are free of the taint of slavery. Smithfield has recognized Lady Frederica's marriage. Matlock still refuses to have any private contact with her, but he acknowledges her in public, which is more than we had hoped for."

Elizabeth's gaze slipped to Mr. Hadley. "How very like you, to see a problem and seek to find a solution, no matter how far it may be from your purview." It was precisely that propensity on his part that had brought her to Darcy's bedside.

He inclined his head. "I believe you share that tendency to a certain degree, my dear."

The butler appeared in the doorway. "Dr. Hackforth-Jones," he announced.

Elizabeth turned back to Darcy. "I suppose that is my cue to step out of the room."

His hand clenched tightly on hers. "Come back," he whispered.

"I promise I will not leave this house without speaking to you first," she said soothingly. But as soon as she released his hand, Darcy's valet thrust a cup in her direction with a pleading look. "Ah, yes," she added. "Will you drink a little more before I go? I will hold it for you."

At his slight nod, she leaned forward to set the cup to his pallid lips. Such an intimate service, so close to him that she could see his throat move as he swallowed and feel the warmth of his breath moving over her fingers, yet it felt so right. When he finished, she impulsively laid her hand on his cheek. Why not, after all? She had no reputation to protect anymore, and he might die. What did it matter?

At least she would have the memory of this moment, of his warm eyes silently thanking her, the sensation of his stubble pricking at the tender skin of her fingers. The two of them in their own tiny bubble.

"Heal quickly, I implore you," she whispered.

He turned his head so that his lips brushed her palm, and a shiver ran through her. But it was only a moment before he looked away, apparently more aware than she was of their audience.

She set down the cup, rose, and forced her feet to carry her out the door, without looking at any of them. She had no time for embarrassment, not when Darcy needed her.

Chapter 33

When they reached the drawing room, Andrew poured wine for Elizabeth without asking if she wanted any, but she was glad to have it, both to steady her nerves and to give her something to do with her hands. This was an awkward meeting, even without her anxiety over Darcy's injuries. Why had Andrew shown no surprise over her apparent closeness to Darcy? Had his brother told him of their past? But this was not the time to question him. She sipped gingerly at her wine, barely tasting it.

He passed a second glass to Mr. Hadley, saying, "Thank you so much for bringing Elizabeth. Fitzwilliam would barely even look at any of us before and refused everything. I feared he had given up completely."

"Surely not," Mr. Hadley said, his eyes darting towards Elizabeth.

"You have not seen him these last months. He has not been himself. That is why I accompanied him to Town; Georgiana and I feared he would not take care of himself otherwise. And then this happened." Andrew collapsed into a chair. "He put himself in danger to save me, knowing he could not escape it, and while I would never say he intended harm to himself, he made no great effort to avoid it, either."

"It sounds as if it all happened quite quickly," Mr. Hadley said. "Doubtless he was acting on pure instinct. You are his brother; of course he would risk himself to save you."

"I think he did not care what happened to him," Andrew said mournfully.

Elizabeth took a large swallow of wine, her heart aching.

Mr. Hadley said, "He is fortunate you were here to watch over him. Is Miss Darcy in London, too?"

"Not yet." Andrew drank off his wine too quickly and coughed. "She and my wife stayed in Derbyshire. I sent them an express, and I expect they are on their way here."

Elizabeth lifted her head. Mary. Her sister would be here soon. An hour ago, she would have been thrilled by the notion of seeing her, but now her fear for Darcy overrode everything else.

"Your wife will no doubt be glad to see her sister," Mr. Hadley said.

Andrew looked as if he had completely forgotten the connection. "Good God, yes. We have been so worried."

"As you can see, I have been in excellent hands," she said. "Despite the circumstances, I will be glad to see her again. I cannot tell you how happy I was to learn of your marriage."

Andrew rubbed the toe of his boot against the carpet. "You were correct that Mary and I would be well suited."

She had no energy for beating around the bush. "I am sure of it, just as I know you and I are best suited to be friends." She added with a teasing air, "This way you can walk away when I become argumentative."

His embarrassed smile gave him away. "There is that."

"I am glad to hear you are pleased with your marriage." Enough of the difficult topic of their broken engagement. "May I impose upon you to answer a less urgent question that has worried me? My puppy, Sir Galahad – do you happen to know what became of him? Did Mary keep him, or is he still at Longbourn?" It had been one of the hardest parts about leaving her home, especially knowing that no one else at Longbourn particularly cared about him.

Andrew's face cleared. "Neither. My brother asked if he could have him. He takes him everywhere. He is in the stables now to keep him from disturbing Fitzwilliam while he is healing."

She half rose in her chair. "Sir Galahad is here?" Oh, how she longed for his puppy comfort! But would he even remember her? It had been three months, half of his short lifetime. Slowly she sank down again.

"Yes. If you would like, I could fetch him."

"Oh, yes, if you please!"

"Very well. I will return shortly." Andrew bowed and left the room.

Once his footsteps had faded away, Mr. Hadley said, "I hope I was not wrong to bring you, but if you wish, we can leave at any time."

She looked down at her hands. "No, you were right. I need to be here." Her voice was not as steady as she would like. "For now, at least. I know I have responsibilities to your sister."

"Nonsense. She can do perfectly well without you for a time, and she would want you to be where you are needed." Sympathy infused his words. "I can only imagine how difficult this must be for you."

"Do you think it is true, what Drew said? That he did not try to avoid being injured?" The words spilled out of her.

Mr. Hadley sighed and sat down beside her. "Have you ever had a period of low spirits, where everything, even the simplest task, seemed a Herculean effort, and it felt as if you are moving through molasses rather than air? From Andrew's description, it sounds as if Darcy has been in such a state. I rather suspect saving Andrew was all Darcy could manage, and that only Andrew's guilt makes him see more in it."

"Of course." She had spent too many days just like that after breaking her engagement, as Mr. Hadley must have guessed. And had not Bingley described a time, after Hunsford, when Darcy had been in a decline? Now he was there again, and, once more, it was because of her. This time he might die of it. Her throat tightened.

Then Sir Galahad raced into the room, a lanky creature almost twice the size she remembered, but still the same familiar puppy, the dark circle around his left eye and his lolling tongue just as she remembered. He charged directly towards her, shoving his wet nose into her hands eagerly, bouncing as if he could barely restrain himself from jumping.

But there was no need, for Elizabeth immediately fell to her knees in front of him, throwing her arms around him and allowing him to lick her nose in greeting as she had trained him to do. "Oh, you darling, you remember me!" She hugged him tightly, burying her face in his soft fur, comforted by the familiar scent of Sir Galahad.

She could have embraced him for hours, but he could not bear to be still for long, and soon he thrust his nose into her face, licking her ears, her cheeks, and anything else he could reach. But she could not scold him, not when she finally had her puppy back. He could take off all her skin with his rough tongue and she would not complain a bit. His enthusiastically wagging tail thumped against a table leg.

He only broke off to race in tight circles around her, round and round until he pushed his face into her arms again. Finally he took a brief break to sniff at Mr. Hadley, who responded by scratching his ears, and then he collapsed on Elizabeth's knees, panting happily.

"Oh, you wonderful, wonderful dog," she told him, rubbing his head in the way he liked.

Mr. Hadley laughed. "I think it has been firmly established that he remembers you."

Andrew stood by the doorway, having dropped Sir Galahad's leash. "He is usually better behaved than this. The Pemberley kennel master has been working with him."

Sir Galahad rolled over on his back, asking for a belly rub. As Elizabeth obliged him, she said, "I think he is perfect."

Darcy's valet entered. "Mr. Andrew, Dr. Hackforth-Jones is preparing to depart."

Andrew glanced at Elizabeth. "Forgive me. I must speak to him." He hurried from the room.

Wilkins bowed to Elizabeth. "Miss Bennet, Mr. Darcy is asking for you, though the doctor plans to tell Mr. Andrew that no callers should be permitted."

Elizabeth's eyes widened at this bit of obvious insubordination. Apparently her ability to convince Mr. Darcy to drink outweighed Andrew's authority, at least in Wilkins' mind. "Then it is fortunate that I am not a caller, but a paid companion hired by Mr. Hadley. Perhaps you should take me to Mr. Darcy now."

The valet wore a satisfied look as he leaned down to collect Sir Galahad's leash. A snap of his fingers brought the dog to sit by his side. The puppy's quick obedience made his new status as Darcy's dog more real, a reminder that Darcy had insisted on adopting her mongrel.

She was more prepared for the sight of Darcy this time, but not for the tug that pulled on her heart as she came near him. The one that told her this was where she belonged. She did not know how she would ever manage to leave again.

Wilkins waved the footman out of the room, leaving just the two of them with Darcy. Leaning over the bed, he said clearly, "Dr. Hackforth-Jones says you may not have callers. Is it your command that Miss Bennet should be permitted to remain?"

"Yes." Darcy's voice was hoarse, but definite. He coughed and then added, "A maid."

"Right away, sir." Wilkins stepped away.

Elizabeth returned to the chair beside his bed, and the puppy immediately leaned up against her leg. "You must be feeling better if you are thinking about chaperones," she teased. "Not that I need one, with Sir Galahad here." She scratched the dog's ears. "I am so pleased that he remembers me. And I thank you for taking him in when I left. That means a great deal to me."

Darcy reached for her hand, and she took it, glad of the contact. She added, "And I am happy to see you again. Will you permit me to give you a little more broth?"

He took only a few sips, and shortly afterwards, the grip of his hand on hers suddenly eased as he slipped into sleep. Some of the tension left Elizabeth's shoulders as she let her eyes feast on his face, now that she no longer need worry about his reaction. How she had missed him! She traced the contours of his beloved face with her gaze. The lines of pain had not faded there, and she ached for the suffering she could not ease.

DARCY ROUSED TWICE more during the evening, speaking only a few words and clinging to Elizabeth's hand. Each time she managed to convince him to take some broth, combining teasing and coaxing.

Finally, well past midnight, she allowed herself to be sent off to bed. She barely even noticed her room before she collapsed and fell into a dreamless sleep, only to wake suddenly before dawn, somehow certain that Darcy was in danger. She wrapped herself in a dressing gown and made her way to his bedchamber, where the manservant reported his condition was unchanged. Still, the terror of the moment would not leave her, so she returned to her room only to dress before going to Darcy's bedside.

During his periods of wakefulness, she tried to find hints of improvement. He was drinking a little more, and even ate a few small bites of bread and jam that Elizabeth fed to him from her breakfast plate. He smiled at her weakly, and brought her hand to his cheek, making heat rise inside her. It was little enough to go on, when he could only say a few words at a time, but it was enough. More than enough, after being starved of his presence for months.

She managed to convince Wilkins, who appeared to have slept little since his master's accident, to rest for a time. Andrew and Mr. Hadley each came to check on her, but she sent them away after a brief greeting. Darcy wanted none but her by his side, and in her heart, she felt the same way. She held his hand and talked to him when he was awake, reading books while he slept.

Late that afternoon, she heard some noise below, but paid little attention to it. Darcy had just slipped into a doze, and she was feeling the strain of the long day. Just then the bedroom door opened to reveal Georgiana, obviously just arrived and still wearing her bonnet and gloves. She tiptoed in, her face carved in lines of worry.

Wilkins moved quickly to intercept her, a finger to his lips, but it was too late. Darcy was already stirring.

"Fitzwilliam? I came as quickly as I could." She perched on the side of the bed nearest the door, across from Elizabeth, whose presence she did not seem to note. "I have been so worried."

Darcy blinked at her, seeming confused. Wilkins said, "Mr. Darcy is doing better today and the doctor hopes he will be back to his usual self soon, but he is fatigued and weak due to the loss of blood. He can understand you, but speaking is difficult for him."

"Oh, my poor brother!" Georgiana took Darcy's hand between both of hers. "I hope you are not in too much pain."

"Not much," he said. "I am sorry to trouble you." Definitely his speech was easier today than yesterday.

"Do not be silly," the girl chided. "How could I stay away?"

She still had not noticed Elizabeth's presence, hardly surprising as she was seated in the shadows and dressed, if not as a servant, certainly not as a lady. Feeling like an interloper, and not anxious to attract attention, Elizabeth stood and moved silently towards the door.

She had almost reached it when she heard her sister Mary's voice outside. "Pray show me to our room instead. I cannot imagine he truly wishes to see me."

"He is ill enough that he likely has no desire to converse, but someone else is in there that you will be very happy to see," said Andrew, sounding more cheerful than earlier.

"What do you mean —" Mary began.

But by then Elizabeth was already in the anteroom, hurrying to her sister's side and crying her name.

Mary's jaw dropped. "Lizzy!" She threw her arms around her and hugged her hard. "You are safe!"

"Quite safe, and very happy to see you, despite the circumstances."

Marriage seemed to have agreed with Mary; the pinched lines between her eyes that had been a constant presence seemed to have been erased, and the tightness around her lips had vanished.

Mary turned to Andrew. "This is such a surprise! You said nothing of it in your letter. How did you find her?"

Elizabeth smiled at her sister's touching faith in her husband. "He only learned of my presence in London yesterday."

Andrew said, "She has been with Hadley and his sister all this time, and he had no idea we were hunting for her. Can you believe it? But let me take you to our room, and then I will leave you to catch up with your sister. I imagine you have a great deal to discuss."

"Yes," Elizabeth said. "I am longing to hear about your wedding, what you think of Kympton, and all the news of our family!" And there was no point in remaining in Darcy's room while Georgiana was there. Her presence would only embarrass the girl. "And you need not worry about keeping my whereabouts a secret. I wrote to our parents and to Jane last night, giving them my direction at Mr. Hadley's house."

"They will be so pleased to hear from you," Mary said.

Andrew showed them into a large bedroom. "I hope you will find this comfortable, Mary. I will be either in Darcy's room or downstairs if you need me."

"Thank you." Mary looked around her as Andrew left them. "How elegant! I am still unaccustomed to the degree of splendor at Pemberley, and it is the same here. But how are you, Lizzy?"

"Quite well, and anxious to hear all about you! But before that, may I ask you a question that has been troubling me? When I left Bath, I thought neither you nor Andrew knew anything of Mr. Darcy's attachment to me, but now Andrew seems to know all about it. I have been too embarrassed to ask him what had happened."

Mary peeled off her gloves and placed them by the wardrobe. "Oh, Fitzwilliam told us, the same day you disappeared. It was quite a shock, especially for poor Andrew, but it has been such an everyday thing since then that it is hard to remember we ever were in ignorance of it."

"An everyday thing? What do you mean?" Elizabeth's throat tightened.

"Why, just that we have not been able to forget it because Fitzwilliam's spirits have been so low, as if your ghost were haunting Pemberley. He can barely stand to be near me because my presence reminds him of what he has lost in you. Oh, he tries to cover it and to be welcoming to me, and I do not think he dislikes me, but he cannot look at me without seeing you." She said it as a practical statement of fact, rather than something that hurt her.

But it did hurt Elizabeth. "I had no idea."

Mary poured water from the ewer and splashed it on her face. "Oh, that is better. The road dust, you know." She patted her face dry. "It was worse at the beginning, when he was absolutely determined to find you and marry you, before he realized... Oh. I am being tactless."

"Before he realized it was impossible?" Elizabeth asked harshly. "Before he could be convinced not to destroy the Darcy name by marrying a ruined woman? Before he acknowledged that doing so would ruin Georgiana's future? You need not pretend to me. I know it all perfectly well. That is why I left."

Mary's newly scrubbed face broke out in red blotches as she started to sob, hiccoughing, shoulder-shaking sobs. "I am so sorry. Please do not hate me, Lizzy!"

"Hate you?" Elizabeth stared at her in astonishment. "Never! Why would you think that?"

"Because I have everything that should be yours! Andrew, that beautiful parsonage, an independent life. I feel as if I stole it all from you."

Elizabeth put her arm around her sister. "You did nothing of the sort. Much as I respect Andrew, I did not want to marry him."

"But how could you possibly prefer to be in service to having your own home? Even when it meant leaving all of us behind?"

Could she ever explain it in a way that would make sense to Mary? "Of course that is not what I wanted, but it was my only other choice. I have missed all of you, but it has given me comfort to know that you and Andrew would be happy together."

"Not as happy as he would have been with you. I know he only took me as a substitute. I am determined to be the best wife I possibly can so he never regrets it, but I am not a fool. No man has ever preferred me to you."

Elizabeth put her hands on Mary's shoulders, forcing her sister to look directly at her. "Andrew does. He admitted it to me in Bath, that he would rather marry you than me. He liked me well enough, but he loves you."

Her eyes grew wide, still full of tears. "He said that?"

"Yes, he did."

Mary wiped at her eyes, her chest heaving. "I never knew. But why would he want me when you are so much prettier and livelier?"

"You underestimate yourself. The thing I admire most about Andrew is his ability to see people for who they truly are. I was so worried about having him meet our mother, yet instead of noticing her silliness and poor manners, he saw her anxiety and need to be heard. You and I – well, it is not easy being a younger sister of the most beautiful girl in the county! We could not compare. Since we would always be second in beauty to Jane, I learned to be witty, and you learned to be accomplished. But Andrew came and saw you as a person, not as a list of accomplishments or how you appeared in comparison to anyone else. And he loved what he saw."

Her sister seemed to consider it. "Yes, he does have that ability, and I will hope it is true, for I love him dearly. He is the best man I know. And I am very glad you do not hate me for it."

"Not at all," Elizabeth reassured her. "And now, I fear, you must wash your face again." At least Mary had not asked her about her feelings for

Darcy, because Elizabeth did not think she could bear to speak about that yet.

ELIZABETH'S PLEASURE in her sister's company lasted only until she realized how much the presence of Mary and Georgiana would change her position in the household. Now that there were ladies present, propriety was the rule of the day again, and she heartily wished them both back in Derbyshire.

"Lizzy, it is only proper for you to dine with us," Mary repeated for the third time. "Do you not think so, Georgiana?"

Georgiana hunched her shoulders and mumbled something. Elizabeth felt sorry for the girl; she had barely dared to look directly at Elizabeth since realizing her presence here. Poor Georgiana must have been told all her life not to associate with ruined women, and she tried so hard to please both her brothers. What could she make of a woman whom one brother loved, yet had jilted the other?

Elizabeth said firmly, "I prefer to help Mr. Darcy with his dinner."

"The servants can do that," said Mary.

Wilkins, who had magically appeared behind her, said deferentially, "It is a dilemma, Mrs. Andrew. The staff is of course capable of assisting Mr. Darcy, but he refuses to eat unless Miss Bennet is present. The doctor was worried about his survival until Miss Bennet arrived and coaxed him to eat. It was a very close thing."

Georgiana raised her head. "Then Elizabeth must remain with Fitzwilliam," she said firmly. "His health must come first."

Elizabeth had already been away from Darcy longer than she could bear, so she immediately turned towards his room. But then a thought struck her, and she said, "Mary, pray tell Andrew that I insisted upon it." Her sister deserved the credit for trying to make her behave.

She paused at the doorway of his bedroom to collect herself, putting on a more cheerful countenance for Darcy's sake before walking in.

He was awake, his face tight with pain, but his expression lightened at the sight of her, and he held out his hand. It only shook slightly.

As she took it in hers, the unsettled, empty feeling inside her vanished, replaced by a warm longing. Oh, it was so right to be with him! Stepping forward, she held the back of his hand to her cheek, not caring how improper it might be. She wanted him to know how good it felt to touch him. And the sensation of his skin against her face sent heat rushing through her. If only she could crawl into that bed and hold him to her.

She only wished she could tell him so. Instead, she said playfully, "Well, you are stuck with me for a couple of hours. I have ungraciously refused to dine with the others in favor of convincing you to drink more beef broth. Now does that not sound exciting beyond measure?"

"Beyond measure." The sweetness of his smile made her heart flutter.

How had she ever thought him ill-tempered? Since he seemed to enjoy her teasing, she added, "Now that Mary and Georgiana are here, Mr. Hadley and Mrs. Todd are returning home, but I fear I have traded my very lax chaperones for rather stricter ones. Fortunately, Wilkins is helping to keep our sisters at bay. He seems to think they will interfere with your beef broth consumption, which is, as you know, the single thing Wilkins cares most about in the entire universe."

Wilkins' lips twitched. "Only because Mr. Darcy despises barley water, which is what the doctor wished him to have. Beef broth is a compromise," he said austerely. Good heavens, had the valet actually made a joke?

"A wise one," Elizabeth said. "I would rather die of thirst than drink nothing but barley water."

"Toast and jam." Darcy spoke slowly, with evident effort. "And dinner for Miss Bennet." He closed his eyes, apparently exhausted by the effort.

An uncharacteristic grin spread across Wilkins' face. "Right away, sir!"

Chapter 34

The following morning, Elizabeth was turned away from Darcy's door, with the news that Darcy would be happy to see her once he was finished being shaved.

"Shaving?" She beamed at the manservant who had given her the news. "That is wonderful news. He must be feeling better, then."

"Seems so, miss," he said. "Very glad to see it."

"Pray inform me when he is ready," she said. She wanted to dance, to sing, to shout the good news out the window, and at the same time, had the strangest urge to cry.

Since there was no hurry, she decided to find the breakfast room, rather than asking for a tray. One of the maids pointed the way to her. How odd to have been in the house for several days, yet to have seen almost nothing of it beyond Darcy's bedroom and his library where she had found a book!

As she approached, she paused as she heard Andrew say, "We will go out after breakfast. Would you prefer to go shopping or to visit one of the museums? Afterwards we can call on Lady Frederica. She will want to take advantage of your presence in Town to prepare for your Season."

"Neither." It was Georgiana's voice. "I want to stay with Fitzwilliam. I did not come all this way to be entertained."

Andrew cleared his throat. "I know you wish to be with him, but we can support him best by staying away. He loves you, but right now he wants to be with Elizabeth, and her presence is helping him recover. Once he is better..." His voice trailed off, as if he were uncertain of that outcome. "While he is injured, she can be with him. He needs this time with her." He left the rest unsaid, that if Darcy improved, Elizabeth would have to leave.

Georgiana's voice was muted. "Could I at least see him briefly before we go?"

"I am certain he would be glad of it," said Andrew.

Unaccountably cheered by the idea of the others going out for the day, Elizabeth abandoned her eavesdropping position and strolled in to find only Georgiana and Andrew there. "Good morning," she said.

Georgiana colored a little at the sight of her.

"Good morning," Andrew replied with a bow. "I hope you slept well."

"Tolerably so. I was pleased with Mr. Darcy's efforts to eat and drink last evening, and I understand he is feeling better for it this morning." She was not about to tell his sister and brother that she had bribed him with the offer of a kiss on his cheek to make him finish an entire bowl of beef broth. In truth, she would happily have given him the kiss for nothing but the pleasure of it, but turning his food into a game seemed to raise his spirits. And it had felt so right. "Is Mary still abed?"

A faint flush rose in Andrew's cheeks. "She sometimes feels a little unwell at breakfast-time, and the journey tired her."

Mary's healthy appetite had been a family joke, and she was always first at the breakfast table at Longbourn. If she was avoiding it, Elizabeth suspected there might be a reason for it. The idea was a reminder of the possibility of happiness.

ANDREW AND GEORGIANA accompanied her to Darcy's room, where they found the freshly-shaved patient propped up in bed. He wore a dark housecoat over his nightshirt, which accentuated his pallor and the circles under his eyes. "Good morning," he said, his voice sounding clearer.

Georgiana kissed his cheek. "How are you?"

"Better, I thank you. I am sorry for giving you such a fright."

"I am so glad you are improved! I will not stay and tire you, though. Drew is taking me to call on Lady Frederica, unless you would rather I remain here." She sounded as if she hoped he would object.

"A good idea. She will no doubt want to take you to her modiste. She was telling me last week about the many preparations to be made for your Season," Darcy said.

A weight lifted from Elizabeth's chest at his ease of speech. It had to be a good sign for his recovery. She stayed in the background as the others chatted with him, but she did not miss how his eyes kept drifting to her. And when Georgiana and Andrew left, his smile was only for her.

Her stomach seemed to be turning somersaults. "Are you desirous of company this morning?" she asked. With his health improving, somehow it seemed as if the rules of propriety ought to return as well, but she did not like it.

"I would be heart-broken if I were deprived of your company," he said gravely. "I pray you, come sit with me."

It was embarrassing how much it meant to her. She hurried to the chair that she already thought of as hers.

When Darcy reached for her hand, she took it, but with a glance at the maid sitting in the chaperone's seat. Not that it had troubled her yesterday, but today everything seemed different. She would not let it stop her, though. It meant too much. "Pray tell me if I am tiring you."

"I will never tire of your company. And I thank you again for coming here." There was heavy meaning in his voice. "Had I known that being trampled by a horse would bring you to my side, I would have thrown myself in front of one much sooner."

"I prefer you untrampled, if you do not mind." She looked down at her hands, wanting to say more, but that discussion was definitely not appropriate in front of a chaperone. "It was quite a surprise to discover you were in London, when I thought you were on a ship somewhere on the Atlantic. I am sorry you could not go on your expedition."

"How could I, when you were missing?" He sounded surprised.

She gave him a teasing look. "I was not missing. I told you I was safe and had found proper employment."

"Would you not have told me the same thing even if you were not safe? Even if your employment was unsuitable?"

"But it *was* true!"

"I could not know that. I was frantic, wondering where you were, under what conditions you were laboring, whether you were in danger. How could I go to the other side of the world, unsure what had happened to you?

What if you needed help, and I did not arrive until three years too late?" He sounded agitated, and he tightened his grip on her hand.

Wilkins, frowning, adjusted his pillows. "You must not fatigue yourself, Mr. Darcy."

Elizabeth took a deep breath. How could she explain herself without distressing him? With a calming smile, she said, "I regret that you were worried, but I am not without any resources. I could always have appealed to my sister or my aunt for relief."

"Still, I suspect you might have chosen to suffer a great deal before you called on them. I do know something of your tenacity."

She could only laugh. "You may as well call it stubbornness, and I believe I am not the only person present who suffers from it."

In a low voice, he said, "Oh, yes, Elizabeth, I can be most marvelously stubborn."

Her pulses leapt at his implication. "First you must apply that stubbornness to improving your health, and then we can discuss other things!" And she needed to change the subject. "I still cannot believe you chose not to go on your expedition. What I would not do for such an opportunity, if only I were a man!"

He chuckled. "I was sorry to miss it, but I am most thankful you are not a man."

She mock-swatted his wrist. "The only time I have ever wished to be a man was when I was twelve years of age and realized I would never be allowed to explore uncharted places because I was female. It utterly broke my heart."

He settled back into his pillows. "You have mentioned that before, wanting to travel in the jungle. How did you come to be interested in such a thing?"

Good. This was a safe topic. "It started with my father. Not that he had any desire to travel, unless he could do so from the comfort of his armchair through the pages of a book, but he loved to read about explorers. When I was young, he would tell us stories from the voyages of Captain Cook. Not quite the normal fare for little girls, but I adored it. I loved hearing about his time in Tahiti for the Transit of Venus. As soon as I could read well enough, I insisted that he allow me to try the book myself, though I doubt I understood half of it. But my imagination was already fired."

He smiled. "So that is how you discovered Captain Cook. And you dreamed of being an explorer?"

"Oh, yes! That was when I started taking long walks, pretending I was carving my way through a vast jungle. I begged my father to teach me to shoot so I could defend myself against jaguars and tigers, which, as you may have heard, are rarely encountered in Hertfordshire. At first, my sisters would play explorer with me, but they gave it up as too boyish. Mary stayed with it longer than the others, though she always wanted to be a missionary converting the savages, and would get angry with me when I would say that the natives were doing quite well without us or our God."

"How very radical of you! It is a pity about the lack of tigers and jaguars, though."

"Indeed! I would have loved to see them, even if it meant being eaten alive. I fell in love with all the strange plants and animals when I read Sir Joseph Banks' *Journals from the Endeavour*. I used to dream of traveling with him."

Darcy laughed. "You should not say that, or I shall be jealous. Sir Joseph is a friend of mine, although he must be seventy years of age by now and crippled by gout. Still, his mind is as sharp as ever."

Her jaw dropped. "You know Sir Joseph Banks?"

"Of course. He helped plan both this expedition and the first one I was invited to join. Many of the plants in my conservatory are descended from the ones he collected."

"Worse and worse!" she teased, although not without a genuine pang of envy. "First you refuse the chance to go on an expedition, and now it turns out you know Sir Joseph Banks himself! I shall never forgive you."

"I would be happy to introduce you to him someday. He is quite charming."

She merely shook her head, forcing herself to keep a smile on her face. Perhaps she might have been able to do so once, when she was a respectable gentleman's daughter, but now she was a servant with a questionable reputation. But her job was to keep Darcy content and cooperative, so she said only, "I should see if they have any of his journals in the circulating library here. It is so much larger than the one in Meryton, which only had two of them."

He smiled, but his eyelids were beginning to droop. "There is a complete set in my library here, along with what I am informed is a ridiculous number of books on exotic flora and fauna."

"Then I shall have plenty to keep me entertained! But before I desert you for your library, I must ask if you have yet enjoyed your morning beef broth or if you have been promoted to a real breakfast."

Wilkins murmured, "I am pleased to report that Mr. Darcy took all his broth and some eggs as well."

Darcy snorted. "Only because you refused to tell Elizabeth I was ready to see her until I finished it."

Wilkins looked down his not-inconsiderable nose at his employer. "You may have failed to notice how much improved you were after Miss Bennet convinced you to drink your broth, but *I* did not."

Elizabeth giggled. "I am glad to know Mr. Darcy is in such good hands."

Chapter 35

Darcy woke again, immediately turning toward Elizabeth's chair, but it was empty. He had to do better than this. He could not afford to keep drifting off to sleep after a few minutes' conversation. He was running out of time; he knew perfectly well that once he was deemed to be out of danger, she would have to leave. "Where is she?" he asked Wilkins.

His valet looked up from whatever he was doing in the wardrobe. "Merely fetching a new book. She should be back shortly."

"I need to talk to her." The words came ripping out of him.

"Yes, sir." Wilkins said, as if he had any control over it. "Is there anything else you would like, sir?" He brought over a comb and tidied Darcy's hair.

"Nothing. Or rather, wine and something to eat." It would please Elizabeth, even if he still had no appetite.

"Right away, sir."

Darcy had just started on the tray of food when Elizabeth returned, carrying a book and followed by her chaperone, the one Darcy had insisted upon and had since come to detest. Not the maid herself, but how her presence kept him from speaking his heart. But Elizabeth's reputation, or what was left of it, had to be protected, if he was to make her his wife.

His heart nearly stopped at the radiant smile she gave him.

"I am glad to see you are eating," she said.

"Anything to please you." He would happily eat his pillow if it would make her smile at him like that.

Wilkins said, "Sir, if I may be excused briefly?"

Darcy waved him away. Elizabeth was all he needed.

She held up the book as Wilkins left. "Look what I found – another of Sir Joseph Banks' journals! I shall have to restrain myself, or I will be up all night reading it. Or perhaps I will read it to you when I run out of conversation, though I think we have talked as much today as in the year and a half since we first met. You will grow tired of hearing me chattering on."

"Never," he said. "Which volume is it?"

She handed it to him, and he opened it to the frontispiece. "Ah, his journey to Iceland and the Hebrides. Not tropical, but still interesting."

"I would be as happy exploring the frozen north as the tropics, although perhaps not as warm," she said.

"You will enjoy his descriptions of Iceland, which is much less icy than its name." He could sit there all day admiring the sparkle in her fine eyes.

"No doubt, but do not allow me to distract you from your repast," she said pointedly.

He laughed, but allowed her to replace the tray in front of him.

Wilkins returned, followed by Mrs. Smith, the housekeeper's assistant, who shuffled in carrying a basket. Taking a seat in the corner, she nodded to Darcy and pulled out some mending. The valet whispered to Elizabeth's chaperone, who followed him from the room.

A disbelieving smile tugged at the corner of Darcy's mouth. "I do not pay Wilkins well enough," he said quietly.

Elizabeth raised her eyebrows. "He has been exhausting himself caring for you. I managed to send him off to rest once by promising to browbeat you into drinking all your broth."

"He must approve of you to allow such a thing," he teased.

She laughed. "I am quite sure he does not approve of me, but he finds me useful, which I daresay is more important in his books! I convinced you to drink, and therefore I am worthy of remaining."

"No, he approves, or he would not have replaced your chaperone with Mrs. Smith." He tapped his ear, wincing as the movement of his arm pulled on his ribs. "Nearly deaf. That is why he deserves a raise."

Her cheeks grew pink. "I see," she said. "We may speak freely, then?"

"At least until someone else comes in." But now that he could speak, there was so much to say that it seemed to stop up his throat. "Elizabeth, promise me one thing, I beg you. If you feel you must go away again, will you tell me first? If you want me to keep my distance, I will respect it, but I pray you, do not leave me in ignorance of your whereabouts again."

Her smile faded. "If you wish it. It seemed for the best at the time."

He forced himself to lighten his tone. "I thank you. And I hope you will not feel the need to depart again, but I will rest easier knowing you will not leave without a word."

She twisted her fingers in the fabric of her skirt. "I never wanted to leave you, but I saw no other choice."

"Did you not know that I would want a future with you?" He had thought his feelings were so obvious, yet she had left anyway.

Glancing away, she said, "I thought you would wish it, but that did not mean it would be possible. If you were someone of no particular importance, it would not matter so much, but you are the Master of Pemberley."

"Pemberley has survived scandal before, as you know," he said in a low voice. "And the scandal may be much less than you think. George Wickham was unable to spread rumors about you, or harm you in any way. You are safe from his machinations."

She looked stunned. "But how? I thought once the news of my broken engagement became public, he would make certain everyone knew I had been compromised in Lambton. Did you pay him?"

"No. I had him imprisoned for debt, as soon as I learned the truth of your engagement. After a few months, he was willing to accept my terms, and he is on his way to India where he will serve in the East India Company Army, never to return to England."

"So now he is India's problem."

"He will cause trouble wherever he goes, but he will not be able to employ his charm against any ladies there; he tried his old tricks in the Marshalsea Prison, and one of the other inmates took a knife to his face. He is badly scarred. I would not have wished it on anyone, but I cannot deny some satisfaction that he will mislead no more women."

She shuddered. "He brought it on himself."

"True, and now you are safe from the scandal he would create." He lowered his voice, staring into her eyes. "Even if that were not true, do not discount my willingness to face the worst society can do, if it means I can have you."

Her face seemed to crumple. "If it were just for you, perhaps you might. But what of your sister? She makes her come-out next year. Even if it is just the matter of the broken engagement, it would affect her chances. Should we seize our own happiness, knowing that she will be mocked, shamed, and rejected because of it? That her choice of husband will be limited to fortune-hunters because we have chosen to throw caution to the wind?"

He closed his eyes, suddenly exhausted. It was true. Andrew had told him the same thing, time and again. "I do not even know if she wishes to have a Season or is only agreeing because it is expected of her."

"Does it matter? Georgiana is too young to make that choice. Especially since she is always so anxious to please you and Drew. If she thought you would be happier if she only had one hand instead of two, she would get out a knife and cut one off. Of course she will say she does not want a Season, or even that she does not wish to marry, if she so much as suspects it is a stumbling block for you. I will not sacrifice her future for my own."

"How fierce you are." There it was: his duty to his family versus his heart's desire. He could never live with himself if he sacrificed Georgiana. "And, to my infinite regret, I cannot argue your point."

"I am fierce because I have thought this through so many times, and the answer is always the same," she said sharply. Then she added something under her breath.

"What was that? I could not hear you."

Her lips twitched. "I should not repeat it, but what I said was, 'At least for now.' Those words have been my small comfort these past months."

A small spark of hope kindled in his chest. "What do you mean?"

Her smile pierced him with its sweet sadness. "It is what I have told myself, late at night, when I could not bear the notion of never seeing you again. That someday, when Georgiana was safely married and you were back from your expedition, I would write to you. If you still cared, and if you were willing to tolerate the scandal of my broken engagement and being in service, and if you had not married someone else – a great many ifs, I grant you – then perhaps you might seek me out. How foolish of me! But it gave me comfort when nothing else could."

His heart seemed to flip in his chest. "You planned to write to me?" He could not believe it.

"Are you shocked that I would do something so improper?" she asked with that arch look that had first won his heart and now haunted his dreams.

"No," he said, feeling her gaze move through his body like molten fire. "Astonished, nay, astounded that you could care that much."

Uncertainty fluttered across her countenance. "I think you must still be confused from your injury. I broke my engagement for your sake, gave up my reputation for your sake, and left my friends and family for your sake. Why in heaven's name would I hesitate to write you a letter?"

"Confused, yes, but not from my injury." Somehow he had to explain this, and quickly, before another servant came in. "I knew you felt a certain warmth towards me, little as I deserved it, and that you felt guilty that your engagement was forcing me to leave England."

"Guilty?" she cried. "I was jealous! I wanted to go with you!"

"I know you said that, but I cannot believe..." He lost track of what he was saying, and he rubbed his hand against his dry mouth.

Elizabeth instantly picked up the wine glass and held it for him. "You must drink. Drink and rest."

He took a swallow, and then another one when she did not move the glass away. "No, I must speak while I can. We both know you disliked me when I first proposed to you. Then you came to Pemberley, engaged to Andrew, and saw me at my worst – angry, jealous, and inhospitable. You had every reason to hate me. That you still trusted me at all was a gift I did not deserve. When you showed me warmth at Longbourn and in Bath, I was grateful, beyond grateful. That you might care more than that – I might wish for it, I might dream of it, but I dare not even hope for it. Especially after you disappeared."

Her eyes grew round. "I could not speak then. You know I could not. It did not mean that I did not feel. I would not have broken my engagement over a tepid sort of liking for you. I am not that noble! I jilted Andrew because the bond I felt between us was so powerful that I knew it would haunt me all my days. And sooner or later, no matter how chaste we were determined to be, Andrew would notice a look, or perhaps a touch, and we would all be plunged into a hellish misery which would destroy both your family and my marriage."

He wanted to get up and dance, and at the same time he wanted to weep. "But why? Why would you care for me, when I showed you nothing but disdain and coldness at Pemberley?"

A sweet smile bloomed on her tempting lips. "Because you showed me so much more than that. You showed me a man who still cared for me despite the bitterness of my refusal and my inexplicable engagement to his brother; a man who was determined to conquer his own needs and desires, no matter the cost, because of his sense of responsibility to his brother and sister. You showed me a man who had created a jungle and had a library full of the same books I love." The words stopped tumbling out as she caught her breath. "And you did apologize quite nicely," she added with a teasing look.

"I do not deserve so much credit."

She tapped his arm in mock reproach. "That is for me to decide, sir! And I am quite certain you do deserve it."

"Will you, then..." Dare he ask it, after his failed proposal? Ought he to wait until he was healthier and more certain of himself? But he could not. He had to know now. "Will you wait for me? Knowing that it may be years before Georgiana is settled, years before I can make you an offer, years before we could be together?"

Her eyes glistened. "Of course I will wait for you, no matter how long it takes. I was already doing that, with almost no hope of success. If you are willing to take me with all my disadvantages, I am yours."

"My love." It was so much more than he had dared to hope for, that she would not only accept him, but long for him as he did for her. He pushed himself up on his elbows, needing to reach out to her, and the room began to spin.

Her eyes widened. "Lie back, I pray you! You must rest. I should not have discussed any of this with you until you were better."

He slumped back, exhausted yet stunned, full of heartfelt delight. "No, my love, you have given me the greatest gift of my life. Now I have a reason to recover." But he could feel the leaden fatigue overtaking him, and he had to force his eyes to stay open. At least the effort gave him the pleasure of watching the loving concern in Elizabeth's eyes.

"You must recover, indeed, after giving me such hope for the future! But first, before you rest, a little more beef broth, or Wilkins will send me off and never permit me to see you again," she teased.

"For you, I will do anything." But it would be easier if the room stopped spinning.

THAT AFTERNOON, DREW had come to Darcy's room after returning from the outing and insisted that Elizabeth come downstairs for dinner. She had left him with a wry smile and a squeeze of his hand. It had felt ridiculously lonely to eat his small meal alone, after becoming accustomed to her constant presence, but he could not keep her by his side forever. Still, no dinner had ever seemed so long.

When Elizabeth reappeared, though, it was obvious that something was troubling her. She offered to read to him, but she did not take his hand, nor did she meet his eyes. Had Drew said something to upset her? Or had her time away given her the opportunity to rethink, and did she now regret their agreement? If only he were not so infernally weak, he could find a way to speak to her privately, but now all he could do was to wait for a time when only trusted servants were in the room. Damn it, why could they not let him be alone with her?

Finally he saw his moment when the maid left the room briefly. There was no time to waste, so he said directly, "Is something the matter, my love?"

"Nothing of note, nothing to compare to my relief that you are better," she said quietly, lowering her head.

"But there is something, I can tell."

She brushed back a curl that had fallen into her face. "It is uncomfortable, being here when Georgiana and Mary are in residence. It is not proper, and I see it in their faces. I cannot stay here much longer, you know."

He knew it all too well, much as he would like to disregard those arguments. "I will miss you. Will you permit me to continue to see you?"

"I would like that."

He breathed a sigh of relief. He had hoped for it, but had not been certain. "Will you return to your family?"

"I think not. I have written them and told them how they may reach me, and I intend to call on the Gardiners. But I do not think I would be happy back at Longbourn. I am comfortable as Mrs. Todd's companion, without the gossip and censure I would face at Longbourn, where everyone would see me as a fallen woman because of my broken engagement."

His throat clenched. "But you are a gentlewoman. You should not be working for your living."

She tilted her head with a wry smile. "Almost all the world does, and I have no objection to my current position." She paused. "And while I do not like to think of it, there is a possibility that you might change your mind or that something might happen to you in the next few years. I must protect my future."

"I will not change my mind." But he could not guarantee he would not be trampled by another horse, or felled by disease. Surely Drew or Bingley would take care of Elizabeth if something happened to him, would they not? His stomach churned at the thought.

She must have noticed his reaction, for she said gently, "I am sorry. I know you dislike my employment, as undemanding as it may be."

"When that day comes when we can be together, it will be hard to explain why you have been in service. If you do not wish to return home, perhaps we can find another option. Bingley has a townhouse where you could stay, and now that he is married to your sister, there would be no impropriety in it."

Her lips tightened. "And I would so enjoy the company of Miss Bingley and Mrs. Hurst, who would never let me forget any of my disgrace."

"What of your aunt and uncle? Could they take you in? I cannot believe they would mistreat you."

She stared down at her skirts, absently smoothing them. "The Gardiners have four children, with another on the way. They do not need a houseguest who stays for years on end, and I would feel obligated to work harder helping to care for their children than I do in my present situation."

If only he could simply pay for a home for her! "We could find lodgings for you, perhaps near them. Bingley would be happy to support you." At least, he would do so if Darcy asked him.

"No matter if Mr. Bingley officially pays for it, it would make me feel like your kept woman, even if you expected nothing for it." Her voice was tight.

"I do not wish to cause you distress. I am only trying to help."

She looked away. "You can help most by allowing me to remain as I am. No, not by allowing me to do so, but by recognizing that it is my choice to make."

"Of course it is your choice. But there will be consequences. It would not look odd for me to call occasionally on Hadley, but if I am there frequently, people will ask questions. If I am seen in public with a lady's companion, people may assume the worst. And Drew is already worrying that my attentions will damage your reputation further."

She rubbed her palms together. "I am sorry that it will be inconvenient for you," she said icily. "But it is my reputation and my life. It is up to you to decide if you can accept that."

Good God, was she suggesting that she would end their understanding over this? "Elizabeth..."

But then the maid walked back into the room, and his tongue was tied once more. How could he explain himself in terms general enough that her chaperone would not understand them?

Elizabeth rose to her feet. "I pray you will excuse me." Her voice shook, and she turned to leave.

"No, I beg you!" He held out his hand, not caring what the maid saw or heard, not if it kept Elizabeth there.

"I think it is better if we discuss this later," she said, and left the room.

He sank back into his pillow. How had that gone so wrong so quickly? To be so close to happiness, and now to have it in danger, was intolerable. He could only hope she returned quickly.

Chapter 36

Darcy felt sick. It was almost midnight. Elizabeth would clearly not be back to speak to him tonight, but there was no point in trying to sleep. He had been given a second chance with her, and he had ruined it.

A barely audible rap raised his spirits for a brief instant, but it came from outside Wilkins' closet, not his own door. The sound of Wilkins' footsteps, followed by a short, soft exchange of words, showed his valet was still awake.

A moment later Wilkins appeared at the adjoining door.

Darcy glared at him. "What is it?"

Wilkins took his time checking the wineglass on Darcy's bedside table and refilling it before he said carefully, "Should it be of interest to you, sir, Miss Bennet is in the library. Alone."

Darcy sat up, uncaring that his head swam with the movement. "I must go to her. Will you help me get there?"

"Of course, sir."

THANK GOD THE LIBRARY was on the same floor. Even with Wilkins supporting his elbow, Darcy did not think he could manage any stairs, not when his ribs kept stabbing him with each step, and he was breathing hard after passing through two rooms. But he was determined to reach Elizabeth.

He paused outside the library to catch his breath. Then, taking the candle from Wilkins, he entered. At first he thought the valet must have been mistaken because the room was dark and seemed empty, but then he saw flickering light spilling from the little alcove in the back. Of course Elizabeth would have gravitated there. It was his favorite spot, too.

His slippers must have made little noise, for she was still absorbed in the book she was reading, curled up in the leather armchair with her feet under her, the delicate lines of her face illuminated by the dancing light from a candle placed on the little round table beside her. She wore a dressing gown, with her hair over her shoulder in a long plait. What little breath he had disappeared at the captivating sight of her, absently twisting one of her ringlets around her finger.

But he could not just stand there and watch her, so he spoke her name.

Obviously startled, she jumped up, her hip knocking against the table beside her. "Mr. Darcy!" She pressed her hand against her chest.

He was so caught up in the vision of her that he barely registered the candle beside her tipping over.

She made a quick attempt to grab at the candlestick, but just missed it as it rolled off the table. She stamped on it as soon as it hit the rug behind her. Crouching down, she slapped fiercely at the floor.

Darcy could see no flames, but the reek of singed wool reached him. Unable to get past her to help, he asked, "Should I fetch water?"

"I think it is out now." She rubbed her fingers into the carpet. "I daresay it will leave a mark. I am sorry."

"It was my fault for surprising you," he said.

She rose, dusting off her hands. "At least it is out. A fire in the library – what a nightmare! I should have been more careful. But you – you are not supposed to be out of your rooms!" Concern filled her voice.

"I had to speak to you." The words tumbled out. "I beg you to accept my apology for pressing you so hard. I was a fool not to listen to you. I would fall on my knees to beg your pardon, except I daresay I would be unable to get up again."

A smile danced across her tempting lips. "Pray do not try! And I accept your apology, though I was not nearly as troubled by your behavior as you seem to believe."

"But you stayed away." He must sound pathetic.

She ducked her head. "I needed to think, and by the time I came to a conclusion, it was too late to come to your room."

His chest tightened. This was it. The dream was ending. "And what did you decide? Have you changed your mind?"

"About staying with Mrs. Todd? No. I am sorry; I know it is not what you want to hear."

"No. About...us. Have you changed your mind about me?"

She blinked twice in rapid succession, looking confused. "Why should I change my mind about you?"

"Because I am an idiot. One who does not listen to you." Dear God, let her not have changed her mind!

A smile blossomed on her face. "I assure you that I am not such a namby-pamby Miss to give up the man I love based on one small disagreement. I am strong enough to argue with you when you are wrong."

The man she loved. She had said it, and he thought he might melt at her feet. Or go up in flames. Or take her into his arms and make passionate love to her until no one could ever deny that he was hers and she was his. But since his legs were not at all convinced that they could hold him up much longer, much less undertake more vigorous activity, instead he asked, "Then why have you stayed away?"

"I needed to gather my courage to tell you something I fear you do not wish to hear, something that might make you change your mind about a future with me." Her voice dropped as she spoke, and was barely audible as she added, "And I could not bear that."

His heart almost stopped. What could be so terrible? "Tell me at once, I beg you. Do not leave me in suspense."

She chewed her lip. "A lady's reputation is a fragile thing. Even if I do nothing else improper for my entire life, some people will see me as damaged. I will never be fully accepted by society."

"I am so very sorry—"

She held up her hand. "I have accepted that, but what I cannot accept is spending the rest of my life begging for approval I will never receive. I will not change my life or my plans in a vain hope of placating those people. I do not care a snap of my fingers for what they think of me. But I think you do care."

"I care nothing for the scandal, only about you."

"Yet you are already trying to make me back into a proper young lady. You think I should not be in service."

Was that all? He almost laughed in relief. "Not because of what anyone will think of you, but because I do not want you to be at someone's beck and call. You deserve the freedom to do what you wish."

Her expression was unsure, as if she did not quite believe him, so he put down his candle and took each of her hands in his. "All I want is you. I do not care at all what society thinks. Shock them as much as you wish." He squeezed her hands for emphasis.

She winced, making a small sound. She pulled away her right hand, bringing her palm to her face, and pressing the base of her thumb against her lips.

"What is the matter?" He still held her left hand.

"A small burn," she said with a degree of embarrassment. "From overenthusiastic quenching of the sparks in your carpet."

"Pray let me see." Gently he grasped her fingers, tilting her hand so the candlelight fell on it. An angry red spot showed on the fleshy part beneath her thumb.

"It is nothing. It does not even really hurt," she said in an oddly quiet voice. "Just when you pressed on it."

"I never wish to cause you pain." He raised her hand and barely brushed his lips against the burn, his eyes fixed on hers. Even in the flickering candlelight, he could see her color rising. The taste of her silken skin went to his head.

He could not help himself. He moved his lips to the uninjured center of her palm, slowly scattering butterfly light kisses across it, letting his senses discover each region and fold of her precious, perfect hand, drinking in the sound of her uneven breathing which told him she was not indifferent to his actions.

Desire flooded him, and he traced his tongue along the crease of her palm, tasting her sweet, womanly scent. What a crime that these precious hands were so often covered with gloves!

She gasped, and he needed no further invitation, moving on to her forefinger, brushing, caressing, and tasting as he went, making love to each segment and tracing the joints with his tongue, taking his time to savor every delicious pleasure of it.

She moaned when he reached the sensitive tip, swirling his tongue across it, and drawing it into his mouth to nibble at and then suck gently until nothing else existed in the world but the two of them in this moment. They were together, and that was all that mattered.

With a wordless sound, she moved towards him and then she was in his arms, and he was employing his lips quite differently, taking and giving the sort of kiss he had spent the last year dreaming of. He knew he should be gentle, given her innocence, but he had longed for this for too long. But she did not seem afraid, not even when he teased her mouth open and finally, finally tasted her apple-sweet breath. After only a moment's hesitation, she met him halfway, her explorations matching his as their tongues fenced together in an age-old dance.

He pressed closer, but it could never be close enough. His ribs stabbed him, but the pleasure of holding Elizabeth far outweighed it. And his damnable weakness did nothing to stop the powerful surge of desire as her soft curves pressed against him. He was drowning in her kisses, kisses that made the room spin around him and his legs weaken, but it was enough to hold onto her for dear life and taste her beloved essence...

"Mr. Darcy!" Elizabeth's voice sounded sharp and seemed to come from a long distance away. "Do not faint, I pray you, for I cannot support you. Can you walk with me to the sofa?"

Of course he could walk to the sofa. Except for the part where he tried to move his legs and nothing happened. "I..." He could not even say the words.

"Wilkins!" she called out.

Somehow his valet materialized beside him, wrapping an arm around his waist and sliding his shoulder under Darcy's arm to support him.

Elizabeth held his other arm. "Let us take him to the sofa."

"Yes, miss," Wilkins said, steering him gently, carrying almost his entire weight. "Here you go, sir. If you will lie down."

Darcy's trembling legs gave way as he collapsed onto the sofa, but at least his head stopped spinning so badly when he lay back. He looked at Elizabeth. "How did you know Wilkins was outside?"

Her lips twitched. "I may still find you remarkably difficult to predict, but I am gaining a tolerable understanding of Wilkins. Or at least enough to know that if you are up to mischief, he is very likely to be near at hand."

ONCE WILKINS HAD DARCY settled on the sofa, he departed to fetch pillows and blankets to keep him warm, but not before asking Elizabeth to stay with him and keep him calm. His voice had suggested this might not be a simple task.

She had nodded, though. Of course she would help Darcy however she could, but the true question was how she was to calm herself, not him, when desire still raged through her body like flickers of lightning along her limbs, as a pool of heaviness sank deep within her. Her insides were a well of liquid heat, engendered by his lips moving across her palm and set afire by his kisses. And now that raging fire in her had nowhere to go.

She glanced down at him, but for once he was not watching her. His eyes were closed, his breathing uneven. "How do you feel?" she asked.

His mouth twisted. "Foolish." Opening his eyes, he added, "I came here desperate to earn your forgiveness, proceeded to behave in an unforgivable manner, and then collapsed. Permit me to say this may not have been my finest moment."

"I thought you did rather well to walk this far," she said lightly. Then, in a more serious tone, she added, "You did nothing that requires forgiveness." To show him she meant it – and because she ached to touch him intimately once more – she reached over and drew her fingertips across his lips in an unmistakably provocative manner. "Perhaps now you will not forgive me," she teased.

His eyes smoldered as he captured her finger with his lips, drawing it into his mouth and nibbling her sensitive fingertip. She caught her breath as a bolt of desire once again shot through her, a melting heat that made her secret places ache with need. God in heaven, how could his slight touch create such a burning agony of need in her?

The echo of loud, shuffling footsteps forced her to snatch her hand away, just as Wilkins, who normally glided alongside so silently as to be impossible to detect, appeared, carrying blankets and pillows.

She stood up hurriedly and backed away to give the valet easier access to his master. She stared down at the floor as he arranged for Darcy's comfort, trying to suppress the throbbing inside her, disturbed by the intensity of her reaction to him. How could she resist such powerful sensations? She rubbed her arms, knowing the goosebumps there had nothing to do with the nighttime chill in the room.

Wilkins said, "I think it best for you to stay here for the rest of the night, sir, just to be safe. We will say you were looking for a book."

Darcy glanced at Elizabeth, and she nodded firmly. If this adventure had risked his health, she would never forgive herself. She said, "I will stay here with you as long as I can."

"Very well, then," Darcy said with a hint of a grumble.

Wilkins went to the fireplace to stir up the banked coals and add more wood, a task that would normally be beneath his dignity.

Elizabeth returned to her chair beside the sofa. "Is there anything I can do for your comfort?"

A smile flickered across his face. "Do not tempt me to tell you what I wish for. I have learned tonight how little I can resist you," he said ruefully.

Her heart flip-flopped, for she knew he spoke her truth as well. "Perhaps it is because we have denied ourselves for so long, thinking it hopeless, that any hope intoxicates us."

"You always intoxicate me, simply by your presence in the room, the tilt of your head when you are amused, the dancing light in your eyes, the way little curls escape your hairpins." He reached up and stroked her plait, his fingers reverent. "I cannot believe I am doing this. That I am so very, very fortunate." His breath caught on his last words.

Her scalp tingled with the slight movement of her plait. "Perhaps you should not try to speak." Her voice sounded husky.

"No, my mind is clear, now that I am lying down again," he said seriously. "Clear enough to know I should not be touching you, much less behaving as I did, when we are not engaged."

Surely he could not mean they should never touch for three years or more? She might lose her mind. "We do have something of an understanding," she said.

"It is not the same thing." He hesitated, his fingers entwining in the loose curls below her plait. "I know it is wrong to ask it, but would you consider agreeing to a secret engagement? If anyone discovers it, there would be even more fodder for gossip, but I would feel better for it."

Heat suffused her. To be truly engaged to him, even in secret – the idea made her heart dance. But it also spoke to her deepest fear. "I would, on one condition."

His relieved smile lit his pale face. "What is that?"

"If you meet another woman and fall in love with her, I want you to promise to tell me and to allow me to end the engagement. I know you would otherwise insist on honoring it." Her voice caught in her throat. "And it would break my heart, that you might marry me out of honor when you loved another."

With a look of horror, he grasped her hand. "That would never happen. It could not."

She had to hold firm. "You would not be the first man to think his love undying, only to discover otherwise. Especially when it could be years before we can marry."

"Elizabeth, no." He tried to sit up, winced, and slowly lay back again. "I could never marry anyone else. Not only because I love you, but because of something else. Do you remember Bingley's wedding, when he and your sister took their vows?"

"Of course." But what had that to do with anything?

"I stood there across from you, looking into your eyes, and silently made those same vows to you, in God's presence and before the altar. It may sound foolish, but since that day I have felt married to you in my heart. For better, for worse, for richer, for poorer, in sickness and in health, to love and to cherish, till death us do part." The reverence in his voice filled the air between them. "Nothing can alter that."

She only became aware that tears were spilling down her cheeks when he reached up to brush them away. What had she done to deserve the devotion of such a man?

"Do not cry, my love," he said tenderly. "It is all the same, a secret engagement or unconsummated vows. As long as I have a future with you, nothing else matters."

Even through her tears, she could not help teasing. "And am I to assume you will wait patiently for three years or more?"

He chuckled. "How well you know me! I am a very selfish soul, so naturally I have been trying to come up with another answer that would allow us to marry sooner."

She caught her breath. "And have you found one?"

He hesitated. "None that are without repercussions for your reputation. The best is that, after my sister's first Season, we could marry secretly and live on a small estate I own in Wales. I cannot see a way to do it sooner, since I must be present for the Season and escort Georgiana to all the events of the marriage mart. If I were on the expedition, my absence could be explained, but not now. And I could not pretend to be unmarried in front of all the young ladies seeking husbands, knowing my wife was waiting for me at home. But that way it would only be a little over a year until we could marry."

A year. Only a year. Dare she hope? "But what of Pemberley? Would it not look odd for you to stay away so long?"

"It might, although I could visit occasionally. But when we appear there together in several years, there will be talk in any case, especially if we have children."

"I would not arrive with a clean slate anyway, even if we waited three years, since everyone there will already know of my engagement to Andrew." And a year would be much easier than an indefinite wait. "Still, I will continue to hope that Georgiana falls madly in love with the perfect gentleman at her very first ball, and that they marry posthaste," she said lightly.

With a look of heartfelt relief, Darcy brought her hand to his lips. "How I adore you!"

Before she could reply, Wilkins appeared at her elbow, carrying a tray with a lamp, decanter, a small bottle, and two glasses. With a minimum of fuss, he set them up on the side table at the end of the sofa.

320

How much of their conversation had the valet heard? But it did not matter, she supposed; his loyalty to Darcy superseded all. She gave him a warm smile. "Thank you for taking such good care of Mr. Darcy, Wilkins."

He inclined his head. "It is my honor." He poured two glasses, and measured a small amount from the stoppered bottle into one of them. He offered the un-doctored one to Elizabeth and the other to Darcy. "It will help you sleep, sir, and you need your rest."

Darcy wrinkled his nose, but allowed Wilkins to prop him up enough to drink it. Elizabeth sipped her wine in silence.

The valet said, "I will need to have a footman help me bring in a cot to sleep on. You may wish to be gone by then, Miss Bennet."

Darcy gripped her hand tightly. "I suppose you must," he said ruefully.

She leaned over and whispered next to his ear, "We are engaged now. You may depend upon me." And then she brushed her lips against his, rejoicing in her power to do so. Wilkins would simply have to accustom himself to this sort of behavior.

"I know. It is simply hard to believe after all we have been through, and as soon as you are gone, the doubts begin."

She could hardly blame him for needing reassurance. He had suffered for love far longer than she had. Surely there must be something she could say or do to make it easier.

Then she knew. With a flirtatious smile, she undid the ribbon that held her plait. "Wilkins, do you have a knife?" she asked.

"Of course, miss." Wilkins produced one and held it out hilt first.

Elizabeth wondered how many other useful items the valet had secreted about his person, but she took the knife, undid her plait, found an unobtrusive tress, and cut it off. Carefully tying the lock of hair with the ribbon, she handed it to Darcy. "For when the doubts arise."

He was staring at her as if mesmerized. "Do you know how often I have dreamed of seeing you with your hair down?" His voice was hoarse as he reached out to touch it.

This time it definitely sent shivers down her back. "You will have many opportunities to do so in the years to come." But she left it loose as he ran his fingers through it. She could rebraid it when she reached her room, after all. "And now I must say good night, although it is practically morning."

"Good night, my dearest, most beloved Elizabeth," he whispered.

How she hated to leave him! But somehow she managed to stand and walk away. At the door, she turned back to see him holding the lock of hair to his chest and smiling gently at her.

Someday he would be her husband. It was beyond anything she had ever thought to be possible. She floated back to her room, hugging herself in happy disbelief.

Chapter 37

E lizabeth stayed at Darcy House another two days. Darcy's setback in the library seemed to resolve after a night's sleep, and by the time she left, he was preparing to take dinner downstairs for the first time since his accident. With Georgiana present, she could no longer sit alone with him in his room, and, more importantly, callers had started to arrive, ones who would not understand why Andrew's disgraced former betrothed was staying in the house. She promised to call regularly, and set out for Mrs. Todd's house.

It was a relief in many ways. There was no further opportunity for private conversation with Darcy, and no matter how right it felt to be with him, the strain of pretending everything was normal in front of Andrew, Mary, and Georgiana had weighed on her, especially given Georgiana's discomfort with her. After all the time she had spent with the girl at Pemberley, Longbourn, and Bath, it was unpleasant to be treated as if she were somehow tainted. But it was what anyone in society would say about a young lady who had jilted one brother and was in some sort of odd, improper relationship with the other.

Just before she left, Mary came to Elizabeth's room to bid her farewell. "I will send you a note every morning to tell you how he is doing."

Elizabeth hugged her sister. "Thank you. I did not like to ask, but that would be a great relief to my mind."

Mary said, "If you feel for him half of what I do for my dear Andrew, then I know how difficult this must be for you. I wish there were a solution for you and Fitzwilliam, but there is no reason to leave you to fret in ignorance."

"I appreciate it greatly." Elizabeth did not know what, if anything, Darcy planned to tell his brother about their plans, so it seemed better to say nothing of them to Mary. "I told Mr. Darcy I would call in a few days."

IT WAS STRANGE TO BE back at the Hadley household. Mrs. Todd fussed over her enough to make Elizabeth certain that Mr. Hadley had explained some of her connection to Darcy, but she did not offer anything.

More importantly, she was no longer isolated from her family. The letters she had written them from Darcy House giving her address had been received. Two days after her return, Mr. and Mrs. Bingley paid a call. Elizabeth and Jane wept with happiness to see each other, and together they visited the Gardiners, who were beside themselves to be reunited with their dear Lizzy again. The subject of Andrew Darcy was tacitly avoided, so that the reunion could be enjoyed by all.

Mr. Bennet bestirred himself so far as to write Elizabeth a short letter, suggesting that she return to Longbourn at once, as he had been deprived of sensible conversation ever since her departure for Bath. Her response promised a visit someday, but made no commitment. Her experience with Georgiana Darcy had not made her look forward to the prospect of being treated as a fallen woman, but she was glad to hear from her father.

Both Mrs. Todd and Mr. Hadley seemed perfectly happy to be regularly invaded by members of Elizabeth's family, especially when it meant that Andrew and Mary were among the callers.

As promised, Elizabeth called at Darcy House after a few days. While she was pleased to see Darcy up and about, his color beginning to return, it was a challenge to be with him among company, where they could discuss little more than pleasantries. But when she took her leave, he held the hand she offered him for a little longer than was proper, and said softly, "As soon as I am able, perhaps we can go out walking." He did not mention that they could be alone that way, but the warmth in his dark eyes told her as much.

That moment kept her going from day to day, along with her memories of the night in the Darcy House library. But it was going to be a long year at this rate.

DREW PAUSED AT THE door of the study. "Is something the matter?" he asked.

Darcy looked up from the book he was glowering at in lieu of reading it. "No. All is well." It was just going to be a very long year. If he was not to draw attention to his connection to Elizabeth, he had to restrict his visits to her to once a week, which meant that most of his time was spent counting days until he could see her again. And even then, they had to be circumspect. His patience was running thin. "Is there something I can do for you?"

"No. The housekeeper just asked me to inform you that your special shipment is here. She is supervising the delivery downstairs."

At least it would be a distraction. "I suppose I should check on it, then." He headed out of the study and down the stairs into the servants' hall, where two burly workmen were hauling in a large wooden crate and placing it beside four others.

"Is this everything?" Darcy asked the man who seemed to be supervising the haulers.

The fellow tipped his cap. "That's the lot of them, sir. I had my best men moving them, and you'll not find a bit of breakage this time, I am sure of it."

"I thank you." Darcy nodded to the housekeeper, who gave the man a few coins.

"Ta, sir." He left, whistling.

Drew's voice came from behind him. "Good Lord, what is all this?"

"Scientific equipment for the expedition."

"But they departed weeks ago."

"Yes, but some of the glassware they had ordered was faulty, so these are replacements."

Drew frowned. "Those are going to the expedition? Does that mean you are joining them after all?"

"No, they just needed someone knowledgeable to inspect them, and I was the obvious choice. It is a small enough service."

Drew expelled a breath. "Oh, good. For a moment I thought you changed your mind, now that we know Elizabeth is safe."

Darcy shook his head silently. Going to South America would mean giving up the little bit of Elizabeth he had. Even if he could only see her once a week, it was something.

If only things were different! Why could they not live in a world where he could take Elizabeth on the expedition? He could imagine her standing beside him on the bow of a ship sailing into the harbor in Surinam, the tropical breeze blowing past them, far from high society and its cruel whispers and vicious gossip. But that dream could never be, either, for the expedition members were just as narrow-minded in a different way, not permitting any women, even as companions. He would much rather make discoveries with Elizabeth by his side. Especially when it was her dream to explore the world.

No, if they were to exile themselves due to the scandal, society would expect it to be in one of the European capitals, even if Elizabeth wanted to explore untamed lands. The expedition would have been perfect, providing an honorable reason for him to leave and keeping them away for years, until Georgiana had a few Seasons under her belt. Damn the expedition rules! He slammed his fist into his palm.

Drew said hastily, "There will be more expeditions in the future, will there not?" His brother was still worrying over him.

Darcy grunted, "Most likely." With the same rules, too.

"Or perhaps you could equip your own someday, a small expedition suited just to your interests," Drew said, as if trying to encourage a sulking child.

His own expedition. His own rules. Elizabeth by his side, with society knowing nothing of it until they returned, years later, with the scandal of their eccentric elopement overwhelming the rumors of the past.

Yes.

He gripped Drew's shoulders, earning a surprised look. "Drew, you are brilliant. Brilliant!"

Drew looked shocked. "I am?" he asked doubtfully.

Chapter 38

"The docks?" Elizabeth shaded her eyes as she looked up at the towering masts of the ships lining the pier, sailors and porters clambering on and off carrying crates, barrels, and parcels. She wrinkled her nose at the odor drifting off the Thames. "This is a rather unusual outing, unless you are planning to kidnap me."

He laughed. "The thought has a certain appeal, but I have an even better idea. One that requires putting you in the mood for travel and adventure." With a boyish grin he pointed to the prow of the boat nearest them. "That is the Ariel. In a few months, it will be sailing into a tropical harbor, palm trees surrounding the turquoise water. Imagine us standing there, side by side. Can you see that?"

"All too easily! You are trying to tempt me."

His face sobered. "Yes, I am. I think I may have found a solution to our dilemma. Will you hear me out, and not reject it immediately?"

"I am not so rash as that," she said with a smile, for she could hear the anxiety he was hiding.

"Then here it is. Do you recall the expedition to South America which I almost went on? I have a shipment of goods for it which is due to travel on the Ariel. No one would be surprised if I decided to take it there myself. Since I was originally going to be on the expedition, everyone would think I plan to remain there as part of it, which would be perfectly acceptable to society, if a little eccentric. Except that you would also be aboard the ship, separately, and once we set sail, we could marry on board. Secretly."

She could not believe her ears. "And join the expedition?"

"We would visit it, but not to stay, as they will not permit a gentlewoman in the encampment. Instead, we will strike off on our own. We could travel through Brazil or Peru, see the ancient ruins of the

Yucatán, or check on the school we are starting in Jamaica. We could sail for the Dutch East Indies. Explore India. Whatever you please, so long as it is far from society."

"Are you serious?"

"Very. In the meantime, Georgiana will have her Season, or perhaps several Seasons, under Lady Frederica's care, with no scandal attached to her, as everyone would think I am with the expedition and no one would know about our marriage. In a few years, we would return, perhaps with a child or two in tow, our marriage an established fact. There will certainly be gossip then, but it will be about our outrageous elopement and how I dragged you through all the savage lands. Compared to that, few will care that you were once engaged to my brother for a short time, or that there was some compromise, because society will be much more shocked at what we have done together."

It was too good to be true. There had to be a catch. "But that scandal will still harm the Darcy name."

"Perhaps, but it smacks more of eccentricity than of shameful behavior. I am willing, more than willing, to make that sacrifice if it means I can have you."

"You cannot know, though. What if the scandal is worse than you think, and it is too late to prevent it? I do not want you to hate me for it."

He took her hand and pressed it to his lips. "I could never hate you. How could I blame you when it is my idea? And should the scandal prove unbearable to you on our return, there is an easy solution." The boyish grin was back.

"What is that?" It was hard not to be infected by his enthusiasm.

"We do it all over again – travel to all parts of the world we missed the first time."

She could hardly breathe. How could it be true, that she could have Darcy and explore the world as well? She pressed her eyes tightly shut and then opened them again. No, it was not a dream. She could sail away with him on this ship. This beautiful, beautiful ship.

"What do you think?" he asked, his voice serious. "You said once that you would do anything to go on an expedition. Does your courage still rise with every attempt to intimidate you?"

"Are you certain you want to do this, to leave Pemberley and your family for so long?"

"I have spent the last day thinking of nothing else, looking at this idea from every direction to see if I could find a flaw, and this much I can tell you: there is nothing I would rather do than to travel the world with you. I will miss my family and Pemberley, but they will be there on our return. I want this." His eyes were full of love.

Her heart seemed to swell inside her chest. "Yes. I will do it." The words burst out of her.

His expression of heartfelt delight was one she would treasure all her life. He stretched out trembling hands as if he could not keep himself still, and then, with a sudden move, he caught her in his arms and whirled her around.

She was dizzy by the time he set her down, dizzy from spinning and dizzy from love. Laughter shook in her throat as she stared into his eyes. She was going to marry him and become his wife, after the long, impossible road they had traversed. It was true.

She glanced around, but the dockworkers and sailors seemed to find nothing interesting in a couple embracing.

"I cannot believe it," he said. "At last!"

"You should believe it. You knew all along what was meant to be," she said breathlessly.

His eyes grew dark, a flush rising in his cheeks. "What I know now is that if I do not find somewhere we can be alone very, very soon, we will have a new scandal on our hands."

Her joy could not be contained. "It will not be long now. How quickly can we be wed on the ship?"

"As soon as we are at sea. A day or two, I would guess."

But she did not wish to wait even that long, and she wanted to share her joy with those she loved. "Could we not marry before we leave, in a quiet, secret ceremony with only a few people present? We would have to tell some of them of our plans, anyway, so that they do not worry when I disappear – Mr. Hadley, Mrs. Todd, Andrew, and Mary."

A broad smile bloomed on his face. "If you wish it. What is your parish church? I will make the arrangements and get a license."

"St. George's, Bloomsbury. If you do not mind."

His eyes bored into her. "Elizabeth, I would happily marry you this very second, standing on these docks, with no one but sailors as our witnesses. I favor anything that makes you my wife sooner."

She could not help smiling. "Good, then."

"Georgiana will wish to attend, of course. Is there anyone else you would like to invite? Your aunt and uncle – could they keep the secret?"

"Oh, yes! I would be so glad to have them there."

"Then we shall do it first thing in the morning, so we can be on the ship when it departs. To preserve secrecy, it is likely better if we arrive there separately."

She laughed, excitement bursting in her. "So much to do! How can I possibly think of everything I will need for such a journey? I must pack everything and call on the Gardiners, and so many other things. I suppose I will have to obtain clothes suitable for the southern climate after we arrive." She could not believe it. She would have her adventure after all, and with Mr. Darcy by her side.

"You need not do it all. Send a list of anything you would like to me. Wilkins is in his glory making arrangements. I believe he enjoys the challenge."

And tomorrow they would be wed.

ELIZABETH LOOKED AROUND the church, happiness filling her. She had given up hope of ever marrying, yet here she was, walking back down the aisle as Mrs. Darcy, passing the pew Georgiana shared with the Gardiners, since Mary and Andrew had been standing up with them. Mr. Hadley and Mrs. Todd were on the other side, both beaming at her. Had she truly only known them a few months? They both felt like dear family. Lady Frederica and Mr. Farleigh were there, too, a reminder of an almost equally quiet wedding in Bath, and sworn to secrecy. So many people were missing; she felt the absence of her father and her sister Jane especially keenly, but it was still a joyous day.

And now Andrew and Georgiana were her family, too. How strange that it should have happened this way, after all those months of expecting to be Mrs. Andrew Darcy! But there was no doubt in her that this was right. Andrew had always felt more like a brother than a lover. The soft, heartfelt looks he gave Mary seemed to belong to a different man than the one she had been engaged to.

She tightened her hand on Darcy's arm. Her husband. It was real. It was all she could do not to laugh aloud for pure delight, right there in the church.

Stopping just inside the church door, Darcy took both her hands in his. "Time is short, but I must tell you that today I am the happiest man in the world, and I thank you with all my heart for your faith in me."

Joy brimmed over in her. "And I thank you for your loyalty, for loving me enough to forgive our past." But she stopped there, conscious of the others coming up behind them.

Andrew cleared his throat. "I am sorry to rush you at such a moment, but the ship is waiting for you."

Mr. Gardiner said, "My wife and I will accompany Lizzy to the docks."

Elizabeth nodded, sudden tears in her eyes as she realized this would be a last farewell. Quickly she embraced Georgiana, who was openly weeping, no doubt dreading her brother's departure. "I look forward to being your sister in truth on my return. Pray watch over Mary and Andrew for me."

The girl gulped and nodded. "I will, I promise. I hope you can forgive me. I hardly knew what to say to you at Darcy House, and I am sorry for that, but I thank you, again and again, for making my brother happy once more. Bring him home safely, I beg you."

"There is nothing to forgive, and I will do my utmost to protect him, for my own sake as well as yours." Elizabeth turned then to Mrs. Todd and Mr. Hadley, taking each by the hand. "Thank you so much for taking me in when I had nowhere to go, and treating me so kindly. I will never forget it."

"Come back and see us on your return." Mr. Hadley's eyes were shiny. "After all, you are now our cousin, too."

She nodded jerkily, afraid she would weep if she said more, and held her hand out to her former betrothed. "Andrew, I cannot tell you how proud I am that you are now my brother twice over. Take care of my sister, I pray you."

Andrew's lips quirked. "I will, and I count on you to keep Fitzwilliam out of trouble."

Elizabeth hugged Mary tightly. "I will miss you," she said. "Will you care for Sir Galahad for me and keep him from being too lonely?" Her voice cracked then. It broke her heart to leave her dog behind, without even time for a final farewell. Not that he would understand the difference, in any case, but still. He would not remember her when they returned in a few years. She would be a stranger to him, and he would love Mary and Andrew instead.

Mary cast a confused glance at Darcy. "But Sir Galahad is going with you."

Elizabeth drew back and stared at Darcy, tears pouring down her cheeks. "He is?" she asked in disbelief.

Darcy nodded. "He is likely already aboard the Ariel waiting for you."

She dashed away the tears with her gloved hand, her smile stretching her mouth. "You are paying to take a mongrel dog halfway around the world?"

He touched her cheek. "I am taking you away from all your family and friends for years. The very least I can do is to bring your dog."

She could not help it. She threw herself into his arms. "You are the best man in the world."

He held her close for a moment, and then freed himself regretfully. "Go now, or I will not be able to let you go." He pressed a gentle kiss to her forehead. "I will see you on the ship soon, and then nothing will separate us again."

She gripped his hands tightly, and then, with one last glance at the beloved faces around her to fix them in her memory, she turned, half blinded by tears, and let the Gardiners lead her out.

THE SHIP'S CABIN WAS larger than the tiny bunk Elizabeth's reading had led her to expect, with room enough to walk a few steps in each direction. Her clothing and belongings were already safely stowed by the maid whom Wilkins had procured for her. He had arranged for different furnishings, and Elizabeth blushed as she looked away from the bed that was much wider than a single officer could possibly use. Sir Galahad was curled up underneath it, with a meaty bone to occupy him.

Where was Darcy? In order to preserve the secret of their marriage, they had agreed she would stay below decks until the ship left the docks, just in case anyone on shore might spot them together. But she could hear the sounds of departure, the shouting of sailors, and the thumping of ropes on the deck, drowning out the soft creaking of the timbers and the slap of wavelets against the ship. She rubbed her arms with a shiver of pleasure. This was real. She was going to sail away on an adventure. With Darcy.

A tap sounded at the door. In the polite world, she should have bid him to enter, but they were leaving that behind. She could do as she pleased, so she flew the short distance to open the door herself. Darcy stood in the shadows, the top of his head only inches from the ceiling. Was it called a ceiling on a ship? There must be a special name for it. But it did not matter.

A slow smile grew on his beloved face. "Mrs. Darcy," he said huskily.

Hot fire burned inside her. She stepped back so he could come in, only to trip over Sir Galahad, rushing out to greet his master, barking and butting against his hand.

Fortunately, Darcy caught her arm and steadied her as the lanky dog ran around his legs. Without removing his eyes from Elizabeth's, Darcy said, "Wilkins, pray take Sir Galahad."

Elizabeth heard the sound of fingers snapping, the padding of Sir Galahad's feet, and the squeak of hinges as the door closed, but she could not have moved from Darcy's smoldering gaze for anything.

"Do you know what the best part of this is?" His voice rumbled in the small cabin, but he did not move.

"Being married?" she suggested.

"Knowing you are my wife is the greatest joy of my life," he said. "But the best part of this voyage is that I will have you to myself, not just for a night or for a few days, but for weeks on end. No one to demand my attention or yours, no distractions, no interminable dinner parties where I cannot sit with you because you are my wife. Just you and me."

How could simply looking at him make her knees grow weak? She licked her tingling lips. "And some dozens of sailors, a puppy, and Wilkins," she teased. Finding her courage, she stepped forward, boldly resting her palms on his chest. "Do you know, when I was in Lyme with Mrs. Todd, I stood each day on the Cobb, dreaming of sailing off on one of those ships with you?"

He made a sound deep in his throat. "I had no idea." But he still did not move, except to cover her fingers with his own.

It was not enough. She needed more of him, so she slid her arms around his neck, tilting her head up to gaze at him provocatively. "Well, Mr. Darcy, now we are all alone. What do you intend to do about it?"

His eyes darkened, his gaze moving to her lips. "Elizabeth. My dearest." His voice trembled. "I am not made of stone, and I have waited for you for so long, despairing of ever calling you my wife. If I kiss you now, I do not know whether I will be able to stop."

She tilted her head to the side. "In that case, my love, it is a very good thing that we are already married." She raised herself onto her tiptoes and brushed her lips against his, sending an uncontrollable tide of desire rushing through her veins.

He needed no second invitation. Crushing her into his arms, he kissed her with all the pent-up desire of their long, troubled courtship.

As all rational thought fled Elizabeth's head, supplanted by exquisite sensation and fulfillment, she knew no other moment in her life would ever match this one.

Epilogue

Pemberley, four years later

"How lovely this is!" Jane Bingley cried as they entered the rose garden at Pemberley. "This must be the work of many years."

"I believe so," Elizabeth said. Glancing over at Bingley, she added, "My first sight of it was in your husband's company, under very different circumstances." The distress of that long-ago day when Andrew had presented her at Pemberley as his future bride seemed so far in the past now.

Bingley cleared his throat. "Ah, yes. Some things are perhaps better forgotten."

Elizabeth smiled at him. "It has always been my philosophy to think of the past only as it gives me pleasure, but my travels have given me new perspective on what might once have seemed painful. Here in England, it is a shocking thing that I was once engaged to Andrew, but in the other societies I have visited, it would be unimportant, even irrelevant. We were all doing the best we could with a situation none of us had asked for, and there is no shame in that."

"I cannot imagine what things you have seen," said Jane diplomatically.

"Oh, the stories I could tell! There was a tribe in Guatemala where the women made all the rules. They were the priests, and the men obeyed them. It did not matter who your father was, only your mother. Can you imagine it? Their life is primitive, by our standards, yet they seemed happy. And it did my heart good to see their female chieftain ordering Darcy around as if he were the least of her servants!" She chuckled at the memory.

"I cannot imagine Darcy taking that well!" said Bingley feelingly.

"Oh, we had seen so many strange things by then that it did not seem to bother him, though afterwards he said it made him understand better what women experience here."

Elizabeth's eldest child, John, erupted into the garden then. His cousin Thomas, his elder by six months, with Andrew's cleft chin and green eyes, kept a more sedate pace, perhaps because he was hanging onto Mr. Hadley's hand.

"Come on, Cousin Hadley!" Thomas cried. "He is getting away!"

Mr. Hadley smiled down at the small boy. "Perhaps I should catch up to you later. My old bones cannot keep your pace."

Thomas hesitated. "Will you promise to play with me later?"

"On my honor." Mr. Hadley shook hands solemnly with the boy.

With that settled, Thomas raced off after John, calling to him and begging him to slow down. Or at least that was what Elizabeth thought he was saying.

"Is that English?" asked Jane, with a note of surprise in her voice.

"Mostly not. They call it Patois in Jamaica. John and even little Marianne can babble away in it, though I cannot understand a quarter of it. Thomas has picked it up from them and their nurse."

"Their nurse speaks it to them?" Now Jane definitely sounded shocked.

"Yes. We hired her for the time we were in Jamaica, but she was so good with the children that we begged her to come back with us. We could not have managed without her! John has always been in some sort of mischief, from the time he could crawl, so we needed all the help we could get. And the children adore her."

Andrew's voice came from behind them. "It will be useful, too, for Thomas to have some familiarity with the language."

Elizabeth turned to smile at him. It had been a relief, on their return, to discover that Drew had found his confidence while they were gone and no longer seemed uncomfortable in her presence. "Useful? Why is that? Does it have anything to do with the secret I am told you will be announcing to me?"

Mary, who stood beside him, said, "Yes, do let us tell them! I cannot keep it inside me one moment longer."

"I cannot wait to hear it! I have been most curious about what serious matter your husband has been discussing with mine for all those hours late at night," Elizabeth said lightly. She actually had a fair idea of Andrew's mysterious business, from something Darcy had let slip. After living together so closely in strange situations, they were unaccustomed to keeping secrets, even the smallest and most benign ones, from each other.

Andrew held out his arm to Mary, and she tucked her hand into it with a proud smile, as he said, "As Elizabeth may have told you, Fitzwilliam found the estate in Jamaica in disarray owing to a dishonest steward, so they were unable to spend as much time starting the school for freed slaves as they had hoped. This spring Mary and I will be sailing for Jamaica, where I shall take over management of the estate, and Mary will run the school. It will most likely only be for a few years, but we have both felt the call to missionary work, so this is a fine opportunity for us."

"It will be hard to say goodbye to you again so quickly, but I must admit you will be a godsend there," Elizabeth declared. "Fitzwilliam has been fretting over trying to manage it from such a great distance, and I understand you have learned a great deal about estate management while we were away." And Darcy had mentioned to her his concern that Drew might feel at loose ends now that he had taken back the reins at Pemberley, after four years of being essentially in charge there.

Mr. Hadley said, "They shall not be going alone, either. I will be accompanying them to assist with their work. My sister is looking forward to seeing her old friends in Jamaica, and we hope the warm climate will help her arthritis."

"That is good news, since I imagine young Thomas would have to be dragged onto the ship if he thought his parents were separating him from his beloved Cousin Hadley!" said Elizabeth lightly. Mary had told her of Mr. Hadley's regular visits to the parsonage at Kympton during the last years, and no one could miss the pleasure the old gentleman took in being part of the life of his unacknowledged grandchildren, nor their adoration of him.

"Oh, Mary, we will miss you! At least it is not for some months," cried Jane. "Lizzy, I beg you, tell me you are not going away again as well."

"No, I am happy to stay here in the comforts of home, having had my chance to travel." At least for now. She and Darcy had discussed it at length, and had agreed to remain in England until the children were grown. Then they might travel again, perhaps to the Dutch East Indies, or to some newly discovered land.

But Jane would never understand her desire to wander. Content with her husband, children, and estate, Jane wanted nothing more.

Elizabeth shaded her eyes as she looked out in the direction the children had gone. "Oh, dear, they are headed towards the lake." But even as she spoke, their nurse caught up with them, accompanied by Sir Galahad, who raced in circles around the children, herding them away from the water. "Sometimes I think it odd that our dog herds children instead of sheep, but mostly I find it a godsend," she said with a laugh. "Especially with a child like John, who never stops running! I doubt your little ones would ever need such a thing." Indeed, Jane's three children were each more adorable and perfectly behaved than the one before, even the baby.

Jane seemed to find this discussion of children in mixed company a little uncomfortable, for she turned to Andrew. "Will you find a vicar to tend to your parish while you are away?"

He grinned. "That is the best part of the plan. My sister's husband is still waiting for a living to come vacant, so he and Georgiana will take over Kympton while we are gone. She will be so happy to be near Fitzwilliam and Pemberley. It is the perfect setting for them."

Elizabeth clapped her hands. "A delightful solution! It will be lovely to have them so nearby, and Kympton could be in no better hands. I will be glad to have them here while Fitzwilliam and I are away during the Season."

Georgiana had surprised everyone when, at the end of her successful first Season, where she had received proposals from and refused no less than three highly eligible gentlemen, she announced that she intended to marry Evan Farleigh's younger brother Stephen, a frequent caller while she had been living with Lady Frederica and Mr. Farleigh. He was destined for the church and had no other ambitions, but he adored Georgiana beyond measure, and she returned his sentiments, even though he lacked the wealth or power of her other suitors. Drew had insisted that they wait a year while a letter could reach Darcy for his opinion of this decidedly unequal, but deliriously happy, match. Georgiana, who had also grown in confidence during their absence, had written to Elizabeth that, while her Season had been exciting, she had disliked the superficiality of it, and was much happier with the prospect of being a country parson's wife.

"You are going to Town for the Season?" asked Jane anxiously. "Are you certain that is a good idea?"

"Lady Frederica insists, and believes we have nothing to worry about," Elizabeth said with a smile. "She says that since the news of our marriage broke, many women are seeing me as a romantic figure rather than a scandalous one. Perhaps I will find one or two who dream of being explorers. Oh, some of the high sticklers may cut me, but I cannot bring myself to care."

Jane sighed. "You are so very brave, Lizzy! I would be frightened."

Elizabeth patted her sister's arm. "Sometime I will tell you the story of the angry puma and young John. After that, nothing will ever frighten me!"

A FEW MINUTES LATER, when everyone's attention was elsewhere, Elizabeth slipped away down the path to the orangery. For some reason, perhaps the light in the sky, it reminded her of her first sight of it, when it had been forbidden to her. Now she could walk in without a second thought, and the heat and humidity within was just a pleasant reminder of the tropical climes she and Darcy had visited.

Just inside the door, Myrtilla stood with a watering can beside a row of seedlings, carefully dripping water by the tender plants. She nodded her head to Elizabeth in lieu of a curtsey.

"How are they coming?" Elizabeth asked, stripping off her gloves as her hands grew hot. During her travels, she had asked local healers for seeds for the plants they used in their remedies, carefully packaged them up with descriptions and drawings, and brought them back to Myrtilla.

"Well enough." Myrtilla's knowledge of healing had earned the respect of the Pemberley housekeeper, and these days the Antiguan woman was as likely to be off caring for the staff and tenants as working in the orangery. "They are growing, at least."

"Good." Elizabeth moved past her along the flagstone path to the rear of the orangery, and found Darcy under the great glass-paned roof, in his shirtsleeves with the neck of his shirt open. It brought back memories of their long days in the tropical sun, when a waistcoat and jacket would not make an appearance for weeks on end. How she had loved the informality of it! She derived a great deal of enjoyment from seeing how handsome her husband looked when dressed formally, but this more relaxed look suited him, too.

He straightened from the ledger where he was recording his findings with a broad smile. "My love, this is a delightful surprise."

She stepped into his arms without a thought, a movement so natural that it would have taken effort to fight it. Even after all these years, the sensation of being in his embrace filled her with pleasure and satisfaction. She laid her head on his shoulder, enjoying the solidity of it and the knowledge that he was always there for her.

He pressed his lips to her forehead. "I hope nothing is the matter."

"No, not really. I am glad to be home, and I love having our family gathered together, but I miss our time alone. I have grown selfishly attached to having you to myself so much," she said.

He bent down to kiss her lightly. "I confess to having similar sentiments. I had forgotten how many demands there are on me here. Perhaps after the Bingleys leave, we should start setting aside time just for each other."

"I would like that." She freed herself, not because of any desire to let go of him, but because the heat made extended embraces uncomfortable. Still, her hands clung to his. "I think Jane does not quite know what to make of me these days. She is worried about the reception we may face in London."

His brows drew together slightly. "We need not go, if you are concerned."

"No, it is not that. It simply reminds me of how worried I once was about the effects of scandal, as if society's view of us was the most important thing in the world. How I have changed since then!"

"Do you think our travels have changed you so much, then?" He raised her hand and pressed his lips into her palm, sending a tingle of desire down her arm.

"I would rather say that they changed my understanding of the world. After visiting places where we were all but worshipped for the mere fact that we were English, and others where we were detested and reviled for the very same reason, among natives who valued my ability to mend a seam over your ownership of Pemberley, and others who considered me less than a child because I did not know how to swim – all those things made me realize that how people think of us does not reflect on who we are, but rather on those who are deciding to accept or reject us. For our children's sake, I hope that no one in London will cut us, but if they do, I will not lose sleep over it."

"I am glad of it. They are not worth a second thought. Nothing they say or do can change our love, and that is all that matters." He pulled her close again. "And you proved very adept at learning to swim."

"When you did not interrupt my lessons with kisses!"

He gave her a look of mock severity. "I do not recall you complaining about it at the time."

She kissed him then. How could she resist, after all? "As for the *ton*, I do not care for myself. I was always far more concerned about the effects on you. You had a social position and a family name to protect. I was no one. The *ton* did not know I existed, so I would have lost nothing if they decided to despise me. But I could not bear to see you lose your standing in society because of me."

"As if that mattered to me! Without you, my place in society meant nothing. My fortune meant nothing. The sparkle in your fine eyes when you smile at me is more valuable than any of them." He twined his finger in the ringlet dancing by her cheek.

She sighed. "I do not know how I ever thought I could give you up. You are right; society means nothing."

His fingertip slid along her face to trace her lips. "You may be certain of one thing, my dearest, loveliest Elizabeth. That no matter what anyone may think of you, no matter who may snub you, no matter what society or country we may inhabit, you will always be first in my heart." And he proceeded to illustrate his point in the most delightful possible manner.

She melted into his arms, grateful beyond measure for his abiding love. Their painful journey from pride to love had been worth the price. Wherever they might go in the years to come, they would be together, and that was what mattered most.

Acknowledgments

It takes a village to write a book! Especially one like this, where a high-angst plot bunny gripped my brain and wouldn't let go. My fabulously insightful critique partners, Shannon Rohane and Susan Meyers, not only helped make this book much tighter and deeper, but also kept me sane and prevented me more than once from throwing the entire manuscript in the digital trash heap. The book has far fewer errors and overly-complex sentences thanks to the tireless efforts of my beta readers, Dave McKee, David Young, Nicola Geiger, J. Dawn King, Jennifer Altman, Carole Steinhardt, Helyn Roberts, Debbie Fortin, and Monica Fairview. They also deserve medals for not throwing rotten fruit at me when I had the brazen nerve to contact them the day before Thanksgiving with a new book and ask them to give me feedback in a week! Extra special thanks to J. Dawn King for coming up with the perfect title for this book.

As always, I couldn't have written this without the faithful support of my beloved husband. Pfeffernusse the Fluffy White Cat kept me entertained throughout it, and I'd like to thank whoever invented online backups for saving the day when our brand-new kittens managed to erase a bunch of the manuscript – and saved their new version, too. Perhaps they objected to Sir Galahad's presence in the story.

Last but far from least, my thanks to you, the reader, for giving me a reason to write this!

About the Author

A bigail Reynolds may be a nationally bestselling author and a physician, but she can't follow a straight line with a ruler. Originally from upstate New York, she studied Russian and theater at Bryn Mawr College and marine biology at the Marine Biological Laboratory in Woods Hole. After a stint in performing arts administration, she decided to attend medical school, and took up writing as a hobby during her years as a physician in private practice.

A life-long lover of Jane Austen's novels, Abigail began writing variations on *Pride & Prejudice* in 2001, then expanded her repertoire to include a series of novels set on her beloved Cape Cod. Her books have won multiple awards and several have been national bestsellers. Her most recent releases are *A Matter of Honor*, *Mr. Darcy's Enchantment*, *Conceit & Concealment*, and *Alone with Mr. Darcy*. Her books have been translated into seven languages. A lifetime member of JASNA, she lives on Cape Cod with her husband and a menagerie of animals. Her hobbies do not include sleeping or cleaning her house.

Visit Abigail's website at www.pemberleyvariations.com

Also by Abigail Reynolds

What Would Mr. Darcy Do?
To Conquer Mr. Darcy
By Force of Instinct
Mr. Darcy's Undoing
Mr. Fitzwilliam Darcy: The Last Man in the World
The Man Who Loved Pride & Prejudice
Morning Light
Mr. Darcy's Obsession
A Pemberley Medley
Mr. Darcy's Letter
Mr. Darcy's Refuge
Mr. Darcy's Noble Connections
The Darcys of Derbyshire
The Darcy Brothers (co-author)
Alone with Mr. Darcy
Mr. Darcy's Journey
Conceit & Concealment
Mr. Darcy's Enchantment
A Matter of Honor

Made in the USA
Las Vegas, NV
23 February 2021